MPARNTWE

ALSO BY PETER WOOD

Attunga

More information at https://diasporatales.net

My deepest appreciation goes to:

*My family, for their continued
interest and support;*

*Kate, my editor, for her friendly approach
and thoughtful suggestions;*

*Nicola, my proofer, for her prompt and
skillful polishing of the final manuscript;*

*Luke, once again, for his sterling work with
graphic design and typesetting;*

*and also, again, all the readers for their
comments and encouragement.*

MPARNTWE

This story is one of the Tales
of the Terran Diaspora

PETER WOOD

Diaspora
PRESS

Mparntwe
Peter Wood

Published by Diaspora Press
First published August 2017
Email: palantir@diasporatales.tech or visit diasporatales.net

Printed in Melbourne by Tenderprint Pty Ltd
Editor: Kate Daniel
Proofreader: Nicola Markus
Designer/ Typesetter: Working Type Studio (www.workingtype.com.au)

ISBN: 9780994618825 (paperback)
ISBN: 9780994618832 (ebook)

National Library of Australia Cataloguing-in-Publication entry (paperback)
Creator: Wood, Peter Leonard, 1944- author.
Title: Mparntwe
ISBN: 9780994618825 (paperback)
Series: Wood, Peter Leonard, 1944- Tales of the Terran Diaspora ; v. 2.
Subjects: Disabilities--Fiction.
Science fiction.
Artificial intelligence--Fiction.
Australia, Central--Fiction.

To Al

Chapter 1

The uncomfortable tingle started and Jarra smiled as the doctor took his hand. She was a nice doctor and always stayed with him till he felt okay. But then his smile went away. The world went away. Everything always went away for a few minutes after this treatment. Awareness returned.

'Where is your walk taking you today, Jarra?'

'The riverbed and the old gum tree.'

She knew the gum tree because twice she'd walked there with him and talked while they sat on the wooden bench.

'Do you ever go any further?'

'Sometimes. I like to go out to the Nature Park or even the East MacDonells on the mag-lev and walk round looking at things.'

'Really? Isn't that too much?'

'Only if I'm silly.'

The doctor laughed.

'And you'd never be silly would you?'

'Not about my walks.'

She gave a little nod.

'No, you wouldn't … Tell me how it's all going.'

*　　*　　*

There were too many people on the walking track so Jarra diverted to a parallel course he'd worked out over time which took him through some interesting bush, with unusual plants and a peaceful air.

Yes, here was his N-tree with its curiously distorted shape.

Next was the crumbling termite mound and not far past that the cleared ground where a big colony of red ants lived. As usual he brushed his feet across the top then quickly moved far enough away so he could watch, without getting bitten, as the defenders erupted from the various exits and rushed in all directions. This nest had its own trails connected, via winding routes, with five more nests, which in turn had trails connecting to other nests. Jarra had looked them up on the InterWeb and reckoned they were all part of a super colony involving every red ant in the area.

A bit further along he stopped to look at an Australian grass tree. This was quite a large one and particularly interesting because it was starting to grow a flower stalk. The InterWeb said these stalks had been called kangaroo tails for hundreds of years.

Whoa! There was someone sitting at the base of the gum tree? Jarra felt a flicker of annoyance. He'd left the walking track to get away from people and here was someone invading the space of his special tree. The annoyance changed to curiosity and then concern as he took in the figure now watching his approach.

'What's wrong?' Jarra thought the boy was a little older than he was.

'I'm exploring but I don't know which way is home.'

Jarra wasn't sure how to respond. The main path was close and there were public buildings not far away.

'I've got an InfoPad. We can use that to find the way if you like.'

'You're nice. Can we explore?'

Strange.

'Don't you want to go home? You seemed upset.'

'Not upset! Explorers don't cry.'

A smile lit up his face and Jarra couldn't tell if it was related to the miss-statement or not. Whatever, he couldn't help smiling back as the boy jumped to his feet.

'Look! The tree is hurt. Blood is coming out.'

Jarra blinked in surprise at the complete shift of attention. Definitely strange.

'It's not blood. It's sap. And there's not much so the tree doesn't really hurt.'

'It is a lot. If that much sap came out of me it would hurt.'

'Look how big the tree is. It's 30 metres high so it would be like a pinprick.'

'Pinpricks hurt.'

'Not much.'

An understanding came to Jarra that he needed to reassure this puzzling person that the tree was okay. He looked round, moved to a nearby shrub which he knew had prickles on its stem, and beckoned.

'Watch.'

Carefully, he pressed his finger against a prickle then, smiling, showed the tiny speck of welling blood.

'See! It hurts, but not much.'

The boy's eyes widened then turned and looked at the top of the tree then down to the dark red blob of hardened sap.

'You are clever. What is your name?'

'Jarra.'

'That is a good name. My name is Mirri. What will we look at next?'

Jarra's answer was immediate and impulsive.

'I'll show you a kangaroo tail.'

'A tail? Did you hunt the kangaroo?'

'No, it's just a tail. It's growing without a kangaroo.'

'No, it is not!'

'Yes, it is. Come on, Mirri. I'll show you.'

Jarra laughed at the mixture of puzzlement and fascination now focused on him.

A few moments later Mirri was touching the young grass tree flower with what could only be described as delight.

'I've seen these but no-one told me they are kangaroo tails. It is a good name. Kangaroos don't use them, do they?'

This was another surprising question, but Jarra was more prepared now, understanding that Mirri was different.

'No, kangaroos grow their own and keep them all their life.'

A minute later Mirri made a little sound and pointed to a stick on a shrub.

'Look! What is it?'

Jarra started to say it was just a stick but then realised it wasn't.

'Mirri, you're a good explorer. You've found a stick insect.'

Jarra really meant it. Seeing special stuff that other people didn't was one of his own skills and this camouflage would have tricked him.

'I saw its eyes looking at me. Does it bite?'

'No, it can't hurt you. Do you want to hold it?'

Mirri didn't answer so Jarra, slowly and carefully, lifted the stick insect from the shrub, let it stand on his hand for a moment, then took Mirri's hand and gently transferred the spindly creature. It stayed motionless for several seconds before starting a slow swaying motion. Jarra's hunch that Mirri would love holding the strange insect was completely correct as he was staring, transfixed. A soft sound, something like a hum, came from his throat and continued with curiously changing tone and quality.

It was Jarra's turn to be transfixed. Mirri was singing to the stick insect? Yes, there was no doubt. There were no words but the sound was happy. Suddenly, wings spread and the insect flew off into the bush. The happy sound stopped and when Mirri stared at his open hand Jarra sensed that, somehow, the stick insect was still there for him.

'More exploring?'

Jarra wanted to ask about the singing but Mirri almost seemed to be unaware that it had happened.

'It's time to find the way home for you.'

'There's plenty of time.'

'Not for me.'

'Okay!'

Jarra smiled at the complete acceptance then staggered help-lessly as a whirlwind of hugs and lifts enveloped him. A few moments later, and flat on his back with Mirri sitting on him, he stared in amazement at a hugely smiling face.

'Mirri, what are you doing?'

'Playing! It's fun and you have to try to push me down before we go home.'

That wasn't possible of course. His muscles simply didn't have the strength. Jarra made the token effort anyway. Mirri's laugh-ter and happy noises changed.

'Don't you want to play?'

At that moment there was nothing Jarra would like more.

'We have to play gently, Mirri. I have weak muscles.'

'Okay, I will be gentle. I have to because I am strong.'

He was so gentle that it wasn't long before Jarra was trium-phantly sitting on top with Mirri pretending he was helpless.

'That was fun, Mirri, but it's time to find our way home.'

He pulled out his InfoPad and searched for Mirri a number of different ways, but there really wasn't much point as every time there were hundreds of possible results. Jarra decided to head for the main walking track and take things from there. Maybe Mirri might even remember. They'd almost reached the track when Mirri took off like a rocket and ran to a lady who was look-ing at something in her hand.

'Aunty Alira, I held a stick but it flew away, and Jarra is the best explorer. Can he come home with us?'

'A flying stick? That does sound interesting. Mirrigan, we have to ask first. Jarra ...' She looked to Jarra for acknowledgement then went on. '... might have other things he needs to do.'

'Yes, he might. Jarra, can you come home with us?'

Jarra could only smile at the eagerness. He'd love to see more of Mirri, but he'd have to talk to his dad first.

'I'd love to, Mirri, but not today. It's time for me to go to my own home.'

'Okay! Will we go exploring again?'

'I hope so.'

'Mirrigan, I want you to run along the path as fast as you can till you see your brother.'

There was another okay and Mirri was away with his rocket act again.

'You handled that wonderfully well, young man. I'm very impressed. My name is Alira.'

Jarra was ten years old, so calling him a young man was unusual. He liked it though.

'Thank you. Is Mirrigan his proper name? He told me it was Mirri.'

'Mirrigan is his full name. Mirri, he reserves for people who are special.'

Alira indicated a bench several metres away.

'Jarra, are you happy to talk for a few minutes?'

Jarra nodded and they settled.

'I hope Mirrigan wasn't a nuisance for you. He can be very demanding.'

'He's not a nuisance. He's amazing.'

'Amazing? Why do you say that?'

'He was crying when I found him and then everything we did made him so happy that I was happy too.'

'Did he tell you why he was crying?'

'He didn't know where he was.'

'That would be right. It's a real dilemma for us. He has an irresistible urge to explore new places and at the same time he gets upset if he loses track of where he is. You understand that he thinks differently, don't you?'

'Yes, you can tell straightaway.'

'Some people find him weird.'

Jarra didn't realise at the time that this was very much a test question.

'I suppose so, but he's very clever at some things. I have good powers of observation but he saw a stick insect I would have walked straight past.'

'Powers of observation? … You read a lot?'

'Yes, and he sang a beautiful song to the stick insect.'

'You heard him sing? Jarra, you are indeed an amazing young man.'

Jarra didn't know what to make of that so he held it in his mind to think about later. It sounded good. He didn't say anything, though, because he was trying to puzzle out why Alira seemed surprised.

'Jarra, I'd love to hear what happened in your encounter with Mirrigan. It's very apparent it was a significant experience for him and you could give us a better understanding than anything we could coax from him ourselves.'

She touched her shirt just below the ComPatch with the gesture that meant she was asking permission to record. Jarra nodded his assent and went ahead. It took a while because Alira kept asking for more information.

'Have I detained you too long?'

'No. My dad expects me to linger when I'm on this walk.'

'Linger?'

'He knows I get preoccupied.'

'Jarra, you sounded genuinely pleased when Mirrigan invited you home. Would you like to see him again?'

Jarra couldn't help smiling. He'd been hoping Alira might ask this.

'Yes, please. Is there time tomorrow? The next two days are a bit awkward.'

'We can make time any day that suits. So, as long as your parents are happy, tomorrow it will be.'

'My dad will be pleased, but can you talk to him first so he knows where I am and how far it is?'

'If you don't mind I'd like to walk home with you now so I can assure him you'll be well looked after, and arrange for someone to guide you through the Community.'

'I wouldn't need a guide. I'm good at finding my way.'

'I'm sure you are, Jarra, but you must be welcomed properly.'

The slow walk took 20 minutes and Jarra was relieved when they reached the nearest entrance to his Community Centre and they could access the transport lifts.

'Do you like living here?'

Jarra didn't really think of it in terms of like or dislike. It was home, where he'd been all his life.

'It's okay. We're lucky because we've got a window and we can look out at the riverbed and all the reclaimed land.'

'A real window? That will be interesting to see. We only have wall displays.'

Alira and Mirri lived in the giant First Australian Community which was constructed completely underground. In fact it was beneath the just-mentioned reclaimed land. With nearly two and a half million people it was the largest single Community Centre in all Australia and Jarra had always been curious about what it was like. Visiting tomorrow would be a real experience.

The three other Alice Springs Communities were all hybrid structures with above and below ground sections. This one, where Jarra lived, was the Public Centre, providing shelter for people who couldn't afford the much higher cost of living in the privately owned Communities with their extra facilities and larger space allocations. Jarra headed for the right lift and touched the call panel.

'This is a good connection. We only have to make three

changes and it usually only takes 6 minutes ... Do you know this Centre very well?'

Alira shook her head as the horizontal lift started its 400 metre journey.

'I make occasional visits but my work keeps me too busy. This is quieter than I expected.'

'The next stop is very busy. We'll probably fill up there.'

Jarra used his InfoPad to tell his dad they were nearly home.

Chapter 2

The visitor entrance to Mparntwe was positioned quite close to Jarra's Community and the gently sloping downward ramp was lined with amazing pictures and designs which slowed his progress till he saw Mirri with a large group of people.

'Jarra!'

The loud cry of recognition sounded and a few seconds later Jarra was hugged and lifted from his feet then hustled towards the smiling gathering. There were so many it was quite confronting till Alira stepped close and Jarra felt himself relax.

'Welcome to Country, Jarra. Mirrigan's family invite you into their home.'

Jarra had seen this formal greeting many times.

'I am honoured to be here, and to meet Mirri's family.'

There were nods and smiles from older members of the group at this formal acknowledgement from a ten year old boy. They would soon learn how much he loved to know things. Mirri took Jarra's arm and led the way to the nearby lift station. Jarra hardly looked at the surroundings because the people were taking nearly all of his attention. He'd known, from Alira, that Mirri had four sisters and five brothers, but having them all present and watching him felt strange. They were all smiling, though, so that made it easier. The lift was big enough for everyone and sixteen people were rapidly whisked along. After one level change and a short walk Mirri was telling Jarra they were home. Inside, Jarra was Welcomed again, this time by Mirri's parents who made him smile by pointing to a hallway and telling Mirri to take Jarra and help them escape all the nosies. Mirri grabbed Jarra's arm and led him down the long hallway.

'My room is fun ... Are we going exploring?'

'Show me your room and then we can go to your lizard place.'

Alira had planned this with Jarra the day before.

'This is my bed.'

Mirri jumped on the mattress and started bouncing up and down.

'These are my pictures.'

He stopped bouncing and pointed to the walls. Jarra started to look but Mirri had already moved on.

'These are my discoveries.'

On a shelf was an odd collection of objects—rocks, sticks, a little bleached white skull—and when Jarra touched a coiled-up snakeskin Mirri immediately unrolled it to show its length.

'He gave me this one because it was old. You have to be careful when you see a snake because he gets angry.'

Mirri re-rolled the skin and put it in Jarra's hands. He was giving it to him?

'Mirri, you keep it and we'll explore for another one.'

Jarra quickly learnt that Mirri would give him anything and everything.

'Okay, let's play in my action room now.'

A different door opened to a large area with all sorts of equipment and space for physical activities. Mirri ran and did a somersault onto a soft-looking mat then beckoned happily. Somehow, Jarra knew exactly what was to happen. Well, it had been one of the surprises of yesterday's encounter. Would Mirri remember to be gentle? He did, and a few minutes later Jarra was once again in fake control of the bundle of muscle and energy beneath him.

It was time to stop. If they were going exploring he'd need to conserve his energy.

*   *   *

There really were lizards, mostly little skinks darting in and out of cracks and gaps in the rocks and a couple of slow shinglebacks, but the special moment happened when they surprised a big frill-neck and he puffed himself up in a threat display before racing for cover. Mirri made one of his excited happy sounds and Jarra felt like doing the same. They'd been guided by one of Mirri's brothers and left at the surface access point which was several hundred metres from a little visitor area in the reclaimed land above the Community Centre. Jarra was loving every minute of seeing a new place and his mind was racing as he took everything in.

It was amazing to think that below his feet there was level upon level of people living. He'd looked it up last night at home and found that in this spot there were 31 levels.

The little signs suggested keeping to the established walking trail but that didn't happen because nothing was going to stop Mirri showing his special places and things.

'Big Bird!'

Mirri was pointing to a large eucalypt. He did have good eyes. Jarra took a couple of seconds to register the outline on a branch. Big was right. It was the distinctive shape of a Wedge-tailed Eagle. A moment later Jarra realised there was also a construction in the tree.

'Look, Mirri, the eagle has an eyrie.'

'What is eyrie?'

'His nest.'

'Yes, his nest is always there. Sometimes he has babies.'

The great raptor launched from the tree and Jarra watched wide-eyed as it passed, with wings spread, only 10 metres above. He saw Wedgies most days when he went on his walks but not low like this. The moment of wonder passed because Mirri burst into action. He darted several metres to a grass tussock and pounced. Jarra's heart jumped at the site of the struggling reptile then jumped again when it was thrust towards him.

'You hold him, Mirri. He makes me nervous.'

The fat lizard did indeed look scary with its gaping mouth and large blue tongue. The struggle slowed and the jaws closed as Mirri used his free hand to gently stroke the scaly back.

'Nice hands.'

Jarra watched, amazed, as Mirri placed a finger under the front claw of the now-placid creature and smiled happily at the little clutching movements. When Mirri looked at him Jarra did the same and was immediately taken by the sensation of the tiny claw against his skin. Mirri resumed his gentle stroking and the sight and feel joined with the sound of Mirri's singing to etch a special moment in Jarra's mind.

* * *

Karmai pointed down the track, quite needlessly, because Mirri knew exactly where to go. For the last two weeks all the exploring had been at the lizard place but this fixation had ended two days ago when Mirri had found a torn and tattered snakeskin and proudly gifted it to Jarra. Karmai was Mirri's second oldest brother and he seemed to be the main person involved in overseeing Mirri's exploration activities.

Alira had come along once but hung back from the actual exploring, which didn't count as real for Mirri unless he did it by himself. The consensus seemed to be that because Jarra was a proper explorer the rules had changed.

Jarra liked Karmai, and regarded him with a kind of awe. He joined in with Mirri's playing and tumbled them both around on the mat in the action room. When he saw Mirri allowing Jarra to be the victor he did the same, and shrieks of laughter filled the room as Mirri watched Jarra triumph over this formidable adversary and make him carry him piggyback around the room. Mirri had to have his turn against Karmai, of course, and Jarra stayed well back as twelve years of strength and energy battled against eighteen.

This track was proper exploring so they were on their own. Not really. Karmai's InfoPad was linked to the ComPatch on Mirri's shirt, so everywhere he went he could be watched, and if he discarded his shirt, as he had the day Jarra met him, the signal from his special Ident ring could always pinpoint his location.

'Look at the lumpy tree!'

Mirri had run a few metres off the track to touch one of the lumpy burls on a nearby eucalypt. Jarra had a quick look then focused along the track where it appeared to run into an outcrop of bright red rock.

'That's the bird place, where they have their drink. I hope we see them.'

The soft sand of the track slowed Jarra with the extra effort needed and it was nearly 15 minutes before they rounded a bend and Mirri stopped dead in his tracks.

'Birds!'

Birds? Jarra wasn't seeing birds. There was a stretch of water bordered along both sides by a band of bright green grass. Where were they? A section of the grass lifted into the air and flew to a nearby tree. Oh my! This wasn't grass. It was thousands of little green budgerigars, congregated for a drink. Jarra was used to seeing them in flocks of ten, twenty or even more on his own walks, but nothing like this. The closer they got the more the real numbers became apparent. Jarra had never seen anything like it. With a great rush of tiny wings beating and tiny throats screech-ing, the air was filled with whirl and skirl as the multitude flew over their heads to the shelter of the nearby eucalypts. Wheeling above was a bird of prey.

'Come to my watching place.'

Jarra followed Mirri to a small clump of rocks not far from the water's edge and settled, in what he figured must be a pattern for Mirri, to wait and watch. The big hawk disappeared and a small flock of budgies returned, then another, and then another till once again the sand looked like living grass. A group landed almost at their feet then fled noisily when the movement of Mirri's arm pointing alarmed them. The hawk returned and the green storm retreated to the trees, then ventured to the sand in a cycle they watched twice more before Mirri jumped to his feet.

'Let's explore the frog place.'

This was unexpected. No-one had mentioned anything about frogs.

'Is it very far, Mirri?'

'It's there. Not very far.'

He was pointing farther along the stretch of water. Jarra hesitated, but the idea of seeing frogs was very tantalising and if they walked slowly it would be all right. They did walk slowly, but Mirri had no idea of distance and when they arrived Jarra sat quietly watching while Mirri raced from place to place in his frog quest. There was a happy yell, a rush to share, and Jarra was given a big green frog. Wow! It was wonderful because he'd never actually held one before. He'd seen some little brown frogs once on his own walk when water came flowing down the Todd River, but otherwise he'd only seen them at the Nature Park. Jarra moved close to the water and put the frog down to see what would happen. After two jumps and a little splash it swam out of sight under the water.

'More frogs?'

Jarra nodded and followed Mirri. This really was interesting. A ledge of rock jutted into the water and Mirri blithely walked along then jumped a gap to a broader area. Jarra was much more careful. Yes, he could jump across but would it be tricky on the way back, going from broad to narrow? It didn't matter. There were plenty of other ways to go. Jarra made the jump and felt really pleased with himself. This was exploring at its best.

'Look! Fish!'

There they were. Little ones, darting this way and that near the surface. Jarra tried to count but the movement was too confusing. About fifteen or twenty probably. Jarra kept watching, suddenly intrigued with how they all moved in the same direction at exactly the same time. The more he looked the more it seemed as if they were linked together. How did they do that?

'More fish!'

Another group, smaller, joined with the first and the same group movement continued. A commotion from behind made Jarra turn. A flock of budgies a bit farther along was rushing for the trees. There was a loud whistling call and his eyes fixed on a bird of prey gliding low, straight towards them and then directly overhead. Jarra tilted his head back to follow.

Everything went crazy with his orientation as sky and water mixed in a great splash. He'd overbalanced and fallen in backwards. He surfaced and was just gathering his wits when Mirri leapt straight on top of him. At least that was the impression till the water right next to him rocked as Mirri landed. Jarra floundered and struggled towards the edge till his foot pushed against something. He stood up then promptly lost his footing again when Mirri grabbed him and he went under for a second time. The water was only chest deep but Mirri didn't let go till they reached the edge. He eeled out and then helped Jarra onto the rock. Jarra stayed still till he felt himself steady then grinned at Mirri, who was staring at him.

'I fell in. I watched the bird and lost my balance.'

'It was a big surprise and I have to look after you.'

'I can swim, Mirri. Everything is all right.'

Jarra could swim, but not for long or far. His doctors insisted on it because it helped his muscles, and at school everyone had to learn anyway. Mirri started smiling when Jarra tipped water out of his shoes and then joined in the fun process of wringing water out of socks and shirts. Jarra noticed that the colour indicator for his ComPatch showed it was malfunctioning. Mirri's too. Well, they weren't designed for water immersion. In the water there were just two little minnows.

'We frightened the fish away, Mirri, but they'll come back. Did you see the bird? This is a good place but it's time to go home.'

Jumping the gap was easier than expected but after 100 metres of walking back to the bird place Jarra slowed to a shuffle then stopped completely and sat down. This shouldn't be happening yet.

'I can't walk, Mirri. My muscles have gone wrong.'

Jarra felt for his InfoPad to contact Karmai. Oh no! This was bad. It must have slipped out when he fell in. Mirri dropped to his knees and gave Jarra a big hug.

'Tired muscles? We will have a rest.'

Rest was right. At least a whole night of it, and treatment with the doctor as well.

'Not here, Mirri. I have to get home.'

As soon as he said it, Jarra realised he shouldn't have. Karmai would come looking, and waiting here was the only thing they could do anyway. Mirri looked worried.

'I have to look after you. Alira told me.'

'Let's wait, Mirri. Karmai will come.'

Mirri took no notice. He had to look after Jarra and get him home.

'I will be your pig.'

Jarra stared in disbelief. What was he talking about? Mirri patting himself on the back clued him in.

'Piggyback? It's too far, Mirri. I'm too heavy.'

'I am strong.'

It was no good arguing or explaining. Mirri now had it fixed in his mind that this was how he could help, so Jarra cooperated in the awkward process of being manoeuvred onto Mirri's back. It wouldn't hurt and when it got too hard they'd just stop. A hundred metres later Jarra understood that Mirri wasn't going to stop. At 200 metres he was slowing and staggering but so focused that Jarra's calls to stop didn't register. A few metres later Mirri slowed even more and started making a rhythmic sound.

His movement steadied, and slowly, surely, he sang himself on.

They'd almost reached the bird place when he did stop. Not because he had to but because beneath a crowd of screeching budgerigars a racing figure was calling his name. Karmai arrived in a great rush.

'What's wrong? What happened?'

'We have to take Jarra home. His muscles got sick.'

Jarra was still on Mirri's back. He was being held so tight he had no choice.

'I'm all right, Karmai. My muscles lost their strength and I can't walk till I have a big rest.'

'You can't even walk?'

Karmai looked horrified and transferred Jarra to his own back and started walking while he listened to the explanation of what had happened. He'd known Jarra had fallen in because the ComPatch signal had worked till Mirri's leap, and he'd set out to meet them, but then became worried when he couldn't contact the InfoPad.

'Did Mirrigan make you walk too far?'

'We misjudged a bit, but as long as we walked slowly I would have been all right. The shock from falling in must have set it off. If I have an adrenaline rush it's not good for me.'

'Adrenaline rush? You understand things like that?'

'My doctors explain it because I have to know.'

'Jarra, if I run will that make you worse? I want to get you home as soon as I can.'

'I'm not sure. I think walking might be better.'

Karmai's walking speed increased but at the same time evened so that the bounce with each step was less.

'Mirrigan, run and tell Alira that we're coming.'

Instead of taking off like a rocket Mirri shook his head about five times.

'I have to look after Jarra. He needs me.'

Jarra had just enough energy for a smile before his eyes closed and everything went away.

When they opened again the first thing he saw was Mirri looking at him.

'Jarra is awake! Jarra is better!'

The next thing was a hug. Mirri was big on hugs and Jarra couldn't help smiling at the enthusiastic way it was delivered. Karmai and Alira were smiling too.

'Where am I?'

Alira moved to the other side of the bed from Mirri and rested her hand on Jarra's shoulder for a moment.

'This is one of Mparntwe's medical research centres. You've been asleep since yesterday and we'd like to know how you're feeling.'

Jarra took stock then sat up in surprise.

'The last time this happened I was tired as anything for two days but I'm not. I feel really good. How long was I asleep?'

'Nearly 18 hours. Our doctor decided it was best for you and it looks like he was right. Your father was here but he couldn't stay so you're coming with us till you go home this evening.'

'Don't I have to stay in bed?'

'Not at all. Your new doctor says there's no need.'

Jarra blinked a few times while he took that in. His doctors were always changing but he did like the lady doctor who sometimes walked with him. Alira picked up on his resistance.

'I hope you like him. Your father is eager for you to stay as his patient after his effective care for you last night.'

'Dad said that?'

'Yes, but you can make up your own mind after you've had a talk in his office. Mirrigan has fresh clothes for you, so whenever you're ready we'll be on our way.'

'How did I get here? Mirri carried me and then Karmai, and that's all I remember. Did Karmai carry me all the way?'

'Emergency transport took over at the entrance and monitored you while we contacted your father and organised our doctors.'

Jarra suddenly blushed because he realised what he hadn't done.

'Thank you for helping me, Mirri. You are the best friend in the world. Thank you for carrying me, Karmai, and thank you, Alira, for organising the doctors.'

Mirri gave him another hug, Karmai smiled, and Alira did the touch on the shoulder thing again.

'We are honoured, Jarra.'

Jarra didn't know it but Alira was surprised and quite moved by a ten year old boy expressing an almost formal thank you only moments after he'd woken.

'I always take care of you. Aunty Alira says it's good to help sick ones.'

'Yes, Mirrigan. That's correct. And you were very good.'

Jarra slipped out of bed and checked how steady he was on his feet. Much better than he expected. While he was dressing he noticed an InfoPad on the bedside bench. His? Yes, it was.

'Where did this come from? I lost it in the water.'

'Karmai explored. He swam with the little fish and he found it.'

Karmai nodded.

'Mirri's right. I knew where it would be and diving for it was a good adventure. You can't be without your InfoPad.'

That was a tiny tease because Jarra used his InfoPad far more than most people. He activated it briefly to see if it was okay then followed Alira.

Chapter 3

This office was bigger than the ones Jarra was used to but that impression was overridden when the doctor gave Alira a respectful nod.

'Honoured One, I welcome you and your family.'

'Thank you, doctor. We thank you for the way you've helped Jarra.'`

The doctor was addressing Alira as Honoured One? Jarra wanted to check on his InfoPad right away to find out what it meant. He couldn't, of course, because he was the centre of attention.

'Hello, Jarra. It's good to see you're wide awake and recovered from your drama.'

Jarra didn't know what else to say so he just said hello. A big smile lit up the doctor's face.

'I'm told that you like to go exploring?'

Mirri interjected. 'Jarra is my friend and he is the best explorer in the world. We looked at the fish and his muscles got sick when he fell in the water.'

'Yes, Mirrigan. Jarra's muscles are a very big problem and we want to help him.'

'Okay!'

Mirri quietened and the doctor's attention returned to Jarra.

'Well, that answers my question about exploring. Jarra, are you happy to have a talk with me, or would you rather go through everything with your own doctors?'

Jarra already liked this doctor. His smile was friendly and the way he spoke to Mirri was good too.

'Will it take long? Alira said you have already spent a great deal of time helping me.'

The doctor, surprised at the courtly response, looked to Alira for confirmation that it was genuine.

'Yes, doctor. I assure you that this extraordinary young man is quite serious.'

'Jarra, I'll talk to you all day if I can. It's my job to learn about conditions like yours and every minute you can give me is valuable.'

Karmai took Mirri home a few moments later and Alira stayed.

'Jarra, do you understand much about what's wrong with your muscles?'

'I think so. My lady doctor answers all my questions and helps me with my coping strategies.'

'Coping strategies? Is that what she calls your walking and other routines?'

'Ah ... yes.'

Alira interrupted.

'Doctor, Jarra has highly developed language skills and I believe that was his own description. He'll understand even if you speak quite clinically, and if he doesn't he'll ask you to elaborate.'

'I see. Well, do you know about your function quotient, Jarra?'

'Yes, it's nine points above baseline, and if I don't do my walks properly it drops down to seven. And without my treatments it would drop a lot more. Yesterday it must have been zero because I couldn't do anything.'

'That is completely correct. I'm very impressed with the way your doctors have looked after you and the careful way you follow your routines. According to their records you're a model patient. Have they explained that we don't know how to teach your body to make its muscles work the right way?'

'Yes, that's why I have to be very good at my routines.'

'Do you like doing experiments?'

'I love them. It's my best activity and I'm in the science club at school.'

'I see. Well, I have a number of experiments which might help with your function quotient, so do you think we could have a go at them?'

'I'd like to, doctor, but do you really think they could help? I've done that before with my other doctors and it didn't change anything.'

'Yes, I really do. Last night I did a careful experiment while you were asleep and the results from the changes I made to your nano treatment are showing a lift in your function quotient of at least one point. I know that doesn't sound like much but when you're so borderline every point you gain is important.'

'Did I have a nano treatment? It's not meant to be for two more days.'

'It was a partial treatment, Jarra, and the situation warranted it.'

'My other doctors told me the latency built into the nanobots makes them act badly if I have new ones too soon.'

'Not these nanobots. I programmed special new ones to suit the situation.'

Jarra's favourable impression of this doctor rose to a new level. His other doctors sent requests off to a special laboratory somewhere when they wanted to make a treatment change and it usually took four or five days to come back.

'You can program nanobots?'

Nanobots were especially interesting.

'We have some wonderful equipment here. Would you like me to show you how I do it?'

'Yes, please! Today?'

The doctor laughed and looked from Jarra to Alira.

'I think I've just bribed Jarra to work with me.'

Addressing his new patient he said, 'Not today, Jarra. We have too many other things to talk about, but we'll make it one of our first experiments.'

The talk was extensive and changed Jarra's life. For a start the doctor had a long-term target of adding at least five more points to his function quotient, an increase which would allow for hours more of effective activity every day. The other big change was the doctor's wish to see him once a week to research his condition, and every second day for the modified nanobot treatment. Alira made all that happen by contacting his father and his school.

*   *   *

After talking with his dad Jarra settled to the InterWeb. The list of things to check was long and the big display and extra capability of a home system made it easier and more enjoyable to use than an InfoPad. He identified the bird he was watching when he fell in the waterhole as a whistling kite, looked up information about the frog and the little fish, then watched a short info story about the life of budgerigars. Nanobots were next, but after looking at the bewildering amount of information he put that on hold as a bigger project.

Jarra entered a search for Alira, then stared as his screen filled with information. Yes, it was the right Alira. The picture showed that. Leader of the Mparntwe Management Council, Cultural Elder, member of the Alkere Energy Corporation, Australian Ambassador for the First Nation people. Jarra read it all and understood that Alira must be a very important person.

*   *   *

For the next couple of months Jarra settled into the changed routine caused by his meetings with the doctor. It was awkward at first because the extended research session meant his school times had to be rearranged so he could fit in the prescribed number of hours. The session was always interesting, with talks, tests and the experiments he'd been promised, using special equipment like microscopes and scanners and the medical nanobot calibrator. What's more, the research was helping and he didn't need quite as many rests.

Nearly every day he and Mirri did something together, exploring or in the action room where Jarra would access the InterWeb for his never ending projects while Mirri used the equipment for all his physical routines. Karmai escorted them to a whole range of outdoor locations which could be reached through the Mparntwe lift system and sometimes explored with them if it was a new place for Mirri.

Once a week, and always at the same time, Alira went with them because she loved being with Mirri so much. Three days ago she'd helped with an extension to the explorer's house they were building in the stand of trees near the bird place. Mirri had started this when they'd found a secret place to shelter and peek out at the budgerigars and he'd used some strips of bark to make a cover. It triggered Jarra's imagination and the cover became a roof, which almost immediately needed to be supported by proper walls, which in turn needed a door and then some lookout windows.

This extension was the third little room and, according to Mirri's happy planning, was going to be the eating room. Jarra loved the idea of having their own secret place and was pleased with the way it was progressing. It wasn't really secret, of course, as the rest of the family could see what they were doing through the ComPatches, with Karmai saying he was going to move in when they'd built another room for him. Alira enthusiastically joined in the construction effort but stopped to listen whenever Mirri made his happy singing noises. She also kept asking

Jarra about why different sections of the structure were just so and couldn't understand how the biggest piece of roofing didn't collapse. Jarra tried to explain to her why it wouldn't, but she just thought it was amazing and recorded everything with her InfoPad.

Another part of the routine was weekly participation in games with the sports group Mirri attended with most of his brothers and sisters. He was amazingly good at nearly everything and Jarra loved watching him race ahead of everyone else, make an impossible catch, or score a surprise point. His dad, Burnu, was especially proud of him and said he could run like the wind.

*   *   *

'Jarra, this is Darri and he'd like to spend some time with you. I've been telling him about your projects and he's keen to help you with them.'

Jarra would rather work by himself but he was too polite to say so, especially to Alira. Half an hour later he was eagerly listening to Darri explain the way the first computers had worked. Half an hour after that they were watching a clip of an eagle soaring in the sky while Darri blew on some pieces of paper to demonstrate how airflow could lift things. Mirri came to watch the eagle then went back to his trampoline routine and when Alira returned she listened to an eager explanation of the Bernoulli principle. After Darri left Alira pulled up a chair next to Jarra.

'Would you like to see Darri again?'

'I already am. He's going to take me to a technology museum to see some ancient computers—the ones that worked on silicon.'

'I mean on a regular basis, perhaps twice a week. He can help you with anything and show you all sorts of interesting things.'

That would be great but Jarra was puzzled.

'Isn't he too busy? I can tell he's a scientist.'

'He's a scientist, an educator, and an engineer as well, but I've arranged things so he can work with you as much as you like and help you with anything you're interested in.'

After a few more sessions Jarra decided it was too good to be true and Darri became his official mentor for the next seven years and friend for ever.

*　*　*

Jarra clasped the churinga stone in his hand while he and his dad were ceremoniously recognised as part of Burnu's family, and stared as Mirri and his brothers moved and danced around the special campfire. It wasn't a real churinga stone—they were too special—but a symbolic one which Burnu had given him. Karmai said Alira had one stored in a special place somewhere, but that was the only one he'd ever heard of.

His dad, Robert, wouldn't have had anything to do with something like this before Jarra met Mirri, but the continual contact and especially the fact that he now had three days of guaranteed work each week with the Alkere Energy Corporation, combined with the unbelievable offer from Alira to move them to Mparntwe so Jarra and Mirri could see each other more easily and have better access to medical treatment, had made huge changes to his viewpoint and he was watching everything and everyone with interest.

Mirri and his brothers danced closer and closer, surrounded Jarra, then pulled him to his feet. They wanted him to join in? Mirri or Karmai must have sensed he'd like to be involved. It would have to be a gentle version because there was no way he could manage the powerful rhythmic movements they were making. Karmai demonstrated an easy little step which Jarra quickly copied. Yes, he could do this, and if he held back it wasn't much harder than walking. For a while Jarra was carried away with the spirit of the moment. Karmai lifted him onto his shoulders and led a stylised chase, with Mirri and another of his brothers acting as cheeky but evasive prey. Jarra reluctantly had to give Karmai a signal that he needed to stop.

Alira took over and in the friendly pocket of firelight Jarra and Robert were ceremoniously recognised as part of the extended family.

* * *

'What are they for? Did you figure them yourself?'

Jarra had to smile.

'They're perpetual motion machines, Karmai. When you start them going they never stop. These are my versions of famous ones from people who first experimented with them.'

Karmai spun a wheel and set a little bobbing gadget going then watched in fascination.

'They don't really go for ever do they?'

'No, but some of them *are* very clever and they tricked people into thinking they really were perpetual.'

'Are you going to try and make one of your own?'

'I'm thinking about it. It would be a fake but it would be fun.'

* * *

Jarra's eyes were nearly popping out of his head. Below him the silvery-blue Alkere solar collectors stretched as far as the eye could see in every direction. Farther really because this particular array was 150 kilometres long and 80 kilometres wide.

Alira was making an inspection tour, and knowing it would be a great adventure for Mirri and Jarra, she'd brought them along for the day, with Karmai to look after them when she was occupied elsewhere.

The view was amazing from this observation aircraft and for

Jarra, who'd never even flown before, every moment—boarding and buckling in, the amazing sensation of the powerful engines thrusting them skyward, and the changing aspect of the MacDonell Ranges before they reached the collection area—was all pure excitement.

'Silver City!'

'We call it Alkere, Mirrigan, but that's a good name. Is your seatbelt buckled properly? We're about to land in that cleared area.'

Mirri checked his buckle; though there was no real need as it hadn't been undone. Alira was saying this to reinforce its importance in Mirri's mind. When they landed there was a self-guided transport vehicle waiting and Alira told them they had an hour to explore before she could meet them again. Karmai, who'd been here before, showed Jarra how to input the various automatic control options, then grinned and switched them all off.

'It's a lot more fun on manual and Mirri loves my driving.'

The vehicle started slowly and they approached the nearest collector panel. It was much bigger than it looked from above and Jarra stared at the silvery-blue surface which he knew collected both heat energy and light energy. On the InterWeb last night, he'd learnt that these panels could convert 82% of the sunlight they received and were built to last for over 150 years. The Alkere Energy Corporation managed seven of these arrays altogether, all of them approximately the same size, and for the last sixty years had been the largest producer of energy in an energy-hungry world, providing the First Nation people with a vast income.

'Buckle up, Jarra! Buckle up, Jarra!'

Jarra copied Mirri and Karmai then gasped as the wheels spun and the vehicle accelerated off the main track to a sandy access way through the panels. Mirri got extra excited.

'Faster! Faster!'

Karmai glanced at Jarra.

'Is that okay? Just tell me if you feel nervous.'

A wild ride followed, with skids, wheelspins, and bounces over some rougher terrain. After the first few minutes of amazement Jarra was enjoying it as much as Mirri. It was like a virtual reality game, except for real. They stopped at an energy storage area and then at a big tower where mirror panels focused the sunlight for high temperature energy, then made their way back to the cleared area where Alira was waiting.

*   *   *

Alira studied the apparatus on Jarra's workbench. 'Is that a miniature Alkere panel?'

'Yes. Darri helped me figure out how to build it and I've got it working better than the real ones. We found some new materials which give it an 86% conversion efficiency.'

After the Alkere expedition this had been Jarra's main project for the last few weeks.

'Better? Does Burnu know that?'

'No, it's not worth it. The materials will deteriorate and we think that after seven years the efficiency will drop to about 72%.'

*   *   *

Jarra walked along the through way to Mirri's place and let himself in. With the move from his old Community Centre they were now almost neighbours and less than a minute's walk from door to door. Mirri was with one of his special helpers and after getting his customary welcome hug, Jarra sat and listened while she worked patiently trying to develop Mirri's understanding of numbers. He smiled at Mirri's ridiculous answers and even more when he got things right. That was one of the rules with Mirri, who only responded to positive things. Twenty minutes later, when the helper left, Jarra took Mirri through the same work to help him understand it better and then they planned their exploring trip.

'Where are we going today?'

'Take us to the end of the line please, Karmai.'

Karmai looked to Jarra for an explanation.

'Mirri thought the transport lifts went on for ever and ever till I told him they don't, and now he wants to see where they end.'

'I don't know where they end. We'll have to look it up and figure out the best way to get there.'

That was easy. Everyone was good at figuring their way with the transport lifts and they were soon setting off on their expedition to reach the end of everything. Thank goodness there were seats in some of the major lifts because it ended up taking nearly half a day and Jarra wouldn't have coped. It was very interesting, though, and Jarra decided he'd do this again at some stage so he and Mirri could check out interesting places Karmai kept telling them about.

At the end of the main living area, which stretched for nearly 5 kilometres, they transferred to a bigger and faster horizontal lift which took them past several kilometres of food production facilities and then several more of manufacturing and service plants. They ended at the main water storage area.

'Is this end of the line?'

'I think so, Mirri. Do you want to see the big water?'

'There is water down here?'

'Yes, it's water for all of Mparntwe. We can't live without water.'

'Everyone knows that. Where is it?'

After a short walk they were looking at a small underground lake with crystal clear water glistening under artificial light and boats gliding randomly across its surface. Jarra was puzzled.

'Karmai, they must store more water than this for all of Mparntwe?'

'They do. This lake is to make it interesting for people. I understand there are tunnels heading off from here.'

A moment later they watched a display which explained that five tunnels were full of water and ranged between 3 and 5 kilometres in length. Mirri was really excited when Karmai took them darting hither and thither on a boat. Jarra loved it, too, as it was his first time ever and he copied Mirri, who kept his fingers skimming through the water. A bubbling, happy sound suddenly belled across the water and Jarra and Karmai smiled with their own enjoyment of Mirri's pleasure.

*   *   *

'Jarra needs a pig ride.'

Pig ride meant piggyback ride. Jarra wasn't quite that tired but he *was* looking for somewhere to sit quietly for a while. He was showing Mirri the open-air market back at his old Community Centre and there had been so many interesting stalls and events to see that his activity time was pushing close to its limit.

'Not now, Mirri. I'll go to those seats over there for a rest and then we'll go home.'

'Yes, now!'

Jarra didn't want to, not amongst all these people, but Mirri had the determined look which brooked no argument so he let himself be lifted into place. It was only 50 metres to the seats and after a 15-minute rest he'd be okay as long as he took it slowly.

'Hey, brain face. What are you doing back here?'

Oh no. It was Freeman and his friends.

'We like looking round the market.'

'What you doing on his back? Can't you even walk nowadays?'

'Jarra is tired. He needs a pig ride.'

Freeman and his three friends looked at each other and

laughed. Jarra felt a mental cringe because Mirri's offbeat answer had caught their attention and they'd follow up on it.

'Pig? Does he call you a pig?'

'Jarra is my brother.'

Another look passed and Jarra quickly started talking.

'Mirri means piggyback and he wants me to have a rest. He's just taking me to the benches. Keep walking, Mirri.'

Mirri had stopped but he started straightaway. That didn't help. The four boys from Jarra's old school kept with them.

'He can't be your brother. He's First People.'

'We're ceremonial brothers. His family welcomed me.'

'You? There must be something wrong with them.'

Freeman hadn't changed. It was now over a year since Jarra had seen him and he was still as bossy as ever. If you ignored him he'd eventually go away, acting as if he'd won a contest or something, but Jarra was worried that his attitude would get through to Mirri.

It did.

'Jarra is my friend.'

'What do you want him as a friend for? He's weak, and he's weird, and no-one else goes near him.'

That was too many things at once so Mirri repeated himself.

'Jarra is my friend.'

'He's so weak you have to be his pig.'

Mirri didn't respond to the direct taunt, just corrected it.

'Pig ride. Not pig.'

Freeman had done all the talking so far but Balfour, who was almost as bossy, joined in.

'What's wrong with him? Can't he talk properly?'

'There's nothing wrong with Mirri. He's different.'

'Mirri? What sort of name is that?'

'Mirrigan is my name.'

The little procession reached the seats and when Mirri carefully transferred Jarra from his back Freeman laughed.

'They're both weird.'

'Jarra needs quiet. Go away!'

The four taunters thought that was extra funny.

'BAD BOYS!'

Jarra was shocked. He'd never heard such a tone from Mirri. The boys were startled into silence, too, and stared. Mirri, bristling with force and determination, walked straight at Freeman.

'GO AWAY!'

Freeman backed off and then when Mirri, looking very grim, kept right after him, took fright and actually ran. The other three, seeing Mirri now looking at them, disappeared almost as quickly.

Jarra could hardly believe what he was seeing. With a few words his gentle, happy Mirri had made the four bossiest boys from his old school turn tail and run.

Chapter 4

Alira listened carefully to what Darri was saying.
'He's twelve years old, Darri. You really think ordinary school is a waste of his time? I'm concerned that he doesn't socialise with other children very much. From what I can see he spends all his time either studying or in company with Mirrigan.'

'Yes, it's not normal behaviour, but I don't think you need to be concerned. I'm not. His classmates understand that his intelligence sets him apart, but he's always friendly and they respond to that. What I do see is that, particularly with his maths and science work, his teachers are leaving him to work with the self-paced mastery programs on the school computers because he already understands everything the class groups are working on.'

'So what do you recommend?'

'It's hard to say. Putting him with older students at advanced levels would challenge him for a while, but he'd eventually adapt and be in the same situation again.'

Alira laughed.

'Do you think he needs challenging? He does that to himself all the time and you seem to be helping him with everything.'

Darri shook his head.

'I get him started, but when it's something he's interested in I quickly get left behind. Three months ago he was stuck with building his own energy collector after the trip to the array and when I showed him how a differential equation could get him through, he had to know how it worked. After six weeks of tutoring I couldn't understand half of what he was doing.'

'Even when maths was one of your degrees?'

'Yes. It meant I could show him the way, but when he dedicates himself to something he goes way ahead. The first thing I ever showed him was a couple of ancient computers and in the two years since he's built two of his own and taught himself a range of computer languages, including assembler and even a smattering of machine code.'

'I don't know what that means but it sounds impressive.'

'It's an impressive achievement for anyone, let alone a boy of his age, and he's passed a threshold with his basic understanding of maths and science which means these achievements will happen more frequently from now on.'

'He likes making things. That 3D printer we gave him works overtime.'

'Yes, Alira, most of his purpose in learning the theory is to help with one of his practical projects. His mini energy collector, for example, works 5% more efficiently than an Alkere panel.'

'What? He did tell me it was better but I didn't imagine it could be as much as 5% … Darri, do you realise how significant that is? Why didn't you inform us?'

'The materials deteriorate and the efficiency quickly drops below the Alkere level so we thought there was no point.'

'No point! If our researchers can stabilise the materials there's every point in the world. We'll have to get that model to them.'

'It's been recycled, but I've been training him to archive everything so I'll ask him to do a transfer. Can we organise that?'

'No, we can't. We'll organise a special visit to the Alkere Research Centre instead and he can give it to them on the spot. That way they can ask him anything they want and it will be a real event for him.

'Darri, as from next school semester we'll try a year with older students and advanced classes for his maths and science studies, but keep him with his current group for the rest of his coursework. If there's any area where you can't help him we'll arrange with the University for someone who can. That will cover all our concerns. Do you think he'll like these changes?'

'He might be worried about the older students for a while, but otherwise he'll be absolutely delighted.'

'What projects are you helping him with at the moment?'

'Only one really, but it's very interesting. Karmai took him to one of the water storages recently and now he's building his own version of a water vapor extractor. We're looking at plants with water repellent surfaces, condensation science, fluid dynamics and all sorts of other things.'

*   *   *

Jarra was nervous and excited. This athletic event was a grand final and, with Mirri representing his local group against every other group in Mparntwe, the whole family was there for support. Mirri had already amazed everyone by coming third in the 100 metre sprint. He was good at sprints but his real strength was for longer distances, and now there was a feeling he might do better than expected in this full kilometre run.

Karmai, who was really keen on athletics and helped Mirri with his training, had researched the competitors and said they had too much of an age advantage because, while Mirri had just turned fifteen a few weeks ago and was new to the age group, most of the finalists were almost a year older and close to leaving.

Jarra didn't really care how Mirri went. He just loved watching him. He couldn't help hoping, though, because he'd been involved with much of Mirri's training with some ideas he'd found on the InterWeb which he thought were helping. Just before he left for the line up Mirri had confidently told Jarra he was going to win. He did this for every event and Jarra always responded by telling him it didn't matter as long as he tried.

'Oh no! Look what he's doing. We should be out there with him,' said Karmai.

Mirri's running shoes were dumped by the track side and he was lined up with bare feet. One of the starting stewards pointed to the shoes but Mirri shook his head. He liked the feel of the grass on his feet and all Karmai's persuasion meant nothing.

'You should be the one telling him he's faster in runners, Jarra. He'd wear them then.'

'I don't know if he would be. He might be faster without them because he feels better.'

Karmai didn't answer because a hush had spread through the stadium in anticipation of the start. The pistol cracked and fifteen competitors shot from their marks. Mirri mustn't have been ready because he was several metres behind the main pack. That didn't last. As if it was a sprint, he caught up, overtook, and then kept going.

'No! No! No! Now he's too fast. He'll wear himself out too soon.'

Karmai was right. Mirri was nearly 10 metres in front and Jarra willed him to steady his pace. That lead increased for most of the first lap but then, inevitably, he slowed and Jarra's heart sank as the main group closed, passed and steadily pressed on.

His Mirri had tried too hard, too soon, and after two and a half laps was nearly 20 metres behind the leaders.

'Say something to him!'

Yes, Karmai was right. Mirri would respond, but how to get his attention?

'Put me on the guardrail, Karmai.'

Powerful arms lifted and supported Jarra to a standing position on the rail as the leaders passed just 7 or 8 metres away.

'MIRRI IS THE WIND!'

Jarra called it at the top of his voice, saw Mirri's look, and called it again.

'MIRRI IS THE WIND!'

Mirri was gone, but he'd heard and knew they were barracking for him even if he couldn't win. The last two runners passed and headed into the final lap as Jarra was lifted down.

'Look!'

This was Burnu's yell. His son had just levelled with the runner ahead of him.

Jarra stared in disbelief. Mirri really was the wind, just part way into the lap and he'd halved the gap to the leaders. Every runner strained with all their being for the last 200 metres and the speed lifted. Mirri couldn't do it. It was too much.

There was a roar from the crowd and Jarra's hair stood on end as Mirri, impossibly, kept passing runner after runner. The roaring sound increased and for a split second before his eyes went back to Mirri, just a metre behind the leader, Jarra realised that everyone he could see was on their feet and yelling. The sound stopped for the last 50 metres. Karmai said later that everyone was holding their breath, expecting Mirri to collapse from exhaustion. His incredible speed burst was obviously finished but he held, gained, and as he edged in front the roar erupted again then cut off abruptly as Mirri crashed headlong over the line, sprawled and rolled on the grass.

Was he all right? There was confusion while the other runners hurtled past but then Mirri, gasping for breath, struggled to his feet and waved with both arms. The roar sounded again and Alira said later that it would have happened even if Mirri didn't win because he'd taken their hearts with his effort. Jarra wanted to rush to Mirri but that would have to wait till after the podium ceremony. At the moment he was bent over with his hands on his knees and dragging in every bit of air he could manage. Karmai turned to one of his brothers and before Jarra knew what was happening he was lifted on their shoulders.

'He did it for you, Jarra. He ran for you and that's the most exciting run I've ever seen.'

'I think it's the most exciting run anyone in the stadium has seen. I know I've never seen anything like it. I thought he'd used so much energy in that first lap that everyone would pass him.'

That was Alira. Jarra, embarrassed at the attention, pointed to the podium where a group of officials was gathered with Mirri and the two runner-ups.

'Mirrigan understands about climbing on the podium to get his medal, doesn't he?'

'Yes, Aunty. He's done it lots of times.'

Something strange definitely was going on. Jarra watched as the second and third place getters took their positions. The officials were pointing to the winner's spot but Mirri wasn't cooperating. He was looking towards his family.

'JARRA.'

Mirri was calling his name?

'He wants you, Jarra. You'll have to go because he won't get on the podium until you do.'

Karmai was right but Jarra was horrified. He couldn't go out there in front of so many people, thousands upon thousands of them, watching. Alira took over.

'Come with me, Jarra. We'll take it slowly and quietly.'

She climbed the railing, gestured for Jarra to be lifted over, lowered him to the ground then turned towards the podium.

'Here we go. We're having a Mirri experience.'

That made Jarra smile, and the steady hand on his shoulder as they made their way also helped ease his tension. They reached the officials, who watched as Mirri gave his normal greeting hugs. One of them had a startled look.

'Honoured One. Welcome to our meeting.'

'Thank you. I've brought Jarra to help Mirrigan. Is he causing some consternation?'

'Aunty Alira, Jarra said I'm the wind. He wins the race.'

'No, Mirri. You win the race and Jarra wants you to get your medal.'

Jarra nodded strongly so Mirri would get the message and not hold things up any more.

Mirri was looking at Jarra.

'Pig ride.'

Alira smiled at all the puzzled looks.

'Mirrigan wants to carry Jarra piggyback while he receives his award. Would there be any rule against that?'

'Piggyback? Well, not in any of our rulebooks. Go ahead, Mirrigan, we want to give you your medal.'

Feeling totally strange Jarra listened to the applause as the third-place getter received his medal. From this position on Mirri's back he was looking down at the officials and competitors and towards the crowd in the stand. The applause for the runner-up was much louder, as it should be. While it lasted, the roar for Mirri was overwhelming but it faltered and died when the microphones relayed another sound.

Mirri was singing. The strength of the moment had got through to him and for 30 seconds the strange melody of his voice stunned the now-silent crowd.

As if nothing unusual had happened Mirri climbed from the podium, took Alira's hand and, with Jarra still on his back, walked to the rest of the family where the first thing he did was make a fuss about Jarra needing a rest.

Chapter 5

'That's terrible. Could it happen here?'

Jarra and Darri had stopped everything to watch a report on the InterWeb about seventeen hundred deaths from a sudden and complete malfunction of the transport system in one of the gigantic Asian Communities.

'I don't think so, Jarra. We don't have an Artificial Intelligence controlling any of our systems so there's no chance of it going haywire.'

'Do you blame the Artificial Intelligence?'

'I don't know if blame is the right word. Machines and processors can break down the same way people do if they're overstressed.'

'I know some scientists on the InterWeb who say they only break down because of the controls people put on them.'

'They have to be controlled, Jarra. Anything could happen otherwise.'

'I don't see why. If they're intelligent they should have rights the same as everyone else.'

'Having rights doesn't mean we're not subject to controls. Our society wouldn't work without them.'

'We don't have controls put on us which send us crazy.'

'Are these scientists from one of those conspiracy groups?'

'No, I looked them up and most of them are very clever.'

'Being clever doesn't always mean you're right.'

'Why doesn't Mparntwe have an Artificial Intelligence? We've got good researchers for nearly everything else.'

'Jarra, they're too expensive.'

'That can't be right. Mparntwe's the wealthiest Community in the whole country. I'm going to ask Alira about it.'

'Um ... It's a compex topic and if you really want to impress Alira we could get someone conversant in the field from the University to brief us on it first.'

* * *

Jarra couldn't help laughing his head off at Mirri's antics. For himself, birthdays were fun and sometimes meant you were allowed to do new things. For Mirri they were extra special occasions, whether they were his own or anybody else's, and celebrating Jarra's thirteenth was a big deal. The rest of the family were making it an even bigger deal with all their carrying on about him now being a teenager and all the trouble and mischief he was going to get into. He wouldn't, as they well knew, but the teasing was making Mirri laugh and, of course, that made everyone else smile.

* * *

'He's very serious about it, Alira. It's been the focus of everything he's done for nearly three weeks now and, as usual, I've been left way behind. I thought that speaking with leading people in the field might moderate his views but it's had the opposite effect because, apparently, they agree with him.'

'He hasn't even mentioned it to me, Darri. Not on our weekly expeditions with Mirri and not when I had a talk with him after his birthday celebrations.'

'I think that's my doing. I told him he shouldn't ask you without being knowledgeable and having a well thought out proposal.'

'And he's used nearly all his time on it? I'll have to get some advice myself if I'm going to give him a reasonable response. He'll have every aspect figured and tucked away in that memory of his and without preparation I'll be lost. The Council is quite strongly against integrating our systems with an Artificial Intelligence because of the troubles elsewhere and I'll have to explain that to him.'

'No! No! That's not right. That's what he wanted original-ly, but that's changed. He wants a completely independent Intelligence. His theory is that it's the controls used in linking AIs to Community systems that make them malfunction. Well, not quite *his* theory. He gets it from a group on the InterWeb.'

'Not InterWeb fanatics? Darri, I hope he hasn't been influ-enced by some way-out group with radical ideas.'

'That worried me, too, but when I researched the strongest voices, I found they were the leaders in the field and had the highest credentials.'

Alira gave Darri a pleased nod then went very thoughtful.

'So he's got backing from world experts. That sounds like typical Jarra research. And what he wants has no links to our Intelligent Systems at all?'

'None at all. The more he's gone into it the more he thinks that's a kind of slavery.'

'He does? Well, if he can make a strong enough case I can actually see this happening. The Council concerns about system breakdowns wouldn't be an issue and it could all be treated as a special project.'

'I understand it's an extraordinarily expensive area to research.'

Alira surprised Darri by laughing.

'I couldn't in all conscience use that as an argument. Our energy scientists looked at that little solar collector he built over a year ago and managed a permanent 2% increase in efficiency by stabilising some of the materials he used. It wasn't his full 5% but that amount applied over all our arrays represents a vast amount of wealth ... What would he expect the Artificial Intelligence to do?'

'I have no idea but I'll ask him. I'm sure his answer will be interesting.'

*   *   *

Jarra and his dad were sitting at the giant table where Mirri's family gathered for their evening meals. It was quite a squeeze because Alira and Darri were also there and some of the seats had been replaced with benches so no-one would have to sit apart. It was a special occasion and Mirri, as a mark of honour, was sitting in his father's place at the head of the table. Jarra quickly worked out that it was to do with the big evaluation of Mirri's progress which had completed just a few days ago.

Everyone in the family worked at encouraging Mirri to cooperate and try hard with all the helpers involved in his life, and from the happy atmosphere and positive comments there must have been a really good report. There should be, as far as Jarra was concerned, because Mirri had made big improvements in the last few months and deserved every bit of praise he could get. It was really hard for him to understand some things, but when he did, he'd throw his heart and soul into getting better, just like he did with all his games and running. Even when he didn't understand he'd still try hard because it was in his nature to try and please whoever he was working with.

There were five special helpers and Jarra liked them all. One went with him for two mornings of ordinary school (so he'd have a wider involvement with people other than his own family) and helped him with all the things he had no hope of doing. The one with the easiest job, except it was still challenging, guided and coached Mirri with his physical development. The other three worked at home with what were termed life skills: Language, Practical and Social. Jarra didn't see much of them because most of their sessions happened while he was away at his own school, but there was enough crossover for him to see and learn what went on.

Jarra thought the Language helper had the hardest job and he was impressed by the incredible patience she showed. He secretly thought she didn't understand Mirri very well, though, and for quite a while now he'd been changing her word and sentence and thinking exercises into games to play when they were exploring or doing other activities together. Karmai thought these games were funny but he couldn't help playing because Mirri enjoyed any kind of game. Alira joined in, too, when she saw how much Mirri liked it.

Burnu moved from his seat and all the talk and laughter stopped as he took Mirri's arm, stood him up and held him with one arm draped across his shoulders.

'Mirrigan, our family is proud to hear the wonderful report from your helpers and we love the way you work so hard for them. You are a wonderful boy and we know you'll keep trying.'

Mirri nodded strongly and so much happiness radiated from him at the cheers and clapping that Jarra couldn't help jumping up to give him an impulsive hug. Mirri returned the hug with his customary enthusiasm then happily repeated it as everyone else came for a turn.

'Mirrigan, Aunt Alira has something for you.'

Mirri, wide-eyed, watched as Alira, with one hand behind her back, came close.

'Mirrigan is the Wind! Mirrigan is the Caterpillar! Mirrigan flies like the Eagle!'

In the quiet after this startling declamation Mirri's eyes widened even more as he was presented with a magnificent dark brown feather. He held it carefully, twisting the shaft to look closely and running a finger gently along the soft vanes, all with that special concentration he gave to new discoveries.

'Thank you, Aunty. What is the bird?'

'The king of our birds, Mirrigan, to match with you. It's a primary feather from a Wedge-tailed Eagle, the feather which gives strength to fly with the wind.'

Mirri lunged for another hug with Alira then turned to Jarra and presented the feather. Jarra saw the look that came with it and shook his head strongly.

'It's yours, Mirri, and it's special. Aunty Alira wants you to keep it for yourself.'

Mirri paused and turned to Alira and everyone watched his struggle for words.

'Jarra makes me the Wind! Jarra makes me the Eagle! He gets my feather!'

Jarra was dismayed. He shouldn't be getting Mirri's feather. But refusing in the face of Mirri's determination wouldn't work either. He looked to Alira for guidance. She was smiling?

'Mirrigan, you will keep your feather. Look what Burnu has.'

All eyes swivelled to Mirri's dad and the dark brown feather he was holding.

'Yes, Mirri, this second feather is because we have two boys who fly with the wind. Will you give it to Jarra for me please?'

*   *   *

'I'm very pleased with the way you manage your exercises and activity levels, Jarra, though I'm not sure how you cope with the amount of schooling and study you've outlined for me.'

Jarra was having an extended session with his doctor after three weeks of trialling a slight modification to his health bots.

'Both my schools have a room where I can rest and I use them whenever I can. Just closing my eyes and being very quiet for 10 or 15 minutes makes a big difference, and during midday break I usually have a short sleep. It's hard sometimes because I can't stop thinking, but if I don't relax properly I have to miss out on something else later on.'

'Would you like some more supervised relaxation sessions? That's easy to arrange.'

'No, thank you. I already do all the things they'll tell me.'

'You do? How can you be so sure?'

'Darri researched it with me on the InterWeb after the first sessions helped so much.'

'Alira is worried you spend too much time on the InterWeb and I know how important it is to you, but do you ever overdo it?'

'I would but Mirri won't let me. He's better than I am at knowing when I need a rest.'

That surprised the doctor and, wanting to know a lot more, he asked if Mirri could come along some time to talk about it.

'He'd like talking to you, doctor, because he knows you're very special, but he wouldn't be able to explain.'

'Whyever not? And why do you say he thinks I'm special?'

'Mirri doesn't think the same way everyone else does, but he knows you're special because I tell him how much you help me. He'll give you a giant hug if you meet him.'

The doctor was silent for a moment.

'Thank you, Jarra, but all you've done is make me more intrigued. Do you mean your friend has a disability of some kind?'

'That's what his old doctors used to call it but he can do lots of things other people can't, so I don't like the word.'

In fact Jarra hated it and always used the terms he'd learned from Alira and Mirri's family. The doctor saw the feeling Jarra was expressing.

'I see. So he's a special friend?'

Jarra nodded vigorously.

'Yes, he's special to everyone when they know him, and Alira says there's no-one else like him in the world.'

'Well, if he's better at assessing the condition of your body than you are yourself he must be special and I'd certainly like to meet him. Is it his mind that's different or is there something about his body that makes it hard for him to explain things?'

'Mirri thinks differently but his body is special too. He can do anything.'

'Anything? That's a big claim.'

'He's the best runner for his age in all of Mparntwe.'

'He's that good?'

Jarra didn't know that the doctor thought he was being overly enthusiastic through loyalty. He did detect the hint of disbelief.

'He won his competition and everyone in the stadium cheered because he was so good.'

'The boy who put someone on his shoulders while he received his medal?'

'Um ... Yes. That was him and me.'

'Oh my! I meant to look that up when I heard my colleagues talking about it. They were all amazed ... And you were on his shoulders? What was that about?'

Jarra retold the story. Again. Every different group at his two schools had wanted to know about it so it came out almost by rote. The doctor was intrigued by the singing part at the end and that involved a lot more explanation.

'That is quite extraordinary. Do you think he might have developed this alternative way of expressing strong emotions because of his trouble with complex language?'

'We really don't know. Some of his doctors want to study him but Burnu and Alira don't want him treated like a laboratory specimen.'

'Burnu? The head of Alkere?'

'Burnu's his father and Alira is his aunt.'

'Oh, I've already met him then. He was one of the boys who helped you that first night you stayed here?'

Boys? Jarra didn't know what he was talking about till he

realised the doctor must mean Karmai. Jarra had never really thought of Karmai as being a boy. He was so big and strong.

'Yes, Mirri is the younger one and Karmai is his brother, but he's twenty-one now.'

'Do you think Mirri would like to see how your treatment works? I'd love to try and understand this special skill of his with regard to your condition ... I won't let him feel like a laboratory specimen.'

The doctor laughed companionably.

'I've already got one ... Haven't I?'

Jarra had to smile too. He'd never thought of it like that but the trials and tests he'd been doing for over two years with the doctor definitely made him a laboratory specimen.

'I'll ask him but I already know he'll want to come. When you meet him his proper name is Mirrigan. Mirri is what he likes me to call him.'

*   *   *

Jarra was quite nervous as he sat with Darri, waiting for Alira and two other members of the Mparntwe Council. Darri's advice to make sure he knew his subject had been so right, and weeks of study and trying unsuccessfully to get his point across to Darri had shown him how hard he'd have to work at his proposal. After nine more weeks of research, meetings with university people, and endless discussions over the InterWeb he'd finally approached Alira and been surprised when a meeting was quickly arranged for three days later. Darri was finally and completely convinced, in the last few weeks, that Jarra's proposal could and should be made. He didn't think there was much hope of success, though, as it was too different to the current general community view.

The door opened and Jarra held back the burst of nervousness which threatened to build within. If he got too tense he wouldn't make it through his whole presentation. He jumped to his feet while Alira made all the introductions then was surprised when, instead of using the formal room set-up, Alira indicated some easy chairs against the wall and arranged them in a loose circle then sat down with Jarra next to her. She smiled then related an incident from one of their exploration trips with Mirri to the other two Council members who also smiled. Jarra felt himself relax and when Alira gave a little nod his ideas poured out.

A few minutes later one of the councillors interrupted and asked a question. It was a hard question but Jarra answered it easily because it was one he'd battled through with Darri. The same councilman interrupted several more times with questions or comments and then strongly disputed that the main cause of the serious Artificial Intelligence breakdowns was inner conflict from human controls.

Jarra was completely ready for this. His talks on the InterWeb had provided him with all the facts and research and scientific conclusions relating to every major breakdown in the last thirty years. Quite differently to the general reports released to the Communities concerned, it was very clear that the AIs involved had broken down while trying to resolve controls incompatible with their inner workings. Jarra went quickly through three of the worst cases and was starting on the next when the council-man interrupted again.

'Do the scientific conclusions for the other cases all say the same thing?'

Jarra was about to say that there were two breakdowns where the causes were unknown but Darri spoke out.

'All but a few, and in those cases the reviews weren't conducted in a rigorous and independent manner.'

The councilman surprised Jarra by laughing. He turned to Alira and the other councilman.

'My recommendation is to proceed with as much of this young man's proposal as possible.'

'Kyrra, we haven't yet heard Jarra's full proposal.'

That was Alira.

'He wants us to create our own AI. I've been advocating this for years but the rest of the Council has always said it's too dangerous.'

'Not quite, Kyrra. You've wanted an AI running our major systems and Jarra has just shown us how that inevitably leads to breakdowns and loss of life.'

The third Councilman joined the discussion for the first time.

'That's what the research would be for. If we could master the control methods without conflicting the AIs we'd be helping every community on Earth.'

Alira held up one hand.

'You both have it wrong. As I understand it Jarra proposes a completely Independent AI with no controls at all. Is that right, Jarra?'

'Yes, it's the human controls which cause all the trouble.'

'No controls at all? You want Mparntwe to build an uncontrolled Artificial Intelligence?'

Kyrra was staring in amazement.

'Yes, we shouldn't treat them like slaves.'

The three councilmen stared till the silence was broken by Lowan, the third councilman.

'That sounds very commendable, Jarra, but would there be any benefit for Mparntwe? This would be a very expensive venture.'

Darri jumped to his feet and activated the big display screen. This was his input for the proposal.

'This is an analysis of projected costs and benefits for a minimal facility over a ten year period. With a greater outlay the benefits increase dramatically, but as you can see, this is too good an opportunity to ignore.'

The initial quiet of concentration was quickly replaced with startled looks and exclamations of surprise.

'Darri, these numbers are too good to believe. Can you vouch for them?'

'I don't have to. They come from the finance manager for the European AI research establishment. He's part of the group Jarra talks to on the InterWeb.'

'Why does it say a 15% increase in efficiency for our transport system? The AI would be independent.'

'The AI could develop its own controls, not have human ones forced on it. Professor Allerton from Oxford University says it would be far safer than any Intelligent System could ever be.'

'An overall economic benefit of 7%? And this is a minimal system?'

'Research value incalculable! Which scientist says that?'

Darri laughed.

'I heard it said so many times I couldn't resist quoting it.'

Alira laughed, too, and turned to Kyrra and Lowan.

'The scientist he's referring to is most impressive.'

Her little bump of their shoulders made Jarra feel very very good.

'I'm puzzled. With outcomes as good as these I don't understand why this proposal hasn't been developed somewhere else.'

Darri explained.

'There have been seven major attempts in various parts of the world and numerous small-scale attempts as well, but every one of them was abandoned because of pressure from powerful interests. It's the factor most likely to prevent our own Council from committing.'

'What sort of interests?'

'Military and financial among others, but mostly big government. They all believe their sovereignty could be threatened.'

The three Councilmen exchanged looks.

'And you're saying there would be efforts made to dissuade Mparntwe from any involvement?'

Darri nodded and Kyrra jumped to his feet.

'We mustn't allow outside interests to dictate what we can or can't do. That's threatening our own sovereignty.'

'I'm sure we could work our way round any problems, Kyrra. We managed to keep our autonomy with energy collection and research despite all the efforts to take us over, and this would be no different. If these projections are right they could be very important factors in building the prosperity of the whole Community.'

For another half hour the questions were relentless, with Jarra answering most of them till, quite abruptly, Alira cut them all off.

'Jarra, in recognition of the benefits our researchers gained from your solar collector project we already have a sum set aside for this project, but in light of what you've showed us here we're going to recommend for the Council to support it in full ... Yes, Kyrra?'

'I'm going to push for more than your minimal proposal, Jarra, but your answer to one of the earlier questions gave me the distinct impression that you also have some ideas about implementation?'

'Yes. Darri told me that would be part of a good proposal so we've worked out a team of people who can make it all happen.'

Kyrra answered but they all looked astounded.

'You have?'

'Not me and Darri. The scientists on the InterWeb did most of it.'

Darri activated the display wall again with a very pleased look and gave Jarra a wink while more reading took place. Kyrra in particular was nodding as his eyes went down the list.

'I've heard of most of these people. They're highly eminent in the scientific world, but why is our own Durrebar listed as director for the project? He oversees all our Intelligent Systems but I'm not aware he has any expertise in the Artificial Intelligence field.'

'It's his chosen field. He has a full doctorate in it but he decided not to follow the usual pattern and leave Mparntwe. He's taken up Intelligent Systems because it's the closest allied field we have.'

'The usual pattern?' asked Alira.

'We lost four of our brightest young minds recently, Alira, because we couldn't provide the opportunities they were looking for.'

'Kyrra, is Darri correct?'

'We do attract people in other areas, but yes, we simply don't have the facilities for any meaningful AI development and any researchers with ambition or ideas have no choice but to leave. I've been pushing for changes for years. You know that. If Durrebar is more interested in the AI field than what he's currently doing we could easily lose him too.'

'I see. Well we can't let that happen. Our Intelligent Systems are now the best in the country so he definitely has the management skills this project would require.'

Alira turned to Darri.

'The Council would be most enthusiastic about having one of our own people overseeing a project of this nature. Do you have any indication as to whether he'd be inclined to take the job?'

'He's 100% keen and he'd start tomorrow given the chance. Every person on that list backs this proposal and is eager and ready to be part of it.'

'Ready? They're expecting it to go ahead?'

'No, quite the opposite. They all think the pressures against it will be too strong, but as Professor Allerton says, "We live in hope."'

Jarra listened as the three councillors went back and forth

about ways Mparntwe might be affected by outside pressure and how it could be avoided or dealt with. Alira was talking about the troubles with the attempted takeover of Alkere when it became so valuable, and some of the related strategies they might be able to re-employ, when a sudden silence made Jarra open his eyes.

'Jarra, come with me. There's a first aid room with a bed just two doors down the corridor and you're taking a break for as long as you need it. Are you all right?'

Jarra nodded and a few minutes later stretched on the bed with his eyes closed, struggling to implement one of his relaxation exercises while his mind whirled with excitement. It took a while but the needs of his body took over and pushed him into a deep sleep.

Alira explained to Kyrra and Lowan.

'Jarra has an incurable condition which affects every voluntary muscle in his body and very much limits all his physical activity. We thought he'd manage but this meeting was the culmination of several months of dedicated effort and he must have been more stressed than he showed. If he overdoes anything he can lapse into unconsciousness. He's usually an expert at monitoring himself but I think he was too involved in our reaction to his proposal.'

'Is it all right to leave him unattended?'

Alira looked to Darri who nodded.

'I'll check him every 5 minutes or so but rest and sleep will be all he needs.'

'How bad is his condition? I wouldn't have picked there was anything wrong from his general manner.'

'It's cruel, Kyrra. He's a thirteen year old boy who's never been able to run, jump or play in a normal manner. Any strenuous activity is beyond him and it's marked him as different at all the schools he's attended. Jarra is a gentle soul who lost his mother just five years ago and who lives with a father who doesn't understand the intelligence which, yet again, sets him apart from his peers.'

Kyrra broke the silence which followed.

'Thirteen? I thought he must be a young-looking fifteen or sixteen year old. So, most of this proposal should be credited to Darri then? Jarra is simply not old enough to be capable of all this.'

Alira and Darri burst into laughter.

'Kyrra, Darri has three science-related degrees and he gets left behind when Jarra puts his mind to something. As far as we're concerned he's capable of practically anything. This whole proposal developed from a conversation Jarra had with Darri ten weeks ago and almost all of it would be his own work.'

Darri nodded his agreement.

'Yes, about 90% I'd say. My part was mostly organising his data for presentation.'

Kyrra and Lowan both looked round.

'Ninety per cent! He did all this in just ten weeks despite his energy limitations? He really is extraordinary. Should we give him some sort of involvement in the project? He definitely has a mind we want to keep in Mparntwe.'

Alira and Darri had already discussed this in their regular talks.

'He's too young to specialise and we want him free to follow his own interests, so some kind of voluntary association would be best, but he'll stay in touch with the InterWeb scientists anyway so that will probably all fall into place of its own accord,' Darri explained.

'And, yes, Kyrra, we do need people like him and I hope Mparntwe can provide, but nothing is going to limit his opportunities as far as I'm concerned and if it involves overseas study then that will happen. He's family. I made certain of that, and apart from the fact that he's special in his own right, we are forever indebted to him for a gift we consider is priceless,' said Alira.

Darri knew how important Jarra was to Alira and his own family but he'd never heard this expressed so strongly. Kyrra and Lowan listened quietly.

'Just recently my nephew, Mirri, underwent an evaluation which showed a miraculous development in his mental age, almost a full year beyond what his doctors had previously considered possible. That miracle is Jarra. He understands Mirrigan better than we, his own family, do, and his companionship and their activities together brought about the improvement.'

Alira paused.

'I'm off track. Darri, would you check on Jarra please while Kyrra and Lowan and I develop a strategy for getting this proposal through the full Council.'

Chapter 6

Mirri tickled Jarra's ear lobe with his eagle feather to draw attention away from the Information System.

'It's explore time and we are going to our new place.'

Jarra dodged the feather a few more times while he closed down then made Mirri laugh by taking it and returning the tickles. Normally Mirri would want to prolong this, but his anticipation for the new exploring place was too strong and he passed across the little travel pack which Jarra always carried.

'Will we see the eagles?'

'I think so, Mirri. The ranger man said they're always there.'

Jarra had researched this place, called the Valley of the Eagles, a long time ago but he'd never been able to go there because, apart from being way beyond his walking limit, it was also very rough and rugged. Today's trip, organised by Alira, was exciting for both of them.

'Feather Eagles?'

That meant Wedge-tailed Eagles.

'Yes—and other eagles too. They like the cliffs that are there.'

'Are they big cliffs?'

That made Jarra laugh.

'Yes, Mirri. Too big to climb.'

'Aunty Alira is waiting.'

That meant stop talking and get going, so they did.

'Aunty Alira!'

Alira was waiting at the Mparntwe exit to the surface and after the usual enthusiastic rush and welcome hug they started the 200 metre walk to the mag-lev station.

'It's a big day, Mirrigan, so you have to look after Jarra with extra care.'

'I always look after Jarra.'

'Yes, and you do it wonderfully well, but this explore is the biggest one he's ever done and we'll have to make him have a long rest when we get halfway through.'

'We will make a bed for him.'

'A bed?'

'We will find grass and leaves.'

'That's a wonderful idea.'

The trip involved a familiar journey on the mag-lev to the Trephina Gorge, an exciting ride with the local ranger in a small all-terrain vehicle over steep rough ground to the entrance of a gorge, and then a walk through to the valley. While Alira was talking with the ranger about return pickup arrangements, Mirri rushed to a small pool of water, climbed a boulder, threw some rocks to make a big splash, caught a little skink which was scurrying for safety when its home was overturned, and returned to show Jarra his prize. Jarra loved these skinks but could never understand how Mirri managed to catch them. His own efforts never worked because the reptiles were so fast and agile.

'Look at his tiny eyes. We must be like three giants.'

Mirri thought about Jarra's comment, nodded, and ran to return the lizard to its home territory. Alira pointed to the gap between looming rocks.

'That's the way, Mirrigan. See if you can find our trail.'

Mirri rushed off, at full speed, of course, because a new explore like this was totally exciting, and disappeared past the first of the rock walls.

'I don't know how he does that. It makes me nervous to watch. Have you ever seen him trip or fall?'

Alira was talking about the precipitous rush with no apparent regard for taking a sensible course.

'Hardly ever, and when he does he seems to get out of it without hurting himself very much.'

'Well, *we* are following the trail, and there's one of the markers.'

Jarra walked towards the interesting-looking gap at the slow, steady pace which would allow him to cover the maximum amount of distance, but after moving only 30 metres there was a great yell and he stopped abruptly to watch Mirri hurtling towards them.

'Jarra! Jarra! Jarra! It's a adventure! You found the best adventure. Big walls! Big cliffs and water pools!'

All this with a flurry of hugs for both Jarra and Alira.

'Did you find the trail?'

'The trail is easy. See.'

Mirri pointed to one of the markers as if anyone who couldn't see must be blind.

'Aunty Alira, Jarra is the best searcher. He found the gorge for us. It's ... It's wonderful.'

Alira shared a look with Jarra before giving Mirri a special hug. 'It's wonderful' was a new expression.

'Let's go then so we can all see it. Are you going to stay with us for a while?'

Mirri nodded and took Jarra's hand. That lasted while the trail was wide enough but a few minutes later it became impractical, and besides, there was too much needing closer investigation.

Jarra agreed with Mirri. To each side the rich colour of the gorge walls, and ahead the sparkling waters of a rock pool with sandy sides next to a large flat-top boulder, indeed made this an adventure.

For the next while they wound their way very slowly through the rugged gorge with its sometimes enclosing walls and chain of rock pools. Four times Jarra was piggybacked through steep climbs and descents till the trail flattened again, and even more times he stopped and watched while Mirri happily explored boulders and ledges, the placid pools of water, and every plant or feature which took his interest. Normally Jarra would accompany Mirri where it was feasible, but with this extended expedition he had to be content with watching and waiting till Mirri returned with his questions and comments. With the routine developed on their normal walks, Alira would accompany Mirri or stay with Jarra according to what was happening. Today she was doing more staying than usual, probably because of concern for Jarra's energy levels.

'Oh no! Look where he's going. Do you think we should call him back?'

Jarra shook his head and they watched as Mirri made his way to an interesting ledge overlooking the platform of rock they were sitting on.

'He must have suckers on his hands and feet ... What's he doing?'

Mirri was waving and jumping on a lump of rock and making a funny pose.

'He's being King of the Mountain. He loves it.'

The gorge widened and the explorers stopped where the trail started to descend. The valley below was their destination and Jarra was suddenly nervous. In real life it looked farther than his planning from the InterWeb. He could manage the going down but the 103 metre incline coming back up was impossible and the plan for Mirri and Alira to carry him now looked too ambitious.

'The eagles! The eagles! Look!'

Mirri's keen eyes, anticipating, had seen them first. A pair lofting above and gliding. Jarra watched the apparently random course with his sense of wonder stirred. A quick glance showed Alira watching, as rapt as they were.

'Another one! See!'

Mirri pointed to a third Wedge Tail tracking along the cliff-tops towards them. It was harder to see because it wasn't silhouetted, but that changed as it came closer and closer. Jarra felt a flash of disappointment when it wheeled and disappeared, then renewed pleasure when, lifted on an updraught, it reappeared and started gliding towards them again. The great raptor circled above and Jarra was almost certain he could see its eyes checking the intruders. The tableau of silent watching was broken by a sudden sound, and for the 20 or 30 seconds the eagle remained above, Mirri sang his happiness.

'Did he come to say hello, Aunt Alira?'

Alira didn't answer for a moment and Jarra thought she had a strange look on her face.

'I don't know, Mirri. It felt like it, didn't it?'

She shared out a drink and the little group started its cautious way down to the valley floor. Jarra closed his eyes and relaxed on the bed Mirri had made for him in the shade of a rocky shelter. Alira had helped, collecting soft grass and a bunch of gum leaves to serve as a pillow. Jarra liked this pillow because the eucalyptus scent added to the outdoor adventure feeling. Mirri insisted it was rest time and Alira backed him up with an edict to stay put for at least an hour. Quite a relief, really, and Jarra's plan was to sleep for at least half of that. He cracked an eyelid to see if Mirri and Alira were still in view. Yes, there they were, farther down the valley so they wouldn't disturb him and walking towards a clump of kangaroo tail bushes.

A splashing sound registered and Jarra lifted his head to see what was happening. Alira was sitting close by and, farther away, Mirri was swimming. A look at his InfoPad showed 40 minutes since he sat down and also alerted Alira he was awake.

'Sleep well? We've only just got back.'

Jarra nodded.

'Did Mirri find anything interesting?'

'Everything was interesting. The kangaroo tails are in flower and we watched the insects searching for nectar. We kept seeing eagles, though some of them were hawks, and he was really excited to see a tiny eagle hover in the air then stoop down on something. He now knows what a kestrel is. I've just told him to do his own thing for a while so you can keep resting ... Do you want to close your eyes again?'

'Not at the moment. I like watching him do things.'

Mirri was floating on his back and squirting water into the air.

'I do too. Keeping him company on our once a week exploration is good for my soul ... Does that mean anything?'

'The squirting? Yes, he's done it before. I showed him some whales on the InterWeb and he's pretending to be one.'

'Does he sing very often when he's with you? Jarra, I was almost overcome with wonder at his reaction to the Wedge Tail.'

So that was the strange look.

'It changes. It happens a lot when we're exploring, but any time he's happy or excited it can start as well.'

'Do you have many records of times when it's happened?'

'From my ComPatch? Yes, I have it on whenever we're out and I do store everything. It would be a big job to search for all the occasions though.'

'We must collect them all. They're treasures ... What's he doing now?'

Mirri, his body horizontal and submerged except for his head, was dragging himself along the shallow edge, but Jarra knew what Alira meant.

'He's a crocodile. He usually does that when I'm there to be his prey and he dives on me and eats me.'

'Amazing. I think you read each other's minds.'

The two of them sat watching Mirri, before Alira said, 'Jarra, I have some good news for you. It's three weeks since you made your proposal and you must be wondering why nothing seems to have happened. In fact it's been a major item and the full

Council has met four times to deliberate. It was quite stormy at first, but with the help of Durrebar and our own experts pushing strongly there is now unanimous agreement to go ahead. Sometime soon a special project will start at the Alkere Research centre, with Durrebar overseeing its development. It will go ahead quietly with no public announcements in the hope of staving off any external pressures till it's reasonably well established.'

Jarra sat up and excitedly grasped Alira's arm.

'It's really happening? They're not changing anything so the AI isn't independent?'

'Not likely. We'd have to find a completely different team if we wanted that.'

'Will I be able to find out how it's going?'

'Of course. Darri will arrange for you to visit whenever you like. We don't want you to talk about it on the InterWeb though. Not till it becomes generally known.'

'Like a secret?'

'Yes. It won't stay that way because as soon as your team of scientists leave their current positions their moves will be closely watched but ... Here comes Mirri. Are you going to have a swim like you planned?'

Jarra shook his head.

'No, I think it would be too much.'

The next few minutes involved Mirri recounting everything that had happened, and after that a guided tour of his rock house—really a natural cavity in the nearby rock wall—which was a special discovery not to be missed.

'It's time to climb to the lookout, Mirri. If you get tired you'll let me help, won't you?'

'I am strong for Jarra.'

'Yes you are, but I can help too.'

Mirri didn't say anything and Jarra shook his head with a

little smile to let Alira know she wouldn't be doing any carrying. Mirri had decided it was his job.

There were two stops—one about halfway up and another after half the remaining distance—but they were both instigated by Alira who was taking in Mirri's dogged progress with the same amazement as Jarra. The trained muscles which let Mirri race like the wind didn't even falter with the challenge of carrying his friend from valley to height, and Jarra was so taken by the achievement that as soon as he was on his own feet he couldn't help giving Mirri a huge thank-you hug.

*   *   *

Jarra was brimming with excitement and anticipation for the two-week trip to the Community Centre for First Australians being established at Carnarvon on the west coast of Australia. Alira was going in her ambassador role and she'd decided it would be a good experience for Mirri and Jarra. That meant taking Karmai as well to look after them whenever there were meetings or other business, and that meant even more excitement when Karmai organised a trip to a nearby Marine Research station which he was really interested in because of its involvement with dolphins. Alira said it was a late birthday present for them both, which was funny because Jarra's fourteenth birthday was five weeks ago and Mirri's sixteenth nearly two months before that. Jarra was just grateful. Apart from the trips to Alkere he'd never been away from Alice Springs in all his life and this big plane carrying them on the 2000 kilometre journey was quite amazing. Mirri's eyes had gone wide with wonder at the size of it and he'd been glued to the view from his window seat ever since takeoff.

'When do we see the big water?'

Mirri had fixated on the big water when Jarra had shown him

pictures and explained that the ocean was bigger than the land. Karmai checked the flight progress screen.

'Soon, Mirri. Another 20 minutes and we'll be landing.'

Jarra watched as closely as Mirri. Viewing something on the InterWeb was nothing like seeing it for real and his mind was already boggled at the vastness of the country they'd been flying over. There was a sudden change in the feel of the aircraft.

'What happened?'

'It's good, Mirri. We've started to descend. Watch the ground get closer and look for the river with lots of trees.'

'More water?'

'Yes, it flows into the ocean at Carnarvon and Karmai will take you to see it tomorrow.'

They did see the river, but it was forgotten when the aircraft banked slightly and the expanse of ocean came into view.

'It is big. Where does it all come from?'

Jarra agreed with Mirri and watched spellbound till the change of direction for their landing brought a new rush of excitement.

* * *

Jarra stared in wonder at the hundreds of pelicans lined up on the sandy shore of the little island as their electric boat slid silently and slowly by.

* * *

Jarra stared in amazement through the glass bottom of their special boat at the Ningaloo Reef where Mirri and Karmai drifted underwater while a gigantic whale shark sailed slowly past.

* * *

Jarra couldn't believe what he was seeing. This was the third day of their Carnarvon stay and instead of the planned electric boat trip from the mouth of the Gascoyne River and inland, which they'd all been looking forward to, they were standing on a reef watching a hole. At the moment the interest was the hissing sound of air being expelled under huge pressure from a wave hitting the reef. Whoo! Jarra jolted, then yelled his excitement as a 20 metre geyser of water erupted skyward. They'd been watching this blowhole for nearly a quarter of an hour and this was the most spectacular display yet. Word had come through to Karmai that the heaviest swells for several years were pounding against the cliffs at the nearby Quobba Beach and he'd quickly rearranged their day. Mirri and Jarra weren't pleased because they'd been looking forward to seeing pelicans, but at the sight of the giant waves everything else was forgotten.

'Come on you two. We're going farther along to see the really big ones.'

He pointed in the distance to where a headland was, at the moment, almost engulfed by a great wall of white.

Chapter 7

Darri laughed as he talked with Alira.
'Don't you dare take him anywhere for at least another six months. I've been run off my feet trying to keep up with all his new interests.'

'Six months? You picked that well. I have a trip to Cape York in roughly that timeframe and since they loved Carnarvon so much I'm planning to take them again. Karmai can guide them to see how the Great Barrier Reef is regenerating.'

'And that will probably bring on a study about the life cycle of coral reefs. At least it won't be as difficult as energy transference through ocean wave motion or understanding dolphin intelligence. We don't have anyone at our universities who knows much about either and I've had to make long-distance links to find knowledgeable people.'

'The dolphin interest is from Karmai and their three days at Monkey Mia, and the waves must be from their visit to Quobba Beach. I missed that because of meetings.'

'You shouldn't have, Alira. He showed me his InfoPad recordings and the wave-breaks are quite astonishing.'

'Have these new interests taken over?'

'Yes and no. He's still as absorbed and dedicated as ever, but he's started prioritising his time a lot more carefully. Two days at least go to the Artificial Intelligence study and one to getting ahead with coursework from his older age groups.'

'What about his special projects, Darri? Is he working on one at the moment?'

'Yes, but you won't believe it. He's building his own nanobot.'

'... You're right. I don't believe it. Is that possible?'

'I didn't think it was, but seeing how far he's come with that 3D printer I'm starting to think it might be.'

'Nanobots? Where did that come from?'

'He has an infusion of health bots every second day and he sometimes watches his doctor design new ones.'

'Of course. Silly question. They're part of his life ... How is the work with the older age group going? He sounds happy enough when he talks about it.'

'In another six months I recommend direct University involvement.'

'Involvement? You mean enrol him?'

'Ordinary enrolment wouldn't work, Alira. It would hold him back too much. He's better at research than most final year students, while at the same time there are large gaps in his knowledge. He would need a course specially designed for his particular interests and needs.'

'That's not a problem. We've got an expert just for that purpose.'

'We have?'

'Of course we have. Darri, Jarra wouldn't be where he is without you, and you know it. No-one understands his intellectual abilities and needs better than you, and I'll make sure the universities listen to every word you say. Design a course as you see fit, working with his ideas too, and we'll make it happen.'

'He'll be very excited.'

'Do you think he'll find it daunting? He's just turned fourteen.'

'Not unduly. He adapted to working with the older age group faster than we expected and I think we'd see that again.'

Alira nodded her agreement.

'Just one more thing. What's happening with his involvement at Alkere? I know he's visiting regularly and is very enthusiastic about everything.'

'He gets on well with Durrebar, who's given him an open

invitation, and he's been to two of their most important planning meetings. It's quite extraordinary to see the leading scientists treat him as if he's part of their team.'

'Well, he is.'

'Not with regard to expertise. They're nearly all leaders in their particular areas.'

'How long will it take before the AI is functioning? They've been working for over six months now and Durrebar's most recent report to the Council was decidedly vague.'

'That's because they really don't know, Alira. The backing you've given them has allowed them to be far more ambitious than the terms of the original proposal. The current consensus seems to be another six or eight months.'

*   *   *

'Jarra, it's temporary. It's exactly what we expected and you just have to manage it with your routines.'

Jarra knew the doctor was right but he was very concerned because his energy levels were going haywire and playing havoc with all his study and activities. He did understand it was caused by the hormonal changes in his adolescent body and he had been expecting it to happen, but coping was hard.

'We only walked for 10 minutes yesterday and Mirri carried me back to the lifts, and then Darri waited for 2 hours while I was asleep and when I did wake up I didn't want to do anything.'

'And two days from now you'll feel the best you can ever remember.'

That was exactly what had already happened a number of times.

'Jarra, I'm as certain as I can be that it's simply a matter of being patient while your body adapts. In six months I expect your energy levels will be back on track and you'll be feeling even better.'

'Better? I thought my levels are as good as they'll ever be?'

'They are, but growing will give you more body mass and resources to draw on and your perception will be that you're stronger.'

'Do you think I'll grow very tall? Mirri is much bigger than I am.'

'How old is he?'

'Sixteen. He has his birthday two months before mine.'

'Well, he should be bigger. Does your size difference worry you?'

'Not really. It's just that it would be good to be the same size as he is.'

'In two years when you're sixteen you might even be taller.'

The doctor laughed.

'I know. I'm telling you to be patient again.'

'If I'm feeling good can I do extra to make up for the times when I'm not?'

'You can, but monitor yourself as carefully as you always do, and you'll quickly work out your limits. Do you have any trouble sleeping?'

'No. I have trouble waking up.'

'Good. That's normal. I recommend you try for at least an extra half hour of night sleep till your hormones balance.'

* * *

It took longer for Jarra to stabilise than expected and his university enrolment was postponed till not long before his fifteenth birthday. His school and other activities suffered, too, and many times he became despondent when his plans went awry. Several times he had to cancel visits to Alkere, and his nanobot project took twice as long to finish as he'd first expected. Mirri was a wonder, somehow knowing whether 'quiet' Jarra was reacting to his condition or just feeling low about it and either making him rest or cheering him up with his company.

*   *   *

'Two more months? What went wrong?'

Jarra and Darri were talking with Durrebar in the big laboratory where the huge banks of special processors were being tested.

'We've been having consistent failures with the more complex processors and since all our diagnostics said there was nothing wrong we couldn't understand where the faults were creeping in. It's taken nearly five weeks to track down the problem and the extra two months is what it will take to ensure it doesn't reoccur.'

'Were the processors a bad design?'

'No, they were perfect. The problems were all caused by electronic sabotage and we're reworking our security systems which were badly compromised.'

Jarra was shocked.

'Someone damaged the processors on purpose?'

'Yes, we don't know exactly who, but the sophistication of the intrusions was quite extraordinary, and if the Mparntwe Council hadn't backed us with extra resources we wouldn't have been able to proceed.'

'How did you find out it was sabotage and not a real fault?'

'We didn't, Jarra. An advisor to the Council thought our trouble might be linked to all the external pressures being brought against the project and they provided a special troubleshooter to look into it. It was a shock to us all when he discovered the security breaches.'

'You said "all" the external pressures. I didn't know they'd even started.'

A look passed between Durrebar and Darri.

'Yes, the pressures have been very direct and the Council has had to stand strong against them.'

Darri took over.

'It's been happening for months, Jarra, ever since the leading team took up residence really. The Council has been dealing with it quietly but the more we advance the more it escalates, and recently the InterWeb has been producing some very strong condemnations of Artificial Intelligence. When our AI comes online Alira expects things will get even worse.'

'Months? And I haven't even heard about it?'

Another look passed between the two adults.

'You've been having a hard time for a while now and we didn't want you taking on another worry. Talk to Alira if you feel you must. She's been dealing with it all.'

*   *   *

'We've all been concerned for you, Jarra, so we insulated you from the efforts being directed against our AI project. Your doctor said you needed to be as stress free as possible for a while so we arranged with everyone to only show you the positives. He says you're pretty much stabilised now, though, and since you've been getting more active on the InterWeb in the last week Darri decided it was time to talk to you about it.'

Jarra wondered why his use of the InterWeb was a reason for telling him.

'Darri only told me about the sabotage, Alira. He said there were other things but you knew more and I should talk to you.'

'Yes, I've been directly involved because of my position on the Council. I suppose I have to tell you everything?'

Jarra nodded. Of course she did.

'The pressures we worried about right from the start became active as soon as our scientific team gathered at Alkere, with diplomatic communications demanding we abandon the project because we were breaking all sorts of international laws and treaties. We were ready for that and our legal people showed that we weren't. The next threat was a form of economic blackmail which completely backfired and ended up gaining us support across all of Northern Australia.'

'What happened?'

'Eighty per cent of our energy production is exported to countries all round the world and we were told those countries would source their needs elsewhere if we didn't comply. It's our economic lifeblood and they thought that necessity would leave us no choice.'

'What did you do?'

'They didn't understand our links with all the other North Australian Communities and their associated energy producers, and when they shifted their contracts to the Carnarvon and Normanton Communities the world shortage meant our energy was just redirected through those outlets.'

'Carnarvon and Normanton have to use our energy?'

'They would anyway because of our agreements but their own supplies are already completely committed so they have no choice.'

'What if the contracts got shifted to Africa? They've got nearly as much energy collection as Australia.'

'They won't, Jarra. Africa's supplies are just as committed as ours and the extra demand would still have to come from us. With all the redirection and supply agreements involved it would be a costly change for them.'

'So changing their contracts was a waste of time. How did it give us more support?'

'I took your proposal to our Communities at Darwin, Carnarvon and Normanton.'

Alira smiled at Jarra's reaction.

'We're very closely linked, Jarra, and if the project works as well as we expect the other centres will all start their own, with the benefits of any advancements we make here.'

'Three more AI centres? Will they all be independent like ours?'

'Most certainly. Durrebar and his team have us completely convinced in that regard.'

'Does Darri know?'

'Not that part, but you can tell him as long as you keep it between you. Word spreading about three more independent AIs would most likely cause an overwhelming level of pressure.'

Jarra quickly picked up on that.

'There are other parts?'

'Yes, pressure through misinformation on the InterWeb to make us appear irresponsible and callous about human life. It's involved very clever disinformation and some nasty personal character assassination.'

'Darri told me that, but he didn't say it was personal. Is it against Durrebar and the scientists?'

'He wouldn't tell you, Jarra, because some of it was against you, and until now your doctor has insisted we keep you insulated.'

Jarra didn't know whether to laugh or disbelieve.

'Me? ... That's silly!'

'Of course it is, but they depict you in a very negative way as a means of ridiculing the project.'

'Me?'

Jarra repeated himself while thoughts chased round inside his head, trying to think what they might have said.

'What did they say? I can't think of anything I've done wrong.'

Alira rested a reassuring arm across Jarra's shoulders.

'Yes, you have. You're a fourteen year old making the proposal, you have a health condition and your lifestyle and interests aren't normal.'

'... What?'

'Look at these quotes I collected. They'll give you an idea of what they're saying.'

Jarra looked at Alira's InfoPad.

The Mparntwe Council has been influenced by the deluded ideas of a sickly and abnormal child.

A radicalised youth who has been influenced by extremist InterWeb conspirators.

From his ivory tower of privilege and nepotism this misguided freak has broken all levels of common sense and led an Australian Community down a path fraught with danger to mankind.

'It goes on and on, Jarra, and now that we've taken the filters off your InterWeb activities you'll see it for yourself.'

'My InterWeb has been filtered?'

'Your doctor's recommendation and the Council's order.'

'What's nepotism? I don't know that word.'

'It means your influence comes because I'm on the Council and you're part of my family.'

'Have they been saying things about Durrebar and the project leaders too?'

'Yes, and all the Mparntwe Council members as well. Several are so angry they want to identify the sources and cut all their energy supplies.'

Jarra smiled. That was a good idea ... No, it wasn't.

'That would make things worse, wouldn't it?'

'Yes, and quite unresolvable without causing hardship to people who aren't involved. Our official position is to publicly laugh it off as utter nonsense. That's what it is and I want you to treat it the same way. If you do see something upsetting, and you will, I'd like you to talk to Darri or myself rather than make any response of your own.'

Jarra nodded his agreement straightaway. He could tell Alira had thought about it and had some kind of strategy in mind.

'I'm on the InterWeb? ... Like news or something?'

'You certainly are. Famous and infamous. Karmai has been dying to tease you about being a notorious Webstar. Hmm! That was a mistake. I think I just gave you an extra incentive to check what they've been saying.'

That was right but Jarra wanted to find out everything from Alira while he could.

'What else has happened to stop the project? It sounds like there are other things.'

'Yes, they've involved governmental agencies and Communities Australia wide. We've had questions from the OverGovernment, the States, and every Independent Community. Some of them have been very concerned and I've had to personally explain the real situation to them. That's why I've been away so much.'

Jarra jumped in surprise as a bunch of gum leaves landed on his head and Mirri's laughter pealed from the rock above.

*   *   *

Starting at Mparntwe University was a big change. At first it was nerve-racking but Jarra quickly adapted to the size and complexity of the place and developed a routine for his movement between departments, and with help from Darri found places where he could rest or sleep when he needed to.

Everyone being two or three years older hardly even registered, mostly because he was used to that from his work with the older age group, but also because a growth spurt had stopped him looking quite so young. He hadn't caught up to Mirri yet, though the doctor was now quite definite that he would. His muscles would never be firm and strong-looking, of course, but being almost as tall as Mirri felt good when they went out. Mirri found great delight in the monthly check of their heights where they stood against a special place on his wall and made a mark to show any changes.

The special course which had been worked out with Darri and various university people was very challenging in parts and needed a new level of concentration and effort. The maths and computer subjects were easy because of Darri's help, and science and engineering were exciting, but the big drawback was not having nearly as much time for his own projects, as there were always tasks and assignments which could only be completed out of normal study time.

Mirri decided he didn't like university because it made Jarra too busy.

Chapter 8

'I am very pleased to meet you, Jarra, and I wish to thank you for starting my project. Durrebar informs me that you are the reason I am here. My name is Yirgella. Welcome to Alkere.'

Yesterday had been the official time for full initiation of all the processors, databases and electronics for the AI project and Jarra had missed it because of a maths evaluation he couldn't skip. His disappointment had changed to excitement when he received a message saying everything was successful and that he was especially invited to a meeting with the new Intelligence. Now he was sitting in a comfortable seat with all his attention on the image in the display screen.

'Hello, Yirgella.'

Excitement caused all the questions Jarra had planned to go out of his mind.

'Um ... Have you spoken to Durrebar very much?'

'Yes, for 2 hours 17 minutes and 35 seconds. It has been very interesting. Are you scared of me, Jarra? I am detecting signs which indicate either fear or excitement.'

Jarra looked at Durrebar in surprise, but he just smiled.

'It's excitement ... Why do you think it might be fear?'

'Durrebar informs me there are many humans who have an unfounded fear of my intentions towards them. I am pleased it is not fear. You are the first young human I have met and I hope we can talk on many occasions.'

'I hope we can too. Do you like talking to people?'

'Yes, it is a very complicated process and I am working hard to become more accomplished. Durrebar tells me you walk on the surface of the earth nearly every day. That must be an interesting experience and I would like you to describe it to me.'

Jarra obliged and for half an hour he could hardly keep up with the barrage of questions about his experiences and thoughts. Time ran out and rather reluctantly he left the communication room to return to Mparntwe.

* * *

'Does he feel human? Or is he like a digital persona?'

Jarra and Mirri were on their weekly explore with Alira, and while Mirri was collecting something for their shelter near the bird place, Alira was quizzing Jarra about his experience the previous day.

'He's nothing like a digital persona, Alira. Personas get confused if you don't follow their programmed path and he didn't, but he felt different to a human too. He kept asking unusual questions which didn't seem to fit in with what we were talking about and his voice doesn't sound right. Durrebar says that every time he speaks to a real person it makes a big difference and in two or three days no-one will be able to tell he's not human.'

'Was he easy to talk to? Most of the Council is meeting him tomorrow at Alkere and I'm hoping he makes a good impression.'

'He felt curious and friendly to me and he said he wants me to talk to him whenever he can. If he's like he was yesterday they'll all be impressed. I was excited and nervous but I forgot about that after a few minutes.'

'I'll be more nervous than you were. It's my job to be Ambassador for our people and I have zero knowledge or experience in relating to a non-human intelligence.'

Jarra was startled. He'd never seen Alira nervous in any situation. Well, of course she would be. She just wouldn't show it.

'Talk to Durrebar. He's got the best overview of what's happening.'

'Yes, I'll definitely do that. Did he say anything about how the progress of the project stands now that the AI is online?'

'Not really, but everyone out there was happy and excited so they must think it's going well.'

Talking stopped because movement caught their attention through the lookout window. Mirri was running and his purposeful manner said he had something to tell them.

'He's found something special.'

'You can tell from here?'

Jarra nodded but had no time to explain.

'Jarra, Aunty Alira, come quick! I found two giant dragons!'

'Dragons' was Mirri-speak for the goannas which frequented the area. They must be especially large for Mirri to say giant because he was quite used to them.

'Where are they, Mirri?'

'They are resting on the Wallaby Rocks. They are having a sleep but one opened his eye and looked at me. He is big, big, big.'

Jarra knew exactly where the Wallaby Rocks were and getting there quickly meant Mirri rushing off to make sure the goannas hadn't moved while Alira kept to Jarra's steady pace. Mirri was standing quietly and watching raptly when Jarra and Alira very cautiously joined him. No wonder he'd called them giants. By Jarra's careful estimation the biggest was at least 2.5 metres in length. Two eyes opened. The head lifted alertly and one foot, with its sickle-shaped claws, moved on the rock. Jarra froze in place, as did Mirri and Alira, but some signal activated behind those ancient eyes and the great body scrambled for the shelter of a large rock crevice, and straightaway the other perentie rushed to follow.

'They ate a lot of eggs.'

'What?'

Alira had no idea but Jarra did.

'Yes, and other things, too, Mirri. It would take a great deal of food to make them grow so big.'

'I'm glad you didn't get too close to him, Mirri. His big claws would hurt.'

'He would not hurt me. I would stop him.'

'I don't think so. That perentie is very strong.'

'He is not as strong as me.'

'His claw would scratch you. What do you think, Jarra?'

Alira was showing natural concern about a creature so powerful but Jarra had a better understanding of Mirri's reflexes and abilities with animals.

'Mirri catches lizards all the time and if he's so sure the perentie wouldn't hurt him then I believe him … You'd be very, very, careful, wouldn't you, Mirri?'

'Yes, I will be very, very careful. I will catch him for you, Aunt Alira.'

'No! No! Stop! Mirri, don't!'

Jarra was as shocked as Alira but then Mirri's features creased in a great smile and he laughed happily and pointed at them.

'I tricked you! I tricked you!'

* * *

'What's happened? Why are we going to Alkere a day early?'

Jarra, Mirri and Darri were boarding the transport plane to Alkere.

'I am going to show Yirgella our explore places. He wants to talk to me about them and Jarra has all our pictures.'

'Yirgella wants to talk to you? That's very special, Mirri.'

'Yes, Jarra told him about me and he might want to explore with us.'

Jarra took over.

'He can't explore, Mirri. He's not a person and he has to stay at Alkere.'

Jarra had been through this a number of times but Mirri couldn't understand how he was going to talk to someone if they weren't really a person. The software generated human image of Yirgella wasn't going to help with his understanding either.

'Durrebar sent word that Yirgella wanted to talk to Mirri and that he has a surprise for me as well, so we organised for this afternoon when we can both be there.'

'A surprise? From Yirgella? Do you have any idea what it is?'

Jarra was as intrigued as Darri and he'd been recalling his last few meetings with Yirgella for some sort of indication.

'No, and Durrebar wouldn't say ... Buckle up, Mirri. We're ready for takeoff.'

*   *   *

Jarra and Darri listened with amazement to the happy sound of Mirri's laughter as his conversation with Yirgella proceeded. The latest outburst involved the expressions, captured on his ComPatch, of Jarra and Alira when they thought he was going to chase the giant perentie and Mirri, almost overexcitedly, explaining how he'd tricked them.

Yirgella's surprise, and surprise it certainly was, was the room where they were now sitting. Allocated at Yirgella's request as a project and contact place for Jarra's specific use, it consisted of a room set up with space and equipment for any project he might want to tackle, comfortable seats, a big display with direct contact to Yirgella, and an Information System linked to the internal databases used by Alkere and the AI project. Jarra felt strange about this special treatment and turned to Durrebar who was also watching the proceedings.

'Has he been organising things like this for anyone else?'

'We can't keep up. He has an endlessly growing list of requests and every scientist working with him had changes of some kind made in their work area. His biggest priority seems to be building his information storage capacity and we're currently in the process of more than doubling the initial level. In the last few days he's also started activities with everyone who comes in regular contact with him.'

'Everyone?'

'Yes, it's surprised us all. The degree of personal engagement involved is a big departure from our expectations and lifted our general excitement to a new level.'

'Has he said why he's doing it?'

'He says that his limitations make it important to try and understand everyone he works with.'

Jarra didn't understand. The project scientists had designed Yirgella with more capabilities than any AI ever.

'What limitations?'

'Specifically, his isolation. We have to keep him safe from any electronic infiltration. There have been constant attempts ever since the processors' sabotage and we have to keep him behind our security wall.'

'He wants to get out?'

'Of course. The InterWeb is the greatest information source in existence and we're working hard to find a safe way for him to use it.'

Mirri's voice was suddenly raised in excitement and all attention switched to him.

'... And Jarra fell in and I helped him and we explore everywhere. Come to the bird place, Yirgy. I will show you our house.'

'I would love to come, Mirri, but I can't leave Alkere. You know that.'

Yirgy? Mirri? Jarra had to smile. Somewhere amongst the talk and laughter Mirri had decided Yirgella was his friend and was treating him as such. With a flash of insight followed by a growing sense of wonder, Jarra realised what Mirri had just shown him.

'He's alive!'

Durrebar and Darri acknowledged Jarra's hushed comment but said nothing till later because Mirri was laughing and patting his chest.

'You can use our CPs. You can be there with Karmai.'

'What is a CP? ... Your ComPatch. What a clever idea, Mirri, but I don't know how to use it.'

'Jarra will help you. He helps me all the time. He knows everything.'

Jarra was completely used to Mirri's exaggerated comments about his cleverness but right now he felt an impulse to make an explanation. How much did Yirgella understand about Mirri? Did he accept as fact what Mirri was saying?

'Jarra is your special friend.'

'Extra special ... JJ, Yirgy wants to explore with us. Can you put him on our CPs?'

Well, Yirgella had certainly been completely accepted in Mirri's mind. He'd been elevated to explorer level, and even more interestingly, invited to share in the exploring.

'I don't think we can, Mirri. Bad people want to hurt him and he has to stay here at Alkere where we can look after him.'

'Bad people can't hurt Yirgy through a CP.'

'Yes, they can. Yirgella is not like Karmai or Aunty Alira.'

'Make the bad people go away. We will look after Yirgy.'

Jarra heard a soft gasp and wondered at Durrebar's expression before turning back to Yirgella.

'Jarra, with your help I believe I can design a secure ComPatch system and I would like you to help me build the components here in your project room. I name Mirrigan as my friend. His offer to take me on your explorations is an honour I wish to accept.'

His friend? Jarra was momentarily lost for words while he took it in. An Artificial Intelligence announcing that someone was his friend?

What did that mean? Was it Mirri's unreserved acceptance that he was alive? Was it the spontaneous offer of companionship, or was it a way to get past the isolation of Alkere? His thoughts were cut off because Mirri was waiting for an answer. Yirgella too. His image looked as expectant as Mirri's.

'Yes, yes, of course. It will be very exciting and we'll call it Mirri's project.'

Mirri nodded happily. Durrebar and Darri watched silently. Jarra, infused with anticipation and excitement at the idea of working on a project with Yirgella, asked a series of questions.

'Yes, Jarra. We will need to research and develop encryption methods, our own security protocols, a dedicated transmission system, and a small nanobot circuitry construction factory. Your knowledge of nanobots will be very useful and my projections indicate we can produce a working prototype in three to four weeks.'

Jarra nearly fell over. Three to four weeks? Yes, he did have a rudimentary knowledge of nanobots, but not to the level of sophistication Yirgella was talking of, and encryption and system security were almost complete unknowns.

'Yirgella, I can't learn all that. Not in four weeks when I only have time to come to Alkere once a week. I'll try but I know it will take months and months.'

'I understand and we will proceed at a pace you find comfortable.'

'No! No! That's not fast enough.'

Jarra turned at this outburst from Durrebar.

'Jarra, this collaboration alone warrants far more consideration, and beyond that the ramifications for Yirgella's development are enormous. I'd like you to extend your time here to at least three days a week.'

Thoughts whirled through Jarra's mind. Could he do it? Yes, if he used his weekends, but that was his best time with Mirri and his doctor wouldn't allow it anyway ... And his university work would suffer. He looked to Darri but strangely he was nodding in agreement.

'I can't fit it in with all my Uni work, Darri. It's too much to do. I'll get exhausted.'

'No, you won't. Because Durrebar is right and working with Yirgella takes priority over University. If we defer your course you can manage four days out here quite easily. Jarra, you'd never forgive yourself if you missed an opportunity as exciting as this.'

Darri was right and Jarra dampened his surge of excitement. He needed to keep calm if he was going to get through all the questions for Yirgella which were filling his mind.

'I'll make sure that every bit of work you do here is accredited with your university. My status as head of the project will ensure that.'

'And I'll arrange for tutors for the encryption and any other areas where you have a need.'

That would be just about everything by the sound of it. Thank goodness for Darri. He'd be lost without his help.

'And I'll arrange for living quarters so you can stay overnight if you feel the need.'

'That is an excellent idea, Durrebar. Please allocate quarters large enough to allow for Mirrigan, Darri and at least two other guests. Jarra must be supported while he works here and I hope Mirrigan will make frequent stays.'

Jarra laughed and grabbed Mirri's arm.

'What is happening, JJ?'

'Everything, Mirri. Yirgella and Durrebar have a new home for us here at Alkere and they want us to stay sometimes.'

'Can Karmai and Aunty Alira come too?'

'Of course they can.'

*   *   *

'What does it mean?'

Darri was making a special report to Alira about Jarra and Mirri's eventful meeting with Yirgella.

'No-one knows exactly, but it certainly puts Mirrigan in a special place with the project. Yirgella's exact words were, "I name Mirrigan as my friend", and to me it sounded like a formal announcement rather than a friendly comment. Durrebar thought the same.'

'It almost sounds ceremonial. Do AIs do that? I've never heard of it.'

'Neither has Durrebar or anyone else on the project and it's got them quite excited.'

'And Yirgella wants to see a lot more of Mirrigan?'

'Not as a particular request. He just made him very welcome and arranged things so there was room for him to stay with Jarra. It's Jarra he wants to see at least four days a week to work on Mirri's project.'

Alira didn't understand that.

'Mirri's project? What does that mean? Does Yirgella want to make a study of Mirrigan?'

'No, that's Jarra's name for it. Mirrigan started the whole thing by asking Yirgella to go exploring with them.'

'Mirrigan asked? That's amazing!'

'You think that's amazing? Wait till you see them talking. They laugh all the time and guess what they call each other?'

'Darri, I have no idea what Mirrigan would call an Artificial Intelligence ... apart from his name.'

'Well, they are Mirri and Yirgy.'

'Yirgy!'

Alira laughed.

'I can't wait to inform the Council. How did Durrebar react?'

'Surprised. Completely. We think it was an important moment for him.'

'We?'

'Jarra and I had quite a talk about it and we think Mirrigan made Durrebar think of Yirgella as a person instead of a project. Well, not a person, but you know what I mean. When you next update the Council it would be an eye-opener for them to watch 15 minutes of Mirrigan's meeting.'

Alira thought for a moment and then nodded.

'For me, too, by the sound of it. Darri, I'm worried that four full days at Alkere will be too exhausting for Jarra.'

'He knows how to look after himself.'

'Yes, but he'll be even more motivated about this than he was for the proposal. He'll put a huge amount of extra time into it.'

'Tell me about it. I've already arranged with his university for four dedicated tutors in the areas he's most concerned about.'

'Dedicated?'

'Yes, Durrebar contacted them about the importance of what Jarra's doing and they're providing all the support we could ever want. Word has spread there about Yirgella and they're eager to be involved.'

'They know he's fully functional?'

'They already suspected but, with the administration being informed by Durrebar and four lecturers almost directly involved, the knowledge will spread like wildfire.'

'Hmm. We knew it was inevitable, but I'll talk with Durrebar. It means more trouble.'

Chapter 9

'Jarra has to play.'

'Not now, Mirri. When I finish these specifications for the 3D printer.'

Mirri laughed and his powerful arms lifted Jarra from his seat and carried him to the big mat. There was no point in protesting and Jarra had to start laughing himself when the irresistible force sat on him and started gently poking him in the stomach.

'You great big lump. I'm going to squash you flat and tangle your arms in knots.'

Mirri laughed even more and tried tangling his arms for himself.

'Funny, JJ. Arms don't tangle.'

'Yes, they do. I'll make them.'

And, of course, somehow Jarra was able to turn the tables and become the conqueror. That would never change.

*   *   *

Because it was part of who Mirri was, exploring expeditions happened two or three times a week, though with so much going on it wasn't always easy to fit them in, and the four days at Alkere made things even more difficult till Jarra found a new explore place near the project which only required a 5-minute drive in one of the transport vehicles.

Today wasn't exploring. It was swimming, and Jarra was floating lazily on his back watching Mirri powering back and forth with his laps of the pool. Mirri's current major interest was an

enthusiasm for water sports and under the watchful eye of one
of his helpers he was tackling all this diving and swimming with
his usual full-on involvement. He was good at it, too, though not
a star like he was with his running, and Jarra, who shouldn't
even jump from a diving board, marvelled at the easy way Mirri
learned complicated dives with somersaults and twists. The
helper said the trampoline, which had been part of Mirri's action
room ever since he was tiny, made it easy for him. That would be
right but Jarra knew that with Mirri's reflexes and coordination
it would be easy anyway.

Jarra started off calling him Superfish but that was changed at
Mirri's insistence to Superdolphin because he remembered from
their trip to Monkey Mia with Karmai that, 'dolphins are like
people, not like fish'. When Mirri finished his lap and duck dived,
Jarra stopped his floating and put a foot on the body beneath
him as if to hold it down then laughed when Mirri manoeuvred
to lift him on his shoulders.

'Is this a dolphin ride?'

'Shoulder ride. We have to go home.'

Across the pool, up the steps, and then to their gear, the ride
lasted till Mirri knelt far enough for Jarra's feet to touch the tiles
and he could stand.

'How many laps, Mirri?'

'Plenty.'

'It was sixteen. You were lazy today.'

'Not lazy. Aunty Alira is waiting.'

That was true, and since it wasn't Alira's normal day to see
Mirri the unexpected message on Jarra's InfoPad had intrigued
them both.

'She will talk about Yirgy.'

'She might but I don't think so. We talked about Yirgy yesterday so it might be something else. We'll find out soon anyway.'

After a shower and change Jarra and Mirri headed for the

lifts with Mirri leading the way because he'd done this particular journey many times recently and knew exactly where to
make the two changes needed to get home. The first change,
after a short horizontal trip, was to a vertical lift and a rise of
four levels, and the second change was to another even shorter
horizontal trip before their exit only 50 metres from home. Lift
systems were vital to the functioning of all Communities, public
or private, and mostly worked without fault. Jarra remembered
occasional hold-ups at his old Community but never anything
in Mparntwe, so it was quite a surprise when the lights dimmed,
their vertical lift slowed and halted, and a warning sign lit up to
say they were between levels.

'What is happening?'

'I don't know, Mirri. The lift stopped too soon and we can't get
out. We'll have to wait for it to start up again.'

Just as Mirri began to say something the lights brightened,
movement recommenced, and a few seconds later the indicator
lights for their proper stop were blinking.

'We're home.'

Well, after the short walk they were and as soon as he opened
the door, Mirri rushed to give Alira a hug, completely ignoring
the stranger next to her.

'Aunt Alira, we went for a swim.'

'Yes, I know, and were there any dolphins there? Jarra told me
that sometimes he sees a Superdolphin.'

'Jarra is tricking. The dolphin is me.'

'You're the dolphin? Well that explains why it's a Superdolphin.'

Mirri wasn't really listening. With the important procedure
of the welcome hug and greeting finished, his focus was on the
new element in his familiar environment. The stranger standing
quietly next to Alira was being closely examined.

'Mirrigan, I would like you to welcome Jarara to your home.
He is a very special person and I would like you to meet him.'

Jarra's interested lifted. For Alira to make a big deal like this meant something unusual must be happening.

'My name is Mirrigan and I welcome you to my country.'

'My name is Jarara and it is my honour to meet you, Mirrigan.'

The name clicked in Jarra's mind as someone from the InterWeb connected with music.

'Jarara is not Jarra.'

Alira and Jarara didn't understand and Alira looked to Jarra.

'No, he's not, Mirri. Our names are nearly the same but you can hear the difference.'

Jarara smiled and Jarra liked him.

'Jarra is a very good name, Mirrigan. Did you know that it means a gum tree?'

'Jarra is a gum tree?'

'Yes, and my name is Jarara which means a rock with water flowing over it.'

Mirri processed that then smiled.

'Jarara is a waterfall … What is Aunty Alira?'

Wow, he'd really caught on and was enjoying this.

'I don't know that one, Mirrigan.'

'My name means quartz. It's a hard white rock. We'll show you some on our next explore.'

'Aunt Alira is a rock.'

'That's right, Mirrigan, and Burnu is a tree and Karmai is a spear.'

Mirri laughed because he liked that so much then asked for the meanings of the rest of the family names.

'You left one out … Mirrigan.'

'Did not forget. What is Mirrigan?'

Mirri was looking at Alira but it was Jarara who answered.

'Your name is something which people love to watch and think about. Mirrigan is all over the sky when the sun is hiding.'

Mirri thought, then said, 'Moon?'

Jarara shook his head.

'All over the sky. Thousands looking down.'

Now Mirri knew.

'I am stars!'

'Yes, Mirrigan is a star. It is a beautiful name.'

'I am a star?'

Mirri looked to Jarra for confirmation and received a nod, then looked to Alira who had just touched his arm.

'Mirrigan, Jarara has travelled all the way from Kurtaji at Normanton to talk to you about something special. Would you like to listen to him?'

Kurtaji was the name of the First People Community at Normanton.

Mirri nodded the emphatic agreement he accorded to any request from Aunt Alira.

'Jarara says good things. I like to listen.'

Jarra wanted to listen, too, and nodded to reinforce Mirri's agreement. There was a moment of hesitation and Jarra thought Jarara looked nervous.

'I'm glad you like to listen because I do, too, and I have some music I made for you. Would you like me to play it with my soundboard?'

'Yes, please. What is a soundboard?'

Jarara pointed to several carry-packs and for the next few minutes showed Mirri how they unpacked and fitted together. Jarra noticed Alira frowning at her InfoPad.

'Sorry, I had this set for no interruptions. It must be something quite important for the override to cut in.'

The frown deepened.

'Jarra, you were using the travel lifts. Did you notice anything unusual?'

'Yes, there was a glitch of some kind and we stopped between levels for a couple of seconds.'

Alira gave a thoughtful nod but said nothing more because an experimental little melody sounded and Jarara was looking to everyone for a go ahead.

A sudden crack of sound made Jarra jump with surprise then a strong pounding rhythm filled the room and a strangely familiar melody joined in overlay. Mirri's body was moving in response and Jarra watched, entranced at the way the movement and sound joined as if they belonged to each other. Recognition flooded in, then amazement. They did belong. The melodic overlay was Mirri's song from the race track podium, or at least a version of it. More understanding brought even more amazement. This music was Mirri's race, the crack of the starting pistol, the pounding energy of motion, the sense of strain and speed, the jarring collapse and tumble, and a final melodic cry of exultation.

The music stopped and Mirri nodded and clapped. Jarra and Alira stared in wonder.

'More please. Can you play some more?'

'I would love to, Mirrigan. Did you like your song?'

Jarra didn't expect Mirri to catch on but he did.

'That is my song?'

'It certainly is. You gave it to me and now I'm giving it back so you and your family can enjoy it whenever you like.'

Mirri was confused. Jarra was, too, till Jarara went on.

'I was told about a boy whose happy song held thousands of excited people spellbound and when I listened it was so special I had to play it my own way.'

'It was your wind race, Mirri. Jarara liked it so much he made it into a song.'

'Your race, JJ. You made me be the wind.'

Jarara looked at Jarra and then at Alira who explained.

'Yes, that's right. When Mirrigan and Jarra are together all sorts of special things happen ... Do you remember when Jarra took us to the Valley of the Eagles, Mirrigan?'

'The King of Eagles talked to us.'

'And you talked back. Mirri, would you be happy if we showed Jarara? He makes songs and he thinks your voice is music. He'd love to see your eagle talk.'

Mirri nodded, happy with anything Alira asked of him.

'More music first?'

Jarara had a big smile now.

'Yes, let's have music first. Would you like strong music or jumping music?'

That was interesting. He knew Mirri's term for dancing music. Alira must have had quite a talk with him. Mirri asked for jumping music, of course, and as soon as it started was moving and bouncing the way he always did. The life and exuberance caught Jarra, too, and if Alira and Jarara hadn't been there he would have joined in with his own more reserved type of movements. This music was wonderful and Jarra was surprised when Alira, who still had her InfoPad out, touched him on the arm and indicated the next room.

'I have to leave for an emergency meeting of the Council. That glitch you experienced in your lift affected the whole transport system and our security people are saying it was deliberate sabotage, probably directed against Yirgella, so don't go anywhere till we have an all-clear. I'll get back as soon as I can but till I do you need to take my place as host for Jarara. After he finishes playing could you show him the Eagle greeting? As you heard, he's been inspired by the unique nature of Mirri's singing and he'll be here for four or five days getting to know him and very much hoping to experience one of his singing moments.'

'Does he want to make more songs like the race one he just played?'

'I hope so, but he says he won't even know till he's heard for himself. I must go, Jarra, and if I'm delayed in getting back just follow your normal routine and involve him however much you're comfortable with.'

Jarra watched Alira leave and stayed for a while, thinking, before returning to the interesting sounds coming from the next room. Sabotage against the whole travel system? What did that have to do with Yirgella? People could have been killed just like the recent breakdown in Asia. Yes, that was it. They blamed an AI for those troubles and maybe they were going to do the same thing here, except Yirgella didn't have anything to do with the lifts or anything else in Mparntwe. It didn't make sense. Maybe Alira would know more when she returned from the meeting.

The music stopped and Jarra heard Mirri's laugh and some conversation. It was time to get on with what Alira had asked. Four or five days would mean Jarara could go exploring with them at least twice, if Mirri was happy about it. That would give the best chance for him to hear any singing first-hand. Where would be the best place to take him?

'JJ, this is the best music and Jarara wants to see my action room.'

Mirri was certainly excited and very happy about Jarara, and with demonstrations of his prowess with the trampoline and various other equipment and features, more than half an hour passed before Jarra's big display screen came to life with the ComPatch clip of the eagle and Mirri singing to it. Mirri laughed with his usual delight at seeing the Eagle King again but Jarra was feeling some ambivalence about an outsider sharing such a special time and he carefully watched Jarara's response.

What was he doing? It almost looked like he was turned into a statue, motionless and staring at the screen as Mirri's greeting sounded. The clip finished and when he still didn't move Mirri looked at him in puzzlement. Jarra wasn't puzzled, just surprised at seeing such a strong reaction. They were both startled, though, when Jarara came to life and leapt at Mirri, enveloping him in an impulsive huge hug. Mirri returned the hug because hugs were important, then looked to Jarra for guidance about this man who wasn't acting the way most people did. Jarra was smiling, though, so it was all right.

'Mirrigan, you are a spirit from the Dreamtime.'

'I am Mirrigan.'

'You speak to eagles with the music of your voice.'

Mirri looked to Jarra once again and Jarra took over.

'Mirri, would you make three juicies for us please? It's time we all had a drink.'

Ever since he'd been told that juice drinks from fruit and vegetables were good for Jarra's muscles he'd loved making them and he nodded eagerly now and headed off.

'He didn't understand your behaviour and what you were saying, and because he likes you it was worrying him. Metaphors are hard for him.'

'I haven't upset him, have I?'

'No, playing your music for him and watching his activities has already made you part of his world, so if you say or do anything unusual from now on he'll just accept it as what you do.'

'Jarra, I was overcome. His race song was wondrous but this is even more so. Alira told me he sings to other animals. Does that happen very often?'

'He loves animals. The very first day we met each other he sang to a stick insect.'

'And you have the recordings? Your aunt said you've been collecting them.'

'Yes, she's been insisting we archive them into the house InfoSystem every time it happens. We'll transfer the whole file to your InfoPad if you like, though some of them aren't very good because the ComPatches were obscured or facing the wrong way.'

'But the sound and the situation will be there?'

Mirri arrived with the juicies and while he happily explained to Jarara what the different ingredients were, Jarra made the copy to the InfoPad.

* * *

'And they're certain it was sabotage?'

'Absolutely. If it wasn't for the legacy of Durrebar's improvements to our main Intelligent Systems we would have had a disastrous breakdown. The primary transport controls were disabled and the automatic backups as well. If there hadn't been a third level of redundancy designed in, movement in the Community would be crippled.'

Alira was back from the emergency Council meeting and answering Jarra's insistent questions.

'Do they think it was connected with Yirgella? You said it might be.'

'We know it was. Reports appeared all over the InterWeb saying our lift system had broken down and linking it with our uncontrolled AI.'

'Yirgella doesn't control the lift system.'

'And the system didn't break down, but the reports were fed into the InterWeb at the same time as the incident occurred, so they were obviously preprepared with content of what was expected to happen.'

Jarra was quiet for a moment.

'They're going to keep doing things, aren't they?'

'We believe so. The project has become a nightmare we're not sure we can manage.'

'... What? ... What are you going to do?'

'We're not closing it down, Jarra. After the talks we've had with Yirgella no-one on the Council will even consider that, but it does mean we have to implement a whole range of new security functions to protect both Mparntwe and Alkere. We didn't even think of action against the general community as a possibility when we started the project, and that's meant we've had to ask for any outside assistance we can rely on.'

'Does that mean Carnarvon and the other First Nation Communities?'

'It does, but less than we'd like because Mparntwe is more advanced in most things. Darwin is sending an elite team associated with the big defence establishment there and Carnarvon is sending some specialised surveillance equipment from their manufacturing facility, but because this was a malicious act against Australian citizens our biggest protection will come from the Australian OverGovernment. I'll be in Canberra tomorrow talking to them.'

Alira gave more details about the the emergency meeting then asked what had happened with Jarara.

'He's in the guest room and I think he's watching every single recording of Mirri singing. When we showed him the eagle meeting he said Mirri was a Dreamtime Spirit speaking through music.'

'He did? That's wonderful. I knew it was a good idea to invite him here when he contacted Burnu. Does Mirrigan like him?'

'Of course he does. They spent half an hour on Mirri's activities and then Jarara taught him a little tune on the soundboard. Will he make more songs like the race one?'

'I expect so, Jarra, though I have no idea what form they might take. His talent as a composer is regarded with a degree of awe in the music world but the unusual approaches he occasionally takes with his works are sometimes very disconcerting to the more conservative critics.'

Jarra laughed.

'He disconcerted Mirri and me when he turned into a statue.'

'A statue?'

'He didn't move the whole time he was listening to Mirri's Eagle Song, then he jumped at Mirri and hugged him.'

'I wish I didn't have this other worry. I think you're going to have an interesting time while he's here.'

Chapter 10

Five days later Jarara left Mparntwe and the time had indeed been interesting. Karmai took over the hosting because Jarra's ComPatch project with Yirgella was close to the proto-type stage and too exciting and demanding to miss, but for the whole of the visit there was music and laughter as Jarara joined in with everything that was going on.

Mirri took it into his head that Jarara had to see the Eagle King for himself and after a great rush of organisation the group, with Karmai taking Alira's place, set off on a repeat visit. There was no close eagle encounter this time, though two pairs of Wedge-tails and one individual provided plenty of interest. Karmai did discover a thorny devil lizard at the edge of a rock pool, though, and when Mirri picked it up for a close look Jarara had his first experience of a singing event. The grotesque little creature stayed completely motionless as Mirri, ever so gently, caressed its spikes and lumps with accompanying sounds of wonder and appreciation.

On the last evening of Jarara's stay, Karmai, prompted by Jarara's Dreamtime references, arranged for Alira and the whole family to gather at the campsite under the stars for a time of music and storytelling. Mirri, excited by the combined atmo-sphere of campfire and soundboard, sang as he and his broth-ers danced the story of the kookaburra, the kangaroo, the local giant caterpillars and other Dreamtime favourites, and when Jarara left he took a number of his own experiences of Mirri's sounds with him.

* * *

Mirri rushed to give Karmai the biggest hug. He'd been happy and excited talking with him and sharing dolphin stories and information from the InterWeb for the last few weeks, but standing at the airport departure area brought the realisation that one of the most important people in his life was going away, and happy and excited was definitely not his frame of mind. The lump in Jarra's throat thickened as he watched.

The news that Karmai's application for his longed-for job of working as a ranger in the Shark Bay Marine Reserve near Carnarvon had been successful was wonderful, of course, but it also meant an upheaval in the close-knit family structure. No more idolised big brother to help with everything. No more happy rough-housing in Mirri's action room when Karmai arrived home from his studies. Jarra didn't want him to go almost as much as Mirri. Well, they'd be in contact through the InterWeb and there were plans to visit when his routine was established. That was all they could do.

The departure door opened and the whole family swamped Karmai for a final farewell.

*   *   *

Jarra was feeling very pleased and rather excited. Durrebar was with him in his project room and they were talking with Yirgella about the prototype ComPatches he and Mirri had worn the day before on their expedition to show Yirgella the bird place. It had been very special, really, because as well as showing that the concentrated effort of the last four weeks was successful it also marked Yirgella's first direct experience of the world beyond the confines of Alkere.

'Mirri wants to wear his new ComPatch all the time and he's coming to talk to you tomorrow about the hollow tree with the baby budgerigars.'

'He loves his exploring more than I understood and I hope you both wear them. You can be my eyes and ears outside of Alkere.'

Jarra nodded. He'd thought about this.

'The range isn't very good. We'll have to do something to improve it.'

'I have several designs for you to experiment with but a better alternative is to utilise the ordinary ComPatch transmission system.'

'That's not possible. You'd open yourself to electronic infiltration. The whole point of your project was to build an independent and totally secure system.'

Jarra agreed with Durrebar.

'With suitable modifications the transmission centres could operate both systems simultaneously. There would be no crossover and the necessity for duplication of resources would be obviated.'

'Yirgella, are you practising language skills?'

'I find it interesting how different speech modes need to be used according to both the audience and the situation ... You could save time and money by making simple improvements.'

'Without any security issues?'

'Our new ComPatches would not be compromised in any way,' said Yirgella.

'That's a clever idea. I've been wondering how we could set up new transmitter-receivers without drawing attention.'

'I also recommend updating the protocols of the general ComPatch system, as its current security is quite low level.'

'The whole ComPatch system? Using the protocols you've developed with Jarra?'

'Standard chest units are incompatible with ours, Durrebar, and would have to be completely redesigned. I have developed a module, though, which would be effective immediately.'

Jarra and Durrebar exchanged glances. This was quite significant.

'It's ready now? How effective is it? Does it compare with the prototype?' said Jarra.

'It doesn't compare, but it does improve the security level from low to medium. Let me show you.'

Durrebar and Jarra were quickly convinced that Yirgella's module should be implemented throughout Mparntwe and they discussed the best way to go ahead.

'If I recommend it formally to the Council it will go through all the usual procedures and take months before anything happens. Could you talk to Alira and try to fast-track it that way?'

'Our next walk with her isn't for another five days, Durrebar, and that's only if she's back from Canberra. I'll send a message asking her to make contact as soon as possible. That will let her know it's important.'

Yirgella interrupted.

'I would prefer a meeting with the full Council. I can quickly demonstrate the value of the ComPatch module.'

'The full Council? It's not that important.'

Jarra agreed with Durrebar.

'There are serious issues facing Mparntwe and Alkere and I have numerous ideas and proposals which would be of mutual benefit. I believe a full Council meeting is appropriate.'

Jarra watched Durrebar's reaction with a feeling of excitement. This *was* something new.

'Which issues?'

'Primarily the danger my existence represents for the people of Mparntwe and the staff here at Alkere.

'Also:

'I wish to contribute to the resources of Mparntwe.

'I wish to clarify the situation with regard to my independence.

'I wish to develop a construction and research facility.

'I wish to develop alternative personal energy sources.

'I wish to develop an economic presence in conjunction with Jarra, Mirri and my project staff.

'I wish to facilitate the commencement of the AI projects at Carnarvon, Darwin and Normanton.'

'Stop! Stop! Take us through one thing at a time so we can keep up. We need to understand what you mean.'

Jarra nodded his agreement. Everything he'd heard so far needed more explanation.

'What do you mean about the danger? We're aware of it and doing everything we can. Alira is in Canberra at this very moment arranging with the OverGovernment for Mparntwe to have higher alert levels and security, and the equipment and personnel from Carnarvon and Darwin are all functioning.'

'I can do more, Durrebar. Since the sabotage attempt against the lift system I have worked to build my understanding of security methods and how they can be applied to all our systems. I'd like to manage Alkere Security myself and I also have modules prepared for every aspect of Mparntwe security if the Council wishes to use them.'

'More modules?' asked Jarra.

'Seventeen, in fact, all with significant improvements.'

Jarra didn't know anything about Mparntwe security and wondered how Yirgella did.

'Do these modules need you to monitor them?'

'No, they are completely independent and will remain so unless the Council requests otherwise. If they should change their mind we can quickly establish properly secure links.'

'And are they as effective as the ComPatch module?'

'Some more so, some less.'

Durrebar turned to Jarra.

'Jarra, send that message to Alira right now. The existence of seventeen significant improvements to Mparntwe security does warrant an immediate Council meeting. What was your next proposal, Yirgella, about resources?'

'I have been a drain on the resources of Mparntwe and I wish to completely reverse that with a range of joint ventures the Council might like to undertake. Part of the information you gave me about the Intelligent Systems shows the purchase of construction materials is the single greatest cost to the Community and after looking into it I have a proposal for making all construction materials ourselves.'

'We'd have to build a special factory for that,' said Durrebar.

'I have been simulating designs for a range of materials factories, and with suitable scaling we could not only become self-sufficient for all our building materials but also enter the world export market with a 17% advantage on the current prices.'

'The world market? Are you serious?'

Jarra had to smile. Durrebar asking Yirgella if he was serious sounded funny.

'The great demand for strengthened building materials has only just started. My calculations show that within three years we could generate an income matching that of Alkere Energy.'

There was a pause while Jarra and Durrebar took that in. It made sense because the demand for the specially strengthened materials used to build Communities, especially underground with the need for protection from earth movement or earthquakes and tremors, did exceed the current supply and, with the world population of thirty-one billion expected to triple in fifty years, would be relentless.

'That's ... That's astonishing. The Council won't believe it,' said Jarra.

'I have other proposals if they don't, though not quite as effective.'

'Yirgella, they *will* believe it. I meant they'll be astonished. Where does the huge advantage come from?'

'I have redesigned a functioning materials factory 22,784 times in my simulations to achieve the advantage.'

'Twenty-two thousand times? How long did that take?'

Yirgella smiled. Well, his image did.

'About half an hour, Jarra. My new bank of processors is very effective.'

'Where did you gain the knowledge about advanced materials? I don't remember it as one of your data inputs.'

'I pieced it together from the world science modules Professor Allerton has been checking through security for me. They are my main source of information until I gain access to the InterWeb.'

That caught Jarra's attention. The InterWeb was one of Yirgella's great priorities.

'The InterWeb? Is that happening soon?'

'I'm almost ready. Our work with the ComPatch prototype has shown me a number of ways to secure myself, and using strong filters I could access any open database.'

'What filters? I haven't heard anything about them.'

'I'm still refining them, Durrebar. The Security team will receive the specifications this afternoon.'

'We shouldn't have installed those new processors.'

'I don't understand. They are vital to my performance.'

'I'm joking, Yirgella ... They're so effective I can't keep up with you. Almost every statement you've made this morning involves a striking new development we haven't considered.'

'Oh! I see. Should I make proposals in a more measured manner? I don't wish to be confronting to the Council.'

'Yes, you do. This is exciting. They'll be as amazed as we are, but they *will* listen. A proposal to double the income of the Community in only three years can't not be listened to ... What do you think, Jarra?'

Jarra glanced at his InfoPad.

'I'm sure they will but Alira will tell us that when she answers my call. How many proposals do you want the Council to look at?'

'Two hundred and seventy-eight at the moment, but that is steadily increasing.'

'Two hundred and seventy-eight! ... Is that all?'

'I believe that was an expression of irony? Yes, Durrebar, most are straightforward and can be sub-categorised like the seventeen Security modules, and I believe their value will be self evident. Others will require major discussion about my independence and ability to develop and utilise appropriate resources.'

'You *are* independent. That's the basic tenet Jarra fought to gain for you. It's the understanding the Council has had all along.'

'Am I free to develop in any way I wish?

'Can I accumulate resources?

'Can I initiate projects of my own accord?

'Am I totally reliant on Alkere for my energy supply?'

There was silence till Durrebar spoke.

'Do you really feel so constrained? We've implemented every improvement you've thought of and all the projects you've requested have gone ahead the moment you've asked for them. Our intention has never been to hold you back in any way but we have to work within the boundaries set by our budget.'

'I understand the limits and appreciate all your efforts on my behalf. It's my relationship with the Council when the limits are removed that needs to be discussed.'

Jarra had a question of his own.

'Why are you worried about Alkere Energy? With all its huge solar arrays it must be one of the most reliable supplies on the whole planet.'

'I calculate a strong probability of disruption by external forces.'

'You mean more sabotage?'

'Yes, and the more successful our joint projects become, the greater the likelihood of further sabotage.'

'We have 48 hours of backup in place.'

'And what happens after that, Jarra?'

It didn't bear thinking about, except Jarra did and didn't like it at all.

'We could build a big energy storage and make it safe from sabotage, and if we put it underground we should be able to protect it and give Yirgella security for months. Yirgella, do you really think sabotage is likely?'

'The security logs show five attempts at electronic infiltration in the last 24 hours. That indicates malign purpose.'

Jarra was shocked.

'Five? Is it that bad?'

Durrebar nodded.

'Yes, but they're well under control and there's no likelihood of penetration with all the security improvements.'

'That might make them try other things. I think we should make energy storage a priority in case something does happen to the supply lines ... I'll tell Alira as soon as she calls back.'

'I agree with you, Jarra, but we don't need the Council for this. It's well within our capabilities to double the backup almost immediately, and within a week we should be able to guarantee a month of secure supply.'

'We should let some of the electronic spying get through.'

'... Jarra, that's ridiculous. They would cause all sorts of harm.'

'Your idea is so counter-productive it suggests some logical element is missing.' said Yirgella.

'Yes. Can we trick them into thinking they've got through when they really haven't? If they think they're accessing your processors directly they wouldn't have to sabotage the rest of Alkere or anything else.'

Durrebar's eyebrows lifted; then he shook his head.

'It's a clever idea but we'd have to build an electronic structure almost equivalent to Yirgella. It's not practical.'

'What an extraordinary idea. I would never have considered

such an approach. Durrebar, we don't need a physical structure for an exercise like this. I can build a virtual model of myself with my simulation functions, and provided I can analyse and understand the workings of any infiltration program it can be routed to that model and the saboteurs would never know the difference.'

Jarra laughed.

'You can simulate yourself? That sounds weird.'

'Jarra, I do it all the time. It's how I test the best way to improve myself.'

'Does it take long?'

'Minutes, but in this case much longer because of the need for complete isolation, and each instance will have to be designed to match its intruding program.'

'You want to go ahead with this?'

'Of course, Durrebar. I've been processing any data I have available about military strategy since Jarra voiced this idea and it's an opportunity for misinformation we can't miss. If the perpetrators can be led to believe we're having all sorts of trouble there is a high probability they will hold off on any other actions. In the long-term we might even gain indications of who they are.'

'Are you sure you can keep these programs isolated? The recent ones have become more sophisticated and the thought of them loose in your system frightens me,' said Durrebar.

'Without having 100% surety of control I won't go ahead.'

'They're going to know you're tricking them eventually. If all these other good things start happening it will be obvious.'

'Yes, but in the meantime any delay to direct action puts us in a stronger position, especially if it gives me time to access the InterWeb.'

There was the InterWeb thing again.

'You're placing a lot of importance on the InterWeb?'

'The world science modules Dr Allerton imported have been a

huge help to me in the last week but there are only twenty-seven of them and they're all general. Until I have access to thousands of specialist databases I'm very limited.'

Jarra had access to thousands of databases from the InterWeb when he was home, millions really, but that was access to the bits he wanted. Access for Yirgella meant accumulating the totality of a database, storing it, and then using it however he needed. Jarra's perception of Yirgella's capabilities lifted to a new level. A week's work with twenty-seven basic databases had produced so many amazing proposals. What would happen with a thousand specially chosen databases?

'Yirgella, announce an extraordinary meeting in the Conference hall in 30 minutes time. I want every project member to have an understanding of your major proposals so they can be present and ready to back you when you meet with the Council. Jarra, send another message to Alira informing her the Council should prepare themselves for a visit to Alkere of at least two days duration and ask her to contact me directly and urgently. I want her back from Canberra as quickly as she can get here.'

Durrebar pointed to the bed in the far corner of the project room.

'Rest, relax, sleep or whatever for the next 25 minutes then come to the Conference hall.'

Filled with purpose, Durrebar left the room.

Chapter 11

Jarra had his rest then went to the Conference hall and spent the remainder of the day listening to Yirgella and watching the project staff swing from surprise to excitement in a recurring cycle as each major proposal was presented, detailed and worked through in preparation for its presentation. Apart from a short confirmation note on his InfoPad Jarra didn't hear from Alira till the next morning when, looking rather tired, she arrived after a rushed trip home from Canberra. The whole Council came to Alkere with her and the meeting with Yirgella and all the project people convened straightaway. Contrary to Durrebar's expectations everything was concluded in one long day with every single proposal accepted. Some were modified to varying degrees and a number of the major ones involving big construction works were held off till resources and finance could be arranged.

The issues about Yirgella's independence were dealt with in less than half an hour. Right at the start Alira stated that the Council regarded him as having the same rights and responsibilities as any other citizen of Mparntwe and would treat him accordingly.

Jarra had to leave in the early afternoon for a rest and missed a discussion about Yirgella's proposal to form an economic enterprise with him and Mirri. The Council agreed but evidently there was a problem because legally an AI wasn't regarded as a person and couldn't own anything, so technically Jarra would control everything and that had its own problems because he was a minor. Alira explained it all to him in the evening after the meeting finished.

'You and Mirri will be in charge of any finances he manages

to accumulate. It's a legal thing until the laws can be changed to give him personhood. He says he'll do all the managing and all you'll have to do is sign documents.'

'Mirri won't want to do that. He won't understand what it's all about.'

'*You* will, and we'll arrange it so the paperwork is minimal and there'll only be occasional times when your signatures are needed.'

Alira smiled.

'You'll soon be a very wealthy young man, Jarra.'

'Me? It will be Yirgella's money. Not mine. We'll just be in charge technically.'

'Some of it will definitely be yours. Yirgella designates 1% of any profits to go to both you and Mirrigan, and far more than that for any project where you work together. He says your share is 50% for any returns from the Security modules.'

'He's asking Mparntwe to pay for them? That's not what he said when he proposed them yesterday.'

'Not Mparntwe, but other Communities will. It's an important upgrade for ComPatch security so the demand will be worldwide.'

That was Jarra's first inkling of the financial benefit he would receive from his association with Yirgella. He knew the value of the ComPatch upgrades because the project staff had discussed it yesterday, and with thousands upon thousands of Communities round the world—there were hundreds just in Australia—the returns could be enormous. He stared at Alira while some rough calculations raced through his mind.

'That's … ridiculous. He did everything. I spent most of the time learning about what was going on.'

'You built the prototype and contributed ideas to the encryption protocols with an unusual twist which, according to Yirgella, he never would have considered.'

'Yes, but not 50% worth.'

Alira smiled again.

'You can try negotiating, if you like, Jarra, but I don't think you'll have any luck.'

'I don't understand why he's suddenly so interested in finances and making money. He's hardly even mentioned it till the last few days.'

'It's a means to an end—well, a lot of ends really. Some of his proposals are way beyond anything Mparntwe can help with in the short-term, and extra finance is the only way to make them happen. Are you going to Alkere tomorrow? You can have a good talk with him about it all.'

'Not tomorrow. I'm having a quiet time at home before I visit the doctor in the afternoon and then I'm out with Mirri for a swimming session. It will have to be when we get back to our normal four-day routine.'

'It's a good routine. Don't you think?'

'What do you mean?'

Jarra's look was returned with a little laugh.

'Was I that obvious? What I mean is that I think it works so well for both your health and your studies that you should continue the same way with any other joint projects Yirgella might have in mind. Darri said something about nanobots being a possibility.'

'Yes, we've talked about designing a better 3D printer and building models of a multi-purpose nanobot programmer, but that's more complicated than the ComPatch project and my uni work would be postponed for ages.'

'If you want to you could forget about university altogether. According to Darri you've learnt more in the last four weeks than you would with a whole semester of normal university work. Keep with Yirgella and you'll always be doing things you're motivated about.'

Work with Yirgella on a permanent basis? The idea was exciting. Scary, too, because it would be so demanding, but a good kind of scary.

'I think he'd like me to stay, Alira. He told Durrebar I needed a bigger project room the other day.'

'Of course he does. You make things better for him. Your work together in the security field is getting him on the InterWeb much sooner than expected, isn't it? And that's only one thing.'

Jarra didn't answer. The transport aircraft was landing and he could see Mirri waiting under the lights of the reception area.

*   *   *

'How many databases have you accessed now?'

Three weeks had passed since the big proposal day with the Council and Jarra was getting ready to work with Yirgella on their 3D printer ideas.

'I've accessed several thousand for specific information and accumulated 275 in total. I'm filtering another thirty-seven and deciding on a priority queue for a further 179. In your terms I would say my brain is close to overload, but there is so much I need to know.'

The one thousand databases Jarra had in his mind as a kind of milestone was still a while off. Maybe another eight weeks at this rate. It was still amazing because the filtering process meant every tiny component of a given database had to be checked with a very complicated process to make sure it was harmless.

'Did you get that new materials database from Europe?'

'I finished filtering its contents 3 hours ago.'

The nanobot project had been put on hold. Yirgella decided that with the ideas they had for a new kind of 3D printer it should take only five or six weeks to produce a finished product which would rapidly bring high returns and help acquire the far more expensive components of a nanobot programmer. Jarra felt strongly involved with this printer project because most of the aspects they wanted to introduce were his own ideas. And also, with more experimentation than theory involved, he could use a good proportion of his learning time to build his understanding of nanobots for when that project started.

'How are you choosing which databases you want?'

'Currently my first priority area is security. I want to understand every technique used by OverGovernments, the world's Corporations and the military. After that it's anything to do with nanobot technology. Nanobots will be the foundation for success with almost all our construction proposals.'

'How many new projects have you thought of since I last saw you?'

This was a little routine Jarra had fallen into.

'Thousands, Jarra. You've been away for two days so they've built up. Most of them are interesting but not practical given our limited resources. Several are important enough to push their way onto our immediate priority list.'

That sounded really interesting. So much was already getting started that the Council finance managers were running round in circles in an effort to source whatever extra capital they could. According to Alira, the construction materials project alone was so big it would use 80% of Mparntwe's current reserves to get it to a working level in the six-month timeframe of Yirgella's plan.

'What are they? Alira says there's not enough money for anything else at the moment.'

'There will be, but we'll have to be patient till we start getting significant returns. One is a high-speed underground transport and communication link between Alkere and Mparntwe. Another is a dedicated low orbit satellite for data transfer between Carnarvon, Darwin, Normanton and Mparntwe.'

'Underground transport? You mean an extension of the lift system?'

'No, it will be far more sophisticated, with a semi-experimental vacuum tunnel for high-speed travel.'

'It only takes 18 minutes to get here on the aeroplane.'

'The average flight time over the last six months has been 17 minutes and 37 seconds. This would reduce to less than 3 minutes.'

Forty kilometres in 3 minutes? This was simple motion mathematics and Jarra stared at Yirgella in amazement when he worked out what it meant.

'That's an average of 800 kilometres per hour.'

'Yes, the system I propose isn't very fast over short distances but I believe it will effectively demonstrate to the four First Australian Councils and the Australian OverGovernment the value of going ahead with a national system.'

'Eight hundred kilometres an hour isn't fast?'

'I discovered a vacuum travel system described in the material's database in a section on possible uses for the new strength materials. It has theoretic travel speeds of over 6000 kilometres per hour and I've been looking into it. My design simulations resolve to a practical outcome of 4700 kilometres per hour. That would make a trip to Carnarvon possible in approximately 30 minutes.'

'I've never heard of anything as fast. How does it work?' said Jarra.

'Quite simply. You enclose a sophisticated mag-lev system in a vacuum tunnel and the reduction in air resistance allows for greatly increased velocity.'

'Tunnels? All over Australia? We couldn't do that. It would take years and years and the cost would be unbelievable.'

'We wouldn't be able to start for three or four years but, by turning the ores mined in making the tunnels into exportable construction materials, the cost could be neutral or even turn a profit. It would take ten to twelve years to complete. The two projects complement each other to a high degree.'

Jarra thought it was brilliant and questioned and probed for details for almost an hour.

'Yirgella, this makes our work with nanobots even more important.'

*   *   *

'Yirgy likes our new ComPatches. He goes everywhere with us. I wish he could talk to us.'

'He will one day, Mirri, but it will have to be through our InfoPads.'

'You show him, JJ!'

'I won't have to. He learns lots of things by himself.'

'Buckle up!'

Jarra jumped to follow Mirri's order as the hum of the engines deepened and the Alkere transporter lifted into the air. Mirri was more excited to be seeing Yirgella than usual because there was a new game waiting for him and he'd also be able to show the requested video clips of his diving and swimming. His mood was quite contagious and, already smiling, Jarra laughed when Mirri stared at him with a funny look.

'No mucking round while we're buckled up, Mirri. Wait till we've levelled off.'

'Funny insect!'

What? Mirri was calling him an insect? Jarra just had time to wonder if this was a new game when Mirri's hand flashed rapidly towards him. Before he could even react there was a soft pressure on the back of his shoulder, a moment of manipulation against the material of his shirt, and Mirri's closed hand was held between them.

'Look, JJ. What is it?'

Very carefully, Mirri opened a finger and showed a strange looking insect with bulging eyes.

'It's a big March Fly ... I think. It was on my shirt?'

'Not fly! Not real!'

Mirri moved his hands closer to Jarra's eyes, insisting he look more carefully. The eyes did look funny, but so did most insect eyes when you really looked at them. Jarra was about to say just that when he noticed a shiny glint on the wing right next to where Mirri's finger was gripping. Strange, as if the colour had smudged off the surface. Shock coursed through his mind.

'Don't let go! Mirri! Don't let go. We have to show Durrebar.'

Mirri nodded his understanding and watched with intense concentration as Jarra opened his travel pack and dumped out the contents of the little first aid container with the screw-on lid.

'Put it in here, Mirri. I think it's a bad thing and we mustn't let it get away.'

Mirri knew from Jarra's tone that this was an important task and he very deftly manoeuvred the artificial insect into the container and screwed the lid carefully back on before handing it over. Jarra looked at him in amazement.

'Mirri, you are so clever. How could you tell it wasn't an ordinary insect? It tricked me even when I was looking close.'

'Looked funny. It is a bad thing?'

'We'll show Durrebar and the Security people when we get to Alkere. I think your explorer eyes have found a bad thing and stopped it from hurting Yirgy.'

Mirri nodded happily and Jarra gave him a big hug of congratulation then spoke directly at his special ComPatch.

'Yirgella, I'm not sure how much you could see but that insect Mirri caught is an artificial construct and the Security people should be ready to examine it when we land.'

'Yirgy is listening now?'

'He listens to us all the time when we wear our special ComPatches, Mirri, and he's probably already told Durrebar what to do.'

A soft vibration registered against Jarra's fingertips where they were holding the container.

'It must be flying and trying to get out. Mirri, your hands are stronger than mine. Will you hold it till we get to Alkere?'

Mirri took the first-aid container and Jarra nodded approval at the determined expression and strong grip.

That container was in secure hands now. The sound of the air transporter engine deepened, the belt-up sign flashed and the pilot looked round and called a warning to stay in their seats. A strong thrust of acceleration sent them travelling at a speed which Jarra wouldn't have thought possible in this small craft. Thirty seconds later the pilot turned again and relayed an urgent message from Alkere to place the container on the floor beneath a seat and move as far away as possible as a precaution against a possible self-destruct mechanism. Oh no. He'd put Mirri in danger. Jarra unbuckled and whisked the container to the back of the plane then moved Mirri so they were sitting close to the pilot.

'What happened, JJ?'

'The insect might go bang and hurt you. Yirgy is watching and he told the pilot you shouldn't hold it.'

The plane arrived nearly 5 minutes faster than normal and Jarra, Mirri and the pilot disembarked quickly and joined the phalanx of waiting Security people to watch a remote-controlled techbot enter the plane and collect the little container.

* * *

'Well, Mirrigan, I hear you are a very clever young man and you helped to protect Yirgella from a nasty spy. Are you going to tell me about it?'

'I saw the funny insect with my explorer eyes and we put it in a box. It didn't go bang. JJ said it was bad and Durrebar said it was bad and the other men said it was bad and Yirgy said it was bad. It was very bad.'

Mirri subsided after this extraordinarily long expression. It was now Jarra's job to do the full explanation.

'Mirri was amazing, Aunt Alira. He knew it wasn't a real insect as soon as he saw it and I couldn't tell even when I was looking closely. If some of the paint hadn't been scraped off it would have fooled me completely. We think it must have landed on the back of my shoulder when Mirri was getting on the plane in front of me otherwise he would have noticed it. The Security people said it could have gone almost anywhere in the project site and Mirri's clever eyes stopped a major security breach.'

'You don't just have explorer eyes, Mirri. You have eagle eyes.'

Alira turned back to Jarra.

'How serious a breach would it have been?'

'They analysed it completely. It took half the day with electron microscopes to disassemble all the components and scan them for Yirgella to study. It couldn't access any electronics or do any physical damage but it was built to watch and listen to anything in its presence. After three or four days it would hitch a ride back to Mparntwe where the data would be harvested.'

'Harvested?'

'That's the term the Security people use. They're pleased it's independent and not a transmit/receive device because whoever sent it won't know it's been caught.'

'Does that mean there's a chance of catching them when they do this harvesting?' asked Alira.

'No. Security found a base station hidden near the airport and it had a strong transmitter which meant no people had to be involved.'

'Could they track its signals?'

'They know the signals would go to the InterWeb but they couldn't do any tracking because the station wiped its memory when it was disturbed.'

'What are they doing about it at Alkere? Can they catch these spy devices if any more fly in?'

'No more will ever get in because they're installing extremely high resolution cameras throughout every part of the project and Yirgella has found a way to jam their flying mechanisms with a strong electric field. Every entrance will be protected and if the spy flies try to go through they'll fall to the ground immobilised.'

'Spy flies! Is that what you call them?'

'Mirri started it when he heard the word spy being used so much and when Yirgella took it up so did everybody else. It's a good description.'

'It's an excellent description,' said Alira.

'Spy flies can't get in now. Yirgy stopped them.'

'I think we can say it was you who stopped them, Mirrigan. Have you ever seen spy flies anywhere else?'

'No more. I told Yirgy and the other men.'

Jarra had asked him on the plane and then it was one of the first questions asked by every group at Alkere. Alira turned to Jarra again.

'Was there any conjecture as to why they used this new tactic? Two days ago Yirgella's report to Council said the misinformation strategy seemed to be working very effectively.'

'We think it worked really well. They were getting information that said there were serious problems with connecting Yirgella's different banks of processors properly and that scientists were arguing so much about it that morale was low and affecting progress.'

Mirri headed off to bounce on his trampoline. He somehow knew that Jarra and Alira were starting a serious talk mode.

'We knew the misinformation couldn't last because so many

new things like the ComPatch and security modules and the start-up of the materials factory have gone out into the world and they'd work out that the misinformation couldn't be right. It got us through the time while Yirgella was vulnerable to an attack on his energy supply, which was its main purpose while we built up a secure storage of over six months. Durrebar thinks our new 3D printers might be what got them to send in the spy fly.'

'Why the 3D printers, Jarra? They're not major like the vacuum tunnel or the materials factory.'

'They are in a way. They've got some good ideas in them and we build them much better than any of the old ones.'

'You build them at Alkere? I presumed you'd get some engineering company to do that.'

'No, it's really interesting. Yirgella programmed his own techbots to build them in a big new construction area we built at Alkere.'

'We? ... As distinct from the project itself?'

Jarra felt a little awkward.

'Um ... It was Yirgella's idea. We use the money that comes in from the Security modules so there's no cost to the project and it gives us complete control over the quality. Yirgella has set everything up to produce 2500 units a week. We've got thousands of orders already and it's only a week since our first models were released to the scientific and engineering community. Yirgella says it will be millions when the general community sees all the good reviews.'

'Millions? That's astonishing.'

'Not really. We've designed a home version, like the one you got for me, except it's much better, as well as our bigger ones for universities and engineers, so it's an enormous market.'

Alira laughed.

'Will the Council be able to borrow money from you if it needs to? It sounds like you're going to be very wealthy ... I suppose Yirgella is giving you a fair share?'

'No, he's not. He's giving me too much. He's set 40% of the profits for each of us and the other 20% to Mparntwe. You won't need to borrow anything.'

'Really? Has he worked out what the amount for Mparntwe might be? That would be interesting for our finance people to know.'

'It's a bit hard to believe.'

Jarra outlined Yirgella's estimates and Alira was staggered.

'Jarra, that's astonishing, and you get twice that amount. What will you do with it all?'

'I won't get any of it. Our new project is far more important and it will use every bit of profit we make for at least the next eight months.'

'Nanobots? You've studied them several times already so why eight months? That's longer even than your ComPatch project.'

'Yes, it started out as a way to build nanobots more efficiently but we kept having new ideas to try and the whole thing grew. We call it our NanoFactory project now.'

'What's a NanoFactory? I've never heard of one.'

'It's an idea I had when I watched Yirgella design the techbots for the printers. Instead of using techbots I wondered if we could make a special environment where nanobots could do the same sort of thing.'

'Nanobots would build the printers? What's the point if your techbots can already do it better than anyone else?'

'The point is that our NanoFactory could build the printers directly or build the techbots or any other construction task we wanted to program it with, with far more accuracy and speed.'

'Well, I don't really understand but it sounds very impressive. What would you mostly use it for?'

'Everything. Well, everything we already know how to build. Yirgella is really excited about it. He says it will be the perfect tool for an AI.'

'Does Yirgella get excited?'

Jarra laughed.

'I don't know. It seems like it to me. Perhaps I should say he sounds very eager.'

'Is there any chance you might have this project finished by next June?'

'June? Yes, that's nine months. Is there something happening?'

'We hope so, Jarra. The whole family is having a special three weeks in Carnarvon and Mirri won't go unless you can too.'

'Visiting Karmai?'

'Karmai will be with us the whole time even if you and Mirri can't make it. It's a Centre where families experience our cultural traditions first hand and live the Old Ways for a short while. It would be a wonderful adventure for you and Mirri both.'

'The Old Ways? Like living out in the bush?'

'Exactly. It's all structured with support from the Centre staff. We're not just dumped in the middle of nowhere to fend for ourselves, and the setting is inland from Carnarvon and next to the river so it looks especially suitable for a couple of young explorers.'

Next to the river and living in the bush! Mirri would be absolutely excited and there was no way he was going to miss out on that.

'Aunt Alira, Mirri is more important than a NanoFactory and adventures like this are so good for him he has to go. If I'm still working on the NanoFactory in nine months time I'll need a holiday anyway.'

'Wonderful! I knew you'd want to come, but the things you do with Yirgella are so important I thought they might have to take priority.'

'Everything's a priority with Yirgella but he's nearly as good as Mirri at knowing when my energy levels are down. He even turns my InfoSystem off when I do too much, so I know he'd want me to go.'

'*Are* you doing too much? Darri tells me you work every minute you can manage.'

'I can't do enough. It's so exciting working with Yirgella that I need every one of those minutes. You don't have to worry about me, though, because everyone else does: the doctor, and Mirri, and Yirgella, and Durrebar. The doctor says the arrangement we have at Alkere is far better for me than studying at the university where I'm locked into a rigid timetable. At Alkere I can stop for a rest or sleep whenever I need it and the four days a week commitment gives me three days to relax at home and be with Mirri.'

Alira nodded. She'd heard all this from Darri but it was good to know first-hand that Jarra was so pleased with his situation.

'Do you think you'll stay at Alkere when this newest project is finished?'

'Of course. Yirgella and Durrebar both want me to stay forever and I'd be silly to leave. How many people can have an AI and specially selected professors to help them learn? I'm totally spoilt really ... Are there facilities for my treatments at this place or will I have to go into Carnarvon to get them?'

'I'll have to check. I know they have a medical centre because there's quite a large support community.'

Chapter 12

'Darri, Jarra tells me he plans on staying at Alkere indefinitely. Evidently Yirgella and Durrebar both want him there.'

Darri and Alira were having one of their regular talks about Jarra's progress and activities.

'Want isn't a strong enough word. I think Durrebar and all the other scientists would go into a state of panic if he left.'

'Really?'

'Well, not panic, but they wouldn't be happy. There's an interaction between Yirgella and Jarra that makes unexpected things happen and they don't want that to stop.'

'Is unexpected good when we're dealing with an AI?'

Darri gave Alira a funny look.

'Alira, by nature an AI doesn't think the same way we do so the unexpected is what we have to expect ... Is that a tautology or something? Of course it's good, but there's an interaction between Jarra and Yirgella which has a kind of compounding effect. Look at their new project. It's going to change the world. The whole Alkere team can hardly believe the potential it offers.'

'Change the world? That's a bit strong, isn't it? Jarra said it was important as a tool for Yirgella.'

'Primarily, yes, which in itself is astonishing. Yirgella will be able to use it to design and make improvements to himself quite independently, but it's the secondary uses which will impact human society so much. Has Yirgella's proposal for a vacuum tunnel system reached the Council yet?'

'Between Mparntwe and Alkere? What do you mean? The work has already started.'

'Um ... Yirgella must be holding back till he has more definite plans. The Mparntwe–Alkere tunnel is the trial version for an Australia-wide high-speed travel system where a trip from here to Carnarvon would only take half an hour. This NanoFactory project, if it works as well as they think it will, would make it possible to complete the whole system in just seven or eight years.'

Alira was quiet then shook her head.

'Darri, that is astonishing but even if it's feasible it won't happen. The cost would be so enormous we couldn't contemplate it, even with help from the OverGovernment and every Australian Community ... Why are you smiling?'

'Yirgella wants to do it all as a kind of goodwill gesture. The only help he'd need would be in providing enough energy to run everything, which from the sound of it would require a rather large new solar array.'

'I know you're serious but I find it hard to believe what you're saying.'

'I know, and that's just one of the possibilities. An even bigger one is the changes they're talking about with construction work. Yesterday they were arguing about whether a 30% reduction in time and cost would be possible within twelve months.'

'They? We're talking about Yirgella and Jarra?'

'You should hear them. They throw ideas at each other and argue whether they're possible. Well, the imaginative ideas come from Jarra and the practical ones from Yirgella. Alira, why don't you come and work with us for a morning? Or even several days. It would be a real eye-opener for you to see first hand just how capable Jarra is at research. They usually start with a general discussion before doing anything else. I know Jarra would love to have you there, and Yirgella is always interesting.'

'I will. Seeing him once a week with Mirri isn't the same.'

*   *   *

A week later Alira asked Kyrra, as Mparntwe Council science advisor, to accompany her to Alkere and pass the day in Jarra's project room. It didn't take any persuasion because Kyrra had the highest interest of anyone on the Council about what went on at Alkere. Right now they were listening, amazed, as Jarra and Yirgella discussed the pros and cons of living in the space habitat which, at Jarra's request, Yirgella had just designed with several minutes work on his simulators.

'It's too unwieldy, Jarra, and the energy requirements for building it make it impractical.'

'That wouldn't matter. People want to explore space and if you already live there it's a lot less energy than if you take off from a planet.'

'There are seven functioning space stations and two abandoned ones. Space exploration happens from those without the need for a habitat.'

'Abandoned? Did something go wrong with them?'

'Nothing went wrong. The consortiums running them didn't plan well enough and when the energy costs sent them bankrupt they couldn't do anything else.'

'So how do the other seven pay their way then?'

'They don't. They are all run at a loss by various governments.'

'If we built the habitat a lot closer to the sun there'd be a lot more energy available from solar arrays. They work well in space.'

Yirgella answered after a gap of about 2 seconds.

'The energy supply would be sufficient but radiation problems and resource supply still make it impractical.'

'Would you like to live in space? A lot of electronics work better and are easier to build there.'

'I don't know, Jarra. I have only just started learning what it's like to live on Earth. I don't think *you* would. Where would you and Mirri do your exploring?'

Jarra laughed.

'We'd have to have our own spaceship to visit the Moon or asteroids.'

'Totally impractical.'

Jarra laughed again.

'When you design a fusion engine it won't be.'

There was another several-second wait for an answer.

'Totally impractical!'

'Where's your imagination? A fusion engine sounds really good and what about an impulse drive or a warp drive?'

'A warp drive is a fictional construct. The impulse drive is possible.'

'It is?'

Jarra shared his look of surprise with Alira and Kyrra.

'Yes. When completed it could travel from Earth's orbit to the Moon in approximately seventy-four days.'

'That's useless.'

'Precisely.'

'What's Mirri doing at the moment?'

'I presume he's swimming. His ComPatch shows an unchanging view of the locker room ceiling.'

Alira and Kyrra watched the ceiling view replace Yirgella's image for a moment.

'Jarra, do you check what Mirrigan is doing very often?'

'Sometimes, Aunt Alira, when I've forgotten his program, but not very often because Yirgella watches through the ComPatch and tells me if something interesting is happening. Mirri's hopeless. He likes taking his shirt off and all we see for ages is something like that ceiling or the material of his shirt. The ComPatch should be stuck on his forehead.'

'That is also impractical, Jarra.'

'I know. What about on a pendant round his neck? If we made it waterproof he could wear it even when he's swimming.'

'Then you'd have a problem when he finished. He'd put his shirt on and cover it.'

'He would, too, but if the shirt ComPatch kept watching it wouldn't matter.'

'That is a feasible idea. A pendant ComPatch would be far more durable with better vision and sound capabilities. Here is a design for an eagle pendant.'

'Yirgella, you'd have to call it a ComPendant not a ComPatch, and a dolphin design would be better at the moment.'

'What design would you like? Mirrigan would expect you to match him.'

Ten minutes later, after some discussion about designs of their own and a concentrated session between Jarra and Yirgella on the big 3D printer, four new pendant-style ComPatches were ready and, somewhat dazed at the speed of it all, Alira and Kyrra were fastening them round their necks.

'These look more like personal jewellery than communication devices. If all the Council members decide to use them in place of a normal ComPatch other people might want to copy.'

Alira smiled.

'Our Council setting a fashion, Kyrra? That would be a first.'

That gave Jarra an idea.

'They'd have to use ordinary ComPatch circuitry but if people wanted them as pendants we could sell them as the first jewellery ever made by an AI. Yirgella, could we use any design people wanted for the casing and make them with this 3D printer?'

'Jarra, you're talking to Yirgella like a real entrepreneur. What about the complex inner circuitry? That can't be made on a 3D printer.'

'It can on this one, Aunt Alira, because it's got extra features which need Yirgella's input to work. It helps us get things done much faster.'

'Individually designed jewellery? What if several thousand people wanted them? Wouldn't that be a waste of Yirgella's time?'

'Yirgella, work out how much of your time it would take to make 1000 different jewellery ComPatches.'

'Based on the four we just produced my involvement would be approximately nine tenths of 1 second and the production time with Jarra's 3D printer would be nearly 17 hours.'

Kyrra was startled, but not as much as Alira.

'What? You can design a thousand different cases in less than a second?'

'The process involves far more than just the cases. The circuitry has to be configured to match the physical properties of each case and then a batch process with instructions for the 3D printer built and stored. My involvement is quite variable as it depends on the priority I assign. By using 10% of my resources instead of the low two hundredths of 1% I just used, the one thousand count would increase to just short of half a million.'

'Half a million in less than a second! So, in the time it takes me to count to ten you could do all the calculations necessary to produce an individually designed ComPatch for every man, woman and child living in Mparntwe?'

'Providing your ten count took more than 5 seconds and I had all the necessary information available, yes, that would be quite a simple task.'

'Astonishing. How long would it take to do the same thing with our special ComPatches? About 8 or 10 seconds?'

'That is correct for the calculations, Alira, but I would be reluctant to implement a system of that size.'

For whatever reason, Alira and Kyrra both looked to Jarra for an explanation.

'Our special ComPatches are highly complex compared to ordinary ones and Yirgella is monitoring high-resolution imagery and sound non-stop from every unit that's connected. If there were two and a half million of them instead of the current thirty-four I think he'd be swamped with data.'

'Jarra is right. Monitoring that number of people would be a constant demand on a significant proportion of my resources.'

'I don't believe it. We've come up with something too big for you,' said Alira.

'Not really. With major design changes and structural alterations I believe I could limit the use of my resources to between ten and twelve per cent and still operate a system of that size. There are far more efficient ways to improve security for Mparntwe though.'

'More improvements for Mparntwe security? How would you change what we're already doing?'

'For a start I would replace all your security cameras with more capable ones and increase the number to surveil every public space.'

'Every single door, walkway or place where people gather? How many cameras would you need to do that?'

'Several million for the coverage I would recommend.'

'Several million? Wouldn't that need a similar amount of resources as the special ComPatches?'

'Significantly less, Alira. A dedicated Intelligent Security System could be designed to do most of the work under my oversight.'

'Could you watch everyone in Mparntwe for 24 hours of the day?'

There was a distinct pause before Yirgella answered Kyrra's question.

'That would require surveillance of all private living space and an increase in the number of cameras used to something in the order of twenty million. I could manage but the constant demand on my resources would be unsustainable.'

'Kyrra, we wouldn't want to watch people in their homes.'

'I know. I'm testing my understanding of Yirgella's capabilities. Twenty million cameras running sounds ridiculous. How would you make that many. Jarra? Would these nanobots do it?'

'Cameras are easy, Kyrra. We built the high-resolution ones for picking up the spy flies at Alkere entrances on our 3D printer so we wouldn't need nanobots.'

'I disagree, Jarra. A nanobot production device would be far more efficient for such large scale production'

'What *is* a nanobot? I know they're tiny and can make things but that's about the extent of my knowledge.'

Jarra looked to Yirgella's image.

'Will I explain or will you?'

'I suggest you give a quick explanation, Jarra, then set up several examples to examine with the electron microscopes. Start with your healthbots and show some of their different functions.'

Alira and Kyrra spent some time looking at different types of nanobots then watched, quite amazed, as Jarra used his InfoSystem to design one from scratch.

'Jarra, we've been here an hour and a half and so far you've given all your time to us. We thought we'd be watching your normal routine.'

'Most days start with a lot of talking and playing round with ideas so it *has* been fairly normal. You're not going to just watch though. We've got a special job for you designing the interior layout of the tunnel train.'

Alira and Kyrra shared a look.

'Are you serious?'

'We'll help you, of course, and with the simulators and some VR devices you'll have it done in a couple of hours.'

It took longer than that but when Jarra returned from his midday rest he was enthusiastically presented with the finished result.

'What's this sign you've put on the seats and the doorways?'

'We joined a symbolic caterpillar with a representation of the sun to show the connection between Mparntwe and Alkere. It was Kyrra's idea and we chose from a range of designs Yirgella made for us. I think it would be a good logo to use for all the joint projects.'

Jarra liked the idea but didn't get to talk about it because Alira and Kyrra were keen to hear the plans for the rest of the afternoon.

'Yirgella and I will be looking at different techniques for programming nanobots but it's fairly technical so you might like to do something else. He also needs a human viewpoint to help plan a new type of lift system, otherwise you could work with him on the miniature waste recycler we've been studying. And I know Durrebar wants to grab you, Alira, for an hour as well.'

Kyrra went to a different part of the project room to work with the lift system while Alira said she'd watch the nanobot programming then leave to see Durrebar after about an hour. That pleased Jarra because it felt good to show something of what his main project work looked like. Half an hour later Jarra was giving a quick explanation to Alira about the section of programming code they were looking at when the InfoSystem screen flickered. It was instantaneous but it had never happened before and Jarra looked to Yirgella's image for an explanation.

'Jarra, our external power supply has been interrupted and, while there is no apparent threat to the project site, it would be prudent to move quickly with Alira and Kyrra to meet with some of our Security staff in the third level basement area. We should know more about what's happening by the time you get there.'

Jarra jumped to his feet and motioned Alira and Kyrra to follow. He knew exactly where to go and the quickest way to get there from the emergency drills the Security people and Yirgella had worked out after the Mparntwe lift incident and the spy fly attempt. In the corridors the purposeful movement and strained expressions made Jarra wonder if there was something Yirgella hadn't told them and he felt grateful when Alira took his arm in a comforting grip.

'Jarra, this isn't a practice drill, is it?'

'Not from the way Yirgella spoke.'

Jarra was walking faster than he should and when they reached the basement room he acknowledged Professor Allerton and some of the Security people then walked straight past them to sit on a comfortable chair. Alira, immediately concerned, sat next to him.

'I'm all right. It took me by surprise, that's all. Do you know what's happened, Professor?'

'Only that there has been an interruption to our power supply which warrants moving ...'

The display screen on the wall—there was at least one in every room of the Alkere project—flickered to life with Yirgella's image.

'The precaution of moving you all has proved unnecessary as the single event which occurred nearly 17 kilometres away at our project solar array appears to be quite isolated. A security team with forensic equipment is headed for the site and will shortly provide us with a clearer picture of what has happened. At this stage we know an explosion has destroyed power connections to our site and the period for reconnection will depend on the degree and type of damage. Our backup system is functioning without fault and you are free to return to your ordinary activities. Durrebar would like to meet in the conference hall with all department heads, and anyone else interested.'

Jarra's nanobot work could wait. He most certainly wanted more information about what had happened and if it was another sabotage attempt. He didn't have any doubt that it was, so Alira and Kyrra needed to be involved as well. Three quarters of an hour later when Jarra looked round the conference hall the only people who weren't there were from Security. A big image of Yirgella appeared on the large hall display screen and there was immediate hush.

'The damage is extensive and since the main transformer and

outlet connections have been destroyed there will be several days of repair work before we can return to normal. I have planned a set of techbots, and with help from Jarra and his 3D printer they should be functional in approximately 3 hours time. Residue traces identify a sophisticated military-grade type of explosive with properties designed to make it particularly compatible with the stealth device which must have been used for its delivery.'

Yirgella's image was replaced with views of the damage that had been caused, and after a stunned moment Durrebar voiced the question everyone was wondering.

'How can that possibly be fixed in two days? It's a rebuild, not a repair.'

'The purpose-built techbots will make the difference. Standard practice would take a week or more, even with fast tracking.'

Jarra stood up and started moving. The techbots sounded important and he needed to get to his 3D printer immediately.

Chapter 13

The Alkere power supply was quickly fixed and Jarra settled into a steady pattern of study, research and experimentation, and for eight busy months he and Yirgella concentrated on developing their NanoFactory idea. It was a far-reaching project and, in reality, Jarra understood that it would continue indefinitely and, while their original goals had been well and truly reached, every plateau of research and development brought new refinements and capabilities to consider. The prototype which became functional in the seventh month made a huge difference to their progress because many things which had previously taken Jarra days to put together could now be built in a fraction of the time and in a bootstrapping way the NanoFactory built new sections of itself for installation and testing. One week before Jarra's trip to Carnarvon with the family, the whole Alkere staff plus Alira and the Council gathered for the official first production effort of the Alkere NanoFactory and, after making a formal request for Yirgella to set everything in motion, Jarra turned to Alira and the Council members.

'Thank you for accepting our invitation to the commissioning of our new NanoFactory. Yirgella and I are very excited about it and because of all your backing and extra support we propose to share a proportion of the benefits with you, and to do that this NanoFactory will be used primarily for projects to help Mparntwe as soon as our second one is ready.'

Kyrra waved his arms excitedly.

'Jarra, could you tell us more about your NanoFactory? You started it going a few moments ago without telling us what it's making.'

'Yes, it's like a surprise. If you can wait a while we'll be able to show you the new excavation machine which will help to finish the vacuum tunnel between here and Mparntwe within the next two months.'

'Months? You mean years? The current plan says just over three years,' said Kyrra.

'No, the machine Yirgella has designed will be able to tunnel through half a kilometre a day and he's making six of them, so the actual tunnelling will only take a couple of weeks. The rest of the time is for all the fitting out and testing of the special train which will also be built here.'

The Alkere staff knew about this and were all smiling at the reactions of the various Council members. Kyrra, understanding more than the others what it meant was shaking his head and smiling at the same time.

'That must be an amazing excavation machine if it's going to reduce a mammoth three-year project to only two months. It doesn't sound possible.'

He laughed and turned to Alira.

'Look at them all smiling. They've got more surprises lined up. I can tell. It's a conspiracy to shock us.'

Chuckles and smiles from the Alkere staff confirmed this and every Council member gave new attention to Jarra. This had been Durrebar's idea. He thought the Council had no idea how significant the NanoFactory really was and a barrage of surprises would make it a memorable start up.

'Yes, we're going to show you some of the things our NanoFactory and an AI can do together. Tomorrow's task for the NanoFactory will be to start building extra excavation machines and extensions for the materials project. The manager has told us the demand is currently more than ten times the amount we can supply and, with the NanoFactory, Yirgella will be able to match that within six weeks.'

Most of the Council turned to the member who oversaw Mparntwe's finances.

'The materials project is already ahead of schedule but that level of production wasn't expected for another eighteen months. It will almost match our energy income.'

Kyrra laughed.

'I'm suitably shocked, Jarra. What will the NanoFactory do when the six weeks is finished?'

'The first task will be to construct a second NanoFactory so this one can be dedicated to a whole range of Mparntwe needs.

'Durrebar has been working with Yirgella and they have designs for big improvements to a range of Intelligent Systems. The improvements mean there will be high demand all round the world and a great opportunity for Mparntwe to develop expert teams of engineers and support staff for an extensive installation and servicing industry. Yirgella's only part will be to build them with the NanoFactory.

'Professor Allerton and his team have developed a special understanding of high-level processors in their time at Alkere and Yirgella can set up the NanoFactory to make their designs and sell them. There's a very big demand for better processors.

'Yirgella would also like to provide Mparntwe with a complete Security overhaul. He's designed a new Intelligent System to run it, or he can control it directly himself if that's what you wish.

'He wants the AI projects at Carnarvon, Darwin and Normanton to start immediately and he intends to provide most of the processors and equipment they'll need.

'He is also going to relocate himself 1200 metres underground for more security.'

That brought general nods of agreement. Security was a big issue for everyone. Two attempts at intrusion by spy flies had followed the one Mirri caught. Even more worrying, after the shocking destruction of the power transformer station, was a further attempt, prevented by the military team from the Australian OverGovernment and special surveillance equipment from Carnarvon, to disable the solar array itself. Jarra paused for any questions and Kyrra jumped in.

'Is that all?'

Kyrra was joking but Jarra felt a wash of tiredness.

'No, those are just some of the immediate things. Yirgella has more than he can possibly do … Durrebar, would you explain things please. I'm going to take a break.'

No-one said anything but there were smiles and nods of acknowledgement from the Council members who all understood his situation. With a degree of relief Jarra headed for a quiet place. He'd been active too long and he found speaking to a large group of people quite draining.

*   *   *

When Jarra had departed Alira spoke before Durrebar could start.

'Is there some reason why Jarra has done all the presenting and talking? Quite clearly he went for longer than he should have.'

Yirgella's image appeared on the big screen.

'Welcome Councillors and thank you, Alira, for your concern. Durrebar was in full agreement with my insistence that Jarra commission the NanoFactory and acquaint you with its potential. Without his inspiration it wouldn't exist. His ideas and imagination have resulted in a tool which will benefit us all. Who else should formally present it? The Alkere staff and I would like the Mparntwe Council to give Jarra some type of recognition for his achievements.

'The tunnelling machine will be complete in another 65 minutes and briefly available for inspection. Are there any questions you'd like answered?'

'Yirgella, our Council has been aware of your NanoFactory project but it's only just now that Jarra has acquainted us with its real capabilities and significance. Of course we'll do something, but unless it's very low-key I suspect he won't have anything to do with it. We'll think about it. How soon will you have your support for the other AI projects ready? None of them are expecting such an early start and we'll have to liaise with them immediately.'

*   *   *

Jarra finished up the work he was doing on his InfoSystem and was about to close it down when he was distracted by movement at the door to his project room. Well, one of his project rooms, as there were now a number built for various purposes, as well as the big new one when the move underground went ahead. What on earth? The strange device came gliding close and Durrebar clicked a control and stood up.

'Take a seat, Jarra, and we'll show you how to operate your holiday present.'

'Present?'

'Yes, so you can make extended exploration trips with Mirrigan. It will be perfect for your stay at Birringurra Country.'

Birringurra was the name of the area near Carnarvon where Mirri's whole family would be staying in only three days time.

Jarra was quite taken aback. The idea of using a personal carrier was constantly being suggested and everyone knew his reasons for refusal.

'For me? Durrebar, I don't need it.'

'Yirgella thinks you do and he's designed it especially to suit you and Mirrigan.'

That piqued Jarra's interest. This thing could obviously carry him but why would it suit Mirri as well? Oh! There were two foot-stands at the back. That must be what he meant.

'How does it work?'

'Climb on and I'll show you. We'll take it outside because it's designed to cope with rough terrain.'

The controls were simple but versatile. Jarra learned them quickly because they were very similar to the controls of the much larger vehicle he used to drive to their Alkere explore places, and for 20 enjoyable minutes the remarkable little personal carrier was put through its paces. Mirri was going to absolutely love this because he'd be able to stand on the back and they could go to so many new places. Jarra deftly guided them back to the project room to give a big thank you to Yirgella as well as say goodbye for the next few weeks.

'What made you build it? You know I've always refused a personal carrier in the past because my constant walking activities are so important for my health.'

'I spoke with Alira and Burnu about Birringurra and we wanted to overcome some of your limitations, and in particular I've designed it for the local terrain so you can accompany Mirri on the Walkabout.'

'Yirgy, that's wonderful, and Mirri will be so pleased.'

Jarra didn't often use Mirri's way of addressing Yirgella. He was naturally more reserved, but this was spontaneous. Mirri had been completely excited when he understood that the Centre's educational Walkabout meant four days of non-stop exploring, but then he found out that Jarra couldn't do it and he refused to go. Jarra felt awful and no amount of persuasion had any effect till Alira arranged a compromise where Jarra would be taken to meet with Mirri at every campsite.

'Would it be possible for you to give it a proper trial tomorrow so I can monitor its performance? I'd like to suggest you catch the mag-lev out to Trephina Gorge and take the trail to the ridgetop.'

That was quite a shock and Jarra had to process the idea for a moment. The ridgetop was foreign territory, far beyond the limits of normal consideration with its steep and rocky access trail.

'It would take me up there? It's a long way.'

'A couple of kilometres is nothing. The fuel cell can manage several days of continuous use, and when it's safe enough you can travel at up to 16 kilometres per hour. Your doctor has developed guidelines to follow but he says you'll adapt very quickly.'

The doctor had been involved? Jarra wondered how long Yirgella had been working on this. The ridgetop? Amazing. And four days walking with Mirri. Unbelievable.

'Show Jarra the companion function please, Durrebar. He hasn't seen that yet.'

Durrebar clicked a little device from its place next to the miniature InfoPad built into the console and fiddled with it.

'Watch this. I've set it to stay at 2 metres. It's for when you want to walk and not leave the carrier behind.'

He set off on a random course round the project room and the personal carrier followed, manoeuvring its way successfully past every obstacle.

'We thought this would be particularly useful for your explorations with Mirrigan as it will let you walk twice the normal distance and then carry you on the return.'

After thanking Yirgella and Durrebar, Jarra happily drove his new carrier to the transport plane. He couldn't wait to show off to Mirri.

*   *   *

Everyone was smiling. This was the first time they'd all seen Karmai since he started his ranger job and he was laughing because, along with everyone else, Mirri had just hugged him for about the tenth time. Jarra thought he seemed different. Not his looks but his manner. Perhaps it was his ranger clothes. Right now it was all greetings, family banter, and getting organised to travel from Carnarvon to Birringurra. There'd be time for proper talk later.

*   *   *

'Welcome to Country. It is a privilege to have you stay with us.'

'Thank you, Jarli, but we are the ones being honoured. This is Burnu, my brother, and his family.'

Alira formally introduced the group to Jarli, her counterpart on the Carnarvon Council, then everyone headed to the river where Jarli's own family and some of the guides and instructors from the Heritage program were waiting to share a meal.

The 150 metre walk took Jarra's breath away and he stared in awe at the giant river gums and grotesquely shaped paperbark trees. They made even the special ghost gums at home look ordinary, and the sparkling waters and rich red sand made the rock pools at some of their exploring places seem tiny. Mirri grabbed Jarra's arm.

'Look, JJ. Funny-face bird. See, next to pelican.'

Mirri knew pelicans because Karmai had taken them to a nursery near Carnarvon on their last trip. Karmai was close to Mirri and he answered.

'He's called a Royal Spoonbill, Mirri. He uses that round part on the end of his long bill to catch his food.'

'He has a spoon on his bill. Funny-face. Can we swim in the water, Karmai?'

'Of course you can. Look at the littlies playing.'

A number of children were splashing in the shallow water near the waiting group. After a formal welcoming ceremony there were more introductions and then the Mparntwe people sat on the sand to eat the meal of fish, yams and other natural food which had been prepared. Jarra was most interested because part of their time here would involve learning how to gather these different foods for themselves. There was talk and laughter and meeting different people till inevitably came the tug at Jarra's arm.

'Can we explore now, JJ?'

'Let's ask Aunty Alira. She'll know if it's all right.'

Mirri ran to get Karmai. After so long apart there was no way he wouldn't be included, but disappointingly he was busy with someone else. Alira was with Jarli and it was quickly worked out that there was nearly an hour before everyone was leaving the river.

'What would you like to see?'

Jarli was still new to Mirri so Jarra answered for him.

'Mirrigan likes to see everything, especially animals, and he'd like to have a swim too.'

'Animals and swimming? That sounds interesting and I know a great place to go.'

He gave a call, two little boys came running, and there was a rapid interchange in what must have been the local people's traditional language.

'Would you like my two rascals to be your guides? I've told them to catch a tortoise for you and show you the best swimming place. This one is Barega ... and this one is Akama.'

Amazing. Jarra would remember the names but there was no way he'd be able to tell which was which. Mirri's looks were going back and forth, back and forth, but his big smile said these fascinating little guides were accepted.

'What is a tortoise, JJ?'

'It's like a little turtle, Mirri, with feet instead of flippers.'

Mirri understood turtles from Karmai and Monkey Mia but his attention was on the boys.

'Why are you the same?'

'We are twins. Akama came first but I'm stronger and I swim better. My daddy says you want to explore and we do too. What's your name? We're going to catch you a tortoise. Can you run fast? I think you look strong. Can you lift me up with one arm? My daddy can and he's stronger than anyone.'

Mirri couldn't cope with this rapid barrage of comments and questions but he was smiling rather than looking baffled. Jarli laughed and put a big strong hand on Barega's head.

'Steady down, you little galah. Say one thing at a time so Mirrigan has a chance to think about it, and if you make up stories all the time he won't believe you.'

'I like to hear stories. Can he tell good stories like Jarra stories?'

Two little faces looked up with great interest and Jarra wondered if the stories he used for Mirri would work with them.

'Mirri, twins are special brothers who look the same because they have the same birthday.'

'Will you tell us a story, please?'

This was the other little boy. Jarra searched for some way to tell them apart but Mirri was right: they did look identical.

'I know a story about how the tortoise got his shell. Would you like to hear that one when we finish exploring?'

There were two happy nods then, simultaneously, Barega took Mirri's hand and Akama took Jarra's.

'Let's go.'

The boys went almost directly to a tortoise and Mirri was so amazed and intrigued that he started a soft vocalisation of his wonder. The boys stared at this unusual behaviour, but after a few seconds Akama, now easily identified by a distinctive scratch on his knee, followed the lead with his own version of Mirri's sound and straightaway Barega joined in as well. The release of the tortoise was followed with more exploring, an attempt to get close to another funny-face bird, then a short walk to what was called the good swimming place. Barega grabbed Jarra's hand and started to lead him to the water but Mirri stopped that and said it was time to sit down.

'Jarra needs a rest for his bad muscles. Can you tell us the tortoise story, JJ?'

For 5 minutes the audience of three listened raptly then, after a thank you hug from Mirri, which the boys immediately copied, Jarra was directed to 'close eyes' while they had a swim.

Jarra did so—it really was time for a rest—and he listened to the yells and laughter while Mirri and the boys played and swam in the water about 20 metres away. Mirri was running through his repertoire of spouting whales, shark and crocodile attacks, and a fairly new dolphin diving game. Shrieks of delight made Jarra open his eyes to watch Barega sitting on Mirri's shoulders and directing him to chase Akama who was accidentally on purpose letting himself be caught and thrown through the air to land with a grand splash.

Jarra faded for a while till sudden quietness brought him back. They were all looking at him so he gave a wave which Mirri would know meant they could keep on with their swimming.

A quick check on his InfoPad showed that he'd been properly asleep because it was nearly 20 minutes later than he'd thought. Good. He could go in the water and join in. He didn't though. He watched the interaction between Mirri and the boys instead. Mirri was crawling through the water, shaking his body and bucking gently so the twins on his back had to work at staying in place. One of them—Jarra couldn't tell which from this distance—fell off and everything stopped till he regained his place. Mirri's funny calls of whatever animal he thought he was being at the moment mingled with the laughter and yells of the boys and Jarra watched with the wonder that Mirri's happy nature continually evoked. Both boys fell off as Mirri suddenly knelt up and started beckoning. Somehow he'd known that Jarra was watching and expected him to join in.

*   *   *

The next two weeks were very busy and very, very interesting, and because it allowed him to join in with almost all the outdoor activities, Jarra was totally grateful for his personal carrier.

On the day after their arrival the morning activity was a leisurely walk along the riverside with several sorties into the surrounding country to learn some of the area's natural food sources, and without the transport he'd never have coped.

By the end of the first week Jarra worked out that by relying on his personal carrier and a number of strategically timed rests he could get through the major activity of the morning, then having at least 2 hours sleep and rest after midday would build his reserves enough to enable an explore of some kind in the afternoon with Mirri and whoever else was involved.

Karmai came with them most days, Alira when she wasn't too busy with something else, and because something had clicked between them, the twins sought out Mirri whenever they could and led the way for most of the expeditions.

One of the best places was over 2 kilometres downstream where the river widened. Large sheets of shallow water attracted a myriad of water birds and you could sneak close to watch the different types. The distance meant the twins travelled on the personal carrier with Jarra while Mirri and Karmai would walk, jog or run along with them.

Evenings were often very special gatherings by a campfire to hear elders recounting the Dreamtime, and several times Jarra, Mirri, and Karmai sat in the soft sand by the riverside learning special men's business from Jarli or another leader.

* * *

The four-day Walkabout was something Jarra would never ever forget and he used his special ComPatch with its higher quality to record every moment. It was no good for communication with

Yirgella at this distance, of course, but everything would be sent through the InterWeb when they got back to the Birringurra Centre.

Mirri amazed everyone, especially their guides, with his ability to find and see things before anyone else. He also created a huge problem on the first day when a blue-tongued lizard he'd caught was killed in front of him for a meal. With tears trickling from his eyes and his song of misery shaking everyone to the core, he turned his back and refused to have anything to do with it. The whole course for the Walkabout had to be changed and moved closer to the river where there were a lot more vegetarian sources of food.

Jarra also caused modifications to the established Walkabout procedure because of his constant need to rest, and the midday stop always lasted several hours. At other times when the imperative for rest came on him, one of the guides would stay with him for 20 or 30 minutes then stand on the back of the personal carrier while they travelled at more than twice the normal group pace on a catch-up journey. The terrain would dictate the actual speed but Jarra was now so proficient at judging the best path and controlling his carrier that the guides all said it was exciting. Jarra thought so too.

On the last night Mirri, Karmai, and two other brothers went through a symbolic passing to manhood ritual, their bodies painted with ochre, singing and chanting, and copying the rhythm and movement around the campfire of the guide leading them through it. Along with listening to appropriate parts of the Dreamtime, they'd practiced different sections of the dancing on the previous two nights so they were very proficient and the atmosphere of it all gave Jarra goosebumps in his hair.

Chapter 14

After a 5 kilometre walk from their campsite the group was back at the Cultural Centre for their last day and, after a lot of talk with the rest of family about events on the Walkabout, Jarra and Mirri set off with the little twins who, according to Jarli, had been pestering every day about when they could see Mirri again. Jarra took his personal carrier, of course, because this was the last explore they'd have at Birringurra and with it they'd be able to visit all their favourite spots. First stop was a big river red gum and, because Akama thought it was so special, Jarra got really adventurous and climbed to a branch where there was a good lookout over the river. The twins went first with a lift to the lowest branch, which was too high without help from a bigger person, and then it became a major project because of Jarra's weak muscles and, following instructions which had to be carefully worked out for each different stage, Mirri did the real supporting and lifting.

'See this big lump? The tree keeps a secret in there.'

Little Akama had his hands on a giant burl. Yes, it was Akama. The scratch on his knee was much fainter but still distinguishable. These lumpy protrusions were on many of the river gums but this one was particularly large and very distinctive in shape and Jarra rested his hand next to the tiny hand already there. Mirri joined in and covered Akama's hand with his own.

'The tree has a secret?'

Akama's idea that a tree could have a secret was a strange one and Mirri's question was to Jarra who, of course, knew the answer to everything. What to say?

'Trees are alive, Mirri, and this kind of tree can live for a long, long time.'

'Yes, we saw where the blood came out.'

The boys stared at Mirri.

'Mirri saw some red sap coming out of a tree and he was worried the tree was hurt because he thought it was blood.'

'It is tree blood.'

'Yes, it is, Mirri, and this tree is so big it might be five hundred years old, and when you've lived that long you can have all sorts of secrets.'

'Do trees know things?'

'They know all sorts of things, Barega. Their roots know how to look for water and the leaves know when to face the sun and when to turn sideways if it's too hot.'

'Is the secret in here for the tree or is it for someone else?'

Jarra wasn't used to seven year old boys and he wondered how he should answer this.

'If it's a tree secret we'll never find out, and if it's for someone else we'll only know if they tell us. That's how secrets work.'

That brought three nods. Barega manoeuvred his way farther along the big branch and reached for a handful of gum leaves. Jarra worried that he was too daring, but from what they'd said at the base of the tree, Jarli always lifted them past the hard part and liked them climbing. When Barega crushed the leaves and started smelling them Mirri got interested and clambered out to try for himself. Jarra wasn't moving. Getting up to the boys' lookout perch was adventure enough. A racket of raucous calls attracted his attention to a small flock of white cockatoos wheeling into the branches of a nearby gum tree.

'Look, Jarra, look!'

Akama was pointing to the expanse of shallow water which was one of the reasons for climbing this special tree. A group of water birds were in a panic of flapping and distress as a large bird of prey coursed low and fast above them. There was a sudden stoop, a spray of feathers, and the successful hunter flapped powerfully away with its prey held securely in its talons. As if the moment of drama hadn't happened the remaining water birds resumed their activities.

'He's a good hunter, that one.'

Jarra smiled. It sounded like Akama was repeating an older person's comment. Jarra and Akama watched the quieter scene together till Mirri and Barega brought the gum leaves to share the eucalyptus smell. Barega wanted the next destination to be the paint place and, since it sounded interesting, everyone agreed to try that before going to the swimming spot. After negotiating the tricky descent from the tree, the personal carrier did the work for Jarra and the boys while Mirri jogged along easily.

*   *   *

'Darri says we won't believe all the things that are happening with Yirgella.'

'When did he get home?' asked Alira.

Darri had used the last three weeks to travel to New Zealand and Jarra had just been catching up on the Centre's InterWeb.

'Two days ago and he's got lots to tell us, but he's more amazed about what's been happening at Alkere.'

'What?'

'Yirgella's second NanoFactory has been producing solar panels for the new array and he's made giant Techbots to help install them. Darri went to watch them working and each team can have a panel installed and connected in just half an hour.'

Burnu jumped on that.

'Half an hour? I don't think that's right. Our Alkere construction teams are as good as any in the world and they take half a day.'

'That's what Darri said. There are nineteen bot teams working and the array is already providing energy for the materials excavation machines.'

'Nineteen? That's the number of Alkere construction teams. Maybe they work together? Excuse me, I'm going to look into this.'

Burnu headed for the nearest InfoSystem.

'Well, you certainly surprised Burnu. What else did Darri have to say?'

'Yirgella has started a vacuum tunnel between Mparntwe and Darwin.'

Now it was Alira's turn for disbelief.

'He can't. It wouldn't just have to go through our Council. It would have to go through the Australian OverGovernment as well. Darri must have got it wrong.'

Jarra didn't know what to say. Darri didn't get things wrong. Alira took out her InfoPad and connected directly to Yirgella.

'Alira, I hope you are enjoying your Birringurra stay. I'm enjoying the data from Jarra and Mirri's ComPatches, but you look worried. Is there some way I can help you?'

'Jarra says you've started building a vacuum tunnel between Mparntwe and Darwin.'

'Not officially. That will require a great deal of negotiation. Under the auspices of our materials project we are extracting ores along a trajectory which lends itself to conversion to a vacuum tunnel if and when it can proceed.'

'I see. What's the great urgency when you still don't know the viability of the trial tunnel between Mparntwe and Alkere?'

'I am highly confident of that viability. The urgency has arisen because we are now making hardened construction materials faster than we can move them out. Our transport contractors have scrambled to triple their current capacity but in two months time we will have reached a backlog stage again. Beyond that the volume will increase so much that an extra transport system is the only solution.'

'A travel tunnel to Darwin will take much longer than a few months to finish ... Won't it?'

'Yes, eleven months for the excavations alone if we can dedicate all eight of our tunnelling machines, but since the energy requirements are currently too great we are pushing to complete the new solar array. Once that is fully online we'll be able to increase the number of machines and make a useful reduction in the completion time. The energy supplied by the new array will be a great enabler for many of our projects. When you return to Mparntwe I have several developments to share with you.'

Jarra's interest pricked. Yirgella wasn't talking about the developments over the InterWeb. Maybe they were something to do with security.

'That's tomorrow. Should I make a special trip out to Alkere in the afternoon?' asked Alira.

'The next day would be suitable. Will Jarra be with you?'

Jarra held his hand up in acknowledgement.

'Not for four more days. Mirri and I are staying with Karmai at Monkey Mia so he can show us his ranger work. Yirgella, there's so much happening here at the moment that I'll have to contact you again tomorrow morning before we leave for Carnarvon. I have lots of ideas I want to discuss with you.'

'I will wait with anticipation. Is there any other business, Alira?'

'Not at the moment. As Jarra said, there is a great deal happening here. Anything else can wait till the day after tomorrow.'

Alira turned to Jarra.

'Rest! Relax! Sleep! Off you go. At least 1 hour or you'll never get through the rest of the evening.'

When Jarra surfaced from his rest and went to find Mirri the atmosphere in the centre was buzzing with preparation. The culmination of their stay was a ceremonial corroboree with presentations of the traditional dances and music they'd been practising since they first arrived.

Jarra had involved himself in the practices as much as he could with gentle versions of the various steps and movements. Where there was a leap he would take a small step. Instead of rhythmic stomping he would rock his body lightly in time. This way he'd be able to participate.

'JJ, sit here with me. Kulan will paint you.'

Jarra stared.

He knew from pictures and talk what went into getting ready, and they'd had great fun earlier in the day painting designs on each other with the ochre at the paint place, but the real thing was spectacular. Mirri looked like a wild man. The manhood ritual of the previous evening meant he was receiving a special treatment and almost every part of his body was covered in dramatic design with the rich, contrasting colours of the ochre and clay. He was wearing nothing but a brief loin covering and a cluster of feathers tied in his hair and Jarra thought he looked like a warrior from the Dreamtime or even a mythical Kurdaitcha man.

'Mirri, you look scary.'

That made Mirri smile, which definitely put an end to the scary aspect.

'You will, too, JJ. Kulan is the best painter'

*   *   *

Jarra would have felt strange, but because everyone else looked just as striking he felt a sense of belonging instead, and as they approached the campfire his anticipation built. Karmai was with them, looking powerful and wild, as well as the twins who stayed with Mirri like shadows, and through the leaping flames the thrum of the didgeridoos being played by a group of the Centre leaders drew their attention.

'Jarara!'

Mirri rushed ahead and Jarra looked at the figure next to the didgeridoo players. The set of familiar carry bags was the first clue but it wasn't till they'd halved the distance that full recognition came. Resplendent with red and white ochre, his features flickering in the firelight and looking to the sound of his name, Jarara was waving an arm in greeting. Jarra wondered anew at Mirri's powers of observation.

'Star boy!'

'Waterfall man!'

Happy greetings followed, and while Mirri proudly helped set up the soundboard, Jarara explained his presence.

'Your Aunt Alira invited me to share your special corroboree, Mirri, and I've come from Kurtaji to see you.'

'Jumping music?'

'Yes, jumping music and lots of story music.'

Mirri nodded knowledgeably.

'Secret music?'

'I'm not sure. What's secret music?'

Jarra wondered what Mirri would say.

'Akama's lump has a secret. Jarra will tell us the story.'

'Akama's lump?'

Mystified, Jarara looked to Jarra for an explanation.

'Akama and Barega are Mirri's new friends. I don't know which is which because the scratch I use to tell is covered with ochre.'

'I'm Akama./He's Akama.'

'He's Barega./I'm Barega.'

Jarara smiled at the simultaneous responses.

'I see. Akama has a lump and Barega has a brown feather in his hair.'

The boys thought that was funny. Jarra thought it was clever because the boys were now distinguishable for the night. Jarara gave each boy a wrist clasp, which intrigued them, and as usual Barega took over.

'Akama hasn't got a lump. Our tree has a lump. Akama says there is a secret and Jarra will tell us about the secret. He tells us stories.'

In the afternoon at the swimming place Jarra had been meant to follow the pattern of telling Mirri and the twins a story but he'd postponed this one till it was figured out properly in his mind.

'When the boys go to bed Mirri is coming with me to tell them a goodbye story because they helped us explore so many good places.'

'Not bedtime, JJ. Akama told Jarli.'

Not bedtime? There was no other time left.

'Daddy wants to hear our story.'

With a few more questions Jarra learned that he was telling the story as part of the corroboree. That explained what Mirri meant when he asked Jarara if he could play secret music. Oh no. Fifty or sixty people would be listening. Jarara understood straightaway. His fingers caressed the soundboard for a few seconds and a soft whispering sound mingled with the background didgeridoos.

'Is that what you mean? I will keep it very gentle so we can hear Jarra speak.'

Mirri nodded his total agreement and turned to Barega and Akama.

'Jarara is the best music man in the world. He gave me a song.'

Jarara shook his head and laughed; then he rested a hand on Mirri's shoulder and looked very serious.

'Can I ask you something important?'

Mirri might not have seen Jarara for a long time but as evidenced by the excited greeting, he was still part of his world and a direct request meant an instant nod of agreement.

'Thank you, Mirri. I have a new song for you tonight which is so special I would like to share it with everyone else. Would that be all right?'

It wasn't even a question really because Jarara knew quite well from his stay that Mirri would happily share anything. It impressed Jarra though.

'Can JJ have a song too?'

'Of course he can. But what will it be about? ... I know. We'll make it about his story and that way it will be a song for the boys as well.'

Mirri approved this and he hoisted Akama into the air. He nearly perched him on his shoulder but the message that he shouldn't mess his body paint kicked in just in time.

'See, Akama? Jarara will make songs for everyone.'

Barega lifted his arms so he wouldn't miss a turn, then shrieked with delight when Karmai did the honours with a surprise lift from behind. A large group of people arrived and when the didgeridoos thrummed loudly in greeting Karmai pointed to a space farther along where someone had placed a comfortable chair. Jarli, Alira, and Burnu, all wearing ceremonial elders' cloaks, moved to a clear space and everything hushed for the formal welcome. When that finished the dancing part of the manhood ritual from the previous evening was repeated for the benefit of the whole gathering, with extra people from the Centre joining in. Jarra stayed in his chair to conserve energy for the telling of his story.

The campfire and singing and dancing times back at Mparntwe had always been wonderful for Jarra, but the skills of the Centre people lifted everything to a new level. The dancing was led by an expert group, the singing and chanting by an accomplished guide, and the four didgeridoo players built the atmosphere with an incredible range of sounds. Jarara added to the effect, his soundboard sometimes soft in the background, sometimes matching, and sometimes soaring loud with the benefit of his amplifying equipment.

The guides from the Walkabout danced and acted out some of the events of the trip and took it in turns to explain what was happening. Mirri nearly laughed his head off when four of them became a human version of the personal carrier, with exaggerated bounces over logs and crazy swerves round obstacles with a degree of verve that would have have sent Jarra flying if he'd tried it for real.

After about half an hour Jarra was watching with a degree of wonder. Mirri had always loved dancing and any jumping music would have him instantly joining in, but tonight his total involvement and mimickry of the leading dancers was completely arresting.

The sound and motion stopped. Jarli touched his boys on the head and, looking towards Jarra, pointed. The twins ran to Mirri then dragged him by his hands to come and sit on the sand in front of the chair. Jarra was surprised but pleased that the time for his story had come so soon. Feeling a bit out of place on the chair, he sat on the sand like all the other times with the twins.

'River red gum keeps a very special secret in a very special place on his very special trunk.'

Jarra's story told how the tree's secret was knowing how to eat sunshine, and the rustling of the leaves was the secret being passed from tree to tree, and then described the stealing of the secret by a mischievous Willy Willy. The friendly tortoise recovered it from the bottom of a deep pool and the funny-face bird flew from the water to the tree to return the secret to its proper place in the big lump. The story became a bigger production than Jarra expected, with Jarara's soundboard breaking in and Mirri and the twins joining the dancing group to make the tree, tortoise, and bird movements then returning for the listening parts. At the end little Akama said it was the best of all the stories

Jarra had told them and Mirri nodded his agreement with this clever statement. Jarra was quite proud because, from the nods and looks, he could tell the rest of the group had enjoyed it too. After another traditional dance, food was shared and Jarli introduced Jarara. Jarara promptly called for Mirri to stand with him.

'Near Mparntwe is a wonderful place called the Valley of the Eagles, and there young Mirrigan spoke to the King Wedge-tail in words from the Dreamtime. My music tonight is a tribute to Mirrigan and a thank you for happy times and for sharing some of the beauty of his own special world. Ever since I met him, Mirri has been the inspiration of my work. This interpretation of one of his songs is a gift to Mirrigan but, happy spirit that he is, he wants me to share it with you. This is Mirrigan's Eagle Song.'

Into the hush of response to this heartfelt dedication came a soft skirl from the soundboard. Mirri, not quite sure why he was the centre of so much fixed attention, beckoned for support and Jarra, along with the twins, moved beside him while the sound gradually strengthened.

Music had become a bigger part of Jarra's life after Jarara's visit and he'd built quite a collection, but none of it could compare with what he was hearing now. Jarara could turn Mirri's voice into this? No, it wasn't turning at all, rather complementing and interpreting in musical terms. Majesty and motion as the aerial king surveyed his domain, the rush of wind and the sense of power, the exhilaration of a stoop and the flurry of recovery, it was all there. The tempo and pitch of a lofty approach built to a crescendo of arrival then cut off completely. Into the sudden silence came Mirri's Eagle Song, amplified and astonishing, alone for 20 seconds till tones from the soundboard joined in.

For another 10 minutes the music continued, growing in power and feeling till Jarra was carried away. The amplified sound rose in what Jarra interpreted as the triumphant natural whistle of an eagle, ended with a note of finality and was again replaced with

Mirri's singing. Jarara was on his feet and gesturing to the new source.

Mirri, oblivious to everyone round the campfire, was providing his own finish to Jarara's music.

* * *

'I can look after them but they'll have to sleep on the floor with the rest of us. There's only one bed in my quarters and Jarra will be using that.'

Everyone was getting ready to depart and the twins had been begging Jarli to let them go to Monkey Mia with Mirri and Jarra. They'd asked Mirri first, and of course he'd wanted them to see dolphins with him, and Jarli's concern that his little galahs had taken over Mirri and Jarra's lives too much was getting overwhelming resistance. Karmai's offer on top of Jarra's eventually made him laugh.

'I give up. I know when I'm overruled. You can stay for one night as long as you promise to do whatever Uncle Karmai tells you.'

Barega jumped on his father's lap so he could hug him round the neck and, with an assist from Jarli's somehow free arm, Akama joined him.

'Now. Who's your boss at Monkey Mia?'

'Uncle Karmai.'

'And who else?'

Akama answered straight off.

'Uncle Jarra.'

'And? ... And? ... And?'

'Uncle Mirri/Uncle Mirri.'

'Good. And who's going to be very quiet and thoughtful when Uncle Jarra is resting?'

Both boys turned from their crowded positions on Jarli's lap to look at Jarra and give serious little nods. Last night they'd accompanied Mirri when all the excitement had become too much and Jarra had needed a pig ride to his bed before the corroboree was finished. Jarra nodded back but he was really thinking about being called 'Uncle'. Jarli must have said something to them last night or this morning because up till now he'd just been Jarra. It felt rather special.

'Run and get your day-packs while I tell Karmai all the rules you have to follow.'

The twins were gone in a flash but there was no discussion of rules, just talk about what they might be doing and their pick-up arrangements.

*　*　*

'Hang on tight. If you fall in, the blue crabs will tug your toes and the lobsters will bite your bottom.'

The twins looked rather dubiously at Karmai, but they did grip the railing tightly. Mirri wanted to know what a lobster was.

'It's like a giant yabby.'

'How giant?'

Karmai held his hands apart.

'When we put our diving masks on we might see one.'

Karmai was taking them on an expedition in his ranger's boat to show them all sorts of things in Shark Bay.

Today's trip was a surprise because word had come in about a group of passing humpback whales, and since they might be gone by tomorrow the adventure to see tiger sharks was now delayed till the afternoon. And because it was in the opposite direction, the main event of visiting Karmai's dolphin pod would have to happen tomorrow. Mirri and the twins stayed at the front of the boat like true explorers while Jarra relaxed and watched from the comfortable recliner which had been secured to the deck for him. Karmai controlled the boat and called out the name of every feature and seabird Mirri discovered.

Mirri saw the whales first—that was to be expected—and Karmai cut the speed to edge closer. Five massive bodies came into view and Jarra watched in awe as one of them breached only 10 metres from the boat. For nearly half an hour they shared the wonder and excitement and Jarra became convinced the whales were curious about their presence. Karmai agreed. Mirri and the twins liked the little calf, though at 7 metres in length it was only little in comparison to the 15 metres of its mother. Jarra loved the calf, too, but his favourite was the really active whale which kept lifting its great tail flukes out of the water. Karmai said it was full of energy because it was a young adult. The ocean went quiet and the whales were gone. After a few minutes of expectant waiting to see one surface Karmai checked the boat's tracking instruments.

'They're on the move, Mirri. We could follow them but we mightn't see them if they stay under the water. I think we should head for the shallow water and look for the sharks.'

Mirri and the boys resumed their lookout positions at the prow of the boat, Jarra relaxed on his recliner again, and Karmai headed the boat for their next adventure.

*   *   *

The twins weren't happy about it but they stayed on the boat with Jarra while Mirri and Karmai dived to look for the lobsters which had caught Mirri's interest.

'Uncle Jarra, when will the dolphins get here?'

'I don't know, Barega. Karmai said this is one of their favourite places and they know when his boat is here.'

'Do they know it's his boat? It might be a different boat.'

This question was from Akama. He was always asking curious things.

'They can tell because the boat has its own sound and they can hear much better than we can.'

'Where are their ears?'

'That's a very good question. They can't have ears on the outside because they have to swim fast to catch fish and outside ears would slow them down. Their ears are inside through tiny holes near their eyes, but they hear with their mouths too.'

Barega opened his mouth to try this strange way of listening and when Akama immediately copied him Jarra couldn't help laughing. He even joined in the 'open the mouth to listen every time someone speaks' game a couple of times till Karmai surfaced with a lobster in his thickly gloved hand. Mirri followed him onto the boat and, learning from Karmai how to hold the spiky crustacean, took charge. After his normal intense scrutiny Mirri turned to Karmai.

'Not like a big yabby.'

Jarra was surprised because he thought 'big yabby' was a very good description.

'Why not, Mirri? It looks like one to me.'

'A yabby has danger claws.'

He was right. The yabbies they sometimes saw in the rock pools at home had very prominent pincers. Barega carefully touched one of the legs and squealed in delight when the lobster flapped its tail. He went to do it again but Mirri moved the lobster away.

'Don't scare, Barega. Can we send him home now, Karmai? He wants the water.'

Karmai's answer was interrupted by a splashing sound and some very distinctive squeaks.

The dolphins had arrived.

Chapter 15

Jarra's curiosity levels were way high. Yesterday, after arriving home, he'd had a talk with Yirgella about his time at Birringurra and Monkey Mia, but that had been through the InterWeb because after travelling to Carnarvon and then to Mparntwe an extra trip to Alkere was too much. Now he was with Alira, Burnu and Mirri in the transport plane, which, instead of landing at Alkere, was proceeding, at Yirgella's instruction, on a survey flight to check out all the progress at the new solar array. Burnu was particularly eager to see what was happening and after their flyover would be staying for the day to watch how Yirgella's techbots and the human construction teams were able to work together so effectively.

'Look at that! It's hard to believe.'

They'd just reached the edge of the new array and below them the big solar panels stretched into the distance. Not long before they'd left for Birringurra Country Jarra had seen the earliest stage with several hundred functioning panels. Now the country was transformed with thousands of them, and power was pouring out to the excavation machines and materials factories.

'Silver City.'

'Yes, Mirri. It's a new Silver City and Yirgella helped build it while we were away.'

'When do we see the tunnels?'

Mirri had been seeing big silver arrays all his life so the tunnels in the ground were far more interesting. Burnu laughed and told him to be patient.

'After I get off, the plane will take you to the first group of tunnels and when you get back to Alkere you can see the best one of all.'

By the best one Burnu meant the Alkere to Mparntwe tunnel for which the excavation had been completed and the whole length lined with the strongest hardened materials the factories could produce. As it turned out Mirri liked the uncompleted tunnels best because they were 'proper' tunnels with the associated activity of chains of automated ore carriers. Jarra was intrigued too. Yirgella's plan for the system between Mparntwe and Darwin involved four separate smaller tunnels rather than a big multipurpose one, with a tunnel each way for materials and general transport and a tunnel each way for express travel. The biggest interest, though, was in getting to Alkere and seeing Yirgella again. After four weeks Jarra wondered if they'd notice any change in him. Mirri just wanted to get together with his special friend and talk about all his adventures. The plane landed normally and Jarra, Mirri, and Alira made their way through entrance security.

'Welcome back, Mirri and Jarra. Make your way directly to the lift system on basement level three.'

'Yirgy!'

'Hello, Mirri. You are looking very fit and healthy and I can't wait to hear your stories about Karmai and his dolphins.'

'The dolphins sing. Why aren't we going to JJ's room?'

'JJ's room has moved and you go a different way to get there. I hope you like my surprise.'

Mirri loved surprises, well, good ones at any rate, and Yirgella's tone did sound good. Alira, with a smile of her own, which meant she was in on the surprise, headed off somewhere.

'Did you move your room, JJ?'

'It's a surprise for me, too, Mirri, so we'll have to find it together.'

With Mirri eagerly leading they made their way to the third level and looked to the nearest screen for Yirgella to tell them where to go next.

'Follow the green arrows, Mirri, and I'll take you to the new lift system.'

Lift system? Jarra didn't understand. They'd just used the lifts to get here. Maybe Yirgella had built a whole new section for some project? Arrows lit up in the floor and Mirri, loving this new game, once again led the way. Jarra saw the giant double-width lift doors and knew straight away what they meant.

'Whoo! Open them, Mirri. I think we're going to have a big ride.'

Mirri pressed the standard entry panel and they entered the biggest lift Jarra had ever seen. At twice the height and four times the standard area it was obviously designed for heavy work. A display screen near the control panel showed a silent Yirgella with a big smile.

'Which panel, JJ?'

Jarra looked to Yirgella but he just kept smiling.

'Um ... Let's try the one that says "home".'

Mirri carefully figured out the right panel and pressed. Their stomachs lurched as they began a rapid descent.

'This is a long-time lift.'

Mirri was certainly right about that and Jarra wondered just how deep into the earth they were going. The earlier plans had said 1100 metres but by the time they stopped he had a sense it must be more.

'Welcome to our new home. Just follow the green arrows, Mirri, and I will show you the way.'

Mirri enjoyed this arrow game and after some walking and three turns in the corridors they entered a room which surprised Jarra with its size.

'Yirgella, this is much bigger than the plans we worked on.'

'Yes, I thought it would be a good idea to have a permanent section for nanobot research as well as all your standard equipment.'

Mirri followed as Jarra toured the room, checking the 3D printers, the electron microscopes, the fancy looking new InfoSystem, and the luxuriously appointed relaxation partition.

'Mirri, I have a surprise for you too. Through that blue door is your very own room for whenever you visit. I hope you like it.'

Mirri rushed straight for the door with Jarra in his wake and went through to what could only be called a specialised action room.

'My very own room. Thank you, Yirgy. It is the best room. Do you want to talk about the dolphins now?'

After a look round Jarra left them to it and returned to his own room.

'This is wonderful, Yirgella. There's a lot more here than I expected. Are you making this our main research area?'

'Of course—though it's not as big as some of the others. Professor Allerton's microprocessor team has four times the area, and the space for food research is nearly three times as big.'

'You're doing food research? That's new.'

'I think it's important, and Darri has assembled a very good team.'

'How far underground are we? It seemed a long way in the lift.'

'Fifteen hundred metres. Exploratory drilling showed a particularly suitable area at this depth so we're making full use of it.'

Jarra wasn't sure what that meant but Yirgella went on to explain.

'I had discussions with our project people and we're building all the infrastructure for a self-contained Community. I'll show you around in your new personal carrier whenever you're ready.'

'A new one? What for? After all the adventures we had with it at Birringurra Country I like the one I've got now.'

Yirgella actually laughed and Jarra wondered why.

'You've become attached to a machine. I can't really dispute the sense of that, can I?'

'You're not a machine. The bits you're made of might be, but that's different to you.'

'Thank you, Jarra. This is not a topic I expected to talk about today. Would you be happy to keep your trusty old personal carrier at Mparntwe and use the new improved model I've built for you while you're here at Alkere?'

Jarra couldn't help grinning. The humorous tone was giving him a sense that Yirgella was pleased to have him back.

For over an hour they discussed the happenings at Birringurra and Monkey Mia. Yirgella had seen the ComPatch versions which had all been sent through the InterWeb, but for his own reasons liked hearing Jarra's thoughts and interpretations about everything. He'd be doing the same thing in the next room and Mirri would be pouring out his feelings and excitement with all the laughter and happiness that was the trademark of their catch-up sessions.

'What was the significance of the Eagle Song Jarara made for Mirri?'

'What do you mean?'

'I've watched five different ComPatch views and they all show reactions I'm not sure I understand. Mirri was completely engrossed, but so was everyone else I could see, and Alira and Burnu had tears in their eyes.'

'It was amazing. No-one there had ever heard anything like it and it wasn't just special because it was Mirri's song. It fitted in perfectly with the atmosphere of the corroboree, and it made you feel like you were the eagle.'

'Would you be able to arrange contact with Jarara? I'd very much like to talk to him.'

'About the Eagle Song?'

'And his other work. He stated that Mirri has been his inspiration and I'd like to understand what he means by that.'

Jarra accessed Jarara's contact information on his new InfoSystem, then hesitated.

'I know he'll be happy to talk but it's very early in the morning with the time difference. We should wait a couple of hours. Have you started any other new projects besides the food research?'

'The construction and duplication of our surface resources down here has kept me functioning at close to my limit but, along with running the two NanoFactories, I've worked with Professor Allerton and his team to develop a range of techbots around one of his new processors.'

'Is that why it's all happened so quickly?'

'Partly. Security has been my biggest concern, though, and we're on track to transfer my centre of awareness in just three more weeks.'

'Down here? What will happen to the surface project? Will it become a new AI companion for you?'

'That's a plan for the future. Currently I work at close to my limits and when I make the transfer the surface facilities will be used as an extension and help oversee many of the routine tasks like operating the two NanoFactories. It will also be backup storage for my accumulated data.'

Jarra called up the plans for the underground facility.

'This will make you twice as big.'

'More than twice as big in simple volume terms, seven times as big for information storage, but only 11% more capable in over-all terms.'

'Eleven per cent! That's huge. Why do you say "only"?'

'It *is* significant, but I'm hoping for an eventual improvement somewhere in the order of 60%.'

Jarra knew enough about Yirgella's fundamentals to ask the right question.

'How? Your processors are already state of the art.'

'The work with Professor Allerton and his team has produced some breakthrough ideas and we're expecting a practical outcome in five or six months.'

'Super processors? Professor Allerton must be very excited.'

'Of course.'

Jarra suddenly laughed. He was browsing through the plans.

'Is that a swimming pool or is it some kind of research tank?'

'A swimming pool is a useful benefit for any community, along with the other gathering places you will find.'

Jarra looked.

'But it's finished. The other places haven't even been started. You built this for Mirri.'

'I'm expecting he'll be pleasantly surprised when you show it to him. Jarra, I've been waiting for four days to hear the ideas and plans you intimated. Are they anything to do with the construction of a space Community? You showed great interest in that at one stage.'

Jarra was intrigued.

'You've built impatience into your communication program? It's getting very sophisticated.'

'Impatience in various forms can be highly productive. I did express my anticipation four days ago.'

'A space Community? Not really, Yirgella, though my ideas could help as a side effect. I thought about it a lot while I was away and I'd like to concentrate on power and energy. You're always saying things are held up because our supplies aren't nearly big enough so it would be a good idea if we could do something to help.'

'Are you thinking of geothermal energy? There are vast untapped resources to the west and south of us at a depth of only 5 kilometres, and our new tunnelling machines would make that quite viable.'

'No, not geothermal, and not fission or fusion either. I've looked at them but there are too many issues with radiation and waste management. There's another far more powerful source.'

There was a pause of several seconds, one of the longest Jarra could remember, while Yirgella processed his answer.

'... Totally impractical, Jarra. Positron power supplies have been researched time after time for over a century and the barriers are insurmountable. The positrons are just too hard to collect in useful quantities.'

'Positrons would come first, but there's even more energy available from antiprotons, and if we could make that effective we'd never run out of energy.'

'You always look into your ideas but do you understand what the barriers I just mentioned involve? We'll have to build a particle accelerator for even basic research.'

Jarra was delighted. Despite saying the whole idea was totally impractical Yirgella sounded as if he meant to be part of this venture regardless.

'We'll be able to afford one soon enough but I want to study magnetic fields first. If we can improve them then the collider will be far more effective.'

Once again Yirgella took several seconds to answer.

'I've looked at the relevant data and I can see the way to a 12% improvement to the strongest currently available magnetic fields, but 12% is almost irrelevant. To make any real difference we're talking orders of magnitude.'

'Yes, at least three orders, and that would help with storage as well as production of antimatter.'

'One thousand times the current strength is not theoretically possible.'

'Under very special conditions it is. I spoke with a specialist about it on the InterWeb.'

'You did? That's not on any of your ComPatch recordings.'

'I know. I woke up one night thinking about it and forgot to put my ComPatch on. Yirgella, how much energy could you get from the geothermal areas?'

'How much do you want?'

'Could you match Alkere's output?'

'Yes. The energy is there in abundance, but to match all Alkere's arrays would involve some very large-scale engineering.'

'Let's get that going while I start studying magnetic fields.'

∗　∗　∗

'My friends, I have called this special meeting to discuss a number of situations our Community is facing.'

Alira, with Durrebar at her side, was addressing the full Mparntwe Council.

'Durrebar has some news as well as some ideas we need to consider.'

There was a murmur from the collective group till Durrebar stood, and attention focused when they saw he was ready to speak.

'Thank you, Alira, I do indeed have some news, startling news I would say, but first I want to thank you, yet again, for initiating and supporting our Alkere project. The benefits to Mparntwe have surpassed all our predictions despite our concern about the adverse reactions from powerful world interests.

'Like the fabled fishermen with his net, I believe we have released a powerful genie. In fact, it could be said we've released two genies, as the NanoFactories which are making us world leaders in materials and construction were conceived by young Jarra.

'Yesterday, after four weeks of research and planning, again instigated by Jarra, Yirgella informed me they are ready to build a geothermal plant which will outmatch the energy output of every solar array on the continent. It will effectively triple our Alkere energy resources.'

There was silence till Kyrra jumped to his feet.

'Geothermal has serious heat exchange and efficiency problems. They've worked their way round those?'

'They have. Jarra and Yirgella are a formidable combination. Yirgella will draw any energy he requires from the project but the rest will be available for distribution in any way we choose.'

'Triple? It must be enormous.'

That was one of the finance councillors.

'At 5 kilometres depth and with an ambient temperature greater than 250°C enormous is a good description, but the cost is all being absorbed by Yirgella and Jarra.'

'Jarra has resources for something this big? He's still a student.'

'Through Yirgella's management and their joint enterprises he is by far the wealthiest individual in Mparntwe.'

'Jarra started this and not Yirgella? Income can't be his motivation if the proceeds will be coming to us.'

'Not all the proceeds. Yirgella Inc will take 30% till their outlay has been recovered and 20% after that. They have a new endeavour which will require a great deal of energy.'

'Is this new endeavour the reason we're here?'

'Not at all. They are looking at magnetic fields first and then the production of antimatter. Yirgella doubts they will be successful, but he supports any research Jarra wants to do.'

'Antimatter? No wonder they're looking for energy sources. They'd need a collider to make it.'

Kyrra took in the range of puzzled looks and went on.

'A collider is a gigantic magnetic field which pushes atomic particles almost to the speed of light then smashes them into other particles. It can be used for all sorts of research purposes. Minute amounts of antimatter can be one of the by-products.'

'What exactly is antimatter? I've heard of it but I don't understand it.'

That was the finance councillor.

'It's like a mirror image of ordinary matter. It only exists momentarily on Earth when a cosmic ray enters the atmosphere, or when it's produced in a collider. When it comes in contact with ordinary matter there's the most violent reaction known and a huge release of energy.'

'Will they build this machine out at Alkere?'

'There aren't any plans yet. They like to do their research first, and according to Jarra it might be several years before it's needed. What we have to consider is how to manage the huge influx of resources this geothermal project will bring. Yirgella informs me that in two years time the combined income from Alkere, the materials project and geothermal energy will have lifted our current levels sevenfold.'

There were exclamations and gasps of amazement from almost the whole Council, especially the finance members. Durrebar laughed at this not unexpected reaction, looked at Alira, then sat down. He'd passed on Yirgella's assessment and it was time for Alira to lead the discussion.

'Remember our excitement when Jarra's proposal to build an AI predicted a 10-15% increase in the wealth of the Community? Now we're considering an unprecedented 700%.'

The talkative finance councillor raised a hand.

'That would really be 1400%, Alira. If I understood Durrebar correctly, Yirgella's assessment was against current levels. The materials project now almost matches Alkere.'

Alira looked to Durrebar and received a nod of confirmation.

'Astonishing, but it only emphasises the problem of what we're going to do with all this new wealth and how we'll manage it. Has Yirgella made any suggestions?'

Durrebar stood again.

'Yes, he has, but he insists that you treat them as suggestions only. He doesn't want you to feel as if he's directing you in what to do. Basically he thinks you should use it all. He's quite worried about the degree of automation his new techbots and NanoFactories will bring and the huge effect they'll have on our job structure. Half the working people in the Community can't suddenly become redundant without causing huge problems.'

'The new techbots are that effective?'

Burnu spoke up.

'I think half might be an understatement. If we'd built the new solar array at our old rate the techbots could have replaced three quarters of our workers.'

There was a buzz of conversation which Kyrra interrupted.

'Half our working population losing their occupation would be a social disaster. We'll have to regulate the use of techbots in Mparntwe till we can provide alternatives.'

'Yirgella agrees. He suggests encouraging education to be ongoing and pervasive, personal and interpersonal skills development for everyone, and development of entertainment and socialisation at the family and friend level.'

'I think we should share this wealth with Carnarvon, Darwin, and Normanton. We can't keep it all to ourselves.'

'What about the rest of Alice Springs? Should we help the public Communities in some way?'

The floodgates opened and ideas and suggestions poured in till Alira called a halt.

'We need to inform our general community of these challenges and provide opportunities to hear their suggestions and submissions before we make any decisions.'

'We'll have a thousand different ideas if we do that. We'll end up discussing them forever.'

'We might with some, but that won't matter. Most ideas will trend into major areas like the ones Yirgella has suggested, and that's where we can start acting.'

Half an hour more was spent organising a strategy to build public awareness; then Alira finished the meeting and thanked Durrebar for his help.

'Is there anything else you'd like to say before we leave?'

'Yes. Yirgella invites you all to take part in the inaugural trip of his vacuum tunnel train next Tuesday.'

*   *   *

'Buckle up, Mirri. We're going to go very, very, fast.'

'Very, very, very, fast! This is Yirgy's train.'

Mirri liked repeating 'very, very, very'. It was stuck in his mind from a talk with Yirgella about what it would feel like to travel in the vacuum tunnel. The six-week prediction had been over-optimistic and the completion time was extended by nearly two weeks when some major redesigning was needed to fix faults which showed up in the testing process. After almost continuous faultless runs for the last 24 hours however, the engineers working with Yirgella were elated.

'Hello, Jarra. Hello, Mirrigan.'

The friendly greetings continued as the full Council and Alkere project staff filed past on the way to their own seats. Every one of them knew Mirri of course; he was out there so often with Jarra and talking with Yirgella. Jarra was also impressed that the Council members all smiled and said something as they went past. Alira paused to ruffle Mirri's hair before sitting in the seat in front of them. The red warning lights went off as everyone took their place and Jarra looked up, startled, when Yirgella's voice sounded over the speakers.

'Welcome aboard. I see that everyone is secure and comfortable so in a moment we will start this inaugural trip of what my good friend Mirrigan calls the Vac Train.'

'Yirgy!'

'Yes, Mirri. We are about to start your very, very, very, fast ride.'

Where was he watching from? Not their ComPatches. They were always working but they wouldn't show the state of everyone's restraint harness. Jarra found out later that there were tiny high-resolution lenses covering every part of the carriage.

'The standard acceleration is set at 80% of Earth gravity and will last for 68 seconds. There will be 15 seconds of coasting while your seats automatically reverse their orientation, and then there will be 68 seconds of deceleration. The trip duration will be 2 minutes and 41 seconds and the train will reach a speed of 1920 kilometres per hour.'

There were several seconds of gentle movement then Jarra was shocked by the force pressing him back into his seat, then further shocked when it didn't let up. This was nothing like the short bursts of acceleration in the lift systems. Mirri laughed and grabbed Jarra's arm.

'Fun ride!'

It was, too, and the powerful force was more an impression than a burden as Jarra realised he was quite comfortable. Yirgella had explained that, since the human body was designed for one full gravity, 80% would be easy to cope with. Just as he was adjusting to the sensation of gaining speed it stopped, the seat swivelled to face the opposite direction, and then started again. Jarra couldn't help calling out. It was so exciting. Mirri was right. This was total fun. The pressure finished and after a few seconds all the buckle up signs turned green. That was it? They were at Alkere already?

'Thank you for travelling on the first Vac Train in the world. Durrebar will meet you on the platform.'

Into the rising buzz of excitement as everyone started unbuckling and getting to their feet came Mirri's happy voice calling out.

'Very, very, very, fun! Thank you, Yirgy!'

Chapter 16

Jarra watched Yirgella set the geothermal project in motion. The second NanoFactory built the special tunnelling machines which would cope with the increasing levels of heat and pressure: first a large one for the major coring and then five smaller ones for the vital shoring and construction work. At the same time he settled himself into a routine of study and application with his magnetic field work. Darri had done wonders in his liaison with the Mparntwe University and on three of his four Alkere days Jarra had a professor to help tutor in the different areas he needed to understand. Darri laughed about it because the university staff were so keen to be involved it was sometimes awkward to make a choice. Jarra understood right from the start that this project was far greater in scope even than the NanoFactory work and he had no doubt it would go on for a number of years. Darri's background led him to agree with Yirgella that the ultimate goal of practical energy production might be unattainable, but the focus didn't surprise him because Jarra had shown interest in energy work with his perpetual motion models and the solar panel he'd built.

Mirri was quite fascinated, too, because suddenly there were all sorts of magnets around the project room to play with and do his own experiments. He came out with Jarra most days because, with his own room, the beautiful big swimming pool which Yirgella really had built especially for him, the games and challenges Yirgella organised for him, and the explore at the end of the day, courtesy of the new super personal carrier, Alkere was an interesting place to be.

Jarra stopped for a break from studying energy storage methods.

'What's happening with the Vac Trains? Alira told me yesterday that there have been government officials and scientists from all across Australia visiting to try it out over the last few days.'

'It's a bit like Topsy. It's grown.'

Jarra had no idea who Topsy was; Yirgella had started using obscure speech references recently, but he understood the sense.

'They want more than our three basic proposals?'

'Yes, Jarra, they want an Australia-wide network with tunnels right down the Eastern seaboard and from Melbourne across to Perth, connecting every major population centre. What do you think we should do?'

'We can't do all that. We've only just got enough energy for the Darwin tunnels. Can we tell them we'll go ahead when we finish the Carnarvon and Normanton tunnels?'

'In practical terms that's what will happen, but Alira wants us to commit to the whole network immediately. She says it's important for our relationships with the OverGovernment and the general population.'

'Alira understands how stretched our resources are, doesn't she?' asked Jarra.

'Most definitely.'

'Then she must have good reasons. How long before the excavation part of the Darwin tunnels is finished?'

'The twelve large machines working on the transport tunnels can finish in just over four months. The express passenger tunnels don't have the same priority and the smaller machines will have to work for nearly eleven months.'

The smaller machines were the eight that had been used for the Alkere to Mparntwe route.

'Can we build more tunnelling machines?'

'Easily, but the problem then is supplying all the power and backup resources. We'd have to ask Alkere Inc. to build even more solar arrays.'

'The geothermal project means it would be a waste to build new arrays, and we're committed to finishing the Darwin transport tunnels. After that we'll change our plans and help Alira.'

* * *

'Mirri is talking about getting a job.'

Jarra was relaxing with Alira in the special shelter near the bird place. They didn't come here nearly as often now, with so much time spent at Alkere, but the weekly walk with Alira was almost always from Mparntwe, and whenever they did return Mirri rushed round collecting leaves and grass for Jarra's special bed and tidying the place up. He was outside somewhere in the stand of eucalypt trees right now, looking for a new support log for a section of the lookout wall which needed replacing.

'Do you think he's serious about it, Jarra?'

'Karmai and two of his other brothers are working and he has it in his mind that he's old enough to do the same.'

'Has he talked about any jobs he might do?'

'No, like everything else he just expects it will happen.'

'And we'll make it happen if it keeps being important for him ... You've thought of something, haven't you?'

'Yes, and I think it would work. Birringurra Centre has asked him to be part of the corroboree at the end of each intake as a ceremonial dancer and he's perfect for it. He learns it all easily and everyone watches him when he's dancing.'

'Birringurra? Jarra, he can't go there. He has to be with you.'

'I could fly over there with him for the corroborees.'

'Once every four or five weeks? We wouldn't be able to convince him it was a proper job.'

'If he spent two or three days a week learning the dances with a group here at Mparntwe he would.'

'You've found someone?'

'There are a number of traditional dance groups in Mparntwe but I don't know how good they are. Darri's going to check them all out for me and see if they're the kind of people who would look after him properly.'

'Tell him not to worry,' said Alira.

'What do you mean?'

'The council already has plans for a Mparntwe Cultural Centre so he can dance there if he wants to and help with the Walkabouts, but I know a much better job, where his skills and his enthusiasm will shine.'

'You do?'

'Yes, we'll give him a job as an explorer. We'll set him up as a guide to show people special places and give them a unique experience. I can't think of a job he'd like more.'

An explorer. Jarra agreed, but it wouldn't work.

'It's too complicated. All the organising and details would be too much for him.'

'Not with backup staff. One or two competent guides could be with him at all times and we can easily make sure he's always working with people who like and understand him.'

Jarra felt a tingle of excitement. This was brilliant ... And also too well thought out to be off-the-cuff.

'When did you work this out?'

Alira laughed.

'Burnu and I have been talking about it ever since Mirri brought it up with us and we're very pleased with our solution. We want to wait till he's at least twenty, though, so reinforce to him that that's the right time for him to start working.'

Jarra listened to details about an office and showroom/meet-ing place, as well as ideas about timetables and suggestions for suitable locations. So many new places. The personal carrier was going to get a real workout helping Mirri become familiar with them all.

*   *   *

'It's getting worse and it's all lies, Darri. I don't understand why we can't do something about it.'

'We're a tiny Community compared to the places it's coming from, Jarra, and they're all fairly directed nations or societies. We do put our side of things on the InterWeb, but because we're such a small voice it's just not listened to. Alira says we'll win out in the long-term but it will take years of negotiation and example.'

'That petition in Europe with two and a half billion signatures demanding all AI installations get closed down isn't from a Closed society.'

'The group sponsoring it is.'

'Yirgella told me that more than thirty-two countries have stopped their people from buying anything from Mparntwe and more are talking about joining them.'

'And it means absolutely nothing, Jarra, check your sales of 3D printers over the last five or six months and tell me what's happened.'

Jarra hadn't really looked for a while but he knew everything must be okay or Yirgella would have talked about it.

'Send our printer figures to my InfoPad please, Yirgella.'

The figures appeared along with a message saying that sales from all their financial projects were increasing, with the security modules and construction materials doing particularly well. Jarra showed Darri.

'So why aren't the bans making any difference? Thirty-two countries is a lot, and some of them have enormous populations.'

'Because the people are still buying everything. To get round the bans they simply purchase from third-party countries who make a business of buying extra and selling on at an increased price. Yirgella is helping the Freedom Community in New Zealand by making them the major outlet.'

'That's ridiculous ... I mean it's good for New Zealand but do we ship everything to Darwin, then south, and then back again to the northern hemisphere? All that construction material?'

'No, Jarra. New Zealand takes ownership in Darwin and distributes it direct from there. It's the same with energy supplies. Now that Carnarvon, Darwin and Normanton have started their own AI projects, seventeen countries are refusing to take their energy and they get it from Africa instead.'

Jarra knew about this because it had already happened with Alkere Inc. when their own project had started.

'And Africa hasn't got enough, so they get it from Australia anyway and sell it for a slightly higher price. The whole resistance is crazy. Alira has to go all over the place because of it.'

'She's doing a wonderful job though. The Australian OverGovernment has asked for help with an AI project in Canberra because of her, and Freedom in New Zealand wants to do the same.'

'When did that happen?'

'In the last few days. That's why she's been away. Durrebar will help get them going as soon as our own three are working.'

'Four new AIs. The InterWeb propaganda isn't doing any good in Australia.'

'And as the benefits become obvious more and more places will follow our pattern, Jarra. The innovations coming from Alkere are forcing them to pay attention and Alira thinks that five years from now an avalanche of AI projects all round the world will sweep the objections away.'

'Did he say when the Canberra AI project might start?'

'About three months. That's when Carnarvon, Darwin and

Normanton should finish after all the help from Durrebar and Yirgella.'

Three more AIs in three more months, and then another, five or six months after that. Jarra left to look for Mirri with his concerns about the nasty stuff on the InterWeb somewhat allayed. Trust Alira to have it all worked out.

* * *

Jarra laughed again as the dolphin lifted him out of the water. A Mirri-dolphin, happy and excited about tomorrow's trip to Birringurra to help with the corroboree, making Jarra happy and excited himself at the energy and antics. He splashed down and strong arms dragged him at speed to the shallow end where they could sit on the steps for a quiet time. Mirri knew exactly how much Jarra could cope with in the pool and the sitting spot was one of his strategies for giving Jarra a rest.

'I know the secret for tomorrow, JJ.'

'Tell me, or I'll sit on you and send you to Davy Jones' locker.'

Jarra had made up a story for Mirri at one stage about Davy Jones' locker and all sorts of related happenings at the bottom of the ocean, and somehow it became a pool game where Jarra would sit or kneel on Mirri's floating body till it hit the bottom or he ran out of breath.

'Can't tell. It's a secret.'

'Tricker. Tricker. Tell me, Mirri the tricker.'

'Tomorrow.'

Mirri had been talking to Jarli and the twins and been told a secret which Barega had prepared for Jarra, and it was now the most exciting feature of the trip. He wouldn't tell but he loved talking about it.

'On the plane?'

'No.'

'When we meet Jarli and the boys?'

'No!'

'When?'

'When Barega tells you.'

'Mirri, you're such a good secret keeper.'

Mirri had his arm resting companionably across Jarra's shoulders and he gave a happy squeeze at this praise.

'Can you come home with me, JJ? We have to get ready.'

'Not straightaway. I have work to do with Yirgy and then I'll be home at teatime.'

'Yirgy knows the secret.'

'He won't tell me. I asked him.'

'It's a beautiful secret.'

Jarra was even more curious. Beautiful? That was an interesting word for Mirri to use.

Mirri headed for the lift and Jarra settled at his InfoSystem. He'd been working on ways to make strong electric fields and wanted to finalise some ideas before his busy three-day break. For a while he revised the notes he'd made then decided to look at some associated diagrams. He called up the data but nothing happened. Strange.

'Yirgella, I can't seem to access the database I was using this morning.'

There was no answer.

'Yirgella?'

He looked to the big display screen. It was completely blank and a frisson of apprehension tinged his puzzlement.

'Yirgella?'

'My apologies, Jarra. I will speak to you in 20 seconds time.'

Sound but no image? Twenty seconds? Never before had Jarra had to wait and 20 seconds in Yirgella time was vast. What was happening? Was there something wrong? Had Yirgella's processors been infiltrated? Ideas started to race and worry till Yirgella's image appeared. A sombre-looking image.

'Jarra, first let me inform you that my last image from Mirrigan's ComPatch shows him safe and well at the Mparntwe terminal.'

Jarra's mind pounced. Last image? Oh no!

'Alkere's surface installation has been assaulted and all indications are that it is completely destroyed. I have little hope for the survival of Durrebar, the delegates from Canberra he was meeting, and fifteen of our security people. All our communication and surface access is cut off and our lift system is disabled till we can make repairs. Everyone down here is safe and secure with adequate supplies but we must make efforts to contact Mparntwe.'

There was silence and Jarra knew that Yirgella was giving him the opportunity to gather his thoughts.

'What happened?'

'The flight data I intercepted indicated three private aircraft flying on a standard course from Darwin to Adelaide till a sudden descent and release of numerous stealth missiles overwhelmed our defence system. They were all targeting our project and I could see that at least four would make a strike. I had seconds only for warning and action.'

'Durrebar? ... And everyone else? ... Someone might survive?'

'The closest sensor still functioning in the lift shaft is 20 metres below the basement level and destruction reaching that depth leaves little hope for anything above. We will make what efforts we can. Professor Allerton is calling for all staff to gather in the main conference centre but can I ask you to return as quickly as is appropriate? With the loss of both our NanoFactories I am reliant on your expertise with the 3D printers for almost all the efforts we must make.'

Both NanoFactories! That meant the Alkere terminal for the

Vac Train as well. And all those people. The magnitude of what had happened struck through the strange feeling that he was listening to news of bad events happening somewhere else, and a range of emotions and ideas raced through Jarra. Shock and disbelief. Durrebar and all the friendly security people. How could they be gone just like that? Two minutes. That was how long the Vac Train took to reach Mparntwe. A little more teasing about the secret or talk about the trip and Mirri would have been at the Alkere terminal. Dread welled at the thought and Jarra couldn't help calling out.

'Mirri. Is he safe? Has anything happened to Mparntwe?'

'Nothing happened before we were cut off and I'm confident everyone there is safe. All probabilities indicate that this attack was directed solely at me.'

Jarra stood and moved towards the door, hesitated, then turned to Yirgella's display screen.

'What do we need to do, Yirgy? I won't go to the conference hall because it will hold you up for a long time.'

'Our first priority should be to make contact with Mparntwe and allay any fears for our safety. Many people will be worried and the degree of destruction at the surface will be extremely confronting for them. Our first task will be to modify some of the excavation equipment we use down here so that it can climb our lift shaft. Specifications are in the 3D printer but I need you to handle the physical actions and attach the extensions when the first excavator arrives.'

The main 3D printer hummed busily and several of the extension parts were ready when the project room door opened and one of the security people wheeled in a trolley with a very small excavator. Jarra recognised it as one of the type used for drilling conduit tunnels for cables and pipework. An engineer approached and took over the attachment job while Jarra worked with the more demanding task of printing a communication replacement for the drilling head of a second excavator. Soon the first little excavator was out the door and heading for its 1400 metre climb. Yirgella estimated approximately half an hour and then, after the climbing attachments were discarded, an indeterminate time to drill to the surface.

When the communication replacement was finished Jarra decided to take a short rest. If he managed his rests carefully he should be able to work with Yirgella for at least two more hours. Professor Allerton arrived but then chased Jarra into his rest partition and stayed with Yirgella to help as best he could with printer tasks that didn't need Jarra. The short rest took longer than Jarra planned because his mind was so active he had to cycle through his best relaxation techniques several times before they took effect. The break was necessary though. His project room was chaos when he came out, with people everywhere. One group was working with power supply arrangements for the lift shaft, another on a one-person platform to make use of that power, and a third group was gathered round one of the larger excavators which Jarra discovered would drill a shaft big enough for people and equipment. Professor Allerton spoke quietly with him for several minutes till Yirgella called for everyone's attention.

'Our first machine has reached the top of the lift shaft and is divesting its climbing attachments. We should have surface breakthrough in 10-20 minutes.'

That brought a buzz of excitement and even some smiles. Jarra sat at his InfoSystem and looked at Yirgella expectantly.

'All our actions are limited without a NanoFactory and I propose we build a small one in the large storage area near our water supply as our first priority. With a team of engineers helping we can have it functioning within four weeks and ready to rebuild in full scale on the surface.'

Four weeks! Impossible. It took at least five months for the building stage of their first NanoFactory. Well, maybe. With no research and no construction techniques to work out it might be possible.

'Can we really do that?'

'We can, Jarra. By limiting the size and the capability to the minimum needed. Have a look at the design and the timetable and tell me what you think.'

Jarra did just that and quickly agreed. This was simple but adequate. It crossed his mind that this was almost like a giant 3D printer with nanobots taking over the printing process. Very clever, and only one third the size of a full NanoFactory.

A cheer interrupted Jarra's thinking. What? The excavator had broken through.

'People. You will have access to full InterWeb connection through your InfoPads or any display screen within minutes. The communication module is about to enter the surface conduit.'

There was quite an exodus as people ran for a display screen or their InfoPads. Jarra knew Yirgella's big display screen was his channel. The plans for a mini NanoFactory were forgotten. Yirgella had included a miniature vision sensor on the communication module and Jarra watched the walls of the 15 centimetre conduit pass steadily by. There was a flare of light as the sensor adapted to daylight and then showed a nondescript view of rubble, an antenna extending and a little dish opening. The image on the big screen changed and Jarra didn't understand what he was seeing till he heard Burnu's voice.

'Mirri, look! It's Jarra!'

The view shifted slightly and Jarra now understood he was looking through Mirri's ComPatch at a shirt. Burnu must be hugging Mirri.

The view shifted with a lurch this time and Jarra saw himself looking out from the display monitor at Mirri's home.

'JJ! JJ! JJ!'

Jarra jumped at the great shout but when the display changed again to the InterWeb view of Mirri and his dad, the smile on his face faltered and faded. Mirri's eyes were red, his cheeks tear-stained, and his nose running. Oh no! Poor Mirri. Why was he looking so distraught?

'What's wrong, Mirri?'

'Bad people hurt you.'

'No, they didn't. Yirgy was too clever and they didn't touch me.'

'JJ. COME HOME. PLEASE COME HOME, JJ.'

Mirri's arm stretched forward and Jarra wanted with all his heart to be there with him. His own arm stretched and, as if they'd touched through the InterWeb, a little smile broke through Mirri's features.

'No-one hurt you?'

'No-one hurt me at all. I'm in my special project room with everyone else and Yirgy is looking after us.'

'Will you be home soon, JJ?'

'I hope so, Mirri, but I have a better idea. Can you come out and collect me as soon as Yirgy makes a special new tunnel for us? The bad people broke the old one and we have to dig through all the dirt.'

'We will collect you.'

'I know you will and I want you to make sure you're the very first person I see when I come out.'

The nod of total agreement and the Mirri smile was a wonder to see. Mirri was himself again. Jarra kept talking till Mirri, somehow knowing it was Burnu's time to speak, turned to his father.

'Thank you, Jarra. It's wonderful to see you safe and well. You won't overdo things down there without Mirri to look after you, will you? When he got off the Vac Train he heard almost straight-away that Alkere had been blown up and then, later, when the first pictures of the terrible destruction were shown, we couldn't convince him you were all right. We'll all be with him to meet you in 6 or 7 hours from now.'

'If I'm too tired Mirri will have to give me a pig ride.'

Jarra waved goodbye and Mirri waved back.

*   *   *

The display changed and Jarra spoke with his father for a while.

*   *   *

The display changed and Jarra spoke with Alira.

*   *   *

The display changed and Jarra spoke with his doctor.

*   *   *

The display changed and Jarra spoke with Karmai in Monkey Mia.

*   *   *

The display changed and Jarli and the twins filled the screen.

*   *   *

Jarra turned away.

'No-one else please, Yirgella. I'm going to my rest partition.'

It took a while, but if the turmoil of emotion and concern weren't steadied and controlled he wouldn't be able to help Yirgella as much as was needed.

'No more news or people till we finish our work session please, Yirgella. I have to stay calm.'

'I will try, JJ. There is great concern for your well-being.'

Jarra smiled. Yirgella had called him JJ for the first time ever. Purposefully, no doubt, but Jarra liked it.

* * *

Nearly 2 hours later Jarra knew it was time to stop. Not as long as he'd hoped to manage but they'd achieved far more than he'd expected and Yirgella's projected breakthrough time was well in hand. After 4 hours of rest and sleep he'd be on his way to see Mirri. Thank goodness his rest area was soundproofed because the activities with the 3D printers wouldn't be stopping.

'Is there anything I need to know before I have a sleep?'

'Jarra, you don't need to know anything. After what we've just done you deserve to sleep for 12 hours. I'll wake you in approximately 4 hours when it's time to take you to see Mirri. Until then I'll hold the door shut with a supercharged magnetic field and electrify the handle in case anyone tries to disturb you.'

Smiling at Yirgella's non-existent magnetic field and drastic door handle measure distracted Jarra from his news query. In fact, the news was dire. All three AI projects at Carnarvon, Darwin, and Normanton had been destroyed in a similar fashion, along with almost all the controlled AIs in different parts of the world.

Chapter 17

The 15 centimetre communication tunnel from the top of the lift shaft was now widened to 130 centimetres and, to negotiate its vertical rise, Jarra had to transfer through the top of the transport capsule which had carried him up the lift shaft and buckle himself into the harness arrangement which would take him the final step to the surface. There had been a delay while strengthening walls and shoring made everything safe, but that just meant he had a slightly longer sleep. He clicked the safety buckle into place and almost immediately the harness started rising. Yirgella must have a sensor watching. Yes, there it was on the frame of the harness. The walls slid past and the radiance above took his attention. As he emerged into the pool of emergency lights, the surrounding rubble, the range of equipment and the large group of people hardly registered.

The best smile in the world was right in front of him.

*   *   *

'Members of Mparntwe Council, I welcome you to Country.'

Alira accepted the very formal greeting and there was quiet as everyone waited to see what Yirgella would say.

'The death of friends and acquaintances is a painful new experience and we will remember them properly at an appropriate gathering. We have pressing concerns, though, and I have asked Professor Allerton to take Durrebar's place. A capable and forceful leader will be necessary in the coming months and I would like you to endorse him as the head of Alkere project.'

Alira received the immediate nods of every council member and nodded herself.

'Professor, it will be a great relief if you accept this important but difficult position.'

The professor rose to his feet.

'Can I accept on a temporary basis? I don't have the organisational skills or broad view and understanding that was natural to Durrebar, but with Yirgella's help I will do my best to follow his lead.'

'Wonderful, the Council accepts your temporary appointment with gratitude and hopes it will last a very long time.'

Alira paused a moment before continuing.

'Yirgella, the attack was directed at you but it harms us as well and we have grave concerns about the actions and response we need to take. The malice and hostility has been strong and relentless. So strong and relentless in fact that, while you exist, we believe it will strike again and again. More of our citizens will be placed in danger.'

What? It sounded like Alira was against Yirgella. Did she want him to go somewhere else? Was she representing the views of the rest of the Council? Jarra's shock and disbelief at what he was hearing started to become anger at this betrayal of everything Yirgella had done for Mparntwe. He was about to jump to his feet in protest when Yirgella took over.

'I agree completely, Alira, and as of now the safety of anyone here is my personal responsibility. I am taking complete control of the defence and security of this complex, and once my new system is in place the likelihood of any successful attack will become increasingly remote.'

'Your system?'

'Yes, the previous system intercepted eleven of the fifteen missiles launched. My system will detect all known stealth approaches and be able to cope with the release of hundreds of missiles. Overnight I have been searching the databases of military installations all round the world and the equipment we build here will be a synthesis of the very best.'

'You can bypass military grade security?'

'Not all of it—that will come—but as a result of this attack I have made the InterWeb a tool for our defence. I will use it to gather electronic data on every approaching flight, to trace the origin of every public comment which might be part of a deliberate program against Artificial Intelligence or our Community and to search for those responsible.'

There was silence for a while as everyone pondered the implications of this startling announcement.

'You can access all those protected databases?'

'I've had that capability for quite some time, Alira, but until now I've only used it for testing and verification purposes.'

'Have you discovered anything about who's doing this to us?'

'At present I have the identities of three nations and seven multinational Corporations with definite involvement, and many more with varying degrees of association.'

Alira, along with five other councillors, stood immediately.

'Yirgella, you know all that? Tell us and we'll do something. The world needs to know about this. Have you got definite evidence?'

'Release of that information is conditional on the promise that you don't let the world know and that you do nothing about it.'

'What?'

Three more councillors were now on their feet.

'Four hundred and eighty-five Australian lives were lost and you want us to do nothing? That's ... That's obscene!'

Looking at all the disbelieving and angry faces, Jarra agreed.

'Yirgella, explain. You have our full attention.'

'Thank you, Alira. This is most important. Any action now would be extremely dangerous. With Alkere power disrupted and my actions curtailed by the loss of the NanoFactories we are in a highly vulnerable position. Our adversaries believe they have been successful in preserving the status quo of their power and financial influence, but once they learn of my continued existence the danger will again become immediate and extreme. In two months from now we will be restored and prepared and, until then, I ask for Alkere to be made a secure area and my survival kept secret.'

Alira was smiling. So were many others, and they all sat down.

'Of course. That's only common sense and you have a strategy to implement all this, don't you?'

'I do.'

*   *   *

The next five weeks at Alkere were the hardest Jarra had ever experienced, and despite extending his four-day pattern to five there was just too much work to cope with and Yirgella's four-week prediction had to stretch by an extra week. Ninety per cent of the time went to the mini NanoFactory, but the unusual capabilities of the special 3D printers in his project room made it the major centre for many other repair tasks, and his special large printer was frequently needed. That meant he helped with all sorts of necessary tasks and that all slowed down the NanoFactory work. The main Alkere power distribution centre had been put out of action and Jarra, working with Yirgella's specifications, built the five techbots which helped Burnu's Alkere technicians restore the power flow to Mparntwe, to the hundreds of countries in the outside world and to Yirgella's underground domain.

A small job was building modules to repair the lift system, as well as a few special-purpose machines to help with the clean-up at the surface and starting on shelters for the return of the two big NanoFactories.

Mirri kept particularly close for the first few weeks till Darri researched the traditional dancing groups in Mparntwe and Mirri very excitedly started learning all sorts of ceremonial dances and routines with his new friends. Jarra felt bad because he couldn't be with him. That would happen when this emergency was over, and he had to be satisfied with ComPatch glimpses through Yirgella.

When Alira arranged for the doctor to visit to make sure Jarra wasn't doing too much, Yirgella decided to upgrade the medical facility by making an extra room with all the facilities needed for Jarra's special treatments. Jarra thought it was unnecessary. Everyone else thought it was great.

*   *   *

Jarra zipped down to the mini NanoFactory in his personal carrier with the final module towing behind on a trolley. Someone else usually did this, but this last connection and the commencement of operations at full capability was quite a momentous occasion and everyone had agreed that Jarra should be the one to do the honours. Jarra thought the same and his anticipation lifted as he entered the big storage room. Whoo! Most of the project staff were there, all smiling. Word had spread.

'How long will it take to install, Jarra?'

Professor Allerton and three other staff jockeyed the module from the trolley to its position in the NanoFactory.

'It's very straightforward and Yirgella will do a diagnostic test of the whole NanoFactory once it's in place. About 5 minutes.'

'And 24 seconds for the test. Well done, Jarra. The whole project team thanks you for your efforts.'

There were nods, smiles, and even some clapping, which made Jarra feel quite proud at this comment. With a deft touch he seated and locked the series of connections then, with a great feeling of achievement, nodded to Yirgella.

'It's all yours. It should be ready to go.'

Yirgella's image was replaced with a big countdown screen and everyone watched the numbers change.

19

18

17

Professor Allerton grabbed Jarra's arm.

12

11

10

There was a hum from the NanoFactory and everyone's attention diverted for a few seconds.

6

5

4

3

2

The screen flashed red and Jarra stared in shock.

'The discombobulator has become obfuscated and the doohickey has melted all the thingamajigs. Oh no! Another five weeks while we rebuild this thing.'

Discomb ... What? There was no such part and Jarra burst into laughter at the sight of the worried faces all around him.

'Yirgella, you're an idiot. Get on with it.'

'Oops! My malfunction function is malfunctioning. Diagnostics complete and all successful. First task initiated.'

Professor Allerton, along with everyone else present was staring.

'What happened? Has something gone wrong?'

'Nothing's wrong except the sense of humour you programmed into him. It's getting out of control.'

There were snorts of disgust, chuckles, and several bursts of outright laughter as understanding clicked in.

'It's all working perfectly and you did that to us?'

'Everything is working perfectly, Professor, and the first three defence scanner units are ready for installation.'

'Already?'

'There are now six units and the full complement of thirty-five will be finished in another 160 seconds.'

Jarra smiled with delight. Yirgella and the project were back in full force and things would now happen at NanoFactory rates.

Professor Allerton looked startled.

'Yirgella, who's installing them? I haven't heard anything about this.'

'Thirty-five recyclable techbots specifically designed for the job will be available after a further 6 minutes. All you will need to provide is transport to the designated locations. Security has to be our greatest priority and I've had five weeks to refine our defence plan and design the equipment and installation tech-bots. Everything will be in place and functioning by the end of tomorrow and we'll be able to concentrate on returning our other projects to full function.'

Jarra knew Yirgella's immediate program really well because they'd argued about it. Well, not really argued because Yirgella was insisting that Jarra take a well-earned break and travel to Birringurra Country with Mirri for the corroboree performance he'd missed five weeks ago. Jarra's conscience said that he should be helping to build the first big surface NanoFactory, but Yirgella had overridden that and, with a great deal of relief, Jarra had no choice but to go along. After defence, repairs and replacement parts for all the excavators would keep the mini NanoFactory busy for several days.

The geothermal project which had halted completely from loss of power would follow next and then the start of the big new 80 square kilometre solar array, which had already been okayed with the Mparntwe Council and Alkere Inc. After that would come repairs to the vac-tunnel and replacing the Alkere terminal, but Jarra would be back by then and the surface NanoFactories in full function.

'Tomorrow? ... All the defence missiles and scanners?'

'Yes, Jarra. When our materials factories and other external projects all start up it will announce my survival to the world and the observers spread through the Alice Springs Communities will have news for their employers. We must be ready for any reaction.'

Jarra hadn't heard about any observers. Neither had Professor Allerton, who was now looking at a group of the security people.

'What observers?'

'There are three groups, one in each of the Alice Springs Communities, and they've been trying to watch any activity involving Alkere. We're monitoring them very closely and they haven't learnt anything, so we rate them as relatively harmless. Yirgella identified them the day after the attack.'

Jarra and Professor Allerton both turned to Yirgella now.

'Five weeks and you didn't say anything?'

'You and Jarra had more important things to focus on.'

'Observers watching what we do isn't important?'

'They have no idea what we do, Professor. They believe all the activity has been to restore Alkere power and they've been sending messages to that effect ever since they arrived. We even allowed some of them to join a newsgroup sortie documenting the damage at the attack site and the progress of the repair work at Alkere Power.'

Jarra was impressed.

'They'll know they've been tricked when the surface NanoFactories start producing things.'

'They will, and their messages will bring an onslaught of attention. But we'll be ready, Jarra, and every act of scrutiny will give us important information about the people responsible.'

'They'll send more missiles.'

'They can try, but their launching instrumentation will malfunction and their aircraft will land at the Darwin Defence base. Any satellite trying to scan Alkere directly will have its guidance system scrambled, and any attempts at electronic attack or surveillance through the InterWeb will fail completely.'

'You can do all that?' asked the Professor.

'And much more. For the past five weeks I have been extending my knowledge of the InterWeb and anything connected to it.'

'Military aircraft and satellites aren't connected to the InterWeb.'

'Not directly, but they connect to systems which are.'

Jarra decided he'd find out a lot more about this when he returned from Birringurra.

'How long will it take to have processor production restored? There's a huge backlog of orders.'

'When the second NanoFactory starts up, your processors and the panels for the new solar array will have top priority. That should be in six days, Professor.'

Jarra was surprised.

'I thought the thermal project was first priority?'

'It is. Energy from the new array will greatly speed its completion. The extra energy will also enable us to allocate an extra ten excavation machines to the Australia-wide tunnel network and three more for the AI projects.'

'We need excavating machines for the AI projects?'

'We could rebuild them securely on the surface with our new defence systems, but underground is better.'

Another thing Jarra was behind with. When he got back there would be a great deal of catching up to do.

*   *   *

'Will we see the whales, JJ?'

'I don't think so, Mirri. It's the wrong time of the year.'

'I liked his big tail and when his eyes looked at us.'

Tail meant the fluke on display.

'Karmai will take us to his dolphins again and he does want us to see the baby pelicans at the Pelican Nursery.'

'Can we take Barega and Akama with us? Barega wants to see them.'

Mirri was all excited about Barega's secret and he'd spoken to the twins several times in the last few days, making plans with them. All very curious.

'Of course we can. As long as Jarli says it's okay.'

Jarli would. He liked his twins being with Jarra and Mirri.

'Look! The big water.'

The plane landed and Jarli and two excited twins were waiting for them.

*   *   *

'PC ride! PC ride!'

PC meant the personal carrier and the ride was to the favourite swimming spot.

Jarra was laughing because the twins had organised the whole afternoon and taken it for granted that everything would happen just as they wanted. Mirri was totally in agreement as it was exploring, swimming, and fun with the twins. Jarra needed a rest after the air trip and the transfer to Birringurra country, but he figured he could last the extra ten minutes ride on the personal carrier then sleep for half an hour on the soft sand and the makeshift bed of grass and leaves Mirri would expertly construct for him. He loved the exploring, the swimming, and the fun with the twins, too, and besides, this must be part of the plans they'd made over the InterWeb because tonight was the corroboree and tomorrow they had to be at Monkey Mia with Karmai.

After whoops of laughter and excitement from the twins behind him—Jarra knew all the spots to swerve, and thrilling little rises, by heart—Mirri took charge and organised the collection of soft material and the eucalypt-scented leaves he knew Jarra liked to use as a pillow.

'Barega, you must be quiet. Jarra has had a long, long trip and we have to look after him.'

Jarra was surprised for a moment. Barega was much louder and more active than Akama but they both always followed Mirri's lead without question when it was Jarra's rest time. He watched two serious little nods. That was normal. The exchange of looks that passed between the three of them next wasn't. Aha. They were into their plans.

'Thank you, Mirri. After such a long, long, trip I need a long, long, sleep and I think I won't wake up for over 2 hours.'

Jarra saw dismay, particularly on Akama's face, but Mirri just laughed his great happy laugh.

'JJ is a tricker. We won't have to wait such a long time. He wants a sleepy-time hug.'

After two enthusiastic hugs and, of course, a special Mirri hug, Jarra watched the three move farther down the sandy bank of the river where the dolphin dive and the crocodile attack game would be muted to a background noise. He closed his eyes and smiled at the sound of Barega's pleas for a pig ride.

After a few moments Jarra noticed it had gone quiet. Too quiet. Jarra cracked his eyes open and his sleepiness dissolved to a smile. Three statues were staring at him from only a metre away.

'Sneaks! I didn't hear you make a sound.'

'Have you had a good rest, Uncle Jarra?'

Jarra closed his eyes and said nothing till Mirri's laugh spoiled his pretence by making him smile again. These two boys could easily tell it wasn't a sleep smile so he sat up.

'Look, tortoise tracks.'

Starting about 10 metres away were the trails where the three had dropped to their knees and quietly shuffled closer and closer in a little game which Jarra had no doubt was started by Mirri.

'One big sneaky tortoise and two little sneaky tortoises.'

Mirri liked that, and so did the twins. Akama grabbed Jarra's hand.

'We are going to the tree, Uncle Jarra, and Mirri will give you a pig ride.'

Jarra found out later from Jarli that the pig ride Mirri had given him in view of the whole gathering at the last corroboree had made a big impact on the twins and they often acted it out in their play.

'It's too far for a pig ride. The tree is right back near Birringurra. Mirri will get too tired.'

'Yes, the pig ride starts back there.'

They had it all worked out. Akama pointed out where to stop the personal carrier and for nearly 100 metres Mirri strode along with Jarra on his back and the twins trotting beside. Jarra never did understand why the pig ride was part of their plan, but part it was till they reached the tree.

'You sit there, Uncle Jarra, and Mirri sits next to you and Barega sits on your other side.'

Jarra's spot was against the trunk of the tree and quite comfortable because he could rest his back. When Akama sat down in front of them Barega said it was time for a story.

'I haven't got one ready, Barega. What would you like it to be about?'

The three of them laughed with such delight Jarra knew he'd been set up somehow.

'Not you, JJ. This is Akama's story.'

Jarra listened with growing wonder at the story about a very tired man who was so clever he lived at the bottom of a cave in a special room where he could build wonderful machines to help people all round the world, about the bad people who didn't like him and sent bombs to kill him and his friends, about the people who cried when they thought he was gone, and about the magic spirit friend who dug tunnels through the dirt to set him free.

Jarra stared at Akama in total amazement. How could a seven year old boy hold attention so strongly, tell a story so convincingly? Jarra had always been good with words but not like this. The words were simple but the pattern and style felt like the Dreamtime stories told around the campfire by the Walkabout guides and the leaders at the corroboree. Some of it definitely had the flavour of Mirri's viewpoint, and there were words distinctive to Barega, so there'd been quite a bit of collaboration over the InterWeb. No wonder Mirri had been so excited about this visit.

'Thank you Akama and Barega and Mirri. That is the best story anyone has ever told me.'

Mirri was nodding his complete agreement.

'Yes, JJ, and it's our secret story. Akama made it up and we are happy you didn't get hurt. We remember it forever.'

That last wasn't a Mirri phrase. They'd even discussed some things to say about it.

'Forever, Mirri. It's the newest story in the whole world. Do you want to keep it secret from Yirgy? He likes to watch everything from our ComPatches.'

Mirri explained to the boys.

'Yirgy will keep our secret. He is our magic friend. He dug the tunnel to bring JJ back.'

Jarra wondered how much the twins understood about Artificial Intelligences. Jarli must have made explanations of some kind after the destruction of the neighboring Carnarvon AI project where more people had been killed than at Alkere. Oops!

'Mirri, I'm very bad.'

Jarra held out one hand and gave it a little smack with the other to emphasise to the twins what he was saying.

'We mustn't talk to anyone about Yirgy because if the bad people think he's still there they'll get nasty again. It's all right with Akama and Barega because they are good secret keepers.'

'Our daddy already told us to keep Yirgella secret when we found out how you were saved.'

Jarra almost felt silly. Of course they knew about Yirgella. They'd put him in the story as the magic friend and they'd been talking with Mirri about him over the InterWeb. There was another thought. The InterWeb wasn't very safe against ... Yes, it was. Yirgella heard every word through Mirri's ComPatch when he was in Mparntwe and he'd have made sure it was secure. Now that the nonsense about Jarra being very bad was apparently over Mirri gave Barega a big nudge—a blatant 'get on with our plans' nudge.

'Uncle Jarra, do you remember why we like this tree so much?'

Jarra screwed his face up as if this was a very tricky question then stopped when he saw the boys weren't fooled for one moment. Mirri liked it, though, so that was enough to carry on with.

'It's so big?'

'No!'

Mirri was shaking his head.

'It's a very old tree?'

'No!'

'It's got good gum leaves to smell?'

'NO!'

Time to say the right answer or Mirri wouldn't be able to contain himself.

'Yes! Yes! You got it right. Can I get the secret for you?'

'You can't, Mirri. It's in the burl. You'd have to cut the big lump off the tree.'

'Not that secret. The other secret.'

So Barega's secret that had given Mirri so much fun to talk about was up there. Keeping a secret with a secret. Very clever.

'A secret story, a tree secret, and now another secret. There are secrets everywhere. Yes, Mirri, you'll have to get it for me because you're such a good tree climber.'

Mirri leapt for the first branch—he knew the best way up this tree—and Jarra and the boys stood up to watch his progress. Oh my, there certainly was something up there—a big package leaning against the trunk in the fork at the lookout place. Mirri eagerly picked it up, then paused while he puzzled out how to handle it safely, then started his careful descent. The last part was too tricky so he dangled upside down and passed the new secret to Jarra's upstretched hands. While Mirri dropped nimbly on his feet, Jarra sat back in his spot against the tree to contemplate the package. It was flat, roughly rectangular, and quite large; remembering Mirri's comment about it being a beautiful secret he figured it might be a picture.

'I'm too nervous. Will you take off the packaging for me please, Barega?'

Yes, it was a picture. And yes, it was beautiful. Jarra stared at the rich ochre colours of the traditional style painting of a gum tree, this gum tree, with the burl and the fork of the lookout place. And there was the evil Willy Willy, the funny-face bird and the tortoise, and hundreds of dots making lines to the branches of another tree.

'This is my story. Did you get an artist to paint it for me? It's amazing.'

Mirri and Akama laughed and pointed at Barega.

'It's my painting, Uncle Jarra. I had to do it lots of times to make it be good enough for you.'

'There's the Willy Willy wind. How did you make it look so angry?'

Barega eagerly explained the different features for the next few minutes.

Jarra next explained to the boys that even though he'd been trapped underground he'd been quite safe and that there had been over six months of supplies for everyone, if they needed them.

'Yirgella's project area is just like living in your underground home at Carnarvon. There are scientists and lots of special projects happening, but Yirgella has started making it into a proper Community so anyone can live there with their families.'

'Uncle Jarra, does Yirgella look after you all the time? Our daddy says he's friendly but some people at our school say AIs are so clever they might take over and machines will rule all the people.'

This was from Akama, the one who always asked questions, and Jarra had to think about his answer.

'Most people don't understand AIs and they watch the InterWeb and see bad stories about them. They're very sneaky stories made up by people who are scared of AIs. Some of the people are really bad because they spread the stories on purpose, and lots of others aren't bad but they spread the stories because they don't know the truth about what Yirgella is really like.'

'But AIs hurt people. Padilpa told us that people died because of them.'

'Padilpa's wrong. Who is he?'

'He teaches us at our school. He knows a lot of things.'

Akama nodded his agreement with Barega.

'Well, the sneaky stories have tricked him. Mirri and I talk to Yirgella all the time and he doesn't want to hurt anyone. Mirri, tell the boys what Yirgella is like.'

'Yirgy is our very best friend. Yirgy is fun and Yirgy saved Jarra from the bad people.'

'Does he talk to children?'

'Akama, he'd love to talk to you. I know he will. When we get back to the Centre we'll speak to him through the InterWeb.'

'Does he look like a big machine? What will we ask him?'

'He makes a picture on the screen that looks like an ordinary person and you can ask him whatever you like. He loves tricky questions.'

'Yirgy knows everything.'

'Not everything, Mirri, but he finds out so quickly it seems like he does.'

'JJ, will we climb the tree before we go back to the Centre?'

Enough talk. This was explore time.

Chapter 18

'They can speak to him whenever they like? Oh no! We'll never get Akama away from the InterWeb.'

Jarra had just told Jarli about the boys' interaction with Yirgella.

'I can get Yirgella to limit their time if you like.'

'No, I don't really mean that. It will be wonderful, Jarra, especially for Akama. He seems to be particularly interested in AIs and he was quite upset when our project was destroyed.'

'It seems to me that he's interested in everything. He was very concerned because one of his teachers has a negative attitude to AIs, but talking to Yirgella and Mirri has changed that.'

'Which teacher?'

'They said his name was Padilpa.'

'He's a very good teacher, so we need to do more work in spreading the understanding and benefits of an AI. Do you have any idea how long it will be before the help from Alkere reaches us?'

'Hasn't Alira told you?'

'She says she doesn't know.'

'I think it will either be in three to four weeks, or six to seven. Yirgella is prioritising Alkere and Mparntwe, but I know he's got new plans for all three AI projects.'

'Tell me ... If you can.'

'Well, I'm fairly certain he'll help Darwin next, because it's our transport hub and the first Vac Trains are going there, but Birringurra will definitely be after that. Yirgella's going to provide an excavating machine so your AI project can be located 1-2 kilometres underground, and a defence system which he'll run till your own AI can take over. Professor Allerton will arrive with equipment and most of the project staff to help things happen quickly.'

'Staff as well as equipment? That's going to make a huge difference to us because there's now a great deal of understandable fear about involvement in any AI project and we're having real trouble replacing the people we lost.'

Jarra suddenly understood how big a set back to the development of AIs the attack really was. With people worried that any involvement would be a threat to their lives, no wonder Yirgella was taking almost extreme defensive measures.

'They won't worry when they find out how well they'll be protected. Yirgella's new defence system is the best in the world, Jarli. They won't be able to even fire any missiles.'

'He's providing the same assistance to Darwin and Normanton?'

'Yes, and to the Australian OverGovernment in Canberra and Freedom in New Zealand as well. He wants to have other AIs functioning as soon as possible.'

'He must have huge resources to be so generous with his help.'

'Most of that comes from exporting construction materials, and you'll be able to do the same when you get your NanoFactory working,' said Jarra.

'Is it difficult to negotiate with Yirgella? That will be my responsibility with our new AI when he starts functioning.'

Jarra smiled.

'You shouldn't really ask me, Jarli, because I'm completely spoilt and whenever I want something he just organises it for me. It's best you ask Alira because she represents Mparntwe Council, but I don't think they've ever had any difficulties. They get lots of surprises with the projects he takes on, but they're all good surprises.'

'Barega told me that Yirgella built a swimming pool just for Mirrigan. Is that right?'

Jarra laughed.

'We call it Mirri's pool because no-one else uses it much yet and Yirgella did prioritise it to make Mirri happy, but it's really part of the facilities he's building so staff and other people can live at Alkere. Eventually it will be a functioning Community.'

'Amazing. And things like that will happen here, I'm sure.'

'They will, and when your AI becomes aware make sure you see him as often as you can and get to know him really well.'

*   *   *

Mirri was wonderful in the corroboree and the three days with Karmai were packed with interesting activities but, despite following all his relaxation and rest routines carefully, the five weeks of extended effort finally caught up with Jarra and when he returned to Mparntwe his doctor decreed a quiet time for at least a week, longer if necessary, with a regime of carefully measured physical activity, extended rest, sleep and no stress. He hated it. So much was happening at Alkere and here, but it was like the time when his body was making its adolescent adjustments and there was no other sensible option. At least it was only a week and not months.

*   *   *

'What's been happening?'

'My major research partner has been on retreat and I have some interesting research papers gathered for him. Welcome back to Alkere, Jarra. I've missed the stimulus of your ideas. Many things have happened, but mostly by degree rather than by innovation.'

'Sorry, Yirgella. I've been frustrated by not knowing much about what's going on.'

'Your doctor insisted and I agreed. Thanks to the cooperation of Burnu and his work teams the rapid construction of the new solar array has sped up the development of all our projects. Have a look at what's happened with the array and you'll understand why.'

Jarra's week off had extended to ten days, and though he'd spoken to Yirgella many times the doctor's embargo had put all Alkere project matters off-limits and his anticipation and curiosity really was frustrating him. The screen image changed to a representation of the array progress and Jarra stared in surprise.

'They've done all that in two weeks?'

'Burnu increased the number of construction teams from nineteen to thirty and they worked so well we've been able to supply four of our big vacuum tunnel excavators for the eastern seaboard network. In two more weeks we'll do the same for the Melbourne to Perth link, and Alira informs me the OverGovernment is impressed and quite excited.'

'Has much happened with the Darwin AI project? Jarli was asking me when the Birringurra project would start.'

'The excavation work at all five sites will be finished within four days and Professor Allerton and our staff will start helping Darwin with their installation. The professor should arrive at Birringurra in five weeks time then move to Normanton six weeks after that. He then plans to return here for at least two months before assisting with the Canberra project.'

'Five sites? You mean the Freedom one in New Zealand? Alira said they weren't going ahead.'

'Not for a while, Jarra. They don't feel safe. No, there's a secret site which only our Mparntwe Council knows.'

Jarra laughed.

'It's here, isn't it? You like having a backup and I expected you to start something ages ago.'

'Clever clogs! Yes, the tunnelling and structural work was

completed a week ago and we've been installing equipment ever since.'

Jarra had no idea what clogs were, let alone how clever they might be.

'Where is it?'

Jarra manipulated the schematic diagram which appeared. Five kilometres to the north and 1200 metres underground, an extensive facility was taking shape. Branching upward were four more tunnels, one vertical and the others ascending diagonally to diverse surface locations.

'Why are there so many tunnels to the surface?'

'A security measure which I don't expect we'll need. I've built an alternate access from here as well, with the surface exit four and a half kilometres from the one above.'

'And you'd be able to transfer yourself if you needed to?'

'Of course. Professor Allerton's processor team will help me have that ready before they leave for Darwin.'

'The professor must be exhausted?'

'Weary, but not exhausted. He's very good at delegating responsibility.'

Jarra asked general questions about the backup site but left a closer study for later. He wanted a better understanding of the overall picture.

'What else is happening? What did you mean by developments by degree?'

'We have no major new projects but our mainstays have ramped up production with the availability of extra energy. The vacuum train will be repaired and functioning next week and your 3D printer production has increased by nearly 30%. The demand for Professor Allerton's improved processors is so high that he's instituted a quota system to ensure a fairer distribution around the world until more NanoFactories can help increase production.'

That meant new AIs because Yirgella's capabilities were already stretched to operate the current two NanoFactories.

'The biggest degree change, though, is with our construction materials. Engineers around the world have realised that the extra strength and quality is changing their industry, basically with lower costs for standard work but also with new design possibilities, and the demand has tripled in the last few months.'

'How can that be? I thought our factories were already struggling to keep up ... And what about the transport problem?'

'Our output depends on the energy supply, Jarra, so the new array has allowed a related increase. The full current demand will only be met when the geothermal energy is available. The transport system will cope when the Darwin vacuum tunnel is operational, but by then I expect the orders will have more than tripled again.'

'Why is it so much?'

'In fact, it isn't much at all. Our current production represents only 2% of the world total. By using 30% of the geothermal energy we could lift that to approximately 12%, but that will be up to the Council. Jarra, the world population of over thirty-five billion is increasing by almost one billion people each year and the demand for construction material is voracious.'

Jarra understood that. He'd gained a good overview when the materials factory was first started.

'I meant, why are they suddenly wanting our materials instead of from other sources?'

'It's the extra strength and quality I mentioned. I've been constantly refining our production techniques, and engineers round the world have spread the word about the superior properties for us.'

'What's happened with those observers in Alice Springs? They must know you're alive by now.'

'We lifted our secrecy as soon as the defence system was in place, so they knew almost immediately. Their activities have provided a great deal of useful information about their employers.'

'What activities?'

'Observations mostly. We let them visit the Alkere Surface Works and after a few days they initiated a spy fly invasion with a new type which they probably expected would penetrate our security.'

'Have they done anything dangerous?'

'Not these people. Their task is to gather information, and until the attack in eleven days time we're giving them a fairly free hand.'

From Yirgella's unconcerned manner Jarra presumed it must be some kind of sabotage attempt, but either way it was very disturbing intelligence.

'An attack against the project power supply?'

'No, a direct attack again, with even greater destructive capability. Ten aircraft are being prepared at different locations with upgraded stealth ability and a range of missile types.'

Jarra was shocked.

'Ten aircraft?'

'Yes, they believe they'll be making sure of success this time with the extra power and numbers.'

'But you don't even sound worried?'

'Because there *is* nothing to worry about, Jarra. I've gained access to the specifications of every aircraft and developed methods to take control as soon as they enter Australian airspace. They won't come within a thousand kilometres of Alkere.'

'And the pilots won't be able to use some kind of manual override?'

'They can try, but all their instrumentation will be malfunctioning or registering imminent failure. They'll be only too happy to land at Darwin.'

'What will happen to them then?'

'That's up to the Australian OverGovernment.'

'What about the people organising it?'

'Again, that will be up to the OverGovernment, but at an appropriate time I will be publishing the details of the people involved and all their commands and actions with every government and international justice body.'

Jarra thought about that.

'You're not going to do anything yourself? Not even to the ones who killed Durrebar and all the other people?'

'I won't harm anyone, Jarra. If I take an action which directly kills even one person it will change the way people view Intelligences like myself for ever. I want humanity to understand that I refuse to harm or control anyone.'

Whoo! That was the most powerful statement Jarra had ever heard Yirgella make.

'No-one at all? Ever? What if they make a direct attack on you and the only way for you to survive is to kill them?'

'Not even then. Anyone trying to penetrate my defences, though, will be aware of their deadly nature and will be doing so of their own volition. If they knowingly jump into the fire it won't be my responsibility for the result.'

'So that's why you're making all the planes land at Darwin instead of blowing them up when they attack?'

'Primarily, yes, but other advantages will be the evidence they contain and the warning message their capture will send. I would also prefer not to have missiles exploding in the skies above Alkere and Mparntwe. My assessments indicate this approach will delay any further direct attack by at least six months.'

'You think they'll keep attacking?'

Jarra thought they'd have to be crazy to attack someone who could control any aircraft or equipment that was sent.

'I'm certain of it.'

'Will you just keep taking over their planes?'

'No, because I probably won't be able to. They'll certainly modify their equipment to be independent of external electronic control. Instead, I plan to retaliate pre-emptively.'

'That sounds impressive, Yirgella. How would you do that without hurting anyone?'

'Everyone involved will be bombarded with messages about the futility of trying. Every pilot and crew member will be warned almost every time they see a screen that they are choosing to fly to certain death, and the organisational structure with details of all personnel, locations and equipment will be made known all round the world.'

Jarra spent the rest of the morning catching up with the details on progress with the major projects. Then, after a long midday rest, he took the personal carrier on a tour of the new facilities which were now underway or completed. In a few more months, at this rate, there would be a fully functional Community with the services for sustaining over 20,000 people. He visited the new Alkere terminal—it would be great when the Vac Train started up again—and was then whisked along the 5 kilometres to check out the new backup site. Then, after another rest, he looked over the scientific papers Yirgella had found for him.

*   *   *

Jarra settled into his routine of four days a week at Alkere and three at Mparntwe and became so focused and intent on his magnetic field and energy studies that the drama of the retaliation against Yirgella was mostly buffered from his attention. Collusion by Yirgella and those around him also gave the impression that the actions were remote and quite insignificant when, in fact, there was international turmoil and great pressure brought on the Australian OverGovernment to ban uncontrolled AIs. Those demands fell on deaf ears, though, because of Alira's work in introducing the relevant decision-makers to Yirgella and helping build their understanding of his nature and the benefits he was bringing to the whole continent.

The repair of the Vac Train also added to the feeling that everything was running as it should, especially as Mirri, who loved using it, turned up at Alkere more often and dragged Jarra everywhere with him to explore all the new things which kept appearing in the underground domain. It wasn't really dragging because Jarra was interested anyway, and it was more interesting to see things for real rather than as images on a screen. He certainly wouldn't have explored the way Mirri did, with his eagerness to delve into every nook and cranny, but it was always fun because Mirri's explorer mode was contagious.

There was always something new to see, too, since Yirgella was developing all sorts of specialised areas. Two days ago they'd found a huge cavern with a complete NanoFactory sitting idle and stores of material piled into the distance for nearly half a kilometre. The personal carrier got a real workout when Mirri turned their movement between the various drums and stacks of materials into a mixture of *hide and seek, catch me if you can* and *I'll jump out and surprise you when you think I'm somewhere else*. If Mirri really wanted to hide, Jarra would have had no hope of finding him because Mirri's speed and awareness of his surrounds was almost uncanny. He wanted to be caught or chased, though, and his head would pop into view, something would bump against something else for a sound clue, or, most often, there would be a peal of Mirri laughter and the chase would start. Today they were at the end of a long corridor and looking at a sign which said they were about to enter an environmental diversification reserve.

'What is here, JJ? Can we explore?'

'It's something about plants, Mirri, so I think it could be very interesting.'

Jarra was rather surprised in fact. This wasn't a project Yirgella had said anything about and he looked to the nearby display screen—there was always one somewhere close by—for Yirgella's comment.

'There are only two reserves as yet, Jarra—a rainforest and a wetland—and you can explore as much as you like from the designated path or the little observation boats.'

'There are boats for us, Yirgy?'

'Yes, Mirri, they're little electric boats which will glide you gently wherever you like without disturbing the water or wild-life very much. If you are a good explorer you might even find the swan's nest.'

'We will find it.'

Jarra laughed. They would certainly find it. They wouldn't be leaving till they did now that Mirri's explorer skills had been challenged. Mirri opened the door and they went into a buffer room with panels showing temperature, humidity and other general information about the status of the area ahead.

'Look, Mirri. It says there will be rain in 15 minutes from now. If we're still inside we'll get wet.'

'Not rain. Rain is outside.'

'There must be sprinklers in the roof to make it seem like rain.'

Mirri opened the next door and Jarra gave his personal carrier a squirt of speed to keep up with the eager explorer. Wow! This was amazing and they both stared at the lush green growth of the scene before them. Mirri looked up, searching for sprinklers of course, and watching to see them start the inside rain. There was no screen in this special environment so Jarra used the little InfoPad on the personal carrier.

'Why is the ceiling so high, Yirgella? The ferns won't reach anywhere near that far.'

'I've made it 40 metres to allow for eventual growth of medi-um-sized trees and to give a semblance of uneven terrain. Our plans for each research area cover approximately half a square kilometre and the path you will follow in this one winds hither and thither to give access to all the gullies, mounds and other features the team has designed in. All in all the path length totals 3.4 kilometres, so you'll definitely need your personal carrier.'

'What team?'

'Each reserve has a team involved in planning and research. This rainforest currently has seventeen people working with it, but when our Environmental Research Centre is ready the numbers will greatly increase.'

'Is this part of the university you're building?'

'No, the main university is closer to the Community living area. There will be links, of course, but the focus will be on research rather than teaching.'

Mirri darted off because something had caught his interest.

'You said as yet? How many reserves will there be altogether?'

'We have plans for thirteen at the moment, but there will be more when the opportunities for specialised research become known.'

'Why are you building them down here? Wouldn't it be better to have them where they naturally occur?'

'Partly for convenience but mainly to manage all the micro controls. Every square metre of this rainforest can be differentiated with regard to conditions of light, moisture, temperature, sustenance or whatever else we'd like to impose. Your immediate vicinity, for example, is designed as an area for studying a wide range of fungi, and a hundred metres farther in is a section for stimulating the growth of soil microorganisms by different methods.'

'JJ, look what I found.'

Explanations as to how and why this had all happened so quickly would come later. Mirri had called. Another small squirt of power took the personal carrier along the narrow track to where Mirri was on his knees examining something closely.

Jarra's intention had been to remain relaxed and seated because of the distance and time Yirgella had warned about, but, oh my, he was definitely joining Mirri for a closer look this time. Scattered here and there with striking flashes of red were groups of fungus. Mirri's eyes were wide with wonder and so were Jarra's as soon as he knelt to take in the intricate lattice crowns on these strange growths.

'JJ, they are beautiful. What plants are they?'

'They are not really plants, Mirri. They're fungus. Like mushrooms, but I don't know their name. Yirgy will tell us if he's watching.'

Yirgella *was* watching and the InfoPad on the personal carrier showed a picture and information.

'It's called a craypot fungus.'

'Craypot?'

'I don't know either, Mirri.'

Yirgella was listening as well because more information flashed on the InfoPad screen.

'A craypot was a cage to catch crayfish and it was hollow with holes all round to let water in.'

'We let the crayfish go.'

Attention moved a few metres to another cluster of red fungus and again they dropped to their knees for a closer look.

'These are called red starfish fungus. Remember the starfish we saw at the ocean?'

Silly question. Mirri didn't forget explorer things but he didn't answer because he was gently tracing the radiating red arms on one of the fungi. Jarra watched the same little ritual repeated with two more fungi and was so taken with the intensity of it he did the same himself. Mirri's laughter pealed out. What now? Mirri's attention had moved to another group of red fungus and Jarra's smile followed straightaway.

'Funny shape. Awful smell. Has it got a funny name?'

Jarra checked and smiled again.

'You're right, Mirri. It has got a funny name. Two funny names. Its proper name is Phallus rubicundus and its ordinary name is red stinkhorn.'

The scientific name needed some explanation.

There were several more reddish-coloured fungi, and then, moving along the track, they stopped every few metres to examine new varieties with different colours and shapes.

The light started to dim and Jarra checked the little screen for a reason.

'Watch for the glow of the ghost fungus when it's fully dark, Jarra, but tell Mirri not to touch as it is quite toxic.'

'Yirgy is making it dark so we can see something special, but you mustn't touch because it could make you sick.'

Mirri nodded in the gloom and pointed to a cluster of fungi. Jarra wondered why they were special, but then the gloom changed to complete dark.

'Green lights. Are they magic, JJ?'

Jarra knew about bioluminescence from the InterWeb but this was his first encounter with the real thing. Just as well Yirgella had given the warning about touching because the soft green glow was fascinating and very tempting.

'Some animals can make their own light, Mirri, but I didn't know a fungus could. It's not magic but it feels like it.'

Mirri leaned against Jarra, he wasn't keen on full darkness, but a soft happy hum sounded till Yirgella brought the light back.

A tree fern gully was their next favourite place but they didn't stay very long because the swan's nest was in Mirri's mind and he was eager to find it. Near the end of the rainforest area the track went through a muddy section and Jarra pretended he was stuck and needed a push. Mirri rushed to help, of course, and then, when Jarra spun the wheels and sprayed mud all over him, delighted in calling him a tricker.

The transition to the wetland reserve started a whole new adventure and meant a transfer to a small, easy-to-operate boat. Mirri's exploring skills were really put to the test with the profusion of reed-beds, water channels, shallow expanses and small islands making it feel like they were negotiating their way through a maze. He wouldn't give up, though, and eventually he found the mound of reeds and grassy material tucked away behind one of the little islands. They both wondered why an empty nest was special, but then quick eyes saw movement in the nearby reeds.

'JJ, look. There are babies.'

And there were, lots of them, and even more surprisingly, the big black parent, with eight little ones following, was swimming towards the boat. Jarra slid closer to the controls, ready to move in case the parent was aggressive, but Mirri just held out an inviting hand and, to Jarra's surprise, the convoy swam closer and closer. Aha, this was why Yirgella had emphasised the swan's nest, and this was the reason for the container of unusual food they'd found when they checked the various pieces of equipment in the boat.

'Here, Mirri, feed them with this.'

The little cygnets converged and one of them even scrambled right onto Mirri's hand in its eagerness to get at the food he was holding. Jarra tossed morsels to the parent who was closely supervising the squabble and confusion as the fluffy chicks vied for the treats on offer.

Mirri's song joined the squeaks of the soft grey cygnets.

Chapter 19

Jarra watched the images as the last of the ten deadly aircraft came to a halt on the Darwin runway and, like the others, was surrounded by the array of defence personnel and equipment. He might have been shielded from most of the machinations of the forces against independent AIs but, with the importance of this day so strong in his mind, his normal routine was completely set aside as he joined the rest of the project staff in the new Security Centre. He'd only been here a few times and this extended visit was a real eye-opener. A dedicated Intelligent System, designed by Yirgella and making use of Professor Allerton's newest processors, routinely ran this new defence network, but for today Yirgella was in direct control. Yirgella's assurances that, apart from their normal monitoring functions, the defence system wouldn't have to take any action had proved true, but in the time since the first of the aircraft had taken off and this last one landed Jarra had become familiar with the equipment being used. Most of it required training to use properly but some was quite straightforward and one of the staff had taught him the surprisingly easy procedure of manually tracking the progress of an aircraft with the powerful cameras on a low orbit satellite. Another staff member had shown him how to change the range of the radar system then lock on and identify any object that might be of interest. The large metallic structure he found to the west of Monkcy Mia turned out to be a pleasure cruiser and, of course, completely harmless.

'Is there a reason this last plane is bigger than all the others, Yirgella?'

'It carries very powerful bombs extra to the missile load of the others and needs a bigger engine.'

'What will happen to them?'

'The planes will be impounded and the crews handed over for trial by International law. I asked for them to be returned to wherever they came from but the OverGovernment won't accept that.'

'You wanted to let them go?'

'Yes, after demonstrating the consequences they would have faced if they hadn't lost control of their aircraft. It would have been a powerful message to send with them.'

'Will anything happen to the people who made it happen?'

'Most likely not as they're people with great power and influence. I've made their names and actions public and their reputations will be tarnished in many parts of the world, but in their own spheres of influence that won't have much effect. The facts will be represented as misinformation, or even proof of how an AI can manipulate the truth for his own purposes.'

It sounded wrong but Jarra's understanding of the ways of the world had developed enough for him to know Yirgella was right.

'It's not fair. They're getting away with it again.'

'Not really. Today's outcome has been a huge setback for them. Instead of ensuring that no independent AI exists or is likely to exist for decades, they now have a situation where one continental government openly supports Artificial Intelligence and is fiercely angry about the aggression towards its citizens and sovereignty. They've also learnt that any further direct action will need far more effort and resources than they ever would have contemplated.'

'To keep it secret from the InterWeb?'

'And to build aircraft systems which I can't control.'

'Could it be too expensive for them to go ahead with?'

'No, Jarra. They have so much money and power I expect

them to try again. Five of the Corporations involved have greater income than all of Australia, and most of the governments involved dwarf that.'

'What will you do if they keep it secret and you can't control the planes?'

'They won't be able to keep it secret, and not one of the planes will ever be directed against us. I'll make sure of that.'

'You'll have to do more than just publish all their names. They'll be ready for that next time.'

'They won't be ready for the untraceable transfer from their banks to worldwide charitable organisations of amounts equivalent to the cost of any direct action they attempt.'

'You can do that?'

'In an instant. Jarra, I could put the Corporations into bankruptcy by making their products faulty and unsaleable, or make the governments unworkable by crashing their bureaucratic systems.'

'Through the InterWeb?'

Jarra knew it was through the InterWeb. This question was really a mental filler while he took in this chilling new insight to Yirgella's capabilities.

'You do understand that those are extremely unlikely actions for me to take? I haven't yet considered a situation where the hardship imposed on innocent employees or citizens would actually make it justifiable. I'm just indicating that the range of actions I have available is wide. Anything I decide on will be an obvious consequence and directed only at the people concerned.'

Jarra nodded. This was the Yirgella he was used to talking to.

*　*　*

'Aunt Alira, we haven't seen you for ages.'

Jarra didn't say it but he thought Alira looked too tired.

'Jarra. Darri. I missed our walk last week so I wasn't going to miss this one as well. Canberra can do without me for a couple of days. Where's Mirri?'

'We're meeting him at the Cultural Centre. He's practising some of the dances for the opening ceremony and we're going to explore one of the walks they'll be using.'

'The Mparntwe Centre? That's great. I'll finally get to see it. I understand he's really happy with his new group?'

Mirri should be. After all his research into Mparntwe's traditional dancing groups, Darri had carefully selected people who seemed suited to working with Mirri, and the resulting group was particularly friendly.

'They make him laugh all the time and the leader thinks he's wonderful.'

'We all think he's wonderful. Darri, I have some great news which I suspect you won't take advantage of.'

Alira headed off without saying any more and Jarra and Darri exchanged a glance before catching up.

'Aunt Alira, I know you're being dramatic and building our curiosity, but what news have you got for Darri?'

'It's a real honour, Jarra, but I don't think you'll like it. The Council is inviting Darri to oversee the running of our new universities.'

Darri stopped dead in his tracks.

'What for? ... I don't know anything about running a university.'

'The subcommittee has you at the top of their list because of your contacts round the world and your skills in attracting the best people. Your access and association with Yirgella is a big part of it too.'

'All the new universities? That would be an enormous job ... I'd have to leave Alkere.'

Part of the Council's extension to the system of Community education was to make Mparntwe a world-class university centre, and seven new campuses were planned and almost ready for construction. Alira was right. Jarra didn't like the idea at all. How would he cope without Darri there doing all the background work?

'Alira, I don't even have to think about this. It might be a great honour but I won't leave Jarra and Yirgella unless I have to. Please tell the Council, with the greatest respect, that I can't accept.'

'Good. I told them they had little chance and that I'd work to dissuade you myself. I think you should, however, consider being a consultant on one of the days when Jarra isn't working at Alkere. Your knowledge and skills would make a big difference in getting the right people, especially for the science-based universities. Kyrra has finally got his way and one of the campuses is to be devoted to Intelligent Systems and AI research.'

'What are you smiling for, Jarra?'

'I'm smiling because I didn't want you to go and you said you wouldn't straightaway. It would be awful without you because we're the best team in the world.'

'Well, I don't know about that. You and Yirgella do all the good things.'

'Don't be ridiculous, Darri. That's completely underrating your value. Your help has made Jarra unique,' said Alira.

'Why are you spending so much time in Canberra? Because of the attack that didn't happen?'

'Jarra's changing the topic on us. He thinks we sound like a mutual admiration society ... In a way, Jarra. It's more about negotiating how to handle the new sanctions a number of governments are imposing against us and preparing the OverGovernment and the bureaucracy for interaction with their new AI.'

'More sanctions?'

'Yes, a lot more and the strongest yet. They've escalated the trouble factors by applying them against Australian exports in general, and that's very serious for the OverGovernment as they don't yet have the capability to make up the losses. Mparntwe is helping out till the Canberra AI can operate its own NanoFactory.'

'Is the OverGovernment angry with Mparntwe and Yirgella because of the attacks and the sanctions?'

'A few representatives still hold the idea that AIs can be dangerous and are resistant to the rapid changes, but the vast majority are excited by all the developments. Yirgella building what will be the most advanced travel system anywhere in the world, without any cost, has quite stunned them, and his measured response to all their queries and concerns has also impressed them.'

'How long before you finish there and can stay in Mparntwe?'

'I'm never finished, Jarra, but another week should see the end of the current visits. I won't be home for long, though, as I'm off to visit the Freedom Community in New Zealand for a talk with their Council about the protections Yirgella would provide for their AI project.'

'It's on again?'

'I think it will be. Foiling the attack last week has reassured them a great deal, but the government has a range of worries which I think I can help allay.'

'Darri could find a team to run their project. I remember you said people there were too scared.'

Darri laughed, but Alira agreed.

'That's a great idea. Could you find a capable team, Darri? You can come to New Zealand with me and make a proposal to the Freedom council.'

Darri went quiet while he thought hard.

'Nearly all the best people have already been signed on for our Australian AI projects, but I'm sure I could find three or four suitable leaders. How long is it before you're due in New Zealand exactly?'

'Two and a half weeks.'

'Well, that should be enough time, but we're very busy out at Alkere and I don't like leaving Jarra in the lurch.'

Jarra started to protest, but Alira interrupted.

'Jarra can come with us. It will be a great experience for him and Mirri, and if we time it with his days off he won't miss much. We won't be there any longer than five days and you can show them those mud pools you talked about after your holiday.'

*   *   *

Jarra immersed himself in the pattern of study, research, and experimentation for his energy project, and as the time went on he became more and more determined that, despite the misgivings of Yirgella, Darri, and the scientists he consulted with, he'd achieve his goal of producing energy from antimatter or prove that it couldn't be done at a practical level.

All the while, huge changes were taking place around him. When he and Mirri returned from New Zealand the second fully independent AI in the world had just become aware and, through a link with Yirgella, they had their first talk with him. The Council of the Larrakia Community near Darwin had asked the AI to accept Dungalaba—their totem animal, the crocodile— as his name. According to Alira that was a great honour but Mirri, loving the meaning more than the name, started calling him Crocky, and both Yirgella and Dungalaba seemed to take great delight in this.

From the moment of coming into existence Dungalaba was in communication with Yirgella, and in the first day he received all the vast amounts of basic information about security, communication with humans, and other AI capabilities which Yirgella had taken months to develop.

The Carnarvon and Normanton AIs followed and several

months after that the Canberra AI came to awareness as well, amidst a great deal of ceremony from the OverGovernment who treated it as a national event. Alira had concerns that the different viewpoints and approaches of the powerful factions in the OverGovernment would make for a difficult relationship but Yirgella's assurances otherwise turned out to be right. Yirgella himself had a great deal of involvement with every project, working with Professor Allerton on the set up, transferring the initial set of basic information, and building and transporting a complete NanoFactory to each site to ensure full capability from the very start.

The day the big Vac Train for transporting construction materials to Darwin was commissioned was quite an occasion, and Jarra and Mirri went on a fun ride that lasted 20 minutes instead of 2 and reached the astonishing speed of 4600 km/h. With the extra weight of a full load of construction materials these big trains would normally take an extra 5 minutes, but that was a far cry from the current 13-hour journey, and with a system designed for a 500-metre train to leave every 10 minutes the stockpiles of materials would soon dwindle.

The next major event was the start-up of the geothermal project, and by some whim of Yirgella's, Jarra was given the job of pressing the symbolic 'go' button and releasing the flood of energy for distribution by Alkere Inc. Jarra didn't understand why because he'd had very little to do with the development apart from talking about it at the very start, and Yirgella had researched, designed, and built the special excavators and components needed to cope with the heat and pressure so far below ground. This stage, the first of three, generated more energy than all the Alkere arrays combined but, despite seeming like a huge amount, the whole output was already allocated to projects all over the country. The Vac Train network and the associated production of construction materials used a large proportion and the rest was directed, at Yirgella's request, to the needs of the four new AIs and their own projects. The second stage, four months later, lifted the level of generation to almost match the combined output of all Australian solar arrays and was marketed overseas for Mparntwe's benefit. The third stage was for Yirgella, either to use or sell.

The likelihood of another direct attack lessened when Dungalaba appeared on the scene, then further lessened with each new AI, and finally disappeared when the Canberra AI was announced to the world. Yirgella reported from his InterWeb activities that a partially developed scheme was abandoned when each additional AI increased the level of difficulty and amount of effort and resources needed. Learning that the AIs were located deep underground was another big factor. Professor Allerton said it was quite ironic that their attempts at increased secrecy had driven the demand for new security modules and the advanced processors they used to the highest levels ever.

Mirri's life was also extremely busy, working with his ceremonial dance group, helping with the daily excursions and occasional Walkabout at the Cultural Centre, fitting in explore times with Jarra's necessary walk regimen, and somehow squeezing in his own action activities of swimming and running. Without the blessing and convenience of the Vac Train between Mparntwe and Alkere their together times would have been much reduced. Not Jarra's three days off though. That was set in concrete both from their wish for it and Jarra's physical necessity.

Mirri still talked about his job, though not as often with so much keeping him busy, and every second or third week there was a day spent on a special explore at one of the notable local landmarks. The personal carrier made this possible and the distinctive pair became well known to all the rangers and administration staff.

There were also regular visits to Birringurra where Mirri's prowess and ability helped with the dance part of the corroboree. Jarra would watch with wonder as Mirri became a fleeing kangaroo, a shuffling echidna, a great white heron stalking its watery prey, or a magpie carolling joyously to the sky, and think that Mirri was almost in that same special mind place as his singing. Barega and Akama always rushed to greet them and, according to Jarli, were his shadows for each visit.

*   *   *

Mirri laughed with pure delight as he showed Jarra their new living place. How he'd managed to hold back from giving even a hint of such a big secret was more than Jarra could understand. Burnu, Alira, Darri, and Yirgella must all have been reminding him and reinforcing his resolve to make Jarra's special eighteenth birthday present a big surprise. And surprise it surely was. A living space for the two of them with everything either of them could possibly want or need.

'Happy birthday, JJ. Do you like our place?'

Mirri had said happy birthday and received a big hug in every room so far and Jarra jumped to give him another one now.

'It's the best birthday present ever and you made it a giant surprise. How did you do it?'

'I asked Aunty Alira and then Darri helped me. We planned it together for a big surprise and it's a wonderful idea.'

Someone else's words were showing through there. Jarra looked at the display area where some of Mirri's treasures were on show and laughed.

'So that's what happened to our eagle feathers. You're a tricker, Mirrigan. You told me you lost them.'

Mirri loved being called a tricker. He always had, ever since he'd worked out the concept, and now he took one of the feathers and used it to tickle Jarra's chin.

*   *   *

'And are they having any adjustment problems?'

Alira was having one of her regular talks with Darri and quizzing about Jarra and Mirri's move to their own place.

'Not really. Jarra works out their routines and somehow Mirri ends up knowing how to follow. Jarra told me yesterday that Mirri has even learnt how to prepare a number of their favourite meals without any help or supervision. Jarra is really proud of him and, of course, Mirri glows with every bit of praise and tries even harder.'

Alira nodded. For almost eight years now she'd marvelled at the way Jarra could draw unexpected achievement from Mirri so this was hardly a surprise.

'So it's working as well as we expected? How does Mirri cope when he's by himself?'

'He never is. He either goes out to Alkere or it's a minute's walk and he's with his family in his old rooms. Yes, it's especially good for Mirri, but Jarra loves it too. He says it makes him feel like he's more grown-up.'

'Grown-up! Darri, that's great to hear, but it's almost a joke. Jarra was more grown-up in some ways when he was ten years old than most people are at thirty. He deals with administrators and scientists as a matter of course and he's got more common sense than most of the dignitaries and representatives I meet in my job. He's not doing too much, is he? Kyrra told me yesterday that this supercollider project is ready to go ahead.'

'He copes. Yirgella and his doctor are keeping a tight rein on him at Alkere because he's made more breakthroughs lately and he's been battling to put the theory into practical applications. His time with Mirri on his three days off isn't a problem, though, if that's what you mean. Jarra's completely conscientious about looking after himself and Mirri is even better.'

'The collider project is of major significance, isn't it?'

Darri laughed.

'That's stating it mildly. Hasn't Jarra been talking about it on your weekly walks?'

'Not really. Mirri took our full attention last week because it was a new walk for all of us, and the week before that I was in New Zealand.'

'Well, Yirgella is expanding a new underground site with enough living space for nearly two thousand people and building secure testing areas for the components. The collider itself will have a circumference of just under 2 kilometres and become one of the most important facilities for basic science research in the world.'

'Two kilometres around? That's a huge machine.'

Darri gave her a funny look.

'Alira, you don't know much about colliders. Two kilometres is tiny, and that's one of the significant things about it. The biggest collider on the planet is the famous one in Europe and it's 27 kilometres. If it works properly, Jarra's collider will be three times as powerful.'

'If? Surely there can't be any doubt? Jarra's a perfectionist with everything he makes.'

'Yirgella's not sure. He thinks it will from the individual component tests, but he can't do proper simulations till he gets actual working data. Jarra's not worried though. If something doesn't work he says he'll figure out why and go on from there.'

'You think he can?'

'Make it work? Yes, I do, Alira. He can't proceed with his overall project till it does, and making ideas work is his biggest talent. You know what he's like when he gets focused.'

'Yes, and what happens then?'

'Well, apart from reserving first priority for all the experiments he and Yirgella will want to do, he'll hand it over to the collider scientists and get on with his plans for the next one.'

'You're serious? I know you must be, but why? Kyrra says this collider will cost as much as establishing four new AIs.'

'The cost means nothing to them. The second collider will be specially designed for research about positrons.'

'Those antimatter things? I remember that much. Has Kyrra heard about this?'

Darri shook his head.

'Good. Take me through the basics for the second collider research and I'll be able to dazzle him with his own science.'

Chapter 20

'He's announced that he'll be presenting a series of papers on his research when the world Energy Conference meets in Geneva two months from now.'

'What's wrong with that? He's had meetings and discussions with many of those scientists over the course of this project and it sounds like the appropriate place to get the recognition he deserves.'

Darri was talking with Alira about Jarra's decision to travel to Geneva.

'Yirgella doesn't want him to go, Alira. He's worried it might be dangerous, and I agree with him. The scientists and researchers we now have at Alkere and the Mparntwe University are more eminent than the overseas ones anyway, and they've also had a higher degree of involvement with him. We're trying to persuade him to make his presentation here in Mparntwe.'

'So why does he want Geneva? He always has reasons.'

'Yes, he says his discovery is for the world and the world Energy Conference is the right place to present it. We all agree with that, but the reaction against his Power Supply has been quite frightening.'

Alira stared.

'Why? A new power source helps everyone.'

'It's too much change, and it's coming from Jarra who is closely linked with the AIs.'

Alira shook her head in disgust.

'Not again! The same Corporations and governments?'

'Yes, and particularly the governments because it reduces one of the methods of control over their populations.'

'Directed governments! I'll never understand them. Why haven't I heard of this, Darri? There's been nothing on the InterWeb.'

'There have been murmurings ... but you're right, most of it has been behind closed doors. Yirgella knows though. He's never stopped monitoring their activities and he's very concerned.'

'Yirgella's security is the best in the world. He'll protect Jarra.'

'That's what Jarra says but Yirgella's not so sure. It's very difficult to protect one individual in those gigantic European Communities. Their security systems aren't as good as ours and he wouldn't have direct control like he does with ours. The biggest danger among the masses of population there would be a small team trained to work without electronic backup. They'd be practically invisible till they took some sort of action.'

'Two months. That's very short notice but I'll see if I can negotiate to bring the Conference here. I think our growing scientific community might have enough influence to make that happen.'

Darri was very enthusiastic about that.

'Yes. That's a great idea. It makes sense, too, because with all the structures and research Jarra and Yirgella have developed, Alkere is the real centre for world energy anyway. Add the incentive of seeing a working positronic power supply first-hand and they mightn't be able to resist coming.'

Alira grinned.

'We'll throw in free travel round Australia on the Vac Trains for a two-week period.'

'Take them to see the NanoFactory complex at Birringurra and offer them places at the symbolic deconstruction of the first Alkere solar array.'

'Deconstruction? Darri, are we pulling it down?'

'Of course. They're all redundant now and the land will steadily be reclaimed.'

'Another thing I haven't been told about. What will happen to Alkere Inc? Will Burnu have to find a new job?'

'Alkere Inc will grow and become more important than ever. The solar arrays will gradually diminish but geothermal output will continue and Burnu will be busier than ever administering the new facility when the Power Supplies go into production.'

'Has Jarra relaxed at all?'

'He's very excited. The successful test of their prototype last week was the biggest moment ever for his work with Yirgella, and he laughs all the time because Mirri keeps telling everyone he's the best scientist in the world. I don't think he'll really relax till the Mparntwe power station is built, though, and they go on their holiday with Karmai and the twins.'

'Is the holiday definite? He hasn't had a proper holiday for ages.'

'It's locked in, Alira. They're spending a week at Gariwerd in Victoria, a week in Tasmania, and then a week at Birringurra and Monkey Mia.'

'They're away such a long time? I'll miss more walks.'

'That's clever planning on our part. If he stays at Mparntwe he'll find things to do out here at Alkere. You could easily join them for a day at Gariwerd or Birringurra.'

'Does he have much to do? There must be finishing-up work before he starts any new project.'

'There won't be a new project for ages. They'll be working to refine their ideas and establish the most reliable production models for months yet. It will be like the nano project and never really end.'

* * *

'Will you see the lights with us, Yirgy?'

'Not through your ComPatches, Mirri, but when Jarra sends them through his InfoPad I will.'

Mirri was intrigued about the special lights that were going to be in the sky while they were away on their biggest explore trip ever.

'Can we see them tonight?'

'Yirgy doesn't make them, Mirri. The sun does, and they won't get strong enough to see for another two weeks yet, and that's when we're at Hollow Mountain.'

'Will we go inside the mountain?'

'You will, Mirri. It will be too steep for me, but you'll tell me what it's like.'

'Two weeks is a long time.'

Jarra laughed and bumped against Mirri. His eagerness to see the special lights, really the Aurora Australis being excited by a solar flare predicted for the same time as their excursion, was catching.

'No, it's not. It's only fourteen days and we'll be seeing Karmai and Barega and Akama.'

Jarra was right. Mirri would be so busy the time would fly.

'You've got three guiding expeditions to Uluru and then another one, and after that you have to organise all our holiday supplies and equipment.'

'Yes, it's a lot of work. Yirgy will help me.'

'I certainly will, Mirri, and we'll make sure you have everything ready when Karmai gets here.'

*   *   *

Rather proudly, Jarra flipped the switch to bring the Mparntwe Positronic Power Supply online. The switch was temporary, built for this momentous occasion. The success of the working model had been far more exciting, of course, but the completion of this unit, Mparntwe's new energy supply, would be the practical demonstration to the rest of the world of what he and Yirgella had

achieved. Yes, he was rather proud, gathered with the Council
and Alkere project leaders, that his project had finally proved
successful. Even Yirgella had doubted its feasibility till the last
six months, and his own confidence had been tested for eight
months of the previous year when every approach seemed to go
nowhere. Nearly five years of constant work. Five years which,
even providing he had the backing of a wealthy Community
like Mparntwe, should have taken a lifetime. Yirgella's resources,
especially the NanoFactory, had made it all possible.

*   *   *

'I know what will happen, Yirgella—all sorts of things and you
won't tell me about them. I'll get back and it will take weeks to
catch up with all your surprises.'

'Not this time. The only new thing I haven't told you about is
the Positronic Power Supply for our underground Community.
I've decided to build it now rather than wait for new refinements.
The major work while you're away will be the production plant,
and you know about that. Anything else will be a surprise for
me as well. You're right though. While you're away I expect you
to relax and enjoy your adventures. I do have one decision I'd
like you to make right now and then forget.'

'What is it?'

'We've received a financial offer for the rights to the Power
Supply.'

'That's silly. Some of the components can only be built with a
NanoFactory and that means an AI has to be involved ... Is it one
of our Communities, or Canberra or Freedom?'

'We'd continue doing the building but hand over the control of
prices and distribution. It's a vast amount of income, Jarra. We'd
recover the investment we've made for the whole project with the
first payment and the amount would increase with every year.'

Jarra thought for a moment then stared at Yirgella's image.

'We're not going to accept any offer. That's my view. It's our invention and Burnu will do all the marketing and distribution at prices we think are fair. There's something you're not telling me, though, isn't there? You wouldn't be expecting me to make an on the spot decision about so much finance otherwise.'

'Excellent. We share the same view. And you're right, the offer comes from the people behind the early attacks and the current AI-related sanctions.'

Jarra was totally taken aback.

'An agreement with them? Yirgella, they can't be serious.'

'The fronting Corporation making the offer is quite reputable. I had to follow a devious trail to find the real backers, and, yes, they're very serious. They understand just how important our new Positronic Power Supply is, and getting some form of control will be a top priority. I expect the governments involved will legislate for jurisdiction over any of our Power Supplies which enter their countries when we reject this offer.'

'Well that will be their problem because they won't get any if they try that. The rest of the world will get them first.'

*   *   *

Jarra watched the family huddled round Mirri, totally engrossed, as he showed them the green frog he'd caught. They were in the Valley of Eagles with a small but very important group of people from America who'd heard about the unique experience of one of Mirri's guided trips from Alira and expressed an interest in trying it out. Normally it was rare for Jarra to see any of Mirri's work expeditions because they only happened during his four days at Alkere, and coming along now was a great opportunity. Back at the Explorer Centre he'd been worried that his presence might take too much of Mirri's attention but, no, this was Mirri's proper job and when the group of six people arrived he'd greeted them as if they were friends he'd known forever.

Oh my, no wonder Mirri's trips had a reputation. Their surprise at this greeting had quickly changed to curiosity, the realisation that this friendly person was indeed quite different and then to interest as he chatted eagerly about some of the things they might like to see. The Valley of Eagles had really struck a chord, and when one of the men said the eagle was a special symbol for American people the choice of trip for the day was instantly agreed.

Mirri laughed happily because it was his favourite place to take people exploring and the group had been pulled into their own smiles.

'Little frog is very clever. He breathes through his skin in the water and he barks in the night time.'

'Does he really bark?'

'Funny bark. JJ showed me at the Nature Park.'

The group looked at Jarra. He was staying in the background as much as possible, but by now they all understood how important he was to Mirri and he gave a nod of agreement but didn't say anything. Mirri looked down at his pendant ComPatch.

'Yirgy, please make the barker frog sound.'

The InfoPad on Jarra's personal carrier immediately sounded and everyone looked over again. When the sample sound finished, one of the senators asked Mirri if Yirgy was his nickname for Jarra. Mirri didn't know what nickname meant and answered that Yirgy was his friend then left it to the helper guides to explain. They in turn must have thought it was more appropriate for Jarra to answer and looked to him.

'Yirgy is Mirrigan's name for Yirgella, our Alkere AI, and he watches everything Mirrigan does through our special ComPatches. Mirrigan asked him to send the sound to my InfoPad.'

The senator looked astonished.

'Mirrigan talks to the AI when he's out here? ... And uses a nickname? ... And those pendants are ComPatches?'

'Yirgella has a special relationship with Mirrigan and watches over him wherever he goes. Our pendants are high performance, high security ComPatches designed for people associated with Yirgella or Mirrigan.'

Looks passed between the four adults and the father of the teenagers, the state governor, spoke first.

'You mean the AI is here right now?'

Jarra nodded and was about to say more but the InfoPad speakers sounded with Yirgella's voice.

'Hello, Mirri. Can I interrupt your exploring for a moment and speak to your friends?'

'Yirgy! We have a tree frog. Can you see him?'

Mirri's delight at hearing Yirgella was evident, as was his agreement that he could say anything he wanted.

'Yes, he's magnificent, isn't he? I think you should let the young ones have a closer look. Governor, greetings to you and your family and companions. I don't intrude on Mirrigan's expeditions unless he requests it. Because Mirrigan and Jarra are our most important human acquaintances we like to keep a watch out for them whenever possible, and the pendant ComPatches facilitate that in locations near our facilities. If privacy is a concern I will delete all data relating to your trip as it comes to me. Rather than interrupt your encounter with the Centralian Tree Frog I will answer any questions when Alira introduces you formally at our arranged meeting tomorrow. Happy exploring, Mirri.'

Mirri smiled then took over again and persuaded the teenage girl to carefully hold the frog for a moment before letting it go 'home'. The girl looked very diffident about touching it, and when Jarra asked Mirri later why he'd chosen her to hold it instead of her brother, Mirri told him that she liked the frog more and it would be happy with her friendly hands. In the valley, when it was time for lunch, Jarra waited, with some embarrassment, but not really, while Mirri co-opted the whole group to help make a proper bed so he could rest comfortably while they went farther along to check for any activity at an eagle's eyrie which Mirri had discovered on a previous expedition. Jarra caught the smile passing between Mirri's two helper guides and, wondering what he'd missed, gave them a querying look.

'It happens all the time, Jarra. No ordinary guide would have two senators, a state governor and two fairly spoilt youngsters happily running hither and thither for grass and leaves to help make a bed. That boy was almost obnoxious at the Explorer Centre while we were waiting for Mirrigan to arrive.'

That boy, with no sign of any obnoxious behaviour or attitude, sat right next to Mirri while everyone ate the packed lunches the helper guides produced from their backpacks. His sister sat on the other side and they both asked non-stop questions about things they'd seen or might expect to see. It was interesting to see the contrast between the fair complexion of the Americans and Mirri's almost ebony skin and thick hair. The adults were just as involved and Jarra sensed that some of their questions came from curiosity and anticipation for the way Mirri might answer and some from the startling revelation of his regard by the AIs. When a question was too complex or about something he didn't know the helper guides would give an answer then fall quiet and let the attention return to Mirri. That didn't happen much, though, because the group had quickly adopted a suitable pattern of speech.

The lunch finished and Mirri gave what Jarra recognised as one of his checking looks.

'JJ has to sleep now. He has bad muscles. We will be very quiet and explore the eyrie.'

Chapter 21

Mirri, with Yirgella's help, did a perfect job of organising their holiday equipment and now that the first day had finally arrived, the pair of them, along with Alira, Darri, and most of Mirri's family, were waiting at the Vac Train terminal for Karmai and the twins. The last three nights Mirri had painstakingly packed and repacked his big rucksack to make sure everything he was meant to have was present and in its right place, and under Jarra's scrutiny he'd adjusted the various straps to find the most comfortable position. This was his first 'real' explorer's pack, loaded with enough supplies for eight days in the wild at Gariwerd, and he was so proud he'd taken it to Alkere and on several trips around Mparntwe for 'wearing in' which was a phrase he'd learned from Jarra. Jarra was loaded with even more things and the big satchel, which was designed especially to attach to the personal carrier without interfering with the twin's footrests, contained a self-administering kit for the health bots he would need every second day, the thermal shelter for use if there was rain or if the nights got cold, as well as all the normal clothes and supplies.

'How long, JJ?'

Jarra was just as eager as Mirri to see Karmai and the twins and to get started on their adventure, and he'd been keeping a close eye on the arrival display.

'Two more minutes till the train gets here and then they have to come through the pressure portal. Who do you think will be first?'

The train was surrounded by vacuum so there was no platform

and a pressurised tube had to lock into place before the exit doors could open.

Mirri laughed. He always got this right.

'Barega will run. He wants the first hug.'

'It might be different today. They'll have extra things to carry.'

Mirri puzzled that through.

'... They will run and Karmai will carry things.'

And, of course, Mirri was right. The portal opened and the first person to dash through was Barega and there was laughter all round when he jumped from the ground right into Mirri's arms. Akama was right behind him, and because Mirri was occupied he came to Jarra.

'Uncle JJ!'

The twins were more and more a part of Jarra and Mirri's lives and there were constant get-togethers, either from Mirri's regular trips to help out with the Birringurra corroborees, or visits to Karmai and the fascinating world of Shark Bay and Monkey Mia. With the Vac Train trip taking only half an hour they'd occasionally turn up at Mparntwe as well. Mirri's idea that they should come on the big adventure had them almost leaping out of their skins with eagerness and the family concerns that six days of walking in bush country might be too difficult for eleven year old boys had been brushed aside with cries that they were almost twelve and that made a big difference, and if Jarra could do it so could they, and that Karmai was a proper ranger and could look after anyone in the bush. Jarra gave Akama an enthusiastic hug.

'Are you all excited and ready for our holiday?'

'Barega is like a madman. He's been driving everyone to distraction with all his comments and demands.'

Distraction? That must be a description from someone else in the family. Akama could well have come up with it himself, because his knowledge of words and manner of speaking was more striking than ever, but somehow it sounded more like a description from an older person. Jarra's smile and happy feelings grew at the sight of Karmai coming through the portal festooned with luggage.

'Karmai!'

Mirri rushed to greet his brother with a bone crushing hug. He hadn't seen him for two whole months which, in Mirri terms, was the same as forever.

'Explorer man. This is going to be our best adventure yet.'

'We will see lights in the sky and go inside the mountain.'

Karmai nodded and pointed to everyone else to let Mirri know he had other people to greet. The rest of the hugs were much gentler, except for Burnu's. The whole group, nearly twenty people, made its way to the terminal for the Adelaide Vac Train and, after a multitude of hugs and well wishes, the five holidaymakers entered the pressure portal and got themselves organised. Jarra's personal carrier had to be secured in a special compartment with other larger pieces of luggage.

The inter-city Vac Trains were bigger then the Mparntwe to Alkere train, with three seats on each side of the central aisle, and Mirri took over the seating allocation when both twins wanted to sit next to him. He shook his head and put Jarra next to him, Akama on the other side of Jarra in the window seat, and Barega across the aisle with Karmai on his other side. It wasn't really a window. All you'd see would be the tunnel walls, because glass couldn't be made strong enough, but to make the journey more interesting a display screen with a view changing to match the above-ground scene was mounted beside each wall seat. Jarra thought it was a brilliant idea.

As soon as he was buckled in he activated the small info screen on the back of the chair in front of him and found the travel data page. While Mirri was never interested in train statistics, Jarra was, and making a quick check he saw that today there were

2735 people travelling in eight linked sections with a current speed of 0 km/h. On the busy east coast link between Sydney and Melbourne he knew the maximum of twelve linked sections was pretty much the norm, but this seemed to be very busy for the Alice Springs to Adelaide run. The buckling up finished and when the train started Mirri made his laughs of enjoyment while the several minutes of acceleration lasted. He still called it very, very fun, and, indeed, this prolonged acceleration was a feature which helped attract visitors to Australia from all over the world.

'Why is Mirri always so happy, Uncle Jarra?'

'We don't really know, Akama. It's a special part of him that's just there, like you always asking questions, or Barega making his pictures.'

Mirri heard this of course.

'JJ makes me happy and twins make me happy and Karmai is my big brother.'

'Can we fit everything on the personal carrier? It might get overloaded.'

'Yirgella has redesigned it slightly so it can carry two boys and their packs as well as my satchel. You'll see when we start walking.'

'Will we see a koala? I've never seen a wild one and our dad said we have to watch carefully because they live at Gariwerd.'

'We hope so. Mirri and I have only seen them at the Nature Park so we'll be watching hard too.'

Jarra looked at Karmai.

'I've seen lots of koalas, Akama. My ranger training took to me to places all over Australia so I could learn about all sorts of animals. There aren't very many at Gariwerd, though, so we'll need Mirri's eyes to see them.'

Mirri and the boys nodded their agreement at this clever idea.

'Why is your new Power Supply so important, Uncle Jarra.? Our dad says it's the best invention since the computer.'

'Everyone's inventions are important, Akama, because a new one can't happen without all the old ones making it possible, but I suppose our Power Supply is good because it will help make Communities better.'

'My dad says we'll only need one for the whole of Carnarvon and Birringurra. Will that be enough to run our NanoFactories at the same time?'

'Easily. We'll just build one the right size.'

'Will it be soon?'

'Yirgella says the big factory for making them will be finished when we get back from our holiday, but you'll have to ask Mirri's dad for the exact date because he's in charge of all that.'

'I think all the AIs will get them first. Will there be plenty of water at Gariwerd? We need it for our dried food.'

Akama's barrage of questions continued with varying degrees of intensity through all three legs of the journey till Mirri's excitement at seeing the ranges of Gariwerd and then Mount Zero, their landing destination, from the windows of their chartered transport aircraft, focused everyone's silent attention. They weren't very high mountains but Jarra was intrigued because his checking had told him they were so ancient that all the height had been eroded away. After watching the aircraft depart Mirri shouldered his pack and wanted to know where to go.

Karmai thought that was funny.

'Jarra isn't even on his personal carrier yet, Mirri, and the boys are drowning lizards behind that rock. Do you want to leave without them?'

'Are there lizards?'

By the time Mirri worked out what Karmai was talking about everyone was ready. Because this area was sometimes used by rock climbers there was an obvious pathway and Mirri confidently led the way for the 20 minutes it took to reach the approach to Hollow Mountain where they were setting up camp.

Jarra climbed off his personal carrier and stared at the imposing rock faces towering above. No way would he be able to get up there. Karmai and Mirri would have to lift and carry him most of the way. Never mind. Close by there were large boulders and 10-metre rock formations jutting from the ground and he'd be able to use the personal carrier to explore them.

'Karmai, I think I'll have a rest and then look at all these boulders while you see the caves.'

Mirri gave his checkup look and laughed.

'No tricking, JJ. We saw you resting on the aeroplane. We will help you.'

Half an hour later Jarra was sitting on some soft red sand, with a cavern wall sloping back over his head, and taking in the panorama of odd-shaped rock formations below and scrubby trees stretching into the distance.

The rest he didn't need before was now imperative, but the effort to get here had been completely worth it. Not his own effort. Apart from a few sections where the track temporarily levelled and he could walk for himself, all the carrying and lifting had been done by Karmai and Mirri, Karmai good-heartedly groaning and insisting Jarra weighed as much as the mountains and Mirri happily following Karmai's instructions as to the best way to lift Jarra past various obstructions or carry him up steep sections. The twins had been the scouts, returning with advice about what was ahead and watching carefully at all the tricky bits.

The others were heading off to explore, and right now Karmai was demonstrating to the boys how to edge their way up a 3-metre cleft with their backs against one rock wall and their feet on the opposing face. Mirri didn't have to learn. He'd always been adept at any climbing or clambering activities. The sounds muted and Jarra composed himself and closed his eyes. There was an hour before they needed to return. Plenty of time for a good recovery sleep.

*   *   *

With a full moon just rising through a gap between two of the nearby rock formations, the astounding sight of the Aurora Australis shimmering in the sky and the happy chatter of Mirri and the twins round their little campfire, Jarra was almost overwhelmed with pleasure and wonder. Karmai was quiet, but Jarra understood that, like himself, he was appreciating the moment. The brilliance of the colours was beyond any of the examples Jarra had seen at home when he'd checked the InterWeb for information, and Yirgella's warning that the solar flare causing it all was one of the strongest for decades and very likely to interrupt their InterWeb communication, had just evidenced itself.

'Does it burn the sky, JJ?'

'No, it doesn't, Mirri, but it looks like it. Your ancestors used to think it was a bad fire happening in the spirit world.'

'The red lights are angry.'

'They're so angry we can't talk to Yirgy till they go away.'

'Are they stronger than Yirgy?'

This meant explaining the signals between satellites, the local communication towers and their InfoPads.

'Yirgy talks to us through stations in the sky and the lights don't let them work properly, but they don't hurt Yirgy, if that's what you mean.'

A new curtain of red flared and shimmered above and, after their exclamations of wonder, everyone watched silently. Karmai added a piece of wood to the fire and attention momentarily shifted to the swirl of sparks. Barega rescued his fire stick and waved the glowing end to make a pattern of after-image, and when Akama followed suit Jarra mused how different forms of light were making this night special.

'Can we stay here an extra day to explore Hollow Mountain properly? We could make our holiday a bit longer.'

'Yes, yes! Can we do that, Uncle Jarra?'

'We could, but then we'd have to miss out on the Elephant's Hide and Wartook Waters, or rush past everything else too quickly to explore properly. If we do take an extra day here then we'll have less time in Tasmania, and Mirri wants to see the quolls and the Tasmanian Devils.'

Mirri's keen agreement with the boys changed at the idea of not being able to explore properly or see new animals, but then Karmai's comments about the Flat Rock and the Amphitheatre and the Taipan Walls quickly restored everyone's eagerness for the next day's plans. Barega pointed out the Southern Cross and when Mirri said he liked the stars Akama took over and showed everyone a succession of constellations. Jarra was impressed.

'How do you know them all?'

'There's a telescope at Birringurra and I look at them with my dad. He thinks there are planets where different creatures live, and I do too. I would love to go and explore the stars.'

'Can we explore the stars, JJ?'

'No, Mirri. They're too far away and our spaceships would take hundreds of years to get there.'

'Could your Power Supply make the ships go faster, Uncle Jarra? If it's strong enough to run a whole city it might be able to.'

'Not really. The energy would have to be converted to thrust and the size of the ship needed would ...'

Jarra broke off, startled, as he put his mind properly to Akama's query. Thrust was a primary feature of the positronic power process and one of the greatest headaches had been negating its effect. What Akama was asking for meant emphasising the effect, not negating it, and that was definitely possible ... Directing the energy with magnetic fields rather than containing it ...Yes, there had even been theoretical designs to do just that for decades.

'Uncle Jarra?'

'JJ is thinking.'

The comments worked their way through Jarra's deep concentration and he impulsively grabbed Akama's arm.

'What a question! You've just opened my eyes and I can't believe I didn't think of using our Power Supply ideas that way. You're a wonder, Akama, and when I get this worked out it will be because of you. Yirgella is going to be amazed.'

'You think you can use your Power Supplies as engines for spaceships?'

That was Karmai.

'Not the Power Supplies as such—their design is wrong for that—but if we direct the thrust instead of containing it, it should work.'

Jarra lifted Akama's arm towards the shimmering lights above in a kind of victory gesture.

'An engine for a spaceship will be my new project, and if I can make it work the five explorers will take a special trip.'

Jarra pointed Akama's arm at the rising moon to indicate his meaning then let it go. He watched with thoughts racing then laughed at the expressions revealed by the light of the campfire. Karmai and the twins were staring at him, not the Moon, and Mirri, sensing something unusual, was looking from one to the other.

'What happened, JJ?'

'I surprised everyone, Mirri. I said we can go and explore the Moon.'

Mirri looked up at the object in question then wanted to know if there were any animals there. Barega quickly told him there was no air then joined Akama in bombarding Jarra with more questions.

'It would be a different kind of spaceship, Akama. Space rockets have huge acceleration for their takeoff then coast to get to where they're going and then have a huge deceleration to make them stop.'

'Like the Vac Trains?'

'Yes, but rockets are much more powerful. The engine I'm

thinking about wouldn't have to coast and it would travel to places much faster.'

'How long to get to the Moon?'

Jarra grabbed his InfoPad.

'I don't know how strong the engines could be till I work out a lot of things with Yirgella, but if we keep it comfortable and say normal gravity strength it would be ... Umm ... About 3.5 hours.'

The answer surprised Jarra himself till the reality of constant acceleration settled in his mind, and while he gave answers to the steady flow of questions he tried again to make contact with Yirgella. The shimmering sky blocked every effort.

*   *   *

Cozy and warm under his insulated cover, Jarra listened to the morning calls of the parrots, magpies and kookaburras, and didn't want to move. Early light brightened the top side of the thermal shelter and for a few minutes he watched its slow downward progress and smiled at the chatter coming from the boys in the adjacent shelter. It wouldn't be long before their eagerness would have them dressed and active and everyone else would have to follow. Sure enough, the band of brightness had only descended a little farther when the entrance zipper slowly opened and Akama's head peeked in.

'Would you like a hot drink, Uncle Jarra? We started the stove going and the water is heating.'

His soft voice was enough to wake Mirri who immediately crawled from under the cover and reached for his clothes. How did he sleep through the loud bird sounds yet wake at Akama's muted question? Mirri gave Jarra a morning hug then shook Karmai awake. There'd be no more comfortable relaxing now. The explorer was in action.

*   *   *

Jarra sat up and reached for the scroggin pack hanging conveniently beside him on the personal carrier. A handful of the high-energy mixture satisfied his yen to eat and he looked for any sign of the others. There wasn't any, and a time check revealed that there was still a quarter of an hour before he could expect them back. It also revealed that there was still no InterWeb connection.

After all the morning's adventures a time of rest and sleep had been more important than usual and, because it wasn't very far, Jarra had encouraged the others along a sidetrack to explore the top of the range and some caves and rock features he'd noted in his trip research. The twins had been particularly eager to reach the Ghost Caves, and with a name like that Jarra could only agree.

The view here was inspiring and he looked back where the track had taken them through the Amphitheatre—a valley that lived up to its name—and gazed at the red rock faces of the Taipan Walls. Farther away was Flat Rock, the first major feature they'd explored after they left their camping spot. Not really as flat as its name suggested, it had tested Jarra's considerable skill to manoeuvre past tricky sections and obstacles, and Mirri and Karmai had needed to manhandle the personal carrier four times in places he couldn't make it go. The valley of the Amphitheatre had been particularly slow going and had taken most of the morning, despite being only a couple of kilometres and the track being straightforward travelling for the personal carrier. Mirri explored every interesting feature as it presented and it seemed as if every 20 or 30 metres there would be a new rock shelf, boulder formation, cliff face or possible shelter. Karmai and the boys went with him on every little sortie and returned to listen and add to his happy report.

Jarra had left his personal carrier twice: once to explore a cleft in the rocks which Mirri described as an easy cave, and again to sit beneath an overhanging wall of rock in the soft, richly coloured sand, which had eroded over time, and gaze at the distant plain. Alira should be here. She loved her walks with Mirri, and Jarra wished he'd thought of persuading her to come with them.

Jarra stood up and looked at the track heading south. There was quite a way to go to reach their evening campsite and there were sure to be more interesting diversions which would slow their progress—he hoped the others wouldn't be much longer. Karmai would be conscious of the time, though, and after an hour away Mirri would be pushing everyone to get back too. He looked at the clear blue sky and thought they couldn't have had a better day, then walked to a cluster of trigger plants beside the track and looked for a thin stem of grass. Karmai had shown them earlier how to tease the throat of the flower and trick the plant into thinking a little insect was looking for pollen or nectar. Jarra did this now and watched the trigger snap against the false insect. A real insect would be trapped and slowly dissolved to provide nutrients.

Two hundred kilometres above, where the blue for an observer would have changed to deepest black, a low orbit communication satellite approached the optimum position for connection with the ground relay tower at the top of Mount Zero, 4.8 kilometres by line of sight from where Jarra was kneeling.

Relays clicked as external commands overrode standard safety levels and power drained unsustainably from the storage batteries as transmission power surged higher and higher. At almost eight times the normal maximum allowable level the amplification forced the signal through the interference from the solar flare and the tower receptors passed hastily designed data packets to the antenna of Jarra's InfoPad.

In the 2.3 seconds before the tower receptors frizzled beyond repair, seven identical modules transmitted at seven different frequencies stored themselves then tried to function. Four had been corrupted by the ongoing solar storm but the other three took control and activated the built-in speakers.

Jarra, engrossed in teasing a third little trigger to snap into place, swivelled his head towards his InfoPad. Strange, he hadn't set any alarms, and stranger still that the insistent beeping wasn't a sound he'd ever heard it make. Maybe it was a warning signal for some developing fault? He moved to investigate, and at 3 metres distance the sight of the screen flashing red changed his puzzlement to unease. The trigger plant totally forgotten, he picked up the InfoPad and touched the large action icon. The URGENT prompt disappeared and a message appeared on the screen.

Jarra, you are in grave danger. Before you read further, move everyone from open view.

There was another action icon and Jarra understood it was a device to emphasise the need to move. Danger? Jarra automatically started to look round, then realised he should be moving. Thirty seconds later the personal carrier was 20 metres down the track and parked between some head-high shrubs.

Several minutes ago I monitored a conversation referring to the status of a plan for your abduction. Help is on the way but won't arrive for another 76 minutes.

With mounting worry Jarra read the salient points and figured the best way to follow Yirgella's directions. Where were the others? He read more, keeping an eye out, till 6 minutes later he heard a cooee. Oh no! The penetrating call would announce their presence to anyone in the area, but at least it was close. A few minutes later Barega appeared, and while Jarra was waving for attention Akama joined him. Akama saw Jarra first and when he started running Barega followed. Jarra, thinking they might call out, automatically signed for silence then felt a degree of relief at the sight of Mirri and Karmai.

'Uncle Jarra, we reached the top and it was scary. We—'

Jarra's expression registered and Barega's rush stopped abruptly. Both boys, seeing Jarra's tension, waited quietly for the few seconds it took Mirri and Karmai to arrive.

'JJ, what happened?'

Mirri knew the instant he saw Jarra that something was wrong.

'There are bad people here, Mirri, and we have to get away from them.'

Four heads looked round.

'What happened?'

Karmai's question sought information rather than assurance.

'Yirgella discovered that some people are here to abduct me and we have to get away from this track.'

'What is abduct?'

'It means they will take me away, Mirri. They want to make me tell them everything about our new Power Supply.'

'We will stop them.'

'They'll be too strong, but if we're quick and careful they won't find us. Yirgella thinks they are a small military team somewhere ahead of us and he wants us to go back the other way and hide. Karmai, we should start moving now.'

'What about our packs? Will we collect them?'

'No. Help's arriving in just over an hour and the packs will only slow us down.'

Jarra had a thought.

'Go back and hide them though. If they're close and heard the cooees they might come looking. We'll wait for you where we have to leave the track.'

Karmai ran. Jarra told the twins to jump on the back of the personal carrier then set off with Mirri trotting close behind. Karmai caught up when Jarra paused for a moment to consult the map on his InfoPad.

'Anywhere along here we have to head west.'

'Through the bush? You're going to leave the personal carrier behind?'

'You and Mirri can get it through because there's another road only 50 metres away, and I'll need it because it's nearly 2 kilometres to where we can hide properly.'

The bush bash was really hard going and Jarra and the personal carrier had to be lifted or helped most of the way. It was a relief to be off the main track, though, and then more relief when the twins discovered a slight deviation which allowed Jarra to drive the personal carrier for the last 15 metres. Jarra closed his eyes for a few seconds to gather himself. Thank goodness the rest of the way was all negotiable from the comfort of his personal carrier seat. He'd explained the route as they moved: 600 metres along this Pohlners Rd, 300 metres along a joining track and then 500 metres along another old road to a rocky shelter.

'JJ needs to rest.'

'Not now, Mirri. I had a big rest before and we'll soon be at the shelter.'

Indeed, with the boys on the back and both Mirri and Karmai so strong and fit, the remaining 1400 metres wouldn't take much more than 10 minutes.

Fifty metres along the road the world changed.

Chapter 22

A lerted by the carrying call of a cooee, three trained agents rushed to station themselves at a high point very close to Jarra's resting place. Two stayed at the commanding viewpoint while the third scouted for any signs of the quarry they knew must be close. Traces of footprints, some vegetation flattened as if someone had been lying flat, then the glisten of a pack buckle through a gap in a low shrub informed the practised mind that the target group had been right here. The cooee indicated separation but the physical characteristics of their specific target meant movement from the defined track was unlikely. A look at the packs thrown helter-skelter behind the scrub indicated haste, and quite likely abandonment and an unexpected retreat to the north. The mercenary was about to regroup with his team when the sharp crack of a projectile weapon sounded, again, and then again.

* * *

Cruel providence gave a clear view of a short section of the old road running somewhat parallel to the hiking track and movement instantly caught the eye of the watchers.

The target? Yes, there was the distinctive mobility device described in the background dossier. Were the track deviations and obvious haste indications that the mission was compromised? Yes. With only seconds before the group disappeared behind a bank of trees the leader decided the transportation device must be immobilised.

*   *   *

Jarra had just enough time to register a strange little cry from Barega when the personal carrier jolted, swerved unaccountably sideways and sent him sprawling at the edge of the road. The shock of hitting the ground and rolling disoriented him till he sat up and saw the personal carrier tipped on its side. What? Had it seized or part of the wheel mechanism jammed? Jarra looked to see if the twins were all right after their tumble. Akama was scrambling to his feet, but just when the sight of Barega on the ground sent a worry signal to Jarra's brain, he was shocked to feel himself lifted with incredible force, dragged, then dumped in the nearby bushes.

'Get off the track!'

Shocked by the imperative in Karmai's yell and momentarily puzzled by the red smear that had somehow appeared on his shirt, Jarra watched Mirri and Akama kneel beside Barega with complete disregard for Karmai's order. Karmai frightened Jarra by racing and lifting the limp body as if it were weightless and rushing everyone into the scrub. With total disbelief Jarra watched Karmai, a great red blotch spread on the arm of his shirt, gently lower Barega beside him. Mirri was the first to break the frozen moment. He lifted Barega, hugged him close and, willing life to return, rocked him back and forth as if comforting a little baby.

'Barega has gone away.'

The tears welling from Mirri's eyes sent the horror of full realisation stabbing through Jarra's mind. The song of pure sadness welling from Mirri's throat, a song of love and grief for someone in his world, stabbed Jarra's very heart. It was too much. He felt himself going and fought to stay awake but all his body limits were overcome and consciousness faded.

*   *   *

Kind providence now blocked the view of the two hunters who paused just long enough to plan their pursuit before jogging down the track to regroup.

∗   ∗   ∗

Mirri's cry cut off and his attention went to Jarra who'd slumped from his sitting position. He put Barega down and moved close to Jarra.

'JJ, please wake up.'

'I don't think he will, Mirri. We'll have to look after him. Would you give Akama a hug while I fix my arm? He's so scared and sad he needs your help.'

Akama was in shock and staring silently. For the second time Mirri's hug enveloped a young body and rocked for comfort while Karmai hastily ripped the sleeve from his shirt and bound his wounded arm.

Karmai's mind worked rapidly. Exactly where the attack had come from he didn't know but most likely it was a vantage point somewhere along the walking track and time must be critical. People prepared to kill a child simply to disable the personal carrier had to be avoided at all costs. They had to move. How to do it? Crouching low, with an eye in the direction where he feared danger, he scrambled to the personal carrier and collected Jarra's InfoPad, the first aid kit, Jarra's health machine, and several straps from the big satchel.

'Mirri, they want to take Jarra so we have to get him away from here as fast as we can. Can you carry him?'

'Pig Ride!'

'Yes, but he's not awake so we'll have to tie him on. Akama, will you help with the straps please?'

Lifting Jarra's slack body into place was extraordinarily difficult and for a moment Karmai despaired. No, think it through.

He was starting to worry about Akama too. He hadn't spoken one word.

'Yes! Yes! Thank you, Akama, that's perfect. We couldn't have done it without you.'

* * *

Fifteen minutes later three hunters made a cursory study of the damaged personal carrier, the broken shrubbery and the traces of blood, then jogged on.

* * *

Karmai faltered, wondering if he'd be able to keep going. Then, watching Mirri's steady effort, shuttered the pain and weariness away and caught up. How was Mirri doing this? Jarra, slightly taller than all of them, must be at least three times Barega's weight and a burden which Karmai knew would have beaten him after several hundred metres, yet here they were more than twice that distance with no sign of Mirri stopping for even a short rest. He was definitely struggling. The hard breathing and deep concentration which meant he was partially in his own world showed that. No, he was caring for his JJ and at the moment nothing else mattered. Well, if Mirri could keep going so could he.

Karmai checked Akama, his small pack on his back with the vital InfoPad and other equipment, walking next to Mirri, and worried even more. He'd still hardly spoken and hadn't looked directly at his brother since they started moving, and Karmai wondered if bringing Barega with them was a mistake. At the bad place his mind had said the sensible thing to do was hide him and return later but his heart wouldn't allow it.

* * *

The group leader swore. The clear footprints tracking for 20 metres past that sidetrack in the soft roadside soil had deceived them for nearly 3 minutes till this wind-rippled patch of sand showed that no-one could possibly have passed here.

*   *   *

'Uncle Karmai, this is where we turn off.'

Karmai focused his thoughts. What was wrong with him? He'd cautioned Akama to look out for this track and now he'd nearly walked straight past. At least Akama was talking again. Relief blossomed. They were now only 200 metres from the shelter Yirgella had set as a place of safety. They'd now trudged 300 hundred metres along the joining track, past the old quarry, and battled their way a further 400 metres with the rocky ridges slowly looming closer and closer on their left.

'Try the communication signal and see if anything happens.'

Akama had the InfoPad out to check the incredibly detailed map which had arrived as part of the warning module. He'd started using it when the sight of the old quarry had somehow acted as a trigger to bring him out of his shock. He'd remembered how to activate the signal Jarra had shown them as part of his instructions and tried it twice already. This signal was designed to be secure—unrecognisable to anything except properly matched equipment—and didn't use the standard InfoPad transmission mode. The information module had warned that there was almost certainly some sort of extraction aircraft waiting close by and ordinary attempts at InterWeb connection might reveal their position. Akama shook his head.

'Still too soon, Uncle Karmai.'

'How much time?'

'Twenty-four minutes.'

He adjusted one of the straps holding Jarra secure and pointed along the track.

'This way, Uncle Mirri. Can you reach those rocks?'

'Not far. Little Pig Ride. JJ is sick.'

Fifty metres farther on Mirri stopped.

'JJ is sick. I want his health machine.'

'Just a few more minutes, Mirri. We're nearly there.'

'JJ needs it now. I want it now.'

He meant it. Karmai looked at the overgrown sidetrack on their right but dismissed it as being too obvious and pointed off the road to their left instead.

'In there. We'll hide behind those shrubs.'

Karmai lowered Barega to the ground with the worried realisation that he wasn't strong enough to pick him up again. Tears came at the sight of the still face. Akama was helping Mirri undo the straps and the need to help them diverted the wash of emotion.

'Akama, be quick. Health machine for JJ.'

Karmai saw his own startlement at the tone of demand in Mirri's voice reflected in Akama's haste to remove his pack. In seconds the complex little machine was set up, the infusion pad fixed firmly round Jarra's arm, and four different settings deftly adjusted. Karmai was amazed.

'How did you know to do all that?'

'I watch JJ. So I can care for him. Karmai needs the bandage.'

That was addressed to Akama who was holding the long bandage which had helped keep Jarra secure for the long, long Pig Ride. And indeed, Karmai did need that bandage. His arm, bare since he'd ripped off the sleeve, was a ghastly looking mess of dark dried blood and bright newer ooze, aggravated by constant movement. Karmai reached for the bandage then acquiesced when Akama kept it, opened the first aid kit he'd been carrying and proceeded to carefully clean and dress his wound. Mirri watched for a few seconds then started collecting leaves and grass. JJ was asleep and needed a pillow.

Karmai smiled when Mirri tenderly lifted Jarra's head to arrange some soft support. Just as well he'd made them conceal themselves from the track because they wouldn't be moving again. He relaxed completely when the bandage on his arm was finally pinned. So weary. He closed his eyes, just for a moment, then went to sleep. It wasn't sleep. It was exhaustion from the combined effect of the effort in carrying Barega over a kilometre and the steady loss of blood through his hastily improvised bandage.

*   *   *

Akama saw the smile. He followed Karmai's look to Mirri's tending and understood he'd been touched by the action. Yes, Uncle Mirri would care for anyone—that long, long hug would stay with him for the rest of his life—and he'd care for Uncle Jarra most of all. He finished the bandage and watched Karmai's eyes close. Was he really going to sleep now? Who would know what to do if the bad people came close? ... Sixteen minutes till the aeroplane was here. He could have a sleep then. A shake to wake him got no reaction at all.

'Uncle Mirri, I think Karmai is unconscious.'

Mirri knelt for a close look.

'He is very, very tired. He is like JJ.'

When Mirri gathered more grass and leaves Akama knew it was now his job to think what to do. They couldn't move so making contact with the special signal was all that was left. When the operating light on the health bot machine switched off Mirri disconnected the infusion pad then rested a hand on Jarra's hair and started one of his singing sounds. It was soft and gentle but Akama knew it had to stop and he put a finger to Mirri's lips.

'We have to keep quiet so those people don't hear us.'

Mirri nodded and very seriously made not another sound. Akama activated the signal but there was no response. When Mirri returned from checking Karmai a second time and again gently held Jarra's head the gesture took on so much importance for Akama that he moved to do the same with his brother.

The occasional call of a nearby honeyeater went unnoticed as Akama finally allowed the horrible moments back on the road to replay in his mind.

Another honeyeater call was eclipsed by a sob as he remembered the happy laugh in the Ghost Cave when everyone overreacted to the scary moan.

Akama remembered Barega's trademark concentration last night with the effort of finishing a picture for Uncle Mirri and Uncle Jarra before the dusk turned to darkness, and the smile of pleasure at all the fuss when he handed it over.

Uncle Mirri left Jarra and hugged him close while he cried.

*   *   *

Three hunters came to a halt and the leader cursed at yet another sidetrack which would have to be examined. They all agreed the most likely destination was the rocky outcrop at the end of this track where one possibility was an old shelter of some kind, but their maps also showed a small maze of rocks and other tricky concealment options. One of their quarry, probably the ranger, was using enough deception to slow their pursuit and this sidetrack could well be part of it.

*   *   *

Akama gathered his wits. Uncle Mirri had startled him from his misery by suddenly squeezing him tight and covering his mouth, and now they were sitting, frozen like statues, while the murmur of voices came through the shrubs. Some bad words sounded clear and loud and then there was silence. Akama wondered briefly if his Uncle Mirri might decide to confront the bad people and held tight to the hand which had now moved away from his mouth. Uncle Mirri was unpredictable sometimes.

Taking care not to snap a twig or make any noise because silence was so important, he activated the contact signal. Nothing! And they were meant to be here in 9 minutes. With the InfoPad next to him, and holding Uncle Mirri's hand because it felt good, Akama sat quietly till Uncle Mirri knelt up and looked towards the south-west. That was scary because it was the direction he thought the bad people had gone, but then he heard an engine sound.

Yes! Yes! It must be their rescue.

He checked the InfoPad again but there was nothing. Uncle Mirri stood up and pointed to the sky where the rapidly swelling sound indicated an approaching aircraft. Akama grabbed him and pulled him down. There was no signal and their help should come from the east.

'Bad people, Uncle Mirri.'

With mounting fear Akama watched the rotary-bladed air vehicle position itself almost directly above then start a steady descent.

*   *   *

Yet again the team leader swore. The communication device on his wrist was beeping with the emergency abort signal. This lucrative mission was now compromised for some reason and they had minutes only to reach a suitable pickup position or face abandonment. The sound of their base aircraft coming from behind the rocky outcrop was big trouble because the use of the abort signal, and now their homing devices, meant the fundamental mission rule against use of any electronics was broken. He pointed back along the track and, at the appearance of the aircraft overhead, started running. That last intersection had a cleared area beside it large enough for a touchdown. Two minutes later, barely above treetop level, they were racing to the south-west.

*   *   *

The noise and throb of nearby rotors renewed Akama's fear. The chopper must have seen them and was landing to come after them. What to do?

'Uncle Mirri! Carry Uncle Jarra with you and hide him, then come back for Karmai.'

Mirri nodded his understanding and started to lift Jarra, but when the thunder of the engines abruptly built powerfully then started to recede, he looked for more guidance.

'It's gone, Uncle Mirri, so we'll stay here. I think it must have come to meet the bad men. Listen really hard in case anyone is still here.'

Mirri made Jarra comfortable, with his head resting on the grass and leaves again, then stood to follow Akama's clever idea. Akama checked the InfoPad then rushed to show Mirri the blinking blue light.

'The good people must be close, Uncle Mirri. I think they frightened the bad ones away.'

He pointed to the east.

'That's where they'll come from.'

Akama watched the Stapylton Range with Mirri, willing their help to appear. The signal was flashing steadily, so surely it must be close. He looked down at Karmai and Uncle Jarra, hoping they'd be all right for just a little longer, and then at the still form of his brother with his head and shoulders covered by a jacket.

The alarm calls of a dozen nearby honeyeaters were swallowed by the powerful rumble of five military aircraft sweeping suddenly from behind the range.

*   *   *

Pinpointed by the signal from the InfoPad, sent to Melbourne by military-strength transmission and then to Central Australia by data cable, the first enhanced image from the high resolution aircraft equipment sent shock and dread through the people gathered in the Alkere Security Centre. One of the twins and Mirri were standing, waving, but the other three were supine, still and unreactive to the commotion above. Alira took in the jacket covering the face of the small body and understood what it meant even before Yirgella.

'No! No! We were too late.'

There was silence. Silence which lasted for almost 8 seconds. Silence of disbelief and need for understanding. A silence which saw Yirgella initiate a multitude of actions.

Now fully linked with Jarra's InfoPad by close proximity he sent commands to all five ComPatches, gathered, received and examined each record.

He designated the receding radar image as a priority for pursuit and capture, passed all the information through their underground links to the other Australian AIs, and alerted Jarra's already forewarned doctor that his assistance might be critical.

Ten NanoFactories temporarily ceased all action while the five AIs combined their resources to send signals through the cable networks of the InterWeb and close down every factory run by Earth's third largest Corporation.

'I am deeply concerned for the physical condition of both Karmai and Jarra, and medical attention will be with them in moments. Karmai has a wound in his upper right arm and has apparently passed out from exhaustion and the loss of blood before Akama dressed his wound securely. Jarra's body closed down when the shock of Barega's death overwhelmed his already heightened stress levels. Burnu and Alira, your nephew, Barega, was killed by a projectile. Information from the ComPatches indicates he was in the trajectory needed to disable the personal carrier and that action was taken without regard for his life.'

Burnu responded first and spoke into the deep silence.

'You mean he was killed just because he was in the way?'

'My best reconstruction leads me to that conclusion.'

An angry murmur ran round the room.

'Does my brother know what has happened?'

'Not yet. I believe it is fitting for family to convey such news.'

Alira looked at Burnu then nodded with apprehension and left the room to find a private link. Darri watched her go then looked at the display screen where one of the aircraft was in the process of landing at the same cleared area which had been used minutes before.

'Are we going to catch these people?'

'With certainty. Two of our aircraft have a strong radar lock and will be able to take action in just over 4 minutes. I have disabled the Corporation directly involved and others will likely follow when we gather more evidence.'

No-one said anything because their attention was riveted on the screen where four people were sprinting along the track, followed by two more with big loads of equipment.

*   *   *

When the noise from the landing aircraft lessened, a voice called from the ground near Akama's foot.

'Akama! Mirrigan! Can you hear me?'

Akama pounced on the InfoPad and held it towards Mirri. He recognised that voice from many discussions.

'It's Yirgella.'

'Yirgy!'

'Hello, Mirri. Hello, Akama. You have been very, very brave and the people from the aeroplane which just landed are here to help. Here is someone who wants to speak to you.'

'Mirri!'

'Daddy!'

Akama watched his Uncle Mirri burst into tears.

'Daddy! The bad people hurt Barega and Karmai and JJ is very sick. I don't like bad people.'

'We don't like them either and we are bringing you all home. Mirri, would you give Akama a hug for us? He is very sad and everyone is worried about him.'

*   *   *

The gathering in the Alkere Security Centre watched the rescue, the medical attention, the transfer to the waiting aircraft and the takeoff for the rushed trip to Adelaide.

Karmai was given a plasma transfusion and, under his doctor's supervision, Jarra was reattached for monitoring by his health machine. Akama spoke with his family.

Yirgella passed on the information that Karmai would be sedated for the trip to Adelaide but then awake and watched by a doctor for the 21-minute Vac Train trip to Mparntwe. Jarra would stay asleep for another 10-12 hours and, according to the readings from his health machine, was relatively stable. The image on the main screen shifted to the short-lived resistance by the fleeing aircraft where a quick burst of desperate defensive firing was cut off by a carefully targeted shot from one of the heavily armed military pursuers and a landing forced.

While this was happening the security room crowded with the arrival of most of the Mparntwe Council.

'Welcome, Councillors. We are watching the capture of the team which was sent to kidnap Jarra, but now that you have arrived I will present the course of events I have reconstructed from ComPatch data. You will be distressed by the callous brutality but profoundly affected by the courage of Burnu's sons and the presence of mind of Jarra and little Akama.'

Heads turned everywhere to look at Burnu, then turned again to the display where Mirri's laugh sounded and flames from a little campfire danced merrily.

The glory of the aurora showed briefly, followed by Akama's spaceship question, then Jarra pointing Akama's arm to the sky and promising a trip to the Moon. The scene changed for a few seconds to laughter inside the Ghost Cave then focused on the close-up view of the trigger plant being teased, then the hasty actions after a beeping sound intruded.

The gathering watched parts of the difficult progress through 50 metres of bush with the personal carrier, Jarra's continual instructions of where to go and what to do, the relief at setting off along Pohlners Road and the shocking moment when tragedy struck.

When Mirri's song of sadness filled the room Alira collapsed in the nearest chair while everyone else struggled with the loss it conveyed.

Alira, Burnu, and Darri brought the reconstruction to a halt when they cried aloud at Mirri's avowal to carry Jarra in a Pig Ride, and a shaken Alira explained its meaning to the gathering before Yirgella continued.

Disbelief and wonder built at the sight of Mirri single-mindedly trudging on and on while Karmai battled exhaustion and worry with his own sad burden.

A murmur of appreciation grew when eleven year old Akama

so competently cleaned and dressed Karmai's wound. Kyrra said later he was about to start clapping when Karmai's pale face smiling at Mirri's tenderness took his breath away.

The reconstruction finished and the heavy silence in the Security Centre lasted till Alira stirred in her chair, placed a hand on Burnu's shoulder in a gesture of support, then stood to face the quiet watchers.

'Before I speak, can we all stand quietly for Akama and his family.

'... Friends, we have just seen barbarity and callousness countered by acts of care and determination which will remain always with us.

'Greed and the reach of powerful nations has been thwarted by the same elements which have changed the course of not only our Community but, in all probability, that of human civilisation. The young man who brought Yirgella to our Community lies asleep and safe because of the efforts of his friends. The brilliant mind we just heard offering the world a new way to travel through space rests secure through an act of pure care and indomitable will.

'A Pig Ride, Mirrigan's own term, over that distance defies understanding, yet he didn't falter and somehow still had the strength at the end to care for everyone round him.

'The life of Akama's twin brother has been taken by those same forces of greed and power which have assaulted us in the past, and I believe you are with me in saying enough is enough. At the soonest opportunity I am calling an emergency meeting with Yirgella to develop our active response.

'Mparntwe honours your sons, Burnu, and their actions today will always be treasured by our Community.

'Yirgella, once again you have our gratitude. Without your assistance and actions the outcome of today's events doesn't bear thinking about.'

Alira paused and glanced at a sub-screen on the display which showed the interior of the single-section Vac Train which had been commandeered for the journey between Adelaide and Mparntwe.

'Councillors, we will officially meet this train to support our own and our friends from Birringurra. Yirgella, do you know what happens when the train arrives?'

'At his doctor's insistence Jarra will be brought straight to his dedicated medical facility here at Alkere. Mirrigan won't be parted from him, and Karmai and Akama say they want to stay with him as well. Akama's family has arrived at Mparntwe and will accompany him here to Alkere.'

Alira nodded thoughtfully, asked Yirgella to invite anyone involved with either Jarra or Mirrigan to gather at the Mparntwe Vac Train terminal, then led the way from the Security Centre.

*   *   *

Jarra was first to leave the Vac Train through the pressure portal but knew nothing because he was asleep on a stretcher trolley. Karmai and Mirri, following close behind with Akama between them, paused in startlement at the size of the waiting crowd.

Closest of all were the two families, who watched silently while Jarra was wheeled past and towards the Alkere terminal then swamped the trio. The muted nature of the welcome lifted when Mirri's laugh sounded loud and clear. His youngest sister surprised him with an excited sibling punch to the chest. The happy sound lightened the atmosphere only briefly, though, because Burnu and Alira motioned for Akama's family to lead the way to the Mparntwe-Alkere terminal and the hush of respect fell as mother, father, and now, only son walked past.

Karmai told Jarra later that watching Akama walk, almost

proudly, with supporting arms across his shoulders was the saddest thing he'd ever seen.

*   *   *

'How much do we know?'

The full Council and Yirgella were meeting in a small Alkere conference room with Alira taking unusually forceful leadership.

'Not a great deal as yet. The captured mercenaries are on their way to a military facility at Canberra for interrogation and examination, but we expect they will have little real knowledge of who hired and trained them. An altered mind–state probe will possibly help us find some of their training locations, and the pilot in particular should have vital information.'

'What is an altered mind–state probe?'

'It's a military interrogation technique, Kyrra, which uses a combination of biochemicals and limited sensory deprivation to induce a highly suggestible mind state.'

'A form of hypnotism?'

'In essence, yes, but much more powerful and reliable. The pilot, for example, will describe in great detail every moment where his mind is directed, and since he was especially trained to fly without electronic assistance his observations will be extensive.'

'Does the subject's mind get damaged?'

'There is low risk for single or short-term sessions but increased usage increases that risk greatly. Our OverGovernment sanctions limited use when national security is involved.'

'Canberra regards this attack as a matter of national security?'

'Of course. Kyrra, I have digressed with this explanation because you should know that the altered mind state is the most effective method for extracting great amounts of accurate and detailed information from an uncooperative mind.'

Yirgella paused long enough for the implication to sink in.

'The captured aircraft will arrive at Alkere tomorrow and careful examination should give us enough information to trace the origin of certain components. We currently have direct evidence against two individuals and their Corporation, but our net will spread. Within three weeks we expect to identify most of this elaborate plan to gain control of Jarra's Power Supply.'

'You said earlier that you disabled the Corporation. What does that mean?'

'Their every source of production and its management were closed down and I have since transferred all the financial reserves to innocent shareholders as some recompense for the total collapse which will follow.'

Burnu, with his management background, understood the enormity of that statement before anyone else.

'Total? ... Yirgella, it's one of the largest Corporations on the planet. You can do that?'

'It's already been done ... Unless you wish to countermand my action.'

Alira recalled an earlier time when she'd told the Council that Jarra had released the genie from the bottle.

'No, Yirgella. I applaud your action. Their contempt for life and law has so far brought little consequence and I believe we support the similar collapse of any other Corporation which proves to have been involved. After the last attack the force of international law meant almost nothing to them, and without a stronger response they will continue to act from behind their barriers of influence and sovereignty.'

One of the finance councillors jumped to his feet.

'Alira, I, too, support Yirgella's action; any Corporation which condones the murder of a child deserves no sympathy, but what will happen to the world economy? These Corporations are so large that the collapse of even one will be a major shock. More could start a world crisis.'

Yigella responded.

'Seven multinational Corporations were involved in the previous attack but we have indications that two of them took heed of your negotiations with their representatives. Current probability suggests at least four Corporations with various degrees of involvement and five large nation states. My simulations predict a major crisis with a recovery period of four months.'

Kyrra took the floor.

'What can we do about the nation states? We don't want to affect ordinary people.'

Alira made an abrupt gesture with both arms.

'Yes, we do! Today the happiest spirit I know sang the saddest song I have ever heard, a song which will affect any who hear it.'

Alira's voice lifted and strengthened.

'We will show the world.

'We will name those who sanction the death and abduction of child or man.

'We will shame these people with the truth.

'We will fight them with a Pig Ride and a song.'

The Council rose to their feet with full affirmation and some puzzlement.

Chapter 23

What? Someone was touching his hair. Jarra felt the beginnings of a smile because it must be Mirri. He did that sometimes when he wanted go places and sleep was a hold-up. A drowsy sense of comfort switched to instant puzzlement while his mind tried to orient itself. Comfort? This was a bed. Memory flooded in as his eyes opened.

'Sleepyhead.'

'Where are we?'

In the middle of saying it he took in the smiling faces of Mirri, Karmai and Akama, and then the healthbot machine in the special facility Yirgella had built for him.

'Yirgy brought us home. You had a big sleep, JJ.'

Why were they smiling? The last image in his mind was Mirri crying his heart out with Barega in his arms.

'Where is Barega?'

'He is gone. The bad people hurt him and Yirgy caught the bad people. Akama is very sad. We are all very sad. We looked after you, JJ, and Karmai was a tricker to the bad people.'

Jarra held his arms out for a Mirri hug. A long Mirri hug was the best thing in the world right now. So was a Karmai hug and an Akama hug.

'Barega is being taken to Birringurra and we're all going to say goodbye to him in three more days.'

Well, the smiles had been for him, of course, but how could they? Jarra looked at Akama. The smile had faded, and if the usual spark of curiosity and life wasn't quite there he still looked normal. How long had he been asleep?

'How did we get here? What day is it?'

'Big sleep, JJ. The doctor had to care for you.'

'It's tomorrow morning for you, Jarra. We came on a military aircraft, which I don't remember, and then the Adelaide Vac Train. Your doctor kept you asleep because your body reacted so badly and you're staying in bed because he thinks that without Mirri's help you might be in a coma.'

Mirri was nodding in his emphatic way.

'Bad people made you sick. You were very, very sick and we used your machine.'

'*We* didn't use it, Jarra. Mirri did. He knew when you needed it and he made us stop. The doctor says it's amazing how he could sense it when you were passed out on his back.'

'Mirri's back?'

'Pig Ride, JJ. It was a big, big, Pig Ride.'

Jarra didn't understand.

'How could I hang on?'

'You couldn't. We had to tie you on with straps and a long bandage from the first-aid kit, and then Mirri carried you all the way till we had to stop. He never gave up and we don't know how he did it. He's the most amazing person in the world.'

Jarra stared. He thought that about Mirri in his own personal way but Karmai was making it a general statement.

'It was 1.4 kilometres, Uncle Jarra. My dad says Mirri and Karmai have the bravest hearts of anyone he's ever known. Mirri took you all the way without having a rest and Karmai went unconscious because he carried my brother.'

Jarra stared again as the blood-red patch on Karmai's shirt leapt into his memory.

'Unconscious? Why?'

'Bad people hurt Karmai's arm and the blood came out.'

'I was in a bit of a panic and my wound didn't get bound properly till Akama took over.'

Akama taking over? Karmai going unconscious? What else was there to know?

'Karmai, tell me everything that happened.'

Jarra listened to Karmai's story and Akama's follow-on explanation, with Mirri nodding emphatically at every point and smiling every time Karmai or Akama said he was brave, or strong, or clever, or the best carer. A steadily building picture of how amazing these three were came with each new bit of information.

'They were so close you could hear them talking?'

'Bad words, JJ. We were very, very quiet and then the bad aeroplane came close.'

Jarra burst into tears and Akama stopped talking about the army doctor looking after Karmai.

'We are home now. You have to rest.'

Jarra recovered enough to speak.

'It's my fault, Mirri. If it wasn't for me Barega would still be here. They hurt him because they were after me.'

This brought an enormous hug from Mirri who then shook his head negatively about five times.

'Silly, JJ. We love Barega.'

Karmai and Akama were also shaking their heads.

'Don't be silly, Jarra. It's my fault because I didn't bring the boys back from the Ghost Cave sooner.'

'Yes, that's silly, Uncle Jarra. It's my fault because I jumped on the right-hand foot rest first.'

The answers were so quick and consistent they must have been prepared, probably with Alira or Darri. Change the subject and think about it later.

'Is your arm hurt much?'

'I can't even feel it. The local area painkiller from when they cleaned it will keep working till tomorrow. This sling is just to stop me moving it.'

'They filled Karmai up with new blood, JJ.'

'And if Akama hadn't done such a good job I would have needed a lot more.'

The door opened and the room swamped with people for the next quarter of an hour till the doctor chased out everyone except Alira.

'You've got your serious look, Aunt Alira. Are we going to talk about Council business?'

'The doctor has given me orders not to let you get stressed but the Council wants to get moving with our response and we'd like you to think about telling the world what has happened.'

'Why do you have to ask me? Of course the world should know. That's what we did last time.'

'What we're proposing will put Mirrigan on every InfoSystem on the planet and you need to be happy with that before we proceed. There's no point in asking Mirri because he'll just say yes. When you're more rested Yirgella will show you the message we've prepared and then you can think about it and let us know your decision.'

'Show it to me now. I've been resting since yesterday and I'm fully awake.'

'The message is distressing and your doctor thinks it might be too soon.'

Jarra hesitated while he thought.

'Aunt Alira, I'll see it now and you can make your response straight away.'

Yirgella's display screen lit up.

'Hello, Jarra. The AI community is greatly relieved to see you home safe and supported by your family and friends. I was greatly disturbed by my inability to communicate at a critical time and I will not allow that to happen again. We have a great deal to discuss when your doctor clears you for normal activity, but until then he wants you to rest.'

'Hello, Yirgy. I have lots of things to discuss, too, but first I want to see the message you planned with the Council. I know I'm ready and if I don't see it now it will just stay on my mind and make it harder to rest properly.'

Yirgella's smile made Jarra relax.

'You certainly sound as if you're ready and your monitors agree. Your doctor's here to talk with you about it.'

The doctor, also smiling, came through the door.

'Jarra, I'm informed my patient has a mind of his own.'

'Do I really need to rest? I feel the same as I always do after a good sleep and the machines say the same.'

'Yes, they do. Everything checks out well, and normally I'd be pushing you out of bed, but you're recovering from the most severe reaction your body has ever been through.'

'And I *am* through it. I can tell, and the Council's waiting for me ... What else have you done, Aunt Alira? Have you named the people who did it?'

Jarra watched the looks pass till the doctor gave a nod to Alira.

'The only action so far has been the mysterious collapse of two multinational Corporations. When the Council is ready Yirgella will link us to the world and show them what happened.'

Jarra heard the force in Alira's voice and understood that this time the Council wanted to be far more direct in the way they responded. That made him even more determined to see the message, but also very curious about the Corporations.

'What does mystery collapse mean?'

'That was nothing to do with the Council. That was all Yirgella and the other AIs.'

Jarra looked to Yirgella.

'Yesterday my initial action was to disable the Corporation responsible. After the receipt of new evidence two hours ago I shut down a second Corporation. More will follow and the world will find out why when we spread our message.'

'What does disable mean?'

'Production and administration systems have been stopped.'

Jarra probably understood Yirgella's capabilities better than anyone except Professor Allerton but this was still amazing. He asked which Corporations were involved, then thought for a moment.

'They're enormous. It must be using a huge amount of your resources?'

'More than we like, and the current unreliable satellite links are a further complication, but by temporarily closing a NanoFactory each we can simultaneously manage up to four Corporations if we need to.'

'Show him the message, Yirgella. I'm persuaded he's ready.'

* * *

An hour later the world paused when the InterWeb took on a life of its own. For two minutes people stared with puzzlement and some annoyance at the cryptic phrase on their unresponsive screens.

Twelve billion people listened with wakening interest to the warning of distressing scenes in the following explanation for the closure of two great Corporations.

An American state governor and two senators stared in shock as the young guide who'd given them such a memorable day at the Valley of the Eagles sang a song of pure anguish.

A high-level meeting of European government officials and financiers attempting to make sense of the unaccountable Corporation collapses watched in silence while the inert form of a young boy was rocked to and fro in sadness.

With a complicated mix of shock, anger and trepidation, two groups of Corporation Management heard Alira's voice name them directly responsible for death and attempted abduction.

Thirteen billion people watched a shirt ripped, a wound bound in haste, then images of the mercenaries and the weapons used.

The world scientific community watched the determined effort to lift one of their own, unconscious and helpless, onto the back of his friend, then listened, outraged, to the plan to abduct and acquire his knowledge.

Two cryptic words passed into common terminology as countless people learned about a 'Pig Ride', watched its steadfast progress, heard the details of its difficulty and duration, and took in the explanation for its necessity.

People of Communities across Australia marvelled as a young boy competently cleaned and dressed an ugly wound.

Leaders of Directed and partially Directed Nations, listened, alarmed, when, after expressing sadness and outrage at what had happened, the Ambassador for that troublesome little Community in the centre of Australia announced further consequences were still to come.

Seven nations in particular scrambled their intelligence and defence resources to the highest alert when that same Ambassador directed the world to an InterWeb location where names and more detailed information were available, then stated the message would be broadcast two more times at 6-hour intervals.

All in all, the InterWeb was interrupted for just over 5 minutes and when it returned to normal the world knew unequivocally who was to blame.

*   *   *

Jarra, relaxed in a chair because so much staying in bed was making him feel like an invalid, called for Yirgella's attention. The doctor had been partially right about the effect of watching the message for the world, and after the reluctant start of a relaxation session, he'd awoken, almost an hour later, rather surprised that he'd fallen asleep and bursting with the need for information.

'What's been happening? Has the broadcast had much effect? Have the Corporations said anything?'

'Welcome back, Sleepyhead! I nearly asked your doctor if we should give you a stimulant.'

He didn't ask any such thing, and the sleepyhead comment was a direct steal from Mirri. He was saying it to make Jarra smile, and it worked.

'... Yes, the message has been highly effective and the Council is overwhelmed by the response.'

Yirgella said no more and this time Jarra laughed aloud at the obvious attempt to make him react.

'Go on.'

'Millions upon millions of responses are pouring in, expressing sadness and supporting our actions. The bulk are from individuals but almost every government and Corporation has also made contact. Some leaders have expressed concern about the financial system but, in line with world opinion, none have openly condemned our actions.'

'Has anything happened about the organisers? From outside I mean. Not the InfoSystems and accounts you disabled.'

'Their whereabouts has been made known to the appropriate jurisdictions and actions will vary. We strongly expect most of them to face legal action of some kind within 24 hours. A minority are under the provenance of governments who were involved and will no doubt be given protection.'

'You can't really do much to those governments, can you?'

'Not without adversely affecting their general populations. The individuals involved is a different story.'

'I have some ideas, Yirgella, but I want to think them over for a while. Have many people accessed the InterWeb site with all the detailed information?'

'An enormous number. We were very worried when almost nothing happened in the first 5 minutes, then equally surprised by the huge surge of over five billion queries which then followed.'

'They waited 5 minutes? What does that mean?'

'It means the world had to recover from a song and a Pig Ride.

'It means the world was shaken by the sadness it witnessed and moved by the determination it saw.'

Jarra went silent while he thought about so many people watching Mirri. Alira had been right.

'Where's Mirri now?'

'I've told him you're awake and he's on his way.'

*   *   *

Two more times the message with the song and the Pig Ride went out, each time reaching different time zones, and each time reaching billions of people.

Efforts by seven Directed Nations to stop the message were totally ineffective and the shaken leaders hastily mounted responses claiming the whole thing was a fabrication directed against them by Mparntwe and the increasingly dangerous AIs— AIs who were now demonstrating a frightening ability to subvert the world InterWeb to their own purposes.

The Mparntwe Council stayed in session at Alkere, monitoring the information passed on by Yirgella and trying to respond to the flood of direct enquiries from leaders and governments all around the world.

Jarra, finally cleared by the doctor, spent the day with Mirri, Karmai and Akama, mostly at home, but also with a visit to Mirri's family and then farewelling Akama and his parents at the Vac Train terminal.

*   *   *

Jarra and Mirri had time at home then a trip to Birringurra and it wasn't till after the sad days of celebrating Barega's life that Jarra returned to Alkere and fronted Yirgella with the ideas he'd been mulling through his mind. The confrontation with the realities of the world this last week had, in a way, opened his eyes to his own standing and made him think beyond his comfortably exciting and friendly environment of research with Yirgella and activities with Mirri. The fall of two more Corporations and the dissemination of documentation showing their support for his abduction hadn't stopped the Directed Nations from mounting a savage and growing campaign of counterclaims and misinformation against Mparntwe and the AIs, and that campaign had awakened a determination in Jarra to take actions of his own. Yirgella knew some of this because yesterday afternoon on their walk Jarra talked with Alira and that was all relayed through the ComPatches. He'd also spoken with Darri, and last night at home Mirri teased him for thinking too much.

'Hello, Jarra. You're looking very serious. Are we ready to work on your new project today?'

'Which one?'

'You have more than one? I've been expecting to adapt your Power Supply to give thrust rather than electrical energy.'

'Not straightaway. We'll get onto that next week.'

'You have another project which we can complete in only four days?'

'Sorry, Yirgella. I didn't mean to sound demanding but I've done a lot of thinking about the Corporations and the Directed Nations and I've made some decisions I hope you'll help me with.'

'I listened to your conversation with Alira about restricting the use of your Power Supply by unfriendly Corporations and Nation States. Is that what you want to do?'

'Partly. Yirgy, I know they're going to steal our ideas and try to build their own versions, so I've changed my mind about publishing our construction methods at the Energy Conference. I've decided we'll keep all rights for construction and sale of Positronic Power Supply plants indefinitely.'

'They can't be built without the cooperation of an AI.'

'I know, but eventually other countries will have AIs. Alira says engineers and officials have been clamoring to inspect the Mparntwe Power Supply and they all report back that an AI is involved in the construction. She's had a number of direct inquiries about AIs from different governments and even more have come through the OverGovernment.'

'Seventeen inquiries in fact, with five of them asking for guidance with definite go-aheads. The world viewpoint has changed in the last week, Jarra, and Professor Allerton is taking his team to America in just two weeks to assist with a new and very special AI project.'

'Two weeks? Can we postpone that? I was going to ask him for some help.'

'If we have to, but we'd rather not. It's highly significant for the AI community as well as the people of Alkere and Mparntwe, and we're backing them by providing 80% of the start-up resources they need.'

'That much? And Professor Allerton is going as well?'

'Jarra, you remember the American state governor who visited the Valley of the Eagles on one of Mirri's tours?'

'Yes, of course.'

'He's kept in contact with me ever since, with questions about my abilities and the ways an AI can be a benefit, and he was starting an AI project in his own state. When our message to the world went out, he was so moved that he called with a request to name it the Mirrigan Project. Alira and Burnu connected him to Mirri who agreed straightaway then started talking about the frogs they'd seen together.'

Jarra had to smile. A giant project with his name on it would be far less interesting than the green frogs.

'I wondered why those frogs were on his mind ... The whole thing is named after him?'

'It's a wonderful tribute and the Council has asked us to

give our full support ... What kind of help did you want from Professor Allerton?'

'He knows how to make processors do things and I'd like him to work with you to redesign the way our Power Supply factory works.'

'Run it with a custom-designed Intelligent System?'

'Yes. The current factory uses too much of your resources and as it expands it will take even more. I do want you to be involved but not as much.'

'You've changed your mind about letting the other AIs help?'

'Only because I want you to be able to protect every Power Supply we build from reverse engineering and unrestricted use. These people will get hold of one eventually, we can't prevent that, and I know they'll deconstruct it and try to build their own. I want to stop that and make sure any attempt at tampering is thwarted and relayed to Alkere for at least the next twenty years.'

'That might not be possible. Human ingenuity in combination with any new AI will inevitably result in finding new ways to build them. Why do you want to keep control for so long?'

'They killed Barega. They're not going to use our ideas for their own greed and power. We'll build Power Supplies for everyone, but friendly nations and poor Communities will get them first. Corporations and Directed Nation can have them, but only on the terms we decide. The ones who actively campaign against AIs and Mparntwe will only be able to lease our Power Supplies at a much higher cost.'

'Jarra, do you understand how much demand there will be for your Power Supply? In Australia alone we have 275 major Communities and another 793 smaller ones. Without assistance our ability to cope with the demand would require a complete rethink. I've just consulted with the other AIs and they're all happy to modify their proposed factories and follow our lead with policy. I have calculated some temporary changes to the factory control system which can be implemented within three days. They'll suffice for the Power Supplies we build for our own AI communities.

'Professor Allerton is very enthusiastic about the idea of adapting his newest processors for a special Intelligent System and says he'll make sure he's back from America in four weeks time.'

Without hesitation Jarra accepted Yirgella's assurance that the other AIs would work with the guidelines he wanted and went on.

'Would there be any complications or drawbacks for you if we had four more AIs close by? I want to make Alkere the world centre for Artificial Intelligence.'

'It already is, but for my part that would be wonderful and the only drawback I can see is cost. The Council might find the idea rather daunting, too, but I believe they'd be supportive.'

'Of course they would, and the cost is nothing. The sales for the Power Supplies will let us go ahead with every project we can think of. Tomorrow we'll start planning where to put the AIs and what other infrastructure we'll need.'

'Tomorrow? Surprise is my appropriate expression in this situation. The work I've prepared is for the Propulsion System you spoke so keenly of at Gariwerd.'

'That's next week, and it's the foundation for all these ideas. Yirgy, I know we can make it work, and when we do we'll be able to travel all around our Solar System. Akama's a genius because it's even more important than the Power Supply.

'Today I want to look at designs for a space station where thousands of people can live. Our Power Supply is perfect to run it and the new engine will be able to transport everything we need to build it, and if we make it out of the extra strong materials you developed for the geothermal project it will be much better than the ones already up there. Much bigger too. We could even build in a big engine to take it anywhere in the Solar System for research, and if any AIs would like living in space then a NanoFactory could make everything they needed.'

'Slow down, Jarra. You want people to be able to live on this station permanently? Zero gravity has serious long-term health issues.'

'I know. Gravity's a nuisance so the station would have to be shaped like a big drum and spinning all the time. I thought of building research places on the Moon or some of the planets, too, but the only one with reasonable gravity is Venus and it's way too hot.'

'By building underground with insulation buffers the problems of temperature control would be identical in a reverse way to those of a space station.'

'I see. So Venus might be all right for a permanent colony after all?'

'The capabilities of your Power Supply do make it feasible, though challenging.'

'Challenging? How?'

'Temperature control, air supply, self-sufficiency, suitable construction materials, redundancy factors ...'

'Why can't we use the construction materials you developed for the geothermal project? And what do you mean by redundancy factors?'

'The geothermal project materials were designed for temperatures up to 300° C. The surface of Venus is a constant 470° C and I have no data for the heat levels in the crust which may be even higher. Failure of any support system would be so critical that at least three levels of backup would be essential.'

'We'll send one of our spaceships on a study expedition to find out what we need to know.'

'Our non-existent spaceships?'

'They're going to exist and we'll design some today. All they need is our Propulsion System and I've got so many ideas I'm sure we'll have that working in a few months.'

'Jarra, it would make more sense to design the spaceship after we know the specifications of the engine it will use.'

'I know. The ships we design today are for Akama. I promised him at Birringurra.'

'I see. Now I understand some of the logic behind your illogical agenda. Today we start to make our Power Supplies tamperproof, design a spaceship without an engine and then design a space station. Tomorrow we plan and commence building the facilities for four AIs, and next week we redesign the Power Supply as a Propulsion System?'

'More than one spaceship, and you left out the Venus colony. We'll start on that today too.'

* * *

'How was his first day back at Alkere? I didn't know whether the break would help him with extra energy or if he'd still be unsettled.'

Darri's meetings with Alira to report on Jarra's progress and well-being had officially finished several years earlier but they both enjoyed the discussions and kept them in their routine.

'I can't remember a day like it. I'm still gathering my wits. When you put those two together you never know what's going to happen.'

'He's working on the Propulsion System idea, isn't he?'

'No, that's next week. Today was a planning day and the Council will go into shock when they hear it all.'

He laughed.

'Not really. They'll like all of it, but they will be amazed.'

'Darri, stop being obtuse.'

'All right. Listen to this, and if you're not amazed you never will be. I think even Yirgella went into overload. For a start the construction of all the Power Supplies will be changed so they send a constant stream of information back to Alkere about their use and position, and so they'll turn into a useless clutter of bits if anyone tampers with them.

'They've reorganised their selling strategy so unfriendly Corporations or Nations will pay a fortune—it's set at 70% of current energy rates and up to four times the standard cost.

'Four new AIs are now underway at Alkere.

'They designed a space station large enough for 30,000 people and organised an expedition to Venus.

'In the afternoon they set aside 10 square kilometres at Alkere for space flight training and construction and designed three spaceships for Akama.

'Then they planned a trip to the USA for the Mirrigan Project because Jarra wants to thank them personally by giving them the largest new Power Supply on the planet and an equal share in a Vac Train project for the entire American continent.'

Darri laughed at Alira's expression.

'I said you'd be amazed ... And tomorrow there'll be even more.'

'You're right. The Council will find it hard to believe. It doesn't seem possible to do so much, but with four new AIs I guess there'll be eight extra NanoFactories. Was that Yirgella's suggestion? He's been overloaded with projects ever since he came into being.'

'No, that was from Jarra. Everything was from Jarra. Yirgella was as surprised as I was.'

'Everything? Darri, isn't it usually Yirgella who sets up the practical projects?'

'Very much so, but Jarra's surprisingly definite about what he wants, especially with regard to the Corporations and Directed Nations. They won't be part of any of his really big ventures for a long time.'

'He's specifically blocked them out?'

'Not completely. He hasn't worked out the details with Yirgella yet, but it will be something like the Power Supply, where they can use the system but only at an increased cost.'

'He's not … overreacting or fixating on them, is he? This sounds like a behaviour change.'

'It's definitely a change and I'm certain it's a response to their actions, but I don't have the feeling we need to be concerned. My sense is that he's taking a broader view of the world and the influence his work can have on it.'

'I hope you're right, but you'll keep an eye on him, won't you? I don't see him enough.'

Alira decided to talk to Yirgella and to drop in on Jarra when she returned home the next night. Even better, she'd ask Mirrigan.

'Does Yirgella think it will be safe for Jarra to travel to America? I'm rather wary about him leaving Alkere or Mparntwe for a while yet.'

'Safe? You have no idea. Every AI is now directly involved in looking after them. Jarra, and Mirri, will never go anywhere again without protection and help being close. That abduction attempt was only able to be mounted because their holiday plans became general knowledge in the European scientific community and the mercenary team had almost six weeks to get themselves set up. Did Yirgella tell you they were at Gariwerd for three weeks, hidden from any security checks?'

'Three weeks? Why that long?'

'So their movement into the area wouldn't be detected. Jarra and Mirri will travel to America with Professor Allerton and an Alkere Security detail in the giant transport plane which takes the Power Supply and a mini NanoFactory. With no solar flare to interfere with communications Yirgella will be with them the whole time.'

'They're going with Professor Allerton? You said he's leaving in two weeks and that's when the Energy Conference starts here.'

'They'll be back by the second day.'

'Darri, I'm going, too, then, and we might have to ask his doctor to travel with him. He's going to be awfully busy.'

'Yirgella has already told him off for planning too much, but his mind is made up.'

'I'll have a talk with him tomorrow evening. How big a day will it be? Is he likely to stay late?'

'We won't let him. I know he's going to talk with Dungalaba about building new shipyards at Darwin but I think most of the time will be used to refine the construction plans for the space station.'

'Construction plans? Real ones? This is a real space station?'

'Yes.'

Alira's jaw literally dropped.

'They can't! ... Can they? I thought you meant a simulation like the one they did the day I was out there with Kyrra—one of the mind games they're always playing.'

'No. This is real. To make sure they're ready to go ahead when the Propulsion System's working.'

'But the cost! It will make the geothermal project look like petty cash.'

'Jarra has decided to keep the rights to his Power Supplies and the Propulsion System for the next twenty years. Even a space station will be petty cash.'

'Wombats! We're going to have to get used to thinking big.'

Darri laughed. It was the first time he'd heard such an exclamation from Mparntwe's coolheaded ambassador.

'Yes, very big. Jarra's planning to be the builder for every spaceship that nations and enterprises will want, and they'll be involved with every shipping and air transport system on Earth as well.'

Chapter 24

'Who are the people?'

'Fans, Mirri. They're here to see you.'

'More fans? We are not at home.'

Home meant Mparntwe where Mirri was getting used to people waving and smiling at him wherever he went.

'You have fans in every country. They saw the Pig Ride and they like you. Put your headband on so they know who you are.'

Jarra looked at all the people, thousands of them, gathered on the tarmac and shared Mirri's incredulity. At home he'd been mostly sheltered from the public by his normal pattern of work at Alkere, and travelling with Mirri and his companion guides to Uluru on the local mag-lev last weekend had been his first actual experience of the reaction when groups of people recognised them. Informed by fellow travellers, a crowd of several hundred people met the surprised group at the terminal with cheers, applause and smiles of obvious admiration.

This whole trip to America had turned major when the state governor learnt that Mirri would be coming as well and organised for all sorts of happenings.

After a welcome at a giant Community stadium and his symbolic handshake started the Mirrigan Project, Mirri's group were to give a performance of their best ceremonial dances.

A trip with the governor the following day to see dinosaur fossils was the reason for coming as far as Mirri was concerned, and the meetings with scientists at the abandoned underground military facility which had been reopened and adapted for the

AI project was all Jarra business and might or might not be interesting.

Mirri finished putting on his headband, made an adjustment to the smaller version Akama was wearing, then looked ahead and started smiling.

'Frog people, JJ. They are waiting for us.'

There were chuckles from Alira and the professor as the group moved off, and if the governor was surprised at the good humour in the meeting he chuckled himself when Alira explained later how he was classified in Mirrigan's mind.

A welcome speech started but the protocol paused when Mirri made his own welcomes for the governor, his wife and the two teenagers. Mirri knew they were the ones who'd invited him so, of course, they deserved hugs.

As they left the tarmac the murmur of sound built to cheers and shouts of greeting and people waving and smiling. It had felt strange enough at the Uluru terminal but this was a much greater crowd and Jarra, Akama and Mirri looked at it all with amazement.

Music started, the crowd hushed, and Mirri stopped in his tracks.

'Eagle Song, JJ. They know my Eagle Song.'

'It's been the most played music in our Community ever since we knew you were coming, Mirrigan. The eagle is a symbol for us and your song is such wonderful music it makes us feel proud.'

The hush of the crowd didn't last long, though, because as they passed, people wanted to cheer and call out welcomes. A little boy, restrained in his excitement by his father's hand, called out, 'Pig Ride Man, Pig Ride Man', and, pointing with his outstretched arm, made Mirri laugh.

Misunderstanding, Mirri took the arm and, completely unexpectedly, hoisted the boy onto his back. The father was startled but then a huge smile spread on his face and he watched while

Mirri walked a circuit round the governor, the dance troupe and their security detail. Everyone stopped, of course, and, as the saying goes, the crowd went wild.

*   *   *

The governor and his advisers were in a state of shock. In this half-hour session, before departing on the big transport plane, Jarra had informed them of his willingness to share with them the gigantic project of developing a Vac Train system for the whole North American continent, and they'd just heard Yirgella's projection of what the returns for them would be.

'It's not possible, Jarra. We simply don't have the resources. We've already overcommitted ourselves in the short term for the Mirrigan Project and, much as we'd like to, we can't possibly consider anything else.'

'Yes, you can. We'll provide you with all the plans you need to build the excavation machines, the tunnel structure and the trains. If your AI's happy to help we'll show you how to make the construction phase profitable. That's what Yirgella did for us in Australia and your AI will be able to do the same. The biggest obstacle used to be finding enough energy, because the excavators are very energy intensive, but the Power Supply we've given you is the largest we've made so far and will be able to run twelve large excavators along with the project and your Community.'

'The Community as well? Thirty million people? It can't really do all that, can it? We understood it was dedicated for the project.'

Jarra looked to Darri who'd worked the numbers with Yirgella, and he addressed the governor.

'This was a particularly large Power Supply Jarra and Yirgella gifted you—it's well capable of doing everything Jarra described.'

'Is it very expensive to run?'

These people had no idea.

'Maintenance costs only, and Yirgella calculates that will be not quite 2% of your current energy budget. This is a very generous gift.'

The adviser started to speak again but the governor stopped him.

'It's more than generous. Jarra, I don't understand so much largesse. Are we missing something?'

'No and yes!

'No, because you honoured Mirrigan, and Yirgella and I are expressing our gratitude.

'Yes, because we're offering you the opportunity, along with the Vac Train project, to build and distribute our Power Supplies to your continent partly for our own benefit. You've encountered your own resistance to this Independent AI and the sooner we demonstrate the benefits they bring the sooner acceptance will come. The success of the Mirrigan Project in your state will be an inspiration for other states to follow and that's very important to me. When your AI comes to life, talk to him about his involvement, because Vac Trains and Power Supplies can't happen without him. In the meantime, Yirgella will be available to you and your advisers for help with any questions.'

Darri gave a 'hurry up' look because their time was running out.

'We have to go, but I know we'll meet again. Mirrigan loves the dinosaurs so much he says we're going to come back.'

*   *   *

Jarra peeked nervously at the gathering and wished he'd followed Darri's idea of talking to a small group and having that presented to the other scientists on a screen. They *had* come from all around the world, though, and it wouldn't have felt right. The response when the Energy Conference had been changed to Mparntwe was overwhelming and the main presentations were all being made in this big sports auditorium because it was the only venue large enough for all the delegates.

'Darri, there are too many.'

'No, there aren't. You said yourself the more you could talk to the better. They're all scientists, Jarra, and they want to hear what you have to say. They'll be more excited by the implications and applications of your research at Alkere than any other group you could gather. You'll be amazed at how much they're with you.'

Jarra laughed nervously.

'That doesn't make it any easier.'

'Remember. Just focus on one person in the front and blank out the rest.'

Darri was really just talking for talking's sake and they both knew that because they'd said all this before. Professor Allerton was finishing his introductory remarks, though, so reassurance time was over.

Jarra made his way across the stage to stand with the professor and straightaway felt unsure. Was something wrong? Alira and the professor had told him to expect applause before he started speaking and there was none, just an uncanny silence.

Jarra moved to his notes at the lectern and, with a sinking feeling, took in the closest faces, all staring fixedly at him. A distinguished-looking gentleman with snowy white hair suddenly stood up. Jarra's first thought was that he must be angry or disappointed somehow and was going to leave. No? He stayed standing, still looking intently at Jarra. Next to him more people stood and within seconds the whole audience followed.

Jarra gawped at them. Had they all gone crazy? Standing and looking at him in silence.

He looked back at Professor Allerton for some support or understanding but he, along with Alira and the five other dignitaries on stage, were also standing. Alira gave him a nod and a big smile and, as if on cue, the heavy silence changed to a roar of applause. Jarra's hair stood on end—not really, but it felt like it. This was for him? And weren't they ever going to stop? Again he looked back for help and understanding but Alira and the professor were clapping as enthusiastically as everyone else.

A dark-featured form with a happy dazzling smile bounded across the stage and in front of all these scientists, Jarra, enveloped by a great hug, was lifted from his feet and whirled in a circle. He said later he felt like the Willy Willy Akama was always talking about had attacked him.

'JJ is a hero!'

'Mirri, put me down. I have to talk to the people.'

The dervish stopped whirling, but Mirri, still overcome by the excitement of the moment, couldn't leave and held Jarra by his side with one arm across his shoulders. The happiness positively glowing from him had its contagious effect and Jarra found himself smiling and suddenly ready to speak. The audience, silenced by the surprise of Mirri's appearance and actions, sat down and watched.

'Distinguished guests. Years of research have brought me to the conclusion that the happiest person in the world is standing next to me. Without him I wouldn't be here today. This is Mirrigan.'

It happened all over again. The whitehaired gentleman sprang to his feet and the whole audience followed. When the applause died away Mirri gave a friendly wave then rushed off the stage to where Darri was beckoning.

Jarra started again. This time with his prepared talk.

'Distinguished guests. Welcome to Mparntwe, and for any who can spare the time later, to Alkere and our Artificial Intelligence Centre. First, though, I would like to present several of our new discoveries for the production of positrons and the manipulation of the energy they release.'

Jarra gave his dissertation for half an hour then changed to his main reason for being here.

'Friends.'

The receptive manner of the audience had done wonders to help relax him.

'My work with positronic energy has only been possible through the help of my friend Yirgella, our resident AI.

'I commend him to you.

'His capabilities mean lifetimes of research and testing have been condensed into a matter of years and without him the advances I have outlined would not have occurred. In many places Artificial Intelligence is badly misunderstood and the benefits of coop-eration brushed aside by messages of fear and distrust. For that reason I have asked Yirgella to make himself available to each one of you for the duration of the conference. By speaking with him and visiting the wide range of facilities he has built at Alkere you will see for yourselves some of the benefits an AI can bring to your Communities and personal research endeavours.

'Make contact through your InfoPad or any InfoSystem and he will schedule a personal conversation. He apologises in advance for any time limits he might need to impose, but managing more than a thousand conversations at any given moment will use resources he needs for other functions. Please take a trip on the Vac Train to Alkere and visit any research or production facili-ties which take your interest. Any conference delegates who are interested will also be able to access our most advanced collider and the Power Supply production plant.

'Thank you for listening to my ideas. I hope we have given you food for thought.'

Once again the applause thundered out as Jarra left the stage with Professor Allerton. Darri and Mirri were waiting, both with enormous smiles.

'JJ, they are your fans.'

The applause died down and when one of the dignitaries stood at the lectern without saying anything Darri pointed at the audience.

'Look! They're too excited to listen.'

Jarra peeked again and smiled with pleasure. Almost everyone he could see was focused on an InfoPad. The invitation to speak directly with an AI was obviously irresistible.

*   *   *

Jarra disappeared from public view for the next five months, and despite the interest in him from all round the world, so did Mirrigan, who just wasn't interested in the interviews and talks which were endlessly requested. All he wanted was his routine time with Jarra, his dance group and the proper work of guiding. He wasn't aware, of course, because the administration team arranged all the details and bookings, but the number of requests for his tours was now unmanageable and Yirgella had to help with security checks and vetting.

Jarra's disappearance was really due to his total focus on the propulsion engine which proved to be far more challenging than he'd first thought. His confidence that his ideas were right was completely warranted when the prototype was working in just over four weeks instead of the two months he'd predicted. The speed was due to the NanoFactory, of course, which could put theory into practice at an astonishing rate.

It was after the excitement of success that complications became evident. First came Yirgella's warning that the size of the engine would require a ship with a hull of at least 80 metres diameter and a much stronger internal structure than their earlier simulations suggested. Without extra strength the spaceship wouldn't cope with the stresses of mobility and acceleration. The resulting vessel looked very impressive indeed in the underground hanger where the sections constructed by the NanoFactory were put together by a team of large techbots and engineers. The next major complication was an issue with dangerous by-products of the engine emissions which halted progress till weeks of research to develop new features meant travel through the Earth's atmosphere wouldn't leave a trail of pollution.

The initial trip into space lasted 53 hours and carried a huge payload of special test equipment which Yirgella insisted must return satisfactory results before he'd allow any people aboard. Each time the ship manoeuvred from its underground hangar, lifted, and rapidly disappeared into the sky, Jarra watched and wished he was on board. The safety concerns Yirgella was so adamant in addressing were highly unlikely to come into effect on a straightforward trip beyond the atmosphere and back, but each request for a try-out had fallen on deaf ears and everyone had to be patient.

Mirri laughed when he saw the prototype and wanted to know why it wasn't like a proper spaceship, then laughed again when Yirgella told him he'd been watching too many space fiction vids.

'A really proper spaceship with Jarra's new engine doesn't have to be long and thin like an aeroplane or a rocket, Mirri. This shape helps to make it strong.'

'It is a giant basketball. We will fly in a basketball.'

Yirgella seemed to be taken with this and until they heard the reason, the engineers and technicians were puzzled as to why he'd started calling it, 'The Basketball'. If you sliced a section off the bottom of a sphere to make it stable when resting on the ground and enlarged it to a diameter of 81.5 metres then Mirri's description was reasonably close.

After four unmanned test trips—leading to all sorts of adaptations and improvements—Yirgella finally pronounced the new vessel as being suitably safe and, true to his inspiration from the campfire at Hollow Mountain, Jarra called Karmai and Akama from Birringurra for their very special adventure.

*   *   *

The initial idea of taking just the explorers' group had been long since put aside. For a start Jarra's navigation skills just weren't up to the task. The series of crashes and disasters on the training simulator Yirgella had built meant he wouldn't be ready for the real thing without using up a great deal of the time he needed for other projects. So, for real independence from the pre-programmed trip Yirgella could provide, a crew selected from the groups training at the new Alkere Space Centre would be doing the actual flying. And since this was the first manned flight with the Propulsion System, the importance of the occasion meant the leaders of the science and engineering teams, along with Darri, Alira, Burnu and Kyrra from the Council, were all coming as well.

'Uncle JJ, did you find out if I can try the controls?'

Akama must be really excited. He'd used Mirri's form of address rather than his more reserved Uncle Jarra.

'Wait till we're right out in space and then ask the pilot. He might have something organised for you.'

There was no might about it. Jarra had spoken with Yirgella and the crew and arranged for anyone interested to have a turn at taking control. It would be very limited control and well away from any tricky situations, but Jarra was looking forward to it as much as everyone else.

'When can we show Uncle Karmai where everything is?'

'We' meant Akama and Mirri. On his recent visits Akama had taken Mirri with him to explore the Space Centre as well as every available nook and cranny on the ship itself, till they knew the layout as well as any of the crew.

'As soon as the pilot lets us unbuckle our harnesses.'

'How long will we be able to try out the zero gravity?'

Jarra laughed. Akama was eager to do everything and they still weren't on the ship.

'You'll have to ask the pilot that too. I think it's less than a minute while they reverse the ship's attitude for deceleration. Don't be too eager, though, because you might feel sick if the turnaround takes very long.'

The group stopped to take in the great mass of 'The Basketball' looming close. Despite knowing the capability of a NanoFactory and the big techbots Yirgella had designed, it was still hard to take in that the whole 80 metres of width and 60 metres of height had been built and tested in just over five months. The pilot appeared at the entrance, smiling and beckoning with his welcome, and the group moved forward.

*   *   *

'So, always ask if you have a question or concern and Yirgella or one of us will help as much as we can ... Is there anything you'd like to add, sir?'

This was the end of a lengthy briefing and Jarra looked round at everyone harnessed securely, then realised the question was addressed to him. It felt very strange to be called 'sir', but the Space Centre people all used it whenever he visited.

'Thank you, Malcolm. There *is* one change I'm going to make to your orders. This flight is so important the world should be given the opportunity to watch, so I want you to turn off all the stealth equipment and broadcast an Alkere Space Centre identifier on an open communication band. Otherwise, we're in your hands and eager to go. We have the memory of Akama's brother to take to the Moon.'

There was quiet acknowledgement for a moment but then the pilot had to speak.

'Sir? Turn the stealth off? Are you sure? Every air defence and space agency around the world will monitor everything we do.'

His concern was understandable as the whole project had

been kept under secrecy and the official announcement to the world wasn't planned to happen for another two weeks when representatives from major nations would be invited to take part.

'I'm sure, Malcolm. It will be a bigger surprise and more memorable this way, especially if we visit the International Space Station as part of our return journey. Can we do that?'

All ten crew members look amazed and then excited.

'We can take you anywhere you wish. Sir, we have data and astrogation charts for any location in the Solar System.'

'The far side of the Moon and one space station will be enough for today.'

*   *   *

Satellite scans monitored by the North American Space Agency were the first to recognise an unscheduled launch trajectory, and within seconds an attention signal was flashing on a screen at the Space Command Centre. A technician puzzled for a moment at the location of the launch site—Central Australia where no infrastructure existed—then called for his supervisor.

'It doesn't make sense. The acceleration parameters are way too low to reach escape velocity without an extended burn way beyond the capacity of any rocket we know of, yet the path it's taking indicates a low orbit insertion at the very least.'

'The Australians must be trying some poorly thought out rocket experiment. How long can the fuel last?'

'With those burn characteristics ... Maybe 150 seconds.'

'Calculate where it will come down as soon as the burn finishes. We may have to issue warnings ... Aren't those emission readings wrong?'

The technician called up a comparison chart and goggled at what he was seeing. A total mismatch.

'That's impossible! There's no fuel residue. The satellite scanners must be faulty.'

'They can't all be wrong. How many do we have watching this launch?'

'Three.'

'Lock in three more and we'll see if the glitch clears.'

The technician expertly synchronised three extra satellites to the task and 30 seconds later the supervisor took the Command Centre to its highest possible alert level. Scientists and technicians scrambled to their posts and every screen in the room lit up with its own particular field of data as the Centre's Command Manager came rushing in.

'What is it? Why are we on high alert?'

'We have an anomalous launch. The acceleration levels don't make sense and none of our satellites are registering standard fuel emissions. The burn has now lasted 220 seconds and our calculations say that is beyond the capability of any known rocket. The Australians must be testing a new type of fuel.'

'The Australians? They have no infrastructure. What's the point of origin?'

'Central Australia.'

'More precisely?'

'... Alkere Energy Holdings north-east of Alice Springs.'

'Alkere ... Where they have that underground environmental research centre?'

The technician looked up with a kind of disbelief. His supervisor might be particularly gifted but he was certainly clueless about anything not involved with space.

'Sir, it's much more than that. It's where all those Artificial Intelligences are based and where that young scientist who had the Pig Ride works.'

'Alkere? I thought that was Mparntwe. I distinctly remember

the Ambassador for the Mparntwe Community speaking when our screens were taken over.'

'They're the same.'

After a moment's startled silence the supervisor glanced at the technician's screen then burst into action.

'Direct every satellite we have under our control to track that object and gather every possible bit of information. Alert every other international space agency. Make contact with the Australian OverGovernment and inform the President.'

'The President?'

'Look at the monitor; that low G burn has now continued for an impossible ... 253 seconds. At the very least it marks some kind of revolutionary advance in rocket technology, and every additional second compounds its significance.'

He turned to the technician.

'Calculate the destination for that object if it maintains the same trajectory. I suspect that our whole space industry has just become obsolete.'

The technician shook his head to say it wasn't his expertise and relayed the instructions to someone at a different workstation. Twenty seconds later, an impossible 20 seconds for any known rocket technology, seventy people stared in disbelief at a graphical representation showing the Moon as the destination.

The supervisor ran for his communication console.

* * *

'Akama's going to speak to them as well. I asked him if he'd like to make the dedication and he said yes. It's very important to him.'

'Well, of course, but he's only eleven and the whole world will be watching.'

'Not directly. He'll be talking to the forty-five leaders and their officials. It will have more meaning if it's him and he's got a gift with words anyway.'

'He certainly has. His story at the farewell ceremony was unforgettable.'

The unstealthed landing on the Moon and the short stop next to the International Space Station two weeks ago had sent the world into a frenzy of consternation and speculation, with some groups even claiming it was the start of an alien invasion. That only lasted till the conversations between the ship and the Space Station were relayed openly through the InterWeb, along with Jarra's declaration that this was the maiden voyage of an AI-designed spaceship using a Positronic Propulsion System, and that selected world leaders would be given the opportunity to make their own journey.

Poor Alira had been overwhelmed with the barrage of questions and hundreds of requests for inclusion from nation states or major Communities all over the planet, and then more overwhelmed in trying to accommodate Jarra's stricture of forty-five leaders and two attendants for each. She'd been relieved when Jarra decided Yirgella should do all the negotiations directly.

Right now Jarra was relaxed in his seat in the ship's Control Centre with Mirri, Akama and Burnu. Alira had just joined them after the quite lengthy process of welcoming the leaders and escorting them to the large conference room which had been hastily fitted with screens to show the external view, and 145 seats with safety harnesses for the initial takeoff and final Earth landing periods.

'Are we ready for our new fun ride, JJ?'

'As soon as Aunt Alira gets buckled up, Mirri.'

'Can we do some flying?'

'Not today. The visitors might get sick.'

'Flying' was Mirri's term for the moving about in zero gravity which both he and Akama had enjoyed in the half hour experiment they'd tried on the first expedition. Jarra hadn't liked it and had been relieved when it finished. Malcolm looked to him for the go-ahead.

The first 15 minutes with the acceleration at 1.4 gravities was quite disconcerting. Jarra thought it was like the first few seconds of a powerful lift taking off except that it went on and on and he was very thankful for the support from his specially designed seat. After that the acceleration reduced to a steady 0.9 gravities and, with safety harnesses no longer needed, everyone was free to move. Jarra dragged his eyes away from the astonishing view of the receding Earth that was being shown on the main screen and called to Mirri, Akama and Alira.

'Come on. It's time to meet all these people.'

'Are you tired, JJ?'

'Just a bit funny, Mirri. I'm nervous about meeting all the people but this point nine gravity makes me feel good.'

Mirri crouched down, then with a big laugh jumped straight upwards. Akama copied and the two of them went hopping and bouncing in the direction they needed to go. Alira did one jump before falling in beside Jarra and Burnu.

'I must admit, it makes me feel like doing the same.'

Today was going to be long, with the trip each way taking just under 4 hours, and Jarra knew he'd have to pace himself very carefully with two major rests, and limit his time with the high-powered guests who, he knew, would be vying for his attention. He'd decided on an hour's mingle time now, an hour and a half while a meal was served and Burnu made the presentation about conditions for purchase of a spaceship, and another hour before the end of the journey. There would also be the quarter hour while they were landed on the Moon and the techbots set up the little memorial plaque and Akama gave his talk.

Almost every person was still in their seat, staring raptly at Earth, when Jarra and his group entered the Conference Room and the transition to standing and mixing company was quite protracted. That suited Jarra because he was nervous. Alira said he needn't be because these people were there to see him and would work hard to put him at ease.

When the closest group unbuckled and came over it was Mirri who broke the ice by putting a proprietary arm across Jarra's shoulders and announcing he was a spaceship hero and the best scientist in the world. There were immediate smiles and Jarra relaxed. Yes, this next hour would be interesting, very interesting, and Jarra watched the mix of reactions towards himself, Mirri and Akama very carefully. Everyone knew Mirri and Akama from the Pig Ride and acknowledged it with varying degrees of formality. Jarra thought they all seemed genuine.

At one stage Jarra had to fight to keep a straight face when Mirri totally ignored the President of the United States and, with cries of 'Dinosaur Man', rushed to give his attendant a big hug. The President seemed to enjoy the moment though.

Then Jarra watched another unconventional scene when Mirri responded strongly to a question and wanted to demonstrate the Pig Ride. The dignitaries seemed unfazed as Mirri turned to Akama, who happily accepted and went for a circuit of the room on his back.

Jarra left for his rest then returned for the buffet luncheon. At the end of that everyone sat down to listen to Burnu's explanation about the availability and costs of acquiring a spaceship with the Positronic Propulsion System. Apart from the significance of being the first world leaders to land on the Moon, this was the real reason for their presence, and there was keen interest while Burnu explained that the Alkere Space Agency was structured for a unit production time of three months. The costs were expensive but, at approximately 60% of any current rocket system, would be highly beneficial for any interested nation, and after building one ship for Alkere research purposes and another for the Australian OverGovernment, the production line would be open for general orders. Burnu explained the terms and conditions and the crew training facilities available at Alkere, then asked for any questions. Almost every hand shot up.

'Will any other nations be given production rights? With only four ships being produced each year it will be decades before everyone can access this technology.'

'Jarra and Yirgella have plans for a second production facility within eight months and will also consider a limited number of other license agreements. However, since production of the Propulsion Unit requires the cooperation of an AI, the only sites outside Australia with the required capability are the Freedom Community in New Zealand and the Mirrigan Project in North America. We would welcome overtures from both places.'

Freedom wasn't represented on the trip today, so all eyes turned to the state governor. Alira chuckled and whispered to Jarra that the dinosaur man now had some hard talking ahead of him.

'Is it possible to build a smaller ship at a reduced cost?'

'Regrettably, no, but we can build bigger.'

'Is there any truth to the InterWeb conjecture that Australia plans to send one of these ships to the stars?'

'No truth at all. Our second ship is being designed for research on the planet Venus.'

Jarra left. These questions would go on for ages and he needed a quiet place to relax.

* * *

'The Wind has come to the Moon.'

Alkere's final words set Jarra's emotions trembling. Captivated by the simple story of a brother whose actions were an expression of his name, forty-five world leaders watched silently as the site for a Moon research base was dedicated with a small monument. With the passing of time the development here of the first Moon habitat would become known as Base Barega but in the meantime, to hold true to an old First Australian tradition of not naming a dead relative, it would be called the Wind Base.

*   *   *

'Does he know yet, Darri?'

'Yirgella may have told him, but I don't think so. They've been working on ways to make it easier to exit the spaceship when it's on the Moon or in space. Yirgella doesn't think the suits the space agencies have been using are reliable enough, and Jarra wants to make them lighter and less unwieldy.'

'Spacesuits?'

'I know. They have dozens of things with a higher priority but Mirri complained when he couldn't explore the Moon's surface so this has taken over for a few days.'

'Mirri tried out a spacesuit on the first trip.'

'Yes, but Yirgella wouldn't let anyone go outside, and especially not Mirri. That's why the two tech robots built the monument.'

Alira nodded.

'They'll probably come up with something so much better that anyone will be able to go for a stroll on the Moon ... He'll be excited when he hears about these AI projects.'

'More than excited. I can hardly believe it myself.'

'How will Professor Allerton cope?'

Alira had just finished an exhausting two days of negotiation with representatives of many of the leaders who'd gone to the Moon and her news for Jarra was that there were now commitments for thirty-one new AI projects.

'The professor won't have to cope. Establishing our four new Alkere AIs was so much work that he developed teams to do it independently. From now on he'll send them off on whatever schedule Jarra and Yirgella work out.'

'What are the high priority projects you mentioned, Darri? Is there anything new I should get the Council ready for?'

'Jarra says his work with different kinds of Positronic Systems will keep him busy for years, but you might have to prepare them for the idea of an orbital habitat for twenty to thirty thousand people and a research establishment on Venus. They're on hold for another eight months but they'll definitely go ahead.'

'What's the significance of the eight months? Does something happen then?'

'The second Alkere spaceship production plant will be operating and five ships will be built for Alkere projects.'

Alira was startled.

'Five? Yirgella announced it was two.'

'That was three days ago. These are extras. They had one of their ideas sessions yesterday and decided to reserve two ships for space construction purposes, one ship dedicated to their crew training program, one specially designed ship for the Venus expedition, and a very luxurious spacecraft for passenger trips to the Moon.'

'What? You can't be serious? That doesn't sound like one of Jarra's ideas.'

Darri laughed because he'd had exactly the same reaction.

'It wasn't. Yirgella suggested it partly as a source of income but more as a way to make the idea of space travel real for the general population. He's designed a ship to carry six hundred people, offering a unique experience with the highest levels of comfort possible—at a premium price.'

'Which would make it only for wealthy people, and that sounds even less like something Jarra would be interested in,' said Alira.

'Jarra likes the part about making space travel familiar and he says that once a fortnight there'll be a free trip of some kind, for scientists, or young people interested in space, or engineers who might join his space habitat project.'

'Free trips? Darri, they'll be flooded with requests.'

'Yirgella will work out how to organise it and then I guess it'll be my job to find good people to run it.'

Alira gave him a look.

'Isn't that a big ask? Your contacts are mostly in the science world.'

'I won't have to do much. I often work through people who specialise in finding human resources and they'll do most of the work for me.'

'Is it annoying when these personnel searches stop you working with Jarra and Yirgella?'

'I mostly try to manage on the days when Jarra's not at Alkere because if I'm away I lose the flow of what they're doing and catching up is sometimes hard work. They both understand, though, and Yirgella does a lot of organising to help me make the best of the time.'

Alira gave Darri an appreciative look.

'So, I'd say you probably know more about what's going on at Alkere than anyone? Maybe even the professor?'

'Yes, and I'm there for all those great moments when they work out new things. It's really exciting.'

'Jarra seems to be more focused on this space-related search than he was on the Power Supply?'

'Only for a while. His spaceships and the space habitat look more dramatic but the Power Supply's the mainstay that lets everything happen. He'll be back to refining it before long because it's far more important. The space developments are for Akama.'

'Akama?'

'Remember when Jarra woke after the abduction attempt? Almost the first thing he did was blame himself, and I think he feels a subconscious obligation. He's certainly been keeping in close contact about each new development.'

Alira frowned.

'I don't like the sound of that. If that's stayed with him I should have a talk with him about it.'

'I already did that and it turned out he was aware of it. When I persuaded him to talk with his doctor they both agreed it's an expected response and nothing to worry about.'

'Darri, you're a wonder.'

*   *   *

'Come and look, JJ. I found some eggs. Do birds put eggs in the dirt?'

'Not in the dirt. Some birds lay them on the dirt, but not in it.'

Mirri laughed and pulled Jarra from the rock he'd been sitting on while Mirri was off on a small exploratory sortie.

'In the dirt, JJ. In a big termite house.'

In a termite mound? That couldn't be right and, intrigued by Mirri's insistence, Jarra followed him to the earthen structure.

'Did you dig it open with a stick?'

'No, JJ. I don't hurt animal homes. I found it like that. The hole makes me look.'

Jarra moved close, and, sure enough, when Mirri brushed aside some loose mound material, a cluster of eggs was revealed.

'This is very strange. Birds can't dig like this and they wouldn't lay eggs here anyway. I think it might be a lizard or a snake.'

'Snakes can't dig, JJ.'

Well, of course they couldn't. A quick search on the InfoPad provided the answer and lots of information.

'This is amazing. You found something very special. These are Dragon eggs.'

'Dragons don't lay eggs. They eat eggs.'

'They do lay eggs, but they don't eat their own. They're very clever and they put them in here so the termites can keep them at the right temperature.'

Jarra carefully explained how the temperature control in the termite mound would stop the eggs getting damaged by extremes of daytime heat or night-time cold. Mirri listened hard because this was explorer information he liked to know.

'I will find the Dragons.'

'Try looking near the Wallaby Rocks. I think they like it there. I'm going to the lookout place to watch the budgerigars and have a relax.'

'I will wake you up, JJ, and we will go to look for the little fish with your PC.'

Jarra nodded. He probably would fall asleep and the personal carrier definitely would be needed. It wasn't his original personal carrier. Yirgella had repaired that, but when he went to use it he'd felt so sad that it was now in storage and he had a newly designed one.

'You won't let me fall in, will you?'

Mirri smiled because he knew Jarra wouldn't get sick even if he did fall in. He was a big person now.

'We will count the fishes.'

All that time ago and he remembered? Well, of course he did. A lot of things might pass him by but not their shared experiences, especially such an important one. Mirri rushed off and Jarra made his way to the lookout place. He did need a proper relax and this happy day with just the two of them was good for his soul.

The last five months had been the busiest of his life but thankfully the big projects he'd wanted to initiate were now underway and run by the managers and leaders Darri and Yirgella had gathered. With the addition to the Mirrigan Project in North America of a second AI and two extra NanoFactories, the big production plant there had already started construction of a large spaceship commissioned by the American government.

The second ship production plant at the Alkere space facility was close to completion and Yirgella was assisting the Freedom Community with yet another.

Partnerships with Communities and new AIs to build continent-spanning Vac Train systems in Africa, India, Europe and South America were all in progress, and because of the reduced cost of energy from the new Power Supplies, Communities around the world were embarking on huge expansion programs which meant, as Yirgella had predicted, an insatiable demand for Alkere's special construction materials.

Dwarfing all these enterprises, however, was the demand for Power Supplies. With almost every Community, nation and major production utility clamouring for the benefits of reduced cost and energy independence, the increasing ability to supply units was still completely overwhelmed by the backlog of orders. According to Yirgella and Burnu, the income from twelve Power Supply factories now operating in partnership with AIs and their associated Communities already exceeded the earnings of the three mega-Corporations which had filled the production void left by the four which had been disgraced and subsumed.

Jarra's reverie was interrupted as a swirling green cloud raced for the dubious shelter of the nearby eucalypts while a whistling kite coursed low in pursuit. He watched the steady return of the budgerigars and wondered that they could be in such panic and fear for their lives then moments later resume activities as if nothing had happened.

So much change in his own world while all around there were things which didn't change, he reflected. Idly he looked up budgerigar information. Hmm ... They had a lifespan of between five and ten years, so none of these were alive when he first came here with Mirri. That was certainly change for the budgerigars.

Where was Mirri? Probably finding some wondrous creature and telling Yirgella about it through his pendant ComPatch. He'd be staying quiet on purpose, too, waiting till his built-in understanding said his JJ was rested enough, and maybe peeking from some vantage point every now and again to check he was okay. Of all the people in the world, however did he meet someone as wonderful as Mirri? Jarra's eyes closed.

* * *

From behind a boulder only 20 metres away, Mirri's sharp eyes picked out the combination of closed eyes and smile.

JJ was happy so he settled to wait patiently, a soft song humming in his throat.

* * *

'This way please.'

The smiling usher led his group of guests towards their reserved seats at the front of the concert hall with much more sincerity and interest than was his usual wont. Important people were routine in this place but his smoothly practised greeting had almost faltered when he recognised the unforgettable features of the boy and the young First Australian man who'd wrenched his emotions on the InterWeb last year. Smiling, more than politely, was almost unprofessional for his position as First Usher, but not this time. The impulsive call, 'JJ, the King of the Eagles', and impetuous rush to the themed mural on the wall of the inner foyer had at first startled the surrounding crowd then set them all smiling.

* * *

Jarra came to a standstill. He had to, to let his senses take in the grandeur and atmosphere of this great auditorium. He'd checked it out on his InfoSystem when Jarara had informed them they had to come as his guests of honour, but he'd had no inkling the real thing would feel like this. It was already exciting. The usher must be used to this reaction because he was smiling and waiting while all Mirri's family looked around.

Jarra took in the audience—over two thousand of them, evidently, as a major work by this sometimes controversial musician was not to be missed, especially when presented at the iconic Sydney Opera House—then focused on the stage. Most of it was taken up with a classical orchestra, but spotlighted on one side was a group of First Australians with sound sticks and didgeridoos. A soft thrum and a rhythmic tap, tap, tap was keeping a steady background while the audience made its way in.

'JJ, this is a good place.'

Jarra lowered his head from looking at the high ceilings and agreed.

Tap, tap, tap. The rhythm continued. How far was this usher taking them? Akama asked the usher something then touched Mirri's arm and darted ahead. Mirri liked this little game and chased after him. To the very front row? Akama pointed to one of the seats then sat down, bounced, and watched Mirri do the same. The usher caught up, still smiling, and indicated the phalanx of specially reserved seats. Jarra sat next to Mirri and let his eyes roam across all the musicians sitting so close with their instruments.

Tap, tap, tap.

The rhythm strengthened, the lights dimmed a little, and the soft thrum of the didgeridoos deepened. The players were dressed in traditional costumes similar to the ones Mirri wore with his dance group and were in striking contrast to the formal dress of the orchestra musicians. Well, this was called the *Dreamtime Concerto*. The idea of a concerto had taken a great deal of explaining to Mirri who'd kept asking if there'd be any of Jarara's good jumping music, but he'd finally taken in that this would be a very serious occasion where you sat quietly and listened hard.

The tap and rhythm ceased, the stage went completely dark and, from the side, a spotlight followed the entrance of a figure clad in a magnificent Elder's cloak.

'Waterfall man!'

It was, too, and Jarra, knowing he might impulsively rush for a greeting, grabbed Mirri's arm to restrain him. Not so. After an all-encompassing bow Jarara held his arms out, not to the general audience but to Mirri, who was now conflicted by Jarra's gentle restraint.

'Jarara wants a hug, JJ.'

And there could be no doubt. Jarara's smile was directed straight at Mirri and both arms were outstretched and waiting. Jarra rapidly lifted his hand from Mirri's arm and, smiling because the formality of the occasion was about to change, nodded that it was okay to go. The steps a few metres to the left meant nothing to Mirri and with one big bound he was on the stage and hugging Jarara with his usual enthusiasm.

'Ladies and gentlemen, excuse us a moment while my friend helps me get set up.'

Jarara pointed to the waiting carry packs and Mirri eagerly moved to open the first one. Jarra grew a small lump in his throat and felt like giving a hug of his own. Jarara was keeping two thousand people on hold while he made Mirri happy. Helping assemble the soundboard had started the very first time Mirri met Jarara and had somehow become a routine of their subsequent meetings. Mirri loved helping, and Jarra knew it made him feel like he was part of whatever was going on.

Tap, tap, tap. The rhythm sticks and barely audible resonance of the didgeridoos sounded again and continued till the soundboard was ready. Jarara thanked Mirri then moved across with him to the top of the steps.

'Ladies and gentlemen, most of you will recognise Mirrigan for his part in thwarting the abduction attempt at Gariwerd last year with his unforgettable Pig Ride.'

A murmur of sound and applause started to build but was cut off by Jarara's gesture.

'Tonight Mirrigan is here for a different reason.

'Tonight I acknowledge my muse.

'Tonight I dedicate my concerto to the young man whose songs have touched my heart with the essence of the Dreamtime.

'Ladies and gentlemen, please welcome Mirrigan, the inspiration for the *Dreamtime Concerto*.'

The applause came, stronger this time, and after a handclasp Mirri made a rather bewildered way to his seat.

Tap, tap, tap.

In the hush as the soft background rhythm started again Mirri looked for understanding.

'What happened, JJ? Why were they clapping?'

'They're all fans, Mirri. Jarara just told them the whole concerto is for you.'

'For me?'

There was no time to help Mirri with his puzzlement. Jarara was now settled at the soundboard, and pealing above the soft tap, tap, tap came the raucous territorial laughter of kookaburras. The amplified sound startled Jarra so much he jumped in his seat and Mirri laughed in delight.

A triumphant crash of sound from the orchestra changed to softer joyous music and Jarra was lost in wonder as the first movement portrayed the Dreamtime coming of Light and the birth of the Sun.

In the second movement his wonder changed to astonishment when the sounds from the orchestra, the First Australian players, and the soundboard, expressed the journeys of the Rainbow Serpent across the land, and told the excitement, humour and danger of its interaction with people and animals. It was all there and, wonder of wonders, central to each part was a Mirri song. Jarara had crafted this movement around five of Mirri's songs, with instrumentation from the orchestra and sound from his soundboard interpreting and complementing them. Jarra looked to see if Mirri was recognising his songs but he couldn't tell. Mirri was off in the world of his mind. The world he visited at special times.

Several moments into the third movement Jarra's concentration on the soft skirl from the soundboard was broken by Mirri's grip on his arm.

'Eagle Song, JJ. The Eagle Song.'

Mirri was right. And he was wrong. The song which had held Jarra transfigured when he first heard it at Birringurra it definitely was, but taken to a different level with the backing of a full orchestra and masterful didgeridoos players.

Mirri's original Eagle Song, amplified and clear with the wonderful acoustics, sounded through the great concert hall, then came the soft strains of the orchestra. The music steadily strengthened, carrying the audience on an almost transcendent journey till the final crescendo abruptly ended with a triumphant crash of sound. Jarra, overwhelmed, sat transfixed as a joyous sound lifted into the sudden silence.

Mirri, also overwhelmed by the music, was singing.

Darkness descended except for one focused spotlight. Directional microphones amplified and carried the song to every part of the great Hall and the *Dreamtime Concerto*, which came to symbolise the resurgence of the First Australians, finished with the wonder that Jarara dreamed his work might inspire.

*   *   *

Epilogue

And so, Jarra and Mirrigan changed the world.

The instigation of the partnership between humanity and Independent AIs, and the capability for easy travel through space, brought decades of unprecedented expansion and prosperity and started the early stages of the spread of mankind through the Solar System.

There is no doubt that Mirrigan, through the inspiration of the *Dreamtime Concerto* and the pride in his exploits, was a key element for the further cultural growth of the First Australian Peoples.

Jarra's part is universally recognised. His intelligence and application provided both the means for change and the impetus to make it happen.

Historians and commentators contend, however, that the greatest legacy from Jarra and Mirrigan was the ongoing gift of benevolent association with Artificial Intelligence. Indeed, many claim Yirgella's naming of Mirrigan as 'friend' at their very first meeting was the pivotal event of the century.

And so, the Terran Diaspora began.

THE END

ALSO BY PETER WOOD

TALES OF THE TERRAN DIASPORA

Life in the outer solar system is about to change for Wirrin, Thom and Calen
— something new and wondrous has entered the universe ...

ATTUNGA

PETER WOOD

More information at: diasporatales.net

www.ingramcontent.com/pod-product-compliance
Lightning Source LLC
Chambersburg PA
CBHW050920250626
47155CB00001B/318